Through the open window s... cry of a bird she couldn't re... flight out of a dark orange sky onto the pearly white cliffs below.

'This is beautiful, this is why I came,' she reminded herself. The wilder, the more remote and removed from the city rush the better. It had been a big decision; the splitting away from friends and a safe job, the cushion of familiarity that life in Camden had provided. Everyone had shaken their heads at her plan. Colleagues warned that a switch to a Dales backwater practice, however beautiful, was not a smart career move . . .

The strongest reason for cutting loose and moving north was to put distance between herself and Tom. Now that the divorce was through, after their long, slow slide through animosity into indifference, she didn't want him living round the corner, or knocking on her door, or sleeping on her sofa when his latest landlord or girlfriend kicked him out . . . Now, as she stared out at the lengthening shadows and listened to the bird's weird cry, she knew she'd found the space to breathe again.

Kate Fielding was born in Yorkshire and read English at University. She has published crime fiction, family sagas and had stories published in magazines such as *Bella*, *Woman & Home* and *Cosmopolitan*, as well as writing books for young adults. Kate Fielding lives in Ilkley with her two daughters.

By the same author

A Winter in Ravensdale

RAVENSDALE

Kate Fielding

ORION

An Orion Paperback
First published in Great Britain by Orion in 1996
as *Untrodden Ways*
This paperback edition published in 1998 by
Orion Books Ltd,
Orion House, 5 Upper St Martin's Lane,
London WC2H 9EA

A CIP catalogue record for this book
is available from the British Library.

Printed and bound in Great Britain by
Clays Ltd, St Ives plc

For My Daughters

'Oh these bleak winds and bittern northern skies, and impassable roads, and dilatory country surgeons!'

Wuthering Heights, Ch. 10.

CHAPTER ONE

Laura Grant pulled her car off the unfenced road. Below her, a sweep of autumn heather melted into misty green as the high moor gave way to fields, bounded by stone walls that dipped and zig-zagged into the valley. The hillside was dotted with low barns, and solitary slanting trees marked the far horizon.

Above, a hazy red sun settled into the arms of a tall ash tree where rooks had made their clumsy nests. It lit the sky with a pale golden glow and threw deep shadows down the length of Ravensdale.

She basked for a moment in its still beauty, and felt the problems in her own past slip away, as gently she put the car into gear and slid down the winding road into the ancient village of Hawkshead.

She mentioned the dry-stone walls to Gerald Scott, the senior partner in her new practice. They stood together on the threshold of the medical centre, a modern, one-storey building backing onto a playing field beside the River Raven. It had an open outlook across the narrow valley, where sheep grazed and the walls criss-crossed the green slopes. 'It amazes me to think they're all built without mortar, just stones slapped on top of one another hundreds of years ago.'

He followed her gaze. 'Two separate walls tied together by through-stones, tapering, filled with rubble, capped with topstones, to be exact. They got paid three bob a rood. That's fifteen pence for six metres to you. They were out there in wind, rain and snow.'

'Slave labour,' she admitted, forced to rein back her romantic vision.

'Work was work in those days.' He led her into the reception area. 'You'll get to see those damned walls in your dreams before too long, believe me. Along with every barn, every dip and curve of the horizon. But it'll mean something different by then. How many minutes past the broken-down stretch by Capon Tower to Warboys' place up at Askby? How far between Knowles' converted barn at Fellside and old Oxtop, with the wind against you and five patients back here in Reception, fretting over their angina, their paranoia, their arthritis and their rutley chests?'

Laura nodded. She realised that she hadn't escaped the crush and roar of London to an entirely peaceful life. These days, being a doctor meant pressure and more pressure, wherever you worked.

Following Gerald through the empty waiting room, she braced herself. Talking to him was like undergoing a viva at medical school. She had to be on her mettle, ready to prove she was worthy of this new partnership.

'And these days there's all this wretched form filling.' He gave an exaggerated shrug. 'Applying for this and that, certifying things, balancing funds.' He shot her a glance. 'I expect you're good at that?'

'I don't know about being good at it. I only know it has to be done.' This was the stance she'd taken during her interview; that administration was a nuisance but could be minimised by good organisation.

'As if we didn't have enough to worry about looking after our patients, without some faceless bureaucrat from the Department of Health dictating how we spend our time.'

Laura let him grumble on. She agreed, but also knew there was plenty of precious time wasted among traditionalists like Gerald on resisting the irresistible.

'Look here,' he said suddenly. He stopped and turned to face her. 'I expect you'll find us a bit out of touch here in Ravensdale.'

'As a matter of fact, no.' She gestured towards the newly computerised system behind the receptionist's desk, and to the airy, well-lit waiting room with its feel of modern efficiency. 'One of the things that attracted me to the job was the fact that the place has come right up to date, unlike some other rural practices I took a look at.'

'If we've invested in the technological revolution, it's due to Philip. He's the moderniser.'

Philip Maskell was the third partner, someone Laura hardly knew yet. But she realised already that it was Philip, not Gerald, who had been responsible for bringing the first female doctor into the practice.

'I'm the stick in the mud.' He paused again. 'A paid-up, card-carrying member of the Doctor Finlay school. Hands on, old fashioned GP, that's me.'

Laura looked him in the eye. 'That suits me fine too.'

'After thirty years I'm not about to change my ways.'

'As long as you don't expect me to change mine.' Laura widened her eyes.

He grunted. 'Well . . .'

And as long as I don't end up as the token lady doctor, Laura thought; overworked and disregarded. She meant to stand her ground and make her mark in her new job.

She glanced over her shoulder as a round-faced, dark-haired woman came through a back door into the cluttered office.

'You've met Sheila? Sheila Knowles, this is Laura Grant,' Gerald said, before he whisked her through to his own room. 'Have you dropped your stuff off at Town Head yet?' He checked his desk for messages, then sifted through the bulging buff envelopes containing the case notes for his next batch of patients. With his lean frame, his head of thick grey hair swept back from a high forehead above sharp, strong features, he seemed younger than his fifty-seven years.

'Not yet.'

He gave her no time to expand. 'No, I suppose you drove straight here. Don't expect the Ritz. Dot Wilson doesn't go in for new-fangled luxuries like showers and central heating. You may find Town Head a bit on the chilly side when winter sets in.'

'It doesn't bother me, honestly.' Laura's glance strayed across the playing field towards the river. The sun had vanished behind the hill and drained the colour from the rugged landscape. 'It's only a temporary arrangement until I find my own place.'

Gerald grunted. 'And take no notice of the village gossips you're bound to bump into. They're best ignored. In fact, apart from Dot, who's a decent sort, you'll give the whole WI clan a wide berth for a start.' He looked up. 'You know what they say around here, if you don't watch out, folk'll look down t'chimney to see what you're having for breakfast!'

Laura tried not to react to the chauvinist picture being painted for her.

3

'The whole bloody village is a minefield of dropped remarks and unguarded moments. That's the women, of course. Now the men, they're a different kettle of fish. You'll be lucky to get a word out of some of the old farmers, what there are left of them.'

'Right.' She nodded firmly, feeling her spirits begin to sink. Gerald's stale opinions were beginning to overcome her delighted reaction to the beautiful dale.

'But I expect you'll want to find out these things for yourself.' He seemed to mirror her thoughts. 'Don't let me colour your first impressions.'

'No.' He already had. 'Thanks anyway. I'll just drop off my bag next door, then I'll be on my way to Town Head.' She felt a tinge of resentment at her senior partner's implied opinion that she would need guiding like a novice. After all, she had four solid years in her north London practice to build on. She thought of herself as a hardworking doctor doing the best she could within the limits of the cash-strapped, changing National Health Service. She felt she was ready for the new challenges of a rural practice. Gerald obviously saw her as still wet behind the ears.

'Fine. See you tomorrow, eight hundred hours.' He signed something in an indecipherable scrawl, ending with a flourish. 'Practice meeting. Come and introduce yourself to the whole team, eh?' His pen hung poised over a pile of unsigned letters.

Laura nodded and left him to it. She went through to her own spotlessly clean consulting room and deposited her bag of books and medical instruments.

She went and sat behind her empty desk, then rearranged chairs so as to make herself more accessible to her as yet invisible, unknown patients. The room was painted a pale sea-green, with deeper curtains, a white blind and blue carpet. It was attractive but impersonal. But a peep through the blind revealed the dramatic, almost sheer, striated limestone cliff that rose to the north of the village. Through the open window she heard the wheezy wail and cry of a bird she couldn't recognise, and saw its tumbling flight out of a dark orange sky onto the pearly white cliffs below.

'This is beautiful, this is why I came,' she reminded herself. The wilder, the more remote and removed from the city rush the better. It had been a big decision; the splitting away from friends and a safe job, the cushion of familiarity that life in Camden had provided. Everyone had shaken their heads at her plan. Colleagues warned that a switch to a Dales backwater practice, however beautiful, was not a smart career move. Friends spun the usual line that culture was dead north of Watford Gap. 'It's all ee-bah-gum and flat caps, and Nora Batty and sheep!' They said she was mad.

'There's Alan Bennett,' she argued.

'He spends half his time here in Camden!'

'There are theatres, galleries, cinemas up there, you know. In Leeds and Bradford.'

'Exactly.' Case proven. They thought it was a decision made in the throes of her separation from Tom. 'You're not in the right frame of mind to be taking such a huge risk. Why not stay put, see what happens?'

But these days surviving the city tired and depressed her. There, Thou Shalt Not Make Contact was written ten feet high on billboards and spray painted in all the underpasses. Thou Shalt Not Meet Another's Gaze, Thou Shalt Not Smile (unless advertising toothpaste). Thou Shalt Make Love While Eating Ice-cream, and then only if the flesh is firm. 'I come from Yorkshire in the first place, remember,' she told them. 'It's not the ends of the earth, believe me.'

But her friends were right. The strongest reason for cutting loose and moving north was to put distance between herself and Tom. Now that the divorce was through, after their long, slow slide through animosity into indifference, she didn't want him living round the corner, or knocking on her door, or sleeping on her sofa when his latest landlord or girlfriend kicked him out.

Tom was a journalist, and she still admired his work, even if she no longer loved the man. She wanted to read his campaigning pieces in the *Guardian*, not listen in person to his embittered accounts of the private lives of right-wing politicians. He said she was an ostrich, turning her back on everything real and relevant to Britain at the end of the millennium. He spoke as he wrote, in grand terms. So, according to him, she was running away to join a rural elite of second-home owners. He called Hawkshead the graveyard of ambition for clapped-out computer programmers and crooked financiers.

'Leave my social conscience alone, Tom. It's none of your business any more. I've been up to Ravensdale for a look round. I've decided to take the job.' Now, as she stared out at the lengthening shadows and listened to the bird's weird cry, she knew she'd found the space to breathe again.

A knock on the door disturbed her reflections. Philip Maskell waited for a response, then came in. She stood up to shake hands.

'Good, I'm glad to see you got here safely.' He thrust his hands into his pockets and nodded. 'When did you arrive?'

'Half an hour ago.'

'I was out on a call.'

'I already feel as if I've been here for days.'

'That wouldn't be because Gerald's been giving you a hard time, would it?'

'Oh no.'

'Don't worry, you'll soon get used to him.' He crossed the room to the door and raised his voice. 'I'm telling Laura she'll soon get used to your crusty old ways, won't she, Gerald?'

There was a grunt by way of reply. Philip came back and sat on the edge of her desk. 'Just to let him know we're talking about him behind his back. He'd be crestfallen if he thought we were ignoring him.'

Laura found herself settling into Philip's genial presence. He was tall and upright, with light grey eyes in a weathered face. She guessed he was nearing fifty. His spare frame suggested regular exercise; there was a suppleness and ease, a steady attractiveness.

'How long will it take you to straighten yourself out, do you reckon?' He picked up a pencil and waggled it between thumb and forefinger.

'First off, I have to find my lodgings.' Laura looked at her watch. It was almost half past six.

'That's Dot Wilson's place?'

'Yes. And please, don't you tell me my new landlady's a dragon with an uncanny ability to sense the ins and outs of my entire personal life whenever I so much as sneeze.'

'I never said that!' Gerald's voice rang out.

'Not sound-proof,' Philip mouthed in a stage whisper. 'New building, thin walls.'

'I just dropped a couple of gentle hints.' Gerald came through, half-moon glasses perched on the tip of his sharp nose. 'Forewarned is forearmed, is it not?'

'Dot's fine,' Philip assured her. 'Trust me.'

'That's what I said, a decent sort.' Gerald tilted his head to one side. Then he hitched his glasses off and twirled them. 'Memory like an elephant. Can tell you exactly what you were doing, who with and where, when the Japs surrendered to the Allies in August 1945. That sort of thing. A walking local history book, a methodical woman is Dot.' He delivered his verdict and departed. 'If anyone wants me, I'm at home.'

Laura gazed after him. 'Methodical?' It sounded ominous.

'That's Gerald being complimentary,' Philip assured her. Then more seriously, 'Don't let him put you off. And listen, as soon as you're settled at Town Head why not come to us for a drink and a spot of painless induction into the mysteries of rural practice?'

'Thanks, I'd like that.' She stood up and raised her hair from her collar. She eased the back of her neck. 'Who's us, and where?'

'Us is me and Juliet. The rest of us Maskells, Simon, Jim and Bean, are at college or off doing good works in far-flung corners of the globe. They're our sons, and they sometimes remember the fact, especially at Christmas and whenever the bank manager gets in touch with a pressing reminder that funds are low.'

'Bean?'

'Ian. Anyway, now it's just Juliet and me rattling around Bridge House all by ourselves, except for a lodger every now and then. You'll find us by the old bridge, surprisingly enough. Would eight-thirty be OK?'

'Sounds good.'

'If you're too tired, give us a ring and say so. We can easily make it another night.' He stood to one side as Laura picked up her keys and headed for the door. 'I'm here for another hour or so, catching up on paperwork, then I'll be at home.'

'I'm fine, really. I'd like to get into the swing of things as soon as I can.'

'It's bound to seem a bit strange at first.' He followed her into the waiting room.

She nodded. 'In one way I can hardly believe I'm doing this; starting something so different.' She looked beyond Philip out of the window at the stunning layers of cliff, the tree-studded horizon. 'Or living somewhere so beautiful.'

'And in another way?'

'I feel as if it was meant to happen.' She tried to explain. 'I mean, as if this was the best and most inevitable decision I ever made.'

'Good. We'll do our best to make sure it is. We'll give you a right Yorkshire welcome, as we say.'

She took a deep breath. 'You already have.'

Any lingering doubts slipped away as she stepped outside. The hills rose and rolled away in all directions, while the high curlews soared and called.

CHAPTER TWO

Philip Maskell watched Laura drive away. So far he liked what he'd seen and was eager to make her feel at home. He expected her to shake the place up a bit. Good; they were stuck in a rut, or he was at any rate. Same faces, same routine. Laura promised a change for the better. But he stopped in the porch to listen to two old-timers sitting in the sun.

The first cast a wary eye in Laura's direction as she emerged from the building. 'What's up with you, Dick?'

'Nay, Tot, that's what I've come here to find out,' came the short reply. The second old man sniffed and stared. Two pairs of disapproving eyes followed Laura's car out of the car park.

Philip, hovering in the doorway, realised that Tot Dinsdale and Dick Metcalfe hadn't registered his presence.

'See yon young woman?' Tot nudged his neighbour in the ribs and set him coughing. He spoke in an exaggerated whisper. 'She's taken over from Dr Williams.'

'She never has!'

'She has.' Tot nodded, then summoned the wisdom of his eighty years. 'If you must know, I reckon nowt to it.'

'How's that?' Dick Metcalfe cleared his throat and leaned forward to rest his elbows on his knees. His breath came in difficult, long-drawn gasps.

'Women doctors. It's the same as them new women vicars. Somehow it don't feel right.'

The two old men sat shaking their heads.

Philip decided it was high time he came forward to break things up. 'Dick, Tot.' He nodded, then leaned against the wall. 'What brings you here? It's after hours, you know.' Afternoon surgery had ended an hour earlier.

'Aye, but I saw your car, Doctor.' Tot sat unperturbed. He didn't mind who heard this opinion of the newcomer. 'And I thought happen you could give me summat for my angina. I ran out of the stuff you gave me last back-end.'

Years of experience had taught Philip that the old farmers were no respecters of official opening times, either here at the surgery, or for that matter at the pub, the vet's, or the village shop. He didn't mind. In fact, he was grateful not to be dragged up on a home visit to Tot's remote farm at Oxtop. 'Come inside and I'll sort it out. And something for your chest, eh, Dick?'

'Aye. I saw Tot had dropped by, and I thought I might as well catch you while you were at it.'

All three went inside, and while Philip checked the details on the two old men's records, he listened to them lay into modern trends with redoubled energy, well aware that they had an audience for their gripes.

'Now, I hope you're not going to make things difficult for Doctor Grant.' Philip handed them both a prescription and tried to appeal to their better natures.

'What was wrong with Dr Williams, that's what I'd like to know.' Dick squinted at his prescription.

'One three times a day before meals,' Philip instructed. He'd forgotten that Dick's better nature lay deep below the surface. 'And no driving if they make you drowsy.'

Dick cackled and coughed.

Tot recognised the cause of his friend's amusement. 'He'd have to be a darned sight worse than he is before it keeps him out of the Falcon of a night. Nodding off or not, he'll be behind the wheel and coming down the hill on automatic pilot, and he won't be happy until he's got his fist around a pint pot, will you, Dick?'

Philip shook his head in defeat, while Dick took up arms against Tot this time. 'Now don't you go giving everyone the idea I can't stay off the booze. Next thing you know, I'll be on the wagon, doctor's orders!'

'I'm saying nothing,' Philip said evenly.

'No, but I can see you thinking plenty.'

'I'm impressed.' Philip began to usher them towards the door. 'I didn't know thought-reading was in your line, Dick.'

'You doctors, you're all the same.' Tot joined forces with Dick again. 'No drinking, no smoking, no eating what you like because it's bad for you.' He spread his arms in a courtroom gesture of appeal. 'Look at the pair of us. We haven't done bad on it, eh?'

Relenting, Philip smiled and held the door open for them. He noticed the muck trail from Dick's boots across the carpet and sighed.

As he went by, Tot leaned confidentially towards him. 'I'd just like to say, I'll be sticking with you and Dr Scott.' With his slight, sparrow-like build and gaunt face, he looked as if the first strong wind would fell him. But he'd farmed up at Oxtop for more than sixty years, and, like Dick, he still drove his rickety Land Rover at breakneck speed down the narrow lane to the Falcon every night without fail. 'Can't teach an old dog new tricks,' he grumbled as he went out.

'I want you back in for a blood test, Dick,' Philip called after them. He thought that the old man looked frailer; perhaps a touch of anaemia along with his rutley chest. 'Come in and see us as soon as you can.'

Dick didn't swerve from his set path, heading for his Land Rover and grabbing the door handle. 'Nay, it's this cough. It's knocked the stuffing out of me, that's all.'

Philip grunted, while Tot veered back towards him. 'You won't see him for dust,' he advised.

'Why's that?'

'He's afraid he'll fall into the clutches of the new doctor. We're not right taken with her, if you must know.'

'Right, Tot, I think I've got the picture.' Philip made as if to end the conversation.

'Only, she's young, isn't she?'

'Not that young. And she comes here with a good reputation, you know.'

'She's nobbut a lass,' Tot persisted.

'Over thirty, Tot, with a string of letters after her name.' Philip looked pointedly at his watch and tried to close the door.

'Book learning,' he said with wheezy contempt. 'Why, I once had a young vet come to my place, blethering on about inoculations and all that fancy stuff. Straight out of school, he were, right swanky. But could he get my best tup back on its legs? Could he heck. Tup pegged out as he was sat in the house, consulting a great thick book he brought along with him.'

Philip stared him out and Tot turned at last and made his way towards his own mud caked Land Rover. Laura would have to

11

break down many such barriers as she started her new job; an uphill struggle which she might not have anticipated.

It hadn't been so in his own early days as a GP in the dale. Twenty years ago, that generation of old farmers had looked on him with nothing worse than wry amusement as he stifled his squeamishness at gashed legs and torn thumbs. He had belonged to the natural order of things as they saw it; a young local man learning his profession through trial and error.

Philip clicked his tongue as he imagined the pub talk about his new colleague. It was partly his own responsibility; he'd been the one to persuade Gerald to move out of the dark ages by bringing in a female partner.

Gerald had resisted, argued that Hawkshead still wasn't ready for it, and had only grudgingly given way when Philip had pointed out all Laura's plus points. She was well qualified and experienced, and in touch with new aspects of the Health Service which the two of them constantly struggled over; the capitation fees, particular fees for night visits, immunisation, cervical cytology and so on. Funding was a nightmare, they had to admit, and Laura seemed willing and able to handle it.

What's more, there were women patients who had delicately broached the subject of a lady doctor with Joy Hartley, their nurse, or with Sheila Knowles on Reception. Without seeming disloyal to Doctors Scott and Maskell, they said they would love to be able to see a woman. In the end, and because Laura was self-evidently the best candidate, Gerald had agreed.

As Philip sat at his desk to confront his pile of paperwork, he nevertheless found himself wondering whether Laura would be up to the challenge. She struck him at the time of the interview as someone with true intelligence and sensitivity. Senior colleagues in Camden wrote about her as sincere and hardworking. Her caring approach was one of her strengths, they said, and her willingness to sympathise with the underdog. The question now was, would she adapt to the more traditional ways here in Ravensdale? It would take a fine balance between tact and resilience to deal with the Tot Dinsdales in this neck of the woods.

A car drove up. He heard a door slam, followed by lively footsteps half-running up the paved ramp, then a loud knock on the door. Going to the window and pulling the blind to one side, he spotted his lodger, Mary Mercer, peering impatiently into the waiting room.

He went straight out, glad of any diversion, but especially pleased to see Mary. He didn't know why, except that she would shake him out of the doldrums, standing there with her pale face and heavily fringed eyes, in her quirky drama-teacher clothes. 'We're closed,' he said through the plate-glass of the door. 'I'm not here!'

She flashed her eyes. 'It's not *you* I want!' She flattened both palms against the glass and pushed.

'Pity!' He opened up. 'I take it this is an emergency?'

She treated him to a disdainful look. 'As a matter of fact, I came to see Laura.'

'Laura Grant?'

'Is there more than one Laura suddenly?' Her accent changed, she became a Jewish momma.

He laughed. 'I forgot. You two know each other.'

'Darling, we're positively prehistoric!' Now she was Hollywood, more Gabor than Garbo. 'We go back forever. We were at school together.' She drawled the words through pouted lips.

'*You* were at school?'

Mary drew breath and returned to her normal, throaty voice. 'Thanks, Philip. It's true they threw me out in the end, but for a time, yes, Laura and I did grace the hockey fields of Wingate Ladies' College together.'

Philip laughed loudly, amused by Mary's habit of wrong-footing him through these rapid changes of persona. It kept him guessing what lay behind the act. 'Well, you missed her. She just left. She's on her way to Town Head.'

'Damn, that's where I came from. I'm coming and going like a bloody yo-yo.'

'Why don't you come and have a drink with us later? Laura's coming.'

'I'm not sure.'

'Why not? You don't exactly have to go out of your way, do you?' Since she'd come to teach drama in the secondary school at the start of term she'd been renting a room in their house.

'So?'

'So!'

Her face lit up. 'Oh, I suppose I can drink at least. No problems about getting home afterwards. We can reminisce about the teachers we seduced and hearts we broke.'

13

'We?' He imagined Laura was too demure ever to have been Mary's accomplice.

'Yes. Laura and me. Laura and I. Which is it?' She seemed reluctant to leave.

'Work that out by yourself, while I shuffle some papers around my desk, would you?' He tried to push aside how pleased he felt that she'd accepted the invitation.

'And they said you were charming. Reliable, polite Dr Maskell. Your reputation goes before you.' She began to pout.

'I don't have time to be charming.'

'OK.' She used her long slim hands in a gesture of surrender. 'I'm going, I'm going. How did Laura seem, by the way? Nervous?'

'No. She seemed – well, she seemed glad to be here. Don't ask me why.'

'She's lucky she's got you to look after her.' Mary retreated down the ramp. 'To protect her from big, bad Gerald.' She grinned and got into her car.

Her driving was as outrageous as the rest of her, Philip noticed. It demanded attention. So why was he so keen to give it? He wouldn't usually fall for such games.

She turned a wide circle in the car park and squealed to a halt where he stood by the door.

'Scott alert! Scott alert!' She leaned out of the window and spoke in an American cop voice. 'Just observed heading this way!'

'Who, Gerald?'

'No, Aimee. I thought I'd better warn you.'

'Thanks.' Aimee, Gerald's sixteen-year-old daughter, was crossing the road. Philip said goodbye to any hope of returning to his desk.

'I wonder what she wants?' Mary looked long and hard at Aimee's slight, denim-clad figure. 'Your father's gone home,' she called. 'If that's who you're looking for.'

'It's not.' Aimee swept past Philip into the waiting room.

Mary's eyebrow shot up. 'Hello, Aimee – Hello, Miss Mercer, how are you?' She shrugged. 'Good luck, see you later,' she said to Philip.

He followed Aimee inside. 'Then it must be me,' he said, recognising that she must have chosen her time specifically to avoid Gerald.

'Actually it's not.' She went to the reception desk, reached through the open glass screen and swivelled the appointment book towards her.

He went and slapped it shut. 'Sorry, top secret.'

'Yeah, yeah. So what if I want to make an appointment?'

'You could ring up like everyone else.' He'd grown used to Aimee's surliness. She'd transformed overnight from serious, dark-eyed child to angry teenager.

'And let everyone in the place know my business?' She frowned. 'I want to keep this private, OK?'

He acknowledged her right to do this. 'OK, so who do you want to see?'

'The new woman.'

That made a nice change, he thought. 'Dr Grant?' He opened the book. 'When?'

'Tomorrow. Early.'

'It'll have to be ten-thirty.'

She nodded. 'I'll get out of school. It's only drama.'

Philip entered the appointment in the book. 'I'll tell Miss Mercer how much you value her lessons.'

Aimee snorted. 'You must be joking. She doesn't even notice who's there.'

'I think you'd be surprised.' He clicked the end of his pen and slipped it back into his top pocket.

Aimee was already on her way out, without thanks, a smile or any sign of acknowledgement that he had done her a favour. She stopped in the doorway. 'Look, don't tell my dad, OK?'

'As I said, highly confidential.'

Satisfied, she went off, head up, straight dark hair swinging down her back.

Suddenly tired, Philip rang home. 'I'm on my way,' he told Juliet. 'Ten minutes.'

'Your dinner's in the dog.'

'Am I late? Sorry.' He checked; it was seven-thirty.

'No more than usual. You sound worn out.'

'No, I'm fine, see you soon.' He put down the phone, found his keys and locked up.

Outside, an evening mist had settled on the river, a forceful reminder that soon the clocks would go back. Autumn had taken hold. Every year he liked it more; leaves decaying into the earth, the smell of damp, the turning of the seasons.

CHAPTER THREE

At Town Head Dot climbed the narrow stairs to the front bedroom for the umpteenth time. Although she knew it was unnecessary – she'd already checked twice that there were clean towels on the rack – she wanted to be sure that the room was in perfect order for Dr Grant. The landing floorboard creaked as usual, but that couldn't be helped. The house, like her, was getting on in years, and since Arthur had passed away there had been no one to attend to all those small jobs. She would have to warn her new lodger about the pitfalls; the creaky floorboard, the sash window that tended to stick, the gurgle in the pipes in the airing-cupboard.

Yes, there were the two best striped towels folded over the wooden frame. Dr Grant was bound to be worn out after her long drive, she would appreciate hot water in the sink in the corner of her room. Dot went to pat the cream eiderdown. She twitched at the net curtain, suspected dust on the dressing-table mirror and flicked at it with the yellow cloth she always carried in her apron pocket.

New soap in the porcelain soapdish by the sink, a toothbrush mug to match. Freshly laundered white cotton sheets, new lining-paper in the bottom of the wardrobe, and the scent of lavender emanating from every polished surface. She nodded, squared the snowy pillow and gave it an extra pummel. There, Dr Grant couldn't possibly find any cause for complaint.

Dot heard an unfamiliar car engine climb the hill. Since Town Head was at the top of a narrow cul de sac, her ear was finely tuned. This was definitely not a car whose sound she recognised; a smooth, powerful engine, no knocks and rattles as it approached along the cobbled street. She went to the window, taking care not to be seen through the nets. She wouldn't want the doctor to think she pried, but she wanted to convince herself that the car carried her long-awaited lodger. Through the gauzy white curtain she spotted a low, silver model. Driving it steadily towards the house was a young woman with shoulder-length, wavy dark hair, complete with a set of good luggage stacked neatly on the back seat.

All male heads in the village square would have turned to follow this sleek car, Dot knew. Hawkshead lay at the top of the dale, where the made-up road came to an end and the wilderness of heather and rock took over. It was a determined sightseer who came off the busy tourist route, up the narrow, single track road to view the fine Georgian houses that fronted the square. True, it boasted a small wine bar, several cafes tucked down side ginnels, a pub and an antique shop, but strangers driving into town on a Wednesday evening were still a rarity.

'There's Dr Scott's new lady assistant.' The word would fly round and be greeted with suspicious silence which signified that judgment was withheld until such time as the observers standing at their doorsteps had found good cause to condemn the new-comer. Her first slip – a misdiagnosis, a delay over referral to hospital in Wingate twenty-five miles down the dale – would bring her critics clustering round the bar at the Falcon to discuss her lack of 'gumption' and 'savvy'.

Dot knew that Laura must already have run the gauntlet of their tight-lipped stares, as she eased through the market square and up the steep hill, past the plain Methodist chapel and the Gothic Anglican church with its adjacent Victorian primary school. The houses further up this street lost their town façades of dressed stone and pillared porticos, reverting to farmhouse style of plain two-storey dwellings with narrow mullioned windows and massive, moss-covered roofs of Yorkshire stone, all crowded together without regard to town planning. The huddle of houses was linked by steps and alleyways into back streets and closes still cobbled and inaccessible by car.

As Dot maintained her bird's eye view, she recognised that she shared the general scepticism about the new doctor. It wasn't just the generation gap, though this was part of it. It was more the suspicion that someone as clever and sophisticated as Dr Grant must inevitably look down on the likes of Dot; been nowhere, done nothing, a dodo chained to tradition.

Laura parked and lifted her cases from the back seat, dumping them on the cobbled area outside the house. Dot waited for footsteps up the short path, the ring of the doorbell. She went downstairs to open the door and came face to face with a self-possessed young woman who smiled eagerly as she introduced herself.

'Mrs Wilson? I'm Laura Grant.'

'How do you do? Come in.' She would be formal, take her own time to size up her new lodger.

'I'm sorry if I'm late.'

'Oh no, it's given me plenty of time to get things ready.' Dot stood to one side, aware of her own regulation uniform of flowered apron over fawn lambswool cardigan and tweed skirt. Beside Laura she felt, as she'd expected, faded and parochial. 'Your room's ready for you. I hope it's to your liking.' No smile softened her face as she turned to show Laura upstairs. 'You can leave your cases where they are, they're quite safe,' she said stiffly. 'And watch your step on the landing. I've a creaky floorboard, I'm afraid.'

Laura obeyed. They went upstairs to check her room; single bed with veneered headboard, matching dressing-table with wing mirrors and a small cast-iron fireplace. There was a huge solid mahogany wardrobe, rich and shiny as horse chestnuts just out of their shells. The wallpaper sported even more flowers than Dot's apron. The lace-curtained sash windows looked down onto the street. There was a heavy washbasin with elaborate iron brackets in the alcove to the far side of the fireplace. A towel-stand and a plain cream rug over polished floorboards completed the spartan effect.

Dot stood in the doorway, awaiting Laura's reaction.

'Fine.' She took in the utility furniture which clashed oddly with the seventies-style wallpaper.

'It's a nice, light room. It catches the morning sun.'

'It'll suit me fine, thanks.' Laura meant it. Town Head, just a couple of minutes from the medical centre, with a view over the square to open hills, would be a good base. She even liked the unfashionable air of the place.

'It's nothing fancy, mind.'

'No, it's just exactly what I need while I get myself sorted out.'

'There's no fitted carpet, so you might get a bit of a draught through the floorboards. Bathroom's down the landing on the left, separate WC.' Dot listed the amenities, keeping a wary eye on

Laura. She knew these modern young women expected refinements such as *en suite* bathrooms and cooking facilities. 'The telephone's in the hall. You'd see it on your way up?'

Laura confessed that she hadn't. She'd spotted the cuckoo clock, the hat stand, the tapestry pictures, and decided that her landlady had a weakness for souvenirs and knick-knacks. This was confirmed when she followed her downstairs into the living room.

'You'll be wanting a cup of tea, I expect?' Dot hovered by the step into the kitchen. 'You've had a long drive.'

Laura seized the chink of sympathy. 'Five and a half hours, actually. Yes please, I'd love a cup.' She sighed and settled into an easy chair by the open fireplace; a massive marble affair with a tiled inset, neatly laid but unlit.

Dot took great pride in keeping things shipshape, from the polished brass teapot-stand in the hearth and the pair of china dogs on the mantelpiece, to the embroidered linen squares on the backs of the chairs.

The room was a devil to dust, with its shelves of glass ornaments, its plate-rack of fine porcelain commemorating coronations and jubilees, births, deaths and marriages of royalty dating back to the last century. But every piece was pristine. Laura praised them as Dot eased her hostess trolley down the step from the kitchen.

When Dot said 'tea', she meant a cup of best Yorkshire blend, followed by sandwiches, followed by scones and jam. Laura heaped the jam onto her plate with a silver spoon, while Dot went back for the fruitcake and fresh tea. 'You'll have a slice of cake with it?' she prompted.

'Oh no,' Laura protested.

Dot gave her a sideways look.

'Oh, go on then.' She relented and held out her plate, realising that refusing Dot's hospitality would be a black mark against her. A good appetite was obviously an essential credential round here.

'So you're from London?' Dot untied her apron and hung it on a hook in the kitchen.

'Not originally, no. I was born in Yorkshire.'

'You don't sound like it,' came the sceptical reply.

'Yes. Wingate.'

'Ah, well.' A significant silence developed. Dot had always thought the spa town toffee-nosed, not true Yorkshire at all. 'But you've been living in London, from what I hear?'

'Yes, I went to university there, and I just sort of stayed. You know how it is.'

'No need to apologise. It's one of them things.'

Laura laughed. 'Was I apologising? I didn't realise.' Defending herself against the charge of having betrayed her roots was something she must have subconsciously conveyed.

'Well, it's nothing to be ashamed of, like I say. These things happen.' Dot was determined to forgive the lapse. 'You're back now, at any rate.'

'I expect you've lived in Hawkshead all your life?'

Dot nodded, still on her guard. 'I was born here in this house. Bred here. And I expect they'll carry me out feet first.'

'Oh, not for a good few years yet!' Laura smiled at the small, upright figure sitting opposite.

'I'm seventy-three!'

And they were away, in a dam-burst of reminiscence. Dot told proudly of her marriage at the end of the war to Arthur Wilson, the village schoolmaster, which had been a step up in the world for her, a farmer's daughter. She told Laura about their two children, John and Valerie, who had sadly both moved away to the town, and about the selling of the farmland behind the house. 'Nothing would shift me out of my home, though; come what may.' Arthur had been dead ten years, but still she clung on, letting a room here and there when money was tight, going cleaning four days a week to the Maskells. 'I never owed a penny in my life, and never will,' she vowed, wondering how this must sound to a young woman who probably didn't understand the value of setting down roots and staying put.

Laura glanced at the framed photograph on the mantelpiece of a young Dot and Arthur, plus children. The four black and white figures squared their shoulders and shyly faced the camera, dressed in Sunday best; white sandals and stiff collars and ties. She picked up a familiar name. 'You say you work for the Maskells?'

'Yes. Down at Bridge House.'

'That's the connection, then. Dr Maskell actually suggested your place for me to stay. And he's invited me down there later on tonight. Is it easy to find?'

'You can't miss it, right by the bridge, the only house that overlooks the river. It's one of the oldest around. It's a fancy sort of place, with carvings and things there was never any need for.'

'And is it posh? Should I dress up?'

'For Dr Maskell?' Dot shook her head. 'They don't stand on ceremony.'

Laura smiled and rode the silence that followed. She had one other reason for being interested in the Maskells' lifestyle. 'Do you know my friend, Mary Mercer?'

'A bit.' Dot didn't elaborate. In her opinion, Juliet Maskell had made a mistake agreeing to have Mary in the house. It didn't do to open the door to temptation like that. You could see at a glance that Mary might not be the sort to keep her hands off another woman's husband. Quickly she switched subjects. 'Now, the Scotts, they're different. Mrs Scott's a stickler for doing things right, and the doctor himself has always liked hobnobbing.'

'Oh.' Judging it best to keep a neutral stance on this one, Laura let the subject hang in mid-air. She felt the ground she'd made up in the eyes of her landlady begin to slip away again.

Dot gave her a piercing glance. 'Yes, and that daughter of theirs, Aimee. She needs a firm hand, but there's fat chance of that, believe me. She's off the rails, is that girl, and no one seems able to put her back on.'

Curiosity got the better of Laura. If Gerald had a problem at home, perhaps she'd better hear it after all.

'They have a position to keep up, of course.'

'And their daughter's out to sabotage them, is that it?'

'You could look at it like that, I suppose. Anyway, she's set on making herself the talk of the village.' Suddenly Dot drew back. She tightened her expression and leaned back in her seat, realising that Laura must think that she went in for non-stop moaning and criticising. 'But then, maybe it's me. Living in London, I'm sure you came across far worse than Aimee Scott.'

'We'll see. Most girls go through that phase.'

To Dot it looked more bizarre, brought up as she was on digging for victory and making suits out of blankets; whatever they had to do to make a decent impression during the war years. Aimee's offence, it had to be said, partly lay in the length of her skirt and the colour of her nail varnish.

Dot pursed her lips then looked pointedly at the empty cups and saucers as the cuckoo clock in the hall chimed seven-thirty. 'Now, I'd better get these things tidied up.'

Laura remembered her luggage, still standing at the gate, and went out to fetch it. Sure enough, the cases stood undisturbed in the dusk, silently watched over by a little girl in jeans and a red sweatshirt. She held the hand of her toddler companion.

Dot watched and listened from a safe distance.

'Them's too heavy to manage, Miss.' The girl shook her blonde ponytail in disbelief as Laura lifted the biggest one clear of the cobbles. 'Are you moving in with Mrs Wilson, then?'

Laura smiled and nodded.

The little girl's eyes sparkled, and she galloped with toddler in tow towards a playground by the river, where she would no doubt spread the news. 'A lady with three big suitcases and a silver car is coming to live at Mrs Wilson's!'

CHAPTER FOUR

'This is quite a place,' Laura told Philip as he opened the door at Bridge House. She'd bathed, and changed into a long, straight skirt with a soft, light sweater, then driven to the Maskells' house, recognising it by its riverside setting. It was an impressively large stone building, bearing the date and the mason's initials above the doorway: WIW 1624.

'Hard to miss, isn't it?' remarked Philip, as he welcomed her in and introduced her to his wife, Juliet.

Laura shook hands with a smiling woman, her face framed by short fair hair. Dressed in a red print blouse and dark trousers, Juliet sounded sincerely pleased to welcome her husband's new partner. 'I'm glad you're here. You'll be a breath of fresh air.' She led the way into a sitting room with a blazing log fire.

'Fresh air? I wouldn't have thought that was in short supply round here.' Laura took in the big stone fireplace and beamed ceiling.

'It is fairly bracing, isn't it?' laughed Juliet.

'The wind was the first thing I noticed. I stopped the car on the hill overlooking the dale to take a look. I found out straight away why all the trees slant heavily in one direction.'

They chatted on while Philip offered drinks. 'It blows from the west,' Juliet said. 'In winter it's bitter. You've only seen it at its best.'

Juliet's unselfconscious manner put her guest at ease. She conveyed a genuine interest in Laura, asking for her first impressions of Hawkshead.

'After all, I don't count the time you came up to look around the medical centre. Interviews are such pressured situations, you can hardly get an accurate feel for a place.'

'I like what I've seen so far. The place and the people. It remains to be seen whether or not they like me.'

Philip stepped in with advice as he handed her a drink. 'Fatal first mistake, expecting your patients to like you. Especially up here. Liking comes way down the list.'

'What's at the top then?' In Camden Laura had found it easy to win the confidence of her patients, particularly among the young.

'Respect comes pretty high up.'

'Fair enough. But how long will that take?' She imagined a trial period, when she would have to prove herself.

'Ask me again in ten years' time.'

'Philip!' Juliet remonstrated. 'Poor Laura will be packing her bags and heading straight back south if you're not careful.' She turned to their guest. 'I take it Gerald gave you your official welcome when you first arrived?'

'Why, is there a connection between the two?'

Juliet thought for a moment. 'Oh I see. Gerald and heading back south. I didn't mean it to sound like that!'

At least Juliet spared her the line about Gerald's bark being worse than his bite. 'I had the ritualistic warnings,' Laura admitted. 'But don't imagine I came up to Ravensdale wearing rose-coloured glasses.' She could have told them that coping with a multicultural, mobile urban list brought its own stresses and hazards, but she resisted. 'I'm probably tougher than I look.'

'I'll go and tell Mary you're here,' Philip announced. 'She missed you earlier when she came down to the centre, but I know for a fact that she's dying to swap news; who's in amongst your group of friends, who's out, who's married, who's divorced.' He stopped short.

'There's me for a start,' she owned up without embarrassment.

Philip cleared his throat and left the room.

'Big feet,' Juliet said with a shrug. 'He must have forgotten. But tact was never Philip's strong point.'

'I don't mind. It's one of the reasons I'm looking forward to a new challenge. After my break with Tom I needed a change of direction.'

'And do you think you've got it?'

'Ask me that in ten years!'

They were laughing when Mary swept into the room and swamped Laura in an expansive hug. 'I didn't hear you arrive. I wanted to give you the full prodigal whatsit treatment, waiting at the threshold with arms outstretched as the wanderer returned.

You know, I never dreamt in a million years that we'd both find ourselves in Yorkshire. But I don't know, it seems to have a way of dragging you back.'

'Not so much of the dragging, please! This is a forward move for me.'

Mary perched on the arm of Laura's chair. 'Lucky you. At my age the parts begin to dry up. Too old for the romantic lead, too young for dotty old ladies. The last thing I did was a manic depressive housewife in some searing psychological drama. We toured the provinces to half-empty houses. After five weeks I was as crazy as the part I was playing.'

She exaggerated, but Laura read the signs of disillusionment in her friend, who had never been able to settle for half measures.

'So what's new, you might say. Anyway, after that it was back to the old standby of teaching. And that's what brought me back here kicking and screaming.' She stood up to join Philip by the fire. 'Actually, I find it's not too bad, much to my surprise. Do you mind if I show Laura round?' she asked Juliet. They went into the hall. 'Well, what do you think? Isn't this an amazing house?'

'Inside and out,' Laura agreed. 'Trust you to find somewhere like this, Mary. Lesser mortals would have to settle for a maisonette when they took a new job.' Her friend had always done things in style.

Mary took Laura across the flagged floor, past another arched stone fireplace and oak panelling as elaborate as any church's, up a magnificent staircase and along a gallery overlooking deep seventeenth-century windows. She glimpsed a bedroom with a four-poster, a bathroom complete with Victorian fittings, and vast overhead beams that listed at an angle of thirty degrees.

'Impressed?' Mary waltzed ahead, pointing out this and that. 'My bedroom. Philip's office.' She pointed to a low door at the end of the gallery. 'Do not disturb!'

Laura paused for breath. 'Mary, how on earth did you land up in a place like this?' She expected the story to be a good one. Mary's life had been a film-script of hair's breadth escapes, passionate affairs and far-flung adventures. She had the looks to match; strikingly tall and thin with a mass of unruly hennaed hair and heavily lashed eyes. It was a consumptive, interesting style, enhanced by dark, flowing clothes, big jewellery and attention-seeking hats.

'Come into my room and I'll reveal all.'

Laura sat down on Mary's bed, expecting to hear how her friend had crammed in a couple of affairs, a serious breakdown and several jobs during the length of time it had taken her to leave Tom.

'How I got here isn't the point really. A friend of a friend, that sort of thing. But the fact is I'm lovelorn.' She leaned back on her elbows on the bed next to Laura. 'A poor lorn thing.'

'Truly?'

'Yes, and before you ask, my lips are sealed over the precise object of my affections. Suffice it to say that he is not free! Convention has a tight hold around here, as you probably remember, and a stiff upper lip is the order of the day. Find the heart and chop it out, in case things get messy.'

'Ouch.'

'We'd better change the subject before I go all feeble and break down. What do you think of the house?'

'Wonderful.' She recalled its impact as she first approached. The builders had worked with little regard to symmetry, so that the roof dipped unaccountably in places, and stone gargoyles leered at odd angles from the scrolled and fluted mullions.

'Let's go back down, shall we? My glass is empty.' Mary led the way out onto the gallery. 'How much do you believe in mind over matter, Laura? I'm asking you from the medical point of view.'

'As far as illness goes?'

'I was thinking more about love, actually. Is love matter? Does it go away if you simply refuse to think about it?'

Laura touched her arm. 'Poor Mary, I don't know. Love hurts, I do know that. And the loss of it. We're the walking wounded, but who isn't these days?'

Mary linked arms and swayed down the corridor. 'The bloody house lists like a ship in a storm, or am I drunk?' She went quiet. 'Juliet.' She came up with an answer to Laura's question before they went down to rejoin their hosts. 'Juliet's not one of the walking wounded, lucky woman.'

CHAPTER FIVE

Laura woke next morning knowing that this was an important day for her; her first eight hundred, as Gerald called his early morning meetings, and her first surgery, when she would make contact with her new patients.

She dressed carefully in grey trousers and matching jacket, with an open-necked white silk blouse. She put on make-up and small gold earrings, took off the latter, put them on again, considered leaving her hair loose, then put a clip at the back to restrain the wavy effect, wanting to get the image just right. She made her way downstairs to negotiate the hazards of Dot's kitchen; the ancient electric kettle, the temperamental toaster and the bread knife, sharp as a surgeon's scalpel.

It seemed that her landlady's attempts to update the Victorian kitchen had faltered some time during the late fifties, pre-fitted units but post-Formica. All was buttercup yellow and scrupulously clean.

Dot had already left the house and gone to work, leaving a note. 'Dear Dr Grant, My work hours at Bridge House are seven until twelve. Please help yourself to breakfast items left out on the table. Dot Wilson.'

Laura made herself toast and coffee, and timed herself to arrive at the centre with just five minutes to spare. She prepared to meet up with the other members of Ravensdale's primary care team: Gerald and Philip, plus Joy Hartley, the practice nurse.

Theirs was a wide brief in more ways than one. Hawkshead was at the centre of a three hundred square mile pitch, which included hundreds of remote farms and almost twenty hamlets, some no bigger than three houses and a pub. The team serviced a sheltered accommodation complex in the village, ran ante-natal clinics and maintained close links with Wingate General. Still, the doctors managed to find time for old fashioned look-in visits to patients in remote areas – a priority as far as Gerald was concerned. His philosophy of cradle-to-grave medical care might be out of step with modern notions of capitation and formula funding, but it was one of the aspects of the job that had drawn Laura to Ravensdale. She shared the belief that time and money shouldn't exert tyrannical sway over the treatment of people who were seriously ill.

Joy Hartley greeted her at the door with a warm smile, then left her to her own devices, explaining that since her husband was in bed with flu, she'd had to make special arrangements to get their three children to school. She went straight into the office to make a phone call to check that all had gone according to plan.

In the event, it was Philip who took Laura under his wing. He spent five minutes filling her in on the building of the new centre, which had moved from an old terraced house in the village square to smart new premises by the river.

In the early days, as a young GP, Philip had lived over the shop, an experience he claimed not to miss when the purpose-built centre was opened ten years previously. 'No more rude awakenings in the dead of night,' he explained to Laura. 'Give me the civilising distance of the telephone any day.'

He'd clearly been proud of the part he'd played with Gerald in planning, building and paying for the riverside site on a fifteen-year government loan. The central waiting room was large and airy, with glass panels in its high sloping roof. There was a play area for children, and racks well stocked with information leaflets and magazines. The consulting rooms led off from three corners of the central area, and the nurse's treatment room occupied the fourth. 'When I first came into practice with Gerald,' he told her, 'I never dreamed that one day we'd be proud owners of a place like this. Mind you, it took some doing. We spent a lot of hours with our sleeves rolled up and paintbrushes at the ready. That was the only way we could make ends meet in those days, a handy spot of DIY.'

He led her into the eight hundred, paying thoughtful attention to her needs; did she want coffee, did she mind the draught from the window?

'No, it's fine. And, yes please, coffee.' She smiled. He just had time to bring it and settle down beside her before the meeting began.

A steady stream of information followed, about diagnoses,

aftercare, referrals and test results. The psycho-geriatric unit at Wingate was full, Philip reported. They must try to find Elspeth Knightley a place elsewhere; her daughter was concerned about her after a recent fall.

Joy said that her case-load was stretched to breaking point by two new cases of osteo-arthritis. She needed to refer them quickly to a physiotherapist. The waiting time for knee and hip replacements at Wingate General was getting worse, she discovered.

Then she reported on the latest hiccough in her liaison with social services over home help for Dick Metcalfe. 'There's a dispute over what constitutes lifting him when he takes a bath,' she told them. 'Dick can't manage to get in and out by himself, but he refuses to have a hoist. And Margaret Utley at social services insists that her home helps aren't qualified to give him the level of assistance he needs. But unless he accepts the hoist, our remit doesn't allow him to qualify for help from a health visitor either. So we're stuck, I'm afraid.'

'Meanwhile the old boy goes without.' Gerald frowned.

'He could always pay for a private nurse, I suppose.' Joy evidently wasn't happy.

'Eight quid a time for a bloody bath?' came the short reply.

'Glad you came?' Philip asked Laura in the awkward silence.

'Tell me something new.' These were familiar problems; a warning that her job here would be beset with the usual practical difficulties. In Camden days she would have gone home and spilled it all out to Tom, whose fury would turn into campaigning zeal and renewed public hounding of the current Health Secretary.

'How about this?' Gerald tapped his pen on the prescription pad on his desk. 'Order a hoist, Joy. Go through the channels to get him set up for the thing. Explain to the old devil that if the hoist stays in place over the bath, he qualifies for your assistance. Make it clear he doesn't have to use it. Then you can get on and give him the help he will actually accept.'

They considered this. It seemed a decent compromise.

'Tell him he'll save a few quid a throw,' Philip suggested.

Joy's face broke into a smile. 'I'm sure he'll snap my hand off in that case.'

'Fine.' Gerald clicked his pen and stabbed the paper one last time. 'Next?'

Philip steered them through latest numbers for ante-natal

clinics, and a case of confirmed Down's syndrome where the parents-to-be had asked for counselling. Then there were follow-ups from Gerald on recently diagnosed cases of diabetes, angina and leukaemia. By nine o'clock, when surgery was due to begin, Laura felt nicely broken in.

'Now for the baptism of fire.' Gerald stood up and faced her across the desk. He didn't trouble to keep his voice down. It boomed through the open door into the crowded waiting room. All heads turned.

'Good luck, Laura. I'm sure you'll be fine.' Philip spoke quietly, heading off to his own room.

'Don't you believe it.' Gerald led her to the door and invited the patients to share the joke. 'But remember, their bark is generally worse than their bite.'

It was all right for him, Laura thought. She fastened her jacket buttons and went through Reception into her own room. Gerald had known most of them all their lives and they evidently appreciated his humorous touch. But she felt her dignity take an unwarranted knock. Then she scolded herself for being hypersensitive. She sat behind her desk and waited for her first patient to present himself.

By half past nine, she'd looked down several ears and throats, checked rashes and temperatures, and advised a new diet for a patient with high cholesterol levels. So far, no one had bitten her.

They came in, some wary of the newcomer, but most ready to welcome any attention paid to their symptoms. A worried mother thanked her for the diagnosis of measles on her three-year-old boy, and Laura suggested immunisation for the rest of the family. She reassured an angina sufferer whose anxiety required a prescription for diazepam. By ten-thirty, she felt thoroughly at home.

She had two memorable patients that first morning, each of whom stuck in her mind for different reasons. The first was Lilian Rigg, a woman in her late sixties, who came in apparently glowing with health, tanned after a summer in the open air, her grey hair cropped, her figure sturdy under a Fair Isle pullover and corduroy trousers, her gaze direct.

'Now look,' she began, 'it's no good. With a job like mine you need to be able to bend and lift and fettle yourself properly. I want you to give me something for these twinges. But I don't want messing about. So what's it to be?'

Laura returned her gaze. 'Where are the twinges exactly, Mrs Rigg?' She checked the computer screen for details of her patient's history. To her surprise, it was completely blank.

'Nay, there's no use looking on there. I don't have much call for medicine as a rule.'

As it turned out, this was an understatement. Lilian Rigg had been registered with the practice since birth, but had never visited the surgery in her life. She ran a little business, she said, managing all right on her own since her husband's death five years earlier. It was a small garden centre, out of town at Abbey Grange, across the river from the Abbey itself at the bottom of Black Gill. 'Nothing fancy,' she said modestly. 'Old varieties of plants, mostly herbaceous and heathers, though I have a nice line in out-of-the-way *primula denticulata*; a pretty little black one with yellow edges. Quite rare.'

Laura nodded. 'Are these twinges in your back?'

'Low down here. I can't dig like I used to. It's a damned nuisance.'

'And no pain anywhere else? How long have you had the problem?'

'I haven't reckoned it up exactly. A few months, a year maybe.'

Laura glanced up from her notes.

'Nay, I've no time in the summer to be bothered coming down here.' Lilian's speech, though it stuck to dialect rhythms, lacked the local pronunciation. There was evidence of wider experience, better education than the dale would have afforded in the thirties and forties.

Laura looked at her sideways. 'Well, it sounds like lumbago, Mrs Rigg. I can give you an anti-inflammatory drug to help, but you know the best treatment is rest, don't you?'

'Aye, I knew you'd say that.'

'Well, it's true. You should put as little strain as possible on your back, give it a chance to recover.'

Lilian stood up, determined to deal with it in her own way. 'Thank you, Doctor. If you just give me my prescription, I'll get out from under your feet.'

Laura handed her the paper. 'This should help.' It was difficult to imagine anyone less inclined than Lilian Rigg to take to her bed and rest. She shook the proffered workworn hand. 'Come back if you've any more problems, OK?'

'I will, doctor. But I'll be right as rain as soon as I get these little chaps down me. I shan't trouble you again.'

Laura smiled as the door swung to. Many more patients like Lilian would soon put her out of a job.

The second memorable consultation came at ten-thirty, the last appointment on the list for Laura's morning surgery. She'd noted the name with a start; Aimee Scott.

Aimee made her entrance with all the hostility and suspicion that an unhappy sixteen-year-old can muster. Her dark, straight hair hung forward in a dense curtain across her pale face. She hung her head, shooting piercing glances round the room with her large grey eyes. It was clear she intended Laura to understand that she regarded the whole episode as a bore.

'Hello, Aimee, how can I help?' Laura, noting the tight black jumper and dangerously short skirt, the silver rings across the knuckles of both hands, the shadows under the made-up eyes, understood Dot's dim view of Gerald's daughter.

'Look, I don't want a fuss, right? I made Philip make this appointment without telling my father. I'm entitled to do that.'

'Sure.' Laura gave no sign that Aimee was doing anything untoward. She met her gaze.

'I'd only get a lecture. And my mum would only worry if she found out.'

'Fine. Tell me what the problem is and then we can take it from there.'

Aimee's gaze grew still more intense. 'I would've thought it was obvious. I need the morning-after pill, or whatever you call it.'

Not so sophisticated, not so very much in control, Laura thought. 'All right, so how long is it since intercourse took place?'

'The night before last.'

'Unprotected?'

She nodded.

Laura was puzzled. Girls with Aimee's attitude usually got it together before the event, not after.

'Don't start,' Aimee warned. 'It was all perfectly straightforward. No one forced me.'

'And now you're having second thoughts?'

'Yeah well, I'm sober now, aren't I?'

Laura looked at the screen for her patient's recent history. Vaccinations to travel to Goa a couple of summers earlier, treatment for migraine attacks connected with menstrual cycle, no prescription before now for the contraceptive pill. 'Are we talking about a long-term relationship, Aimee?'

'Why?'

'Because if we are, perhaps you and your boyfriend would like to come in and discuss the various options.' She was trying not to pry or push.

'I don't think you could call one night long term, do you?' Aimee said. 'I took a risk, that's all, a one-off. God, do I have to spell it out?'

'Of course not. If we go through to the treatment room, Joy will be able to fix you up.' Laura stood up. If her patient wouldn't be drawn, all that remained was to reassure her that this particular pill would be effective up to forty-eight hours after the event, with no side effects.

Relief flickered briefly across Aimee's face, then vanished. 'I said I didn't want anyone else to know.'

'But Joy is a nurse. She doesn't discuss her patients any more than I do.'

'I came to you because I've never seen you before. Joy's known me for ages.' Aimee clamped her mouth shut.

'Fair enough. I'll bring it in here. I'll just be one minute.' She left the room and closed the door behind her.

'Everything all right?' Sheila Knowles glanced up from behind her desk.

'Yes, but just keep an eye on my door and make sure my patient doesn't bolt, would you?' She went into the nurse's treatment room, collected the necessary contraceptive and returned to Aimee. The girl was still there, sitting on the edge of her seat. She took the pill and stuffed it into her mouth. Then she rearranged her features into the earlier show of bravado.

'Thanks.' She got up and was halfway to the door before Laura could reply.

Leaving her room shortly afterwards, Laura saw Sheila raise her eyebrows.

'How did it go?' she asked.

'Fine. No problem.' Ravensdale, Camden; the dilemmas were

33

identical. You could be a stoical old woman or a rebellious teenager in either place. It didn't take a genius to realise that.

But there was a sharp edge to her curiosity about Gerald and his relationship with his wayward daughter. It wasn't difficult to imagine the lecture that Aimee had been so anxious to avoid, but it seemed to go deeper than that. There was more at stake than an early sexual blunder and a father reluctantly coming to terms with his daughter's maturity.

Aimee had been ferocious over the issue of confidentiality; it had even spilled over to Joy and Sheila. In fact, the only person she'd been prepared to trust was a complete stranger. Laura could picture her dilemma with painful clarity; a desperate fear of pregnancy pitted against an instinct for privacy. This withdrawn behaviour was surely a symptom, but whatever was troubling her lay deeply hidden.

Laura put on her jacket to set out on her first round of home visits. She must let it alone. All she could do was wait to see whether or not Aimee came back to the surgery. Meanwhile there was a full case-load to take over, an ordnance survey map in her pocket to help her find her bearings, and a kind smile from Sheila to send her on her way.

CHAPTER SIX

The next time Laura came across Aimee Scott was not at the surgery but at Philip's house, where she went to meet Mary. It was a week after her arrival in the dale, a breezy Sunday, the last in October. As she walked down to Bridge House, she saw the wind at work stripping the sparse trees and sending crisp golden leaves spiralling down the valley.

She arrived at the house with her face tingling, intrigued to discover whether Mary had kept her resolution to fall out of love as quickly and quietly as possible. She hadn't expected to share her friend's company with Gerald's daughter.

'Laura, come in.' Mary had spotted her before she rang the bell. 'I'm all alone. Philip and Juliet have gone to Paris for the weekend. Aimee dropped by, as you can see.'

'Paris?' She unzipped her jacket and followed Mary into the kitchen.

'Yes, *très* romantic, no?' Mary cleared a space at the table. 'Excuse the mess. Washing up isn't one of my strong points.' The sink was piled high with coffee cups, the table hidden under a landslide of magazines. Evidently resenting the interruption, Aimee scowled at some fashion pages.

'This is Aimee, Gerald's daughter.' Mary introduced them. 'She's one of my A-level students, for my sins. I'm helping her to catch up on an assignment.'

Laura offered to wait in another room until they'd finished.

'No, it's OK, we just did, didn't we, Aimee?'

Laura smiled and said hello. The girl's eyelids flicked up, then down. Neither mentioned their previous meeting.

'The problem is, how to convince someone they have talent when they're dead set on telling themselves they're useless.' Mary pondered aloud as she fished out two mugs and swilled them under the tap. 'I suppose that's the million-dollar question that all teachers ask. No, don't worry about this little lot.' She shoved Laura to one side as she half-heartedly volunteered to help with the washing-up. 'Dot comes in tomorrow morning at some ungodly hour. I'll whisk through the place tonight before I go to bed.' She picked up a sticky teaspoon and delved into the coffee jar.

Aimee stood and stuffed a folder into a leather rucksack.

'You're sure you've finished?' Laura connected her own arrival with Aimee's surly departure.

The girl shrugged. 'It'll be a lousy assignment anyway. I hate doing them.' She headed for the door. Today, her skin-tight black jeans emphasised her slim legs. A heavy-ribbed jumper, the colour of mud and badly frayed at the cuffs, fell shapelessly from her slight shoulders. 'Bye,' she said to Mary, slamming the door as she went.

'See?' Mary handed Laura her coffee. 'Low self-esteem. Don't take it personally.'

'She seems to get on with you all right though.'

'Oh, like a house on fire while we're out of school. Inside the place she ignores me and misses all my lessons. That's why she's fallen behind.'

'How does she get on with the other teachers?'

'Don't ask. Poor Gerald and Janet, they're in for a terrible shock when they come to the next parents' evening. However you couch it, we're all going to have to come clean and tell them the kid doesn't do a stroke of work, rarely shows up in school, and is likely to fail all her exams unless she bucks up.'

'Well, it strikes me that if she wants extra help from you, all's not lost.' Laura thought through Aimee's problems. 'Does she have a boyfriend?'

'Not as far as I know. She does seem to hang out with older men, though. Another worrying sign?' Mary gathered her hair in an untidy coil on top of her head. 'Enough of that. So, how's the new doctor getting along?'

Laura thought back over a week of surgeries and home visits stretched more or less end to end, with few gaps for relaxation. Responses from patients had ranged from caution to downright hostility, with a light smattering of friendliness from some of her younger patients. She'd driven long roads on her rounds, out to a distant farm to see an elderly woman enduring the last stages of cancer, the farmer himself telling her he wasn't taken with the new-fangled treatments that left his wife feeling poorly and still going downhill fast. More cheerfully, she'd attended Joy's ante-natal clinic on the Thursday morning, and once, after a ten-mile drive, had actually been greeted with a smile and the invitation to, 'Come thi ways, sit thee-sen down and reach to'; the old fashioned Yorkshire welcome to a pot of hot tea and a plate of home-made scones.

'I suppose you could say I'm finding my way,' she told Mary cautiously.

'You look well on it.' She studied Laura's oval face and clear complexion. 'But then, you always thrived on hard work. And you're not missing the smoke?'

'London? No, not for a minute.'

'Or your sleaze-digging husband?'

'Ex-husband.' Laura sighed.

'Fascists,' Mary murmured, letting some of her bravado drop. 'I mean, men and their expectations.'

'How about you?'

Mary rolled her dark eyes. 'Com-pli-cated!' she drawled.

'Still not ready to talk?'

'Later, maybe. Say, let's get out into the fresh air.' She jumped to her feet and scrambled for a jacket beneath a heap of outdoor clothes piled onto a chair.

Laura mimicked astonishment. 'Mary Mercer, I thought you were allergic to fresh air. Remember all those cross-country races they made us run? Weren't you the one with sudden stomach cramps and mysterious headaches?'

'I should think so too. God, that gym mistress was a sadist, sending us tender young things out in our aertex vests and gym knickers to contend with the elements and the local builders.' Mary looked round vaguely. 'Can you see a tartan scarf anywhere? Oh, never mind. Come on, let's go for a walk along the moor.' She'd grabbed a black velvet hat with a soft brim and stuffed her hair inside, fixing it low on her forehead. 'I'll meet you outside in a couple of secs.'

From Bridge House, they walked through the village and climbed onto the moortop, through a dramatic change of scenery, from sloping green fields dotted with trees and barns to a wind- and rain-scoured landscape of exposed limestone pavements. There were dizzying drops into natural pits carved out by rainwater eating away at the stone. Laura stopped to peer over the edge of the beautifully fluted rock faces, sometimes scores of feet deep. She held her breath as Mary leapt neatly over a chasm.

'Is it ever not windy up here?' she yelled to Mary, who held fast to her hat.

'No, it's never not windy. And you never see another soul, unless you're dead unlucky.'

They stood on the summit, bridging Ravensdale and Swiredale, feeling the wind tug at their clothes and freshen their faces. Laura felt as close as she'd ever been to heaven on earth. Then Mary led the way along the ridge, pointing out the steel-blue stretch of water in the distance. 'Over there's Ravensdale Tarn, and you see the house beyond?'

Laura made out a fairly grand building, more than a farmhouse with its three storeys, tall chimneys and arched doorway.

'Ravenscar Hall. Built by Quakers. It's run as an outdoor pursuits centre now. There's something bracing about it, don't you think? I'll bring you up here in winter when it's snowing. Come on.' Mary rushed on, turning away from the summit and setting off down a steep gulley where rainwater gushed and splashed down a darker rock than the pale limestone they'd left behind. Here, ferns clung to ledges and saplings leaned over the foaming stream. Laura caught hold of the low branches to ease her descent, planting her boots firmly on the wet, mossy surface of the rocks.

She looked up at the network of branches. A weak sun shone through white clouds, but the gulley felt permanently damp and dark. The water splashed and played amongst the rocks and the place smelt of sharp, wet earth.

'Where are we now?'

'Black Gill. We're going to see something really special. Come on.'

'Are we on a proper footpath?' Laura hesitated. 'It feels as if no one has set foot here before.' The light cast green shadows off the damp Gill sides.

Mary laughed. ' "She dwelt among the untrodden ways",' she quoted. ' "Beside the springs of Dove." Do you remember that one?' She grabbed a sapling as she slid into the water, then drenched them both with a shake of her long scarf.

' "A maid whom there were none to praise, And very few to

love." ' Laura smiled. 'I certainly do. Something about violets and mossy stones and living unknown.'

Mary took up the verse. ' "She lived unknown, and few could know When Lucy ceased to be; But she is in her grave, and, oh, The difference to me!" ' Her eyes filled with tears. 'Oh, don't start me off, Laura.'

'I didn't.' She walked on. 'Do you want to talk about it now?'

'I don't know. You promise not to tell me what I should do? Sorry, I didn't mean that. It's just that you doctors are always so logical and practical about things like aching souls. You say, what's an aching soul beside quadraplegia or cancer of the oesophagus?'

Laura managed to laugh. 'Only other people's souls.' Not her own. Leaving Tom had been the hardest thing she'd ever done. 'So tell me.' She linked arms with her friend and they walked together down the narrow gorge.

'I shouldn't be saying anything. I promised myself I wouldn't make me the centre of the universe for a change.'

'So suddenly you're superhuman?'

'No. But you don't go on and on about things like I do.'

'Who's to say I'm right? If I don't go into details, it's only because I don't want you to see me in a bad light. And you would, if I told you what went on between Tom and me at our worst.'

'You don't mean to say you actually fought?'

'Fisticuffs? No, I'm too much of a physical coward. But I do have a wicked tongue. And I used it to hurt him as much as I could.'

'To get your own back, I expect. Who won, you or him?'

Laura considered for a while. 'I did, on the tiebreaker.'

Mary nodded. 'Well done.'

'I'm not sure about that.' Laura went ahead down the rocky slope by the side of the stream. 'Not when winning costs you everything you ever tried to build up within the marriage; stability, companionship and all the rest.'

'Sex?'

'Oh, that.' She knew that she and Mary would differ over this. Her friend's indiscretions, as she liked to call them, were brief and spectacular and were always sparked off – and usually ended – by physical attraction.

There was a pause as they found their way down another muddy slope. 'This time, though,' Mary continued, 'it's not that I fancy the man – well, I do – but it's not just that. I think I'm actually falling in love with him.'

'And this is making you unhappy?'

'Miserable. I ache with it, I cry myself to sleep, it's pitiful.'

'It's Philip, isn't it?' Laura guessed.

Mary gave a sudden intake of breath. 'Oh my God, is it that obvious?'

There were signs: Mary's uneasy jokiness with Philip, the conscious effort to keep up a light flirtation that she'd seen during the first evening. 'No, not obvious. I don't think Philip would take it seriously.'

'Do you think Juliet's spotted it?'

'Pretty certainly not, though I hardly know her. She seems friendly enough though.'

'That's just it, she's so nice!' Mary wailed. 'I genuinely like the woman. She's been great about letting me have the run of the house since I moved in, and she's introduced me to their set of friends.

'The thing is, Philip's on my mind all the time, lurking somewhere. Then, just as I've kidded myself that I've got it under control, he walks through the door and the whole thing kicks off again. I mean it; he just has to come into the kitchen and ask if I want a drink and my knees turn to jelly, I can't trust myself to speak. On the other hand, if he doesn't come in, I start to wonder where he is and whether I might risk running into him at the Falcon to see what might develop.'

'But he's not even your usual type.'

'No bohemian credentials? No magnetic stare?'

'Exactly. Philip's so – well, he's so stable.' So far, Laura hadn't seen him in any kind of romantic light.

'– And wildly attractive, and lean and strong. He's a man you can be sure of.'

Laura didn't take her up on this, but there was a lack of logic here. If Philip were suddenly to change the habit of a lifetime and jettison Juliet for Mary, he would no longer be the sort of man any woman could rely on. It was her turn to walk on, almost wishing that Mary had left her in the dark. How would she deal with Philip now?

'Where's this place you want to show me?' she asked.

'Joan's Foss. It's my secret place.' Mary overtook her again, bringing them to a ledge where a waterfall spilled over a crescent of rock into a crystal clear pool some twenty feet below.

'What are you doing?' Laura stared at Mary, who had kicked off her boots and was already halfway out of her jacket. 'You're not going to jump in, are you?'

'I certainly am.' She struggled out of the rest of her clothes, bundled them inside her jacket and flung the lot onto the pebble shore by the pool.

'Mary, this is Yorkshire! This is Methodist country, this is a Sunday afternoon! It's nearly November!' And what's more, she thought she'd heard footsteps following them down the hill. She glanced quickly over her shoulder. Nothing.

'Coward.'

'Oh God,' Laura groaned, following suit. 'I must be mad.' She felt the autumn air cold against her skin.

Mary stepped into the water. She stood shivering on the ledge and held her breath. Then she leapt. Her body, white in the shadow, plummeted and splashed into the pool.

Still groaning, Laura stepped towards the edge of the waterfall and felt the clear water swirl around her own ankles. Below, she saw Mary rise to the surface, her dark hair fanned wide.

'It's bloody brilliant!' she called.

Laura stepped closer still to the edge. A boy's face peered out of a bush growing close to the waterfall, then another. Closing her eyes, she jumped into the ice-green depths, touched the bottom and kicked upwards, her body surrounded by bubbles, her face pointing upwards to the bright, white, swirling surface.

CHAPTER SEVEN

Philip stood at the bar of the Falcon later that night, an awkward smile spreading across his face as he listened in to the latest scandal.

'Bloody barmy!' Tot Dinsdale sank his face into a frothy head of beer. 'Swimming, you say? Up at Joan's Foss? Without togs?'

Reports had flown down to the village. Now he must endure the after-shock.

Ancient longings stirred in the old farmer. 'By gum!'

'They was caught at it by a couple of young lads. They say it was a sight for sore eyes.'

'Now, Dick.' Dot's monosyllabic warning from her seat in the corner with Lilian Rigg spoke volumes.

'Don't you now-Dick me, Dorothy. You know what I'm saying's the gospel truth.'

'And what if it is?'

By now the old man was unstoppable. 'Didn't the new doctor come home with her hair wet through at teatime? And isn't that all the proof you need?'

Dot refused to rise to the bait.

'But it'd be a bit nippy,' Tot put in, thoroughly enjoying himself.

Philip grinned at Brian Lawson behind the bar. 'I see the old imagination still works well enough, Tot?'

'Aye, it's a pity I can't say the same for the bits that count.'

Dick took up the reins once more. 'All I'm saying is, it's a free country. I hear Dr Scott got wind of what went on up at the Foss and he was in a right lather. There's talk he intends to drop in a word at the Hall.'

'Why's that?' Brian encouraged him to continue, though Dot and Lilian sat stiff backed, determined to ignore the gossip.

Philip realised that the two old men liked to make mountains out of molehills and wasn't worried by any of it. Nevertheless, he put in a word of defence on behalf of the practice. 'You don't want to believe a word you hear,' he warned.

'Dr Scott thinks Mrs Aire should know,' Dick insisted.

'What's it to do with her ladyship?' Tot growled.

'The Foss is on Aire land, of course. So what goes on there is her business, according to some. Course, she'll reckon nowt to these kind of goings-on.'

Tot shook his head. 'Dr Maskell's right, people should keep their noses out. Before you know it, Maisie Aire will have it all fenced off, with notices to stop people from swimming. You know what she's like.'

'Don't worry, Tot,' Philip told him, getting over the shock of suddenly having him on his side. 'Black Gill is a public right of way. They can't touch it.'

'Quite right.' Tot downed his pint.

'Nay, you old sod, when did you bother about rights of way?' Dick chuntered on. He took the chance of one last dig. 'Aye, but the new doctor and the schoolteacher!'

This time Philip's smile was more forced. On the whole things were less complicated if he didn't try too hard to picture the scene. He guessed that it had been Mary's idea.

It was the landlord who eventually eclipsed this prime piece of gossip with one of his own. 'It's not fencing and notices you need to bother about.' He spoke to Philip, but intended his news for general consumption. 'From what I hear, those surveyors from the quarry company have been snooping around up there again.'

Immediately, Lilian and Dot turned round to listen. Philip found himself paying attention; any news spread by Brian Lawson tended to be reliable. After all, the pub was the centre of the village, a kind of crossroads for information both trivial and important. 'Are you sure?' he asked. 'I thought the quarry idea was dead and buried.'

'The only thing round here that's dead and buried is old Geoffrey Aire, and that's why the surveyors are on the job again.' Brian leaned over his shiny copper bar. 'Mr Aire would never hear of that quarry starting up in the dale. But I wouldn't be so sure about that wife of his.'

Philip weighed it up and couldn't quite dismiss his fears. 'Not if the stone company has sent their men in again. And on the quiet too.'

'That's worse, see.' Brian pressed home the bad tidings. 'They're not going round shouting their heads off. They know how folks round here feel about the quarrying.'

'Ah, it'll never come off.' Tot tried to dismiss it. 'It's all a load of nowt. We've had Aires in this valley since way back, and none of them has started belting holes in them hills yet.'

'It'll be over my dead body and all,' Dick insisted.

Philip listened to the buzz of conversation. He noticed that Dot and Lilian had joined forces with Dick and Tot for a change, and he could see why. A quarry would be the last thing most people would want, himself amongst them.

The idea turned slowly. He considered the angles and concluded, along with the traditionalists, that the landscape was the only thing that remained the same. Generations of farmers were born and died, the old barns on the hillsides fell into disuse or suffered the curse of conversion. But the horizon was timeless. They should never be allowed to interfere with that.

He used the subject to break the ice when, a few days later, Brian Lawson and his wife, Alison, came to the medical centre to keep an appointment with him.

'Any more news of the stone company surveyors?' he asked. Brian looked nervous in these surroundings and it struck Philip how rarely he saw the landlord beyond the four walls of the pub. According to his file, Brian was thirty-eight, though Philip thought he looked younger, which he put down to a good exercise routine, kept up since his cricket playing days. He knew that Brian had played at county level and made a decent career of it through his twenties and into his mid-thirties, before he'd turned to the pub trade. This had been three years earlier, when he'd married for the second time and moved into the dale with Alison to take up the tenancy at the Falcon.

'Not that I've heard. It's as well to keep our ears open, though. The whole thing could slide through without us noticing if we're not careful.'

Philip glanced at Alison. 'You've heard about this latest development?'

'I did hear something. I don't think it'll come to anything, do you?' She spoke without conviction, her mind obviously on other matters.

Alison was younger than Brian, in her mid-twenties, but in a way she looked older than her years, having abandoned the attempt to keep up with fashion and adopted a matronly style. She usually gave the impression of easy-going sociability. Now she sat with her hands clasped, unable to let her gaze settle. She looked at the ceiling, then quickly at Brian, who interpreted this as a signal to begin.

'We need your advice.' He swallowed. Alison stared at her hands.

Brian shrugged; a helpless gesture. 'You must come across this sort of thing a fair amount. I bet your heart sinks. I know mine does.'

'You haven't said what it is yet,' Alison reminded him.

Philip could see the red flush on her neck rising towards her chin. He offered a helping hand. 'As a rule, most couples who make an appointment together want to discuss one of two things; contraception or conception. Not having babies or having them. That's what it comes down to.'

'Yep.' Brian seized the opportunity. 'It's the second.'

'We'd like to have one. Or more.' Alison launched off for herself. 'Only, it's not happening.'

'We've been married three years.'

'And trying for two of those. I mean, I came off the Pill and naturally we assumed that I'd soon get pregnant and we could start a family more or less straight away.'

Philip nodded. 'OK, but I need a bit more background. Alison, this is your first marriage, and Brian, your second?'

They quickly confirmed this, relieved to have got over the first hurdle.

'But Brian, you have a daughter?'

'Nina. She's sixteen. She comes up to stay in the holidays. You've probably seen her around.'

'And Alison, I need to check; you have no previous pregnancies?'

Their histories would take some time to build up. Philip warned them that they would probably only have time for a general chat, then he would send them away with some printed information about fertility; statistics about what might be regarded as a normal incidence of pregnancy, advice on how to optimise their chances and so on. Later, they might have to embark on a series of tests.

Later still, if the situation didn't alter, he could refer them to a specialist in Wingate.

'How long will all this take?' Alison was the one whose expression conveyed most disappointment at the prospect ahead. 'Is there a waiting list to see this specialist?'

Philip consulted another file on the computer. 'I'm afraid so. It could be six to eight months.'

'I said we wouldn't get a solution straight off,' Brian told her gently.

She pressed a hand over her mouth and tears came to her eyes. 'Six months?'

'Perhaps it won't be necessary to refer you.' Philip tried to reassure her. 'Sometimes it's the anxiety that causes the problem. You may find that coming to discuss things here relieves some of that, and pregnancy can follow quite naturally as a result.'

But Alison had gone beyond being consoled. 'I'm sorry.' She huddled forward, rejecting Brian's helping hand. 'It's going to turn out to be my fault, I know it is. What if I can't have babies? What are we going to do?'

Philip handed her a tissue. 'Let's not jump ahead of ourselves. Fertility is a complex issue, there's no blame attached. Let's get that clear.'

'But I know it's me. Look at Brian, he's already got a child of his own. It must be something to do with me, mustn't it?' Her head sank further onto her chest.

'Not necessarily.'

'That's it, see. She thinks like this all the time. She says she's useless. All she ever wanted since we got married was to start a family. I keep telling her she's got plenty of time, she's young. But she won't listen.'

'That's certainly true. How about you? How do you feel about it?'

'I'd like a family, but I'm not desperate.'

Alison pulled herself upright and sniffed. 'That's it, he's not desperate.'

'Meaning what?' Brian cut in.

'Meaning, you wanted children badly enough when you were with Ginny. You went ahead and had Nina. But now, this time, you're not bothered.'

'I never said I didn't want one. I'm here, aren't I?'

Philip listened to what was evidently a well-worn argument. As so often, he saw that the baby issue was opening up cracks in their relationship. Alison seemed to want a baby as a means of cementing their marriage, but Brian was unable to see how much it meant to her. 'What about Nina? How does she feel about the possibility of having a half-sister or brother?'

'She couldn't care less,' Alison said, her voice guarded.

'How do you know? We never asked her.' Brian got up and went to stand at the window.

'So? What are we meant to do, get her permission? It's bad enough you dancing attendance on her every minute without having to get her approval to start our own family!'

Brian turned his back in a stubborn gesture that signified end-of-conversation.

'I'm sorry,' Alison told Philip. 'It's just that I feel he doesn't really want a baby, not deep down. He thinks it might upset Nina.'

'It might,' Philip conceded. 'Children do sometimes find it difficult to adjust to one of their parents starting up another family. On the other hand, she might be pleased.'

'Nina wouldn't be pleased,' Alison insisted. 'You can't talk to Nina about things like that. She has only one word in her vocabulary when she talks to me, and that's n-o, no.'

'That's not fair,' Brian said quietly.

'It is. It's true.'

They were over-running their time, and as usual Philip recognised dimensions to this that had nothing to do with the possible fertility problem. 'Let's take it one step at a time,' he suggested. 'You took the first one by coming here. Let me give you the information I mentioned.' He went to a rack and extracted a couple of leaflets. 'If you read them you can pinpoint for yourselves whether or not you have anything to worry about. Meanwhile, we'll make another appointment. I think it might be as well to see you again in a couple of weeks. At that stage we could well consider going ahead with the business of getting you to see a specialist.' He was upbeat, trying to raise their spirits before they left.

Brian took the leaflets. 'OK, thanks.'

'And try not to worry. This kind of thing is more common than you might realise, and the good news is that the treatments that are available are pretty effective, once the diagnosis is complete.' He turned to Alison. 'Are you happy with the way we're leaving it?'

'Yes. I'm sorry to make a fuss. It's been getting me down lately.'

'That's all right. There's a lot for you two to talk through. Let's see how we go next time.' He showed them to the door. 'Make an appointment with Sheila on your way out, will you?'

They shook hands and the door closed behind them. Philip sat back, relieved to see that they were the last patients on his list. This kind of tangle between people he knew and liked was tiring to deal with. If only it were simply a matter of producing a longed-for baby through a process of screening, pinpointing a difficulty and eliminating it, wouldn't modern medicine deservedly be called a miracle?

He shook himself out of his involvement in the problem by going in search of a coffee and a chat with whoever else happened to be taking a break. The waiting room was mercifully quiet, with toys scattered in the children's corner and magazines open on the low central tables. He glimpsed Joy setting out in her coat and hat, and Sheila busy on the telephone. Laura's door was open, her room empty. He found her in the small kitchen, pouring herself a cup of coffee.

'Want one?' She handed him the one she'd just poured.

'Thanks.'

'Sugar?'

'No, none for me, thanks.' In the cramped space they edged around one another. 'Had a good morning?'

'Pretty straightforward.'

'No teething problems?' She was well into her second week, giving the impression that work was a challenge she constantly relished.

'Not that I'm aware of.' She paused. 'Not with the patients, that is.' She took her own coffee and leaned against the window sill.

He studied her for a moment. 'Is it worth talking about?'

'What?'

'The teething problem that has nothing to do with your patients.'

She wrinkled her nose. 'It's Gerald. He's not speaking to me.'

'Do you know why not?'

'No, it's a complete mystery. As far as I know, I haven't committed any major crime. But he's definitely sent me to Coventry. Has he said anything to you?'

'Not a dicky bird. How long has he been keeping it up?' Philip knew that this was one of Gerald's specialities; the absent-minded gazing into space when a person came into the room, the deliberate forgetting of a name. The offence was usually trivial; a letter that should have gone by first-class post, a request for time off that clashed with Gerald's prior arrangements.

'Since yesterday morning.'

'I shouldn't worry. Why not just enjoy it?' It was best to make light of Gerald's moods, which had certainly been growing more unpredictable lately.

'I'm hoping it hasn't anything to do with Aimee,' she said quietly.

Philip couldn't see the link. 'How come?'

'No, forget I mentioned that, will you? But if you do hear what's eating him, let me know.'

'Eating who?' Gerald's grey-maned head appeared round the kitchen door. He'd done his trick of hearing through walls. Though it was Laura who had spoken, he addressed his question to Philip.

Philip didn't hesitate. 'You, Gerald, as if you didn't know.'

'I wasn't aware that anything was eating me.'

'Well, Laura thinks there is.'

Their senior partner pretended to dig deep into his memory as he busied himself with getting coffee. 'Oh, you must mean the business with Maisie Aire?' He rattled the spoon around the rim of his cup.

Laura looked nonplussed. It wasn't a name that meant anything to her.

'I had a letter from her while you and Juliet were off gadding in Paris. Charming and gracious as ever, written on that distinctive notepaper of hers.'

'What did it say?'

'It thanked me for the many years of exemplary attendance on her and her family, blah blah. She said she was particularly grateful for the care I'd provided during Geoffrey's last illness.'

'And?'

'She went on to say that she now wished to transfer to the list of the new doctor in the practice. No offence and all that, only she felt that at her time of life she would be more comfortable with a female doctor. There were certain problems which it would be more suitable to discuss with a woman, etcetera, etcetera.'

'But you don't take that personally, surely?' Laura came in. 'It happens that way. In fact, presumably that's one of the reasons you brought me into the partnership.' She sounded rational, glad to discuss whatever it was that was bothering Gerald.

'How can I help taking it personally? We're a personal practice. I've looked after Maisie Aire for thirty years. Of course it affects me when she suddenly decides to transfer to someone practically half my age. I don't understand why she has to do it.'

'But you don't think I actively poached your patient, do you?' Laura grew animated. 'Look, I've never even met the woman. I have nothing whatever to do with this.'

He grunted. 'But I never imagined in a million years – Maisie! Here am I pinning my value to this community, such as it is, on the fact that I've known most of them since they were babes in arms. You can't expect me to take it quietly when suddenly one ups and leaves me without a word.'

'She did write to you,' Philip pointed out.

'Only because she'd already rung to make an appointment with Laura and she knew Sheila would let me know the score if she didn't.'

Laura put her cup in the sink with an impatient rattle. 'OK, at least we've cleared *that* up. Thanks, Philip.' She left them to it and set out on her round.

Philip shook his head and watched her go, as Gerald cleared his throat. 'Don't go on at me. I'll apologise next time I see her. Only, sometimes it does feel as if the women gang up, don't you think?'

'No.' Philip wouldn't let him off the hook.

'You think I made too much of it?'

'Yes.'

'And wouldn't you be offended, if you were me?'

'I'm not saying that I wouldn't be disappointed, Gerald. We all like to feel we're indispensable. But I wouldn't let it affect my working relationship with Laura.'

'No,' Gerald conceded. 'I intend to say I'm sorry.'

'Let's hope she accepts your apology.' Philip headed off in time to catch up with Laura in the car park.

When she spotted him, she leaned her head out of the car window, keeping the engine ticking over. 'Thanks again. At least it's nothing major. I'd no idea Gerald was so sensitive about these things.'

Philip had to turn up the collar of his jacket against the strong wind. There were heavy spots of rain in the air and the hills had disappeared beneath low, grey cloud. 'If anyone's at fault, it's Maisie.'

'What's so special about her?'

'You'll know when you meet her. She owns Hawkshead Hall. It's the main house for miles around, been in the Aire family since the year dot. They're a symbol of sorts. You know, tradition, the old ways. I expect Gerald feels it's a sign of the times, Maisie asking for a change of GP.'

Laura gripped the steering wheel and sighed. 'Oh, I am sorry, Philip. It must be harder than I thought for him.'

'To add insult to injury, he and Maisie mix socially as well.' He cast an expert eye on the cloudy hilltops. 'You're heading into some rain over Askby. Watch the roads.'

'I will.' She began to reverse, but stopped when Philip raised a hand and followed her.

'There was something you said earlier about Aimee.'

Laura looked down.

'You may be right, Aimee probably does have something to do with Gerald's bad mood right now. Janet and he are finding her a bit of a handful; the usual thing with teenagers. I must say, I sympathise, having been through it myself. Three times.'

'But there's nothing in particular?'

'Not as far as I know. Gerald's always been keen for Aimee to go to college, originally to read medicine like her elder brother, Nick. But she would have none of that and went all arty on them. Now she's being pretty outrageous, I gather. Gerald isn't sweetness and light at the best of times, but this problem at home certainly isn't helping.'

She relaxed. 'OK, thanks. I'd best be off.'

As she drove away, Philip looked at his watch. There was just time to call in at home before he drove to Wingate for an afternoon meeting of GP fundholders. Juliet had a day off from her job as a dental receptionist in Merton. Perhaps they could have lunch together.

But when he arrived, he was surprised to find Mary there too, and a frosty atmosphere. The two women sat in silence across the kitchen table. He paused in the hall to give himself time to gather his wits. 'What's up? Have you two had a row?' He gave Juliet a peck on the cheek. Mary didn't want to look up to acknowledge him. She looked pale. 'Have you had to come home ill?'

She shook her head.

'She knew I was at home. She came out of school during her lunch hour to hand in her notice,' Juliet said.

'At school?' At first he couldn't grasp what was going on. Why was Juliet aggrieved?

'No, here at home. She wants to give up her room.'

Now Mary managed to look at him. 'I've been thinking of it for quite a while.'

'Why, what's wrong?' He knew instantly that he didn't want her to go.

'That's what I was trying to find out,' Juliet interrupted. 'I mean, a person doesn't disrupt everything for no good reason. It must mean she's unhappy here.'

Mary protested. 'I'm not. It's me. I think it's time to move on.' She sounded dull and defeated.

Philip looked at her. Mary made a big difference; her larger than life presence, her improbable anecdotes. 'Can't we try to change your mind?'

'No, I need my own place, that's all.'

He sat down beside her. 'Have you got somewhere else?'

'Not yet. I wanted to tell you before I started looking. It shouldn't take me long.'

Juliet got up and went back to her sewing work at the window. 'Talk some sense into her, Philip.' She bent over and steered the fabric to the steady whirr of the machine.

'Are you sure?' he asked. Mary's sudden decision intrigued him. It struck him again that there might be hidden meanings to her words and actions. He wasn't skilled in picking up and interpreting the signals of extrovert flirts like Mary.

But now he suspected that in fact she did nothing lightly. She must have a reason for moving out and there was a dawning awareness that it might be to do with him. Or to do with him and her. The pairing in his mind jolted him to his feet. It was absurd, he was making this up. Women like Mary didn't hide their feelings. They went for their men without hesitation. Anyway, he wasn't Mary's type.

All this flashed through his mind as she explained that she would in any case pay her rent until the end of November.

He shrugged at Juliet as Mary left them alone together. 'Don't ask me,' he said. He didn't stay for lunch after all, but left for work, irritated and confused.

CHAPTER EIGHT

Dot had made up her mind to get something off her chest. 'I bumped into Lilian Rigg in the market today,' she told Laura. They were watching television.

'How was she?'

'Not well, if you ask me. That's why I mentioned it. Of course, I don't like to break into your time off. You get little enough as it is.' She admired Laura's appetite for hard work, and the two women had quickly fallen into a sympathetic rhythm.

'No, that's OK, go ahead. I was thinking about Lilian the other day, when I took a walk out past the Abbey. I tried to spot her garden centre.'

'It's tucked away along the lane at the bottom of the Gill. The fact is, she didn't look good. And that's not like Lilian. She's never had a day's illness, as far as I know. Even when Walter died, she kept right on going.'

'Did you have a word with her?'

Dot shook her head. 'Not really. She runs a little stall, you know, though there's not much happening in the gardening line at this time of year. She makes and sells posies of dried flowers for Christmas presents, that kind of thing.' Dot looked thoughtful. 'It wasn't what she said, so much as the way she moved about. She was just packing up for the day.'

'Perhaps I should call in?'

'But don't say I mentioned it. I wouldn't want her thinking I was poking my nose in.'

'I'll be careful,' Laura promised.

'You see, the thing about Dr Grant is that she doesn't alter my routine.' Dot took up the topic of lodgers with Juliet Maskell when she went to clean at Bridge House next day. Juliet mentioned that they were to lose theirs, and Dot set about comparing their merits and disadvantages. 'I don't have to cook for her, of course. I make it a rule that I don't do meals. It's too tying. But with someone like Dr Grant, you'd hardly know she was there.' It was her morning for polishing the oak settle in the hall.

'Mary's not been any trouble. It was her decision to leave, not the other way around.'

'Well, I shouldn't worry.' Dot didn't bother to disguise the dim view she held of Mary Mercer, especially after the escapade at the Foss. In fact, it was a puzzle to her why she and Laura stayed such friends. To her mind they were complete opposites. Juliet told her Mary was upstairs, packing her things. 'You'll find someone else to take the room in no time,' she reassured her.

'I'm not sure that we'll bother.' Juliet looked vaguely for her car keys, ready to set off for work.

Dot picked them up and handed them to her. 'That's right; if you don't need the money, why go to the trouble?'

'Well, I like having someone around, I suppose. It livens the place up a bit.' She buttoned her coat, checked her reflection in the hall mirror.

Dot disagreed. 'Peace and quiet, that's what I like.' Then she thought again. 'I expect you miss your boys?'

'That's it.' Juliet sighed. 'I wouldn't mind if I could see a good reason for Mary to move out. Her job is only temporary, until the summer. You wouldn't have thought it was worth moving into a place of your own just for those few months, would you?'

'Look on the bright side.' Dot got to work with a tin of polish. 'Think how much easier the place will be to manage.'

'I'm late. I'd better be off.' Juliet still lingered by the door. 'I asked Philip to use his charm to persuade her to stay, but he said Mary knew her own mind, and if she was set on taking the room above the bread shop in the High Street, that was her decision.'

'Next to the Falcon?'

'Yes. It's that poky little place through the courtyard. It was the first advert she answered in last week's paper.'

'It won't be a patch on here.' Thus far Dot was prepared to agree. Swapping the solid grace of Bridge House for the noise and cramped conditions of a room above a shop did strike her as a peculiar move.

'You don't think it's *us*?' Juliet made one last attempt to rid herself of the suspicion. 'We're probably too boring.'

'Of course not.' Dot polished in small circles with even pressure. The settle came up lovely.

'You're right.' Juliet clutched her keys decisively. 'Thanks, Dot.'

The door closed and Dot straightened up, her job completed to her own satisfaction. Juliet's problem was plain to see; she missed those three sons of hers. But you couldn't fill your house with strangers and expect them to stop the gap. Dot knew this well enough; nothing had replaced Valerie and John when they left home, not all the cleaning and dusting, and little part-time jobs and finding herself an interest outside the home. Say what you like, when the phone went and she heard their voices far away in their bed-sitters, or in a telephone box amidst the roar of traffic, she knew that she'd lost them. Then came the marrying and grandchildren. That's what Juliet would have to look forward to now. They would come back to visit granny, and that was a great consolation.

Dot worked her way slowly upstairs, polishing the edges of each tread until she reached the gallery. She could hear Mary opening and closing cupboards and drawers inside her own room.

She must have heard Dot's approach. 'Don't come in here,' she called. 'It looks like a bomb's dropped.'

'I'll carry on in Dr Maskell's office, then.' She didn't break her stride. After a few minutes, she heard more things being dragged or pushed, and an exasperated cry from Mary.

'That's it, I give in!' Mary burst from her room, her hair awry. 'How come it all fitted in when I first arrived?'

Dot surrendered the calm of Dr Maskell's study to go and investigate. 'What's the problem?'

'Look, I've got three enormous cases, and I can't get a single one of them to shut.'

Clothes lay piled high, spilling from cases onto the floor; bright flashes of blue and purple scarves amongst the mainly dark items. And she hadn't begun to pack her shoes and other bulky items that still lay on the bed. 'You'll have to make more than one journey,' Dot suggested. It wasn't far from Bridge House onto the High Street, only a couple of minutes by car.

Suddenly Mary laughed. 'For once in my life I wanted to be organised.' She glanced at Dot. 'Yes, I know, pigs might fly.'

'Here.' Dot warmed to anyone who acknowledged their own weaknesses. She put down her duster. 'I'll fetch some big cardboard boxes from the cellar. I think I know just the thing.'

She went down for the boxes, and came back to find Mary in the kitchen making coffee. They took this up with them. Dot placed the boxes by the side of Mary's cluttered bed.

'This reminds me of that challenge about how many people you can squeeze into a telephone box.' Mary piled shoes into one of the boxes. 'Thanks, Dot, this was a good idea.'

'How will you get it all across?' She knew Mary didn't have a car.

'Taxi. I'll call one when I've finished packing.'

'He'll have to come all the way from Merton. It'll be expensive.'

'I know. And he's going to love me when he sees this lot.' Gradually she cleared the bed and began tugging at the zips of her overstuffed suitcases. 'This is like trying to squeeze a size fourteen lady into a size eight dress. I'm hopeless, aren't I?'

'I've seen better packing.' Beneath her sharpness she felt a twinge of sympathy. 'Do you want my help or not? Because if not, I can get on with my work.'

They were struggling downstairs with the first pair of cases when the front door opened and Philip came in. Mary straightened up at once.

'How are you getting on?' He went to help Dot down the last few steps.

'Fine. I just have to ring the taxi.' Mary pointed to the phone by the door.

'Forget the taxi. I dropped by to give you a lift.'

It was clear from Mary's protests that she hadn't expected any help from Philip. He took the stairs two at a time and fetched down the final case.

'I wouldn't mind a coffee while I'm here, Dot.' He went upstairs again. Mary stood quietly in the hall.

Dot went off to boil the kettle. When she brought the cup out to him, the front door was open and most of Mary's possessions were safely stowed in the back of Philip's estate car.

He took a couple of gulps of coffee while Mary got into the front seat. 'I'd better dash,' Philip told Dot. He left half the cup undrunk. 'I've just got time to drop these off for Mary before I drive up to Ginnersby for ten-thirty.'

Dot heaved a sigh of relief when they finally left. It had begun to drizzle; another reason for Mary to be thankful for Philip's help, she imagined. Now she could settle into the business of getting Mary's room back to rights. It would be in use again at Christmas when the

CHAPTER NINE

If there was one patient on her new list about whom Laura felt apprehensive, it was Maisie Aire. Her appointment had been fixed for the Friday morning of her second week in Hawkshead.

Firstly, there was the fuss Gerald had made. True, he'd got round to saying sorry, but in doing so he had again built Maisie up as a figure of great local importance. 'I get on with her perfectly well,' he said. 'And her husband, Geoffrey, was very straightforward and easy. No side, as they say. You know, not at all stand-offish.'

'But what about Maisie?' She thought she detected a hint of criticism.

'Fine most of the time. On occasion she can be a wee bit difficult, until you get to know her. At the moment we're all waiting to see how she gets by without Geoffrey.'

Laura didn't know how much Gerald's opinion had been coloured by his recent rebuff. But there was another reason to be nervous and this had to do with her own attitude towards Maisie Aire's status. She was at home with most kinds of people, but especially sympathetic towards victims of one kind or another; battered women, children involved in accidents, addicts, and patients whose health deteriorated through homelessness and poverty. She was less sure of her ground with those bolstered by social advantage. She'd let herself build up a whole set of prejudices on the basis that this woman's wealth set her apart from others.

There was a polite knock at the door and Maisie came in, shook hands and sat down.

Struck by her elegance, Laura noticed how surprisingly small she was; not much over five feet tall and very slight. She wore her smooth grey hair swept up and coiled on her head, her nose was small and straight over dark red lips. Her black wool suit was plain and well cut, with a simple white blouse beneath. One thing was sure; there would be no need to put her at her ease.

'I'm pleased to meet you, Dr Grant, though I must confess I was a little worried,' Maisie began disarmingly. 'I've been with Gerald for so many years that it was a wrench to leave him.'

'Yes, we've spoken about it.' Laura was surprised by Maisie's accent. Though her style was thoroughly English, her intonation was American.

'And he didn't mind?'

'He understands your reasons.'

'I must say, it is nice to come to a woman.' Maisie leaned forward slightly. 'I would never have done it while Geoffrey was alive, of course, but he died last spring.' She accepted Laura's condolences. 'And since I'm on my own now, I give myself more freedom of choice. Only, I do hope Gerald wasn't too offended.'

Laura smiled and turned to the computer. She brought up Maisie's file. Nothing surprising there, at least, except perhaps Maisie's age – seventy-one. Laura would have put her down as ten years younger. Her medical record showed regular cervical checks, and recent tests for cholesterol, blood pressure, weight and so on, which were all perfectly satisfactory. There was a prescription for an anti-depressant in May, shortly after her husband's death, probably. The dosage had been written up for six weeks and had not been renewed.

'So how can I help? You seem to have done well on the fluoxetine prescribed by Gerald.'

'Marvellously. I was wretched, of course, but it allowed me to take a step back and tell myself that it was natural to feel that way after losing Geoffrey, instead of letting the grief swallow me up whole. After six weeks I was back on my feet, emotionally speaking. And so far, so good.'

Laura nodded her approval.

'I still miss him dreadfully, that goes without saying.'

'Do you have good support from your family?'

There was the slightest pause. 'I have two sons; one living at home at present, the other dividing his time between Hawkshead and Italy. And I have two adorable grandchildren.'

Laura noticed that she'd evaded the question.

'In any case, I'm here to discuss something completely separate from all of that. You'll think it's a minor thing, I guess, but I find it a little disfiguring and I wanted to have it looked at.'

Laura placed the gentle, lilting voice. Refined New England disguised by the years in Yorkshire. She soon learned that the problem was a sudden appearance of several large moles on Maisie's neck and upper chest. She stood up to examine them as Maisie unbuttoned her blouse with a thin hand which sported a plain wedding ring and another with a large diamond.

'It's terribly vain, I know.' She tilted back her head and pointed out the offending marks.

'Not at all.' Laura quickly confirmed in her own mind that the moles were harmless. 'There are some quite large ones, but nothing sinister, you'll be pleased to hear. The skin undergoes many changes at various stages. It's best to have them checked, but I'm confident that they're normal and nothing at all to worry about.'

Maisie drew her blouse into position and did up her buttons. 'Thank you, that sets my mind at rest. But could I have them removed for cosmetic reasons?'

'You could.' Laura typed at the keyboard. 'But I wouldn't necessarily advise it. Of course, only minor surgery is involved, but it's surgery nonetheless. Then there would be some discomfort, especially where the skin is stretched over the bone, as on the collarbone, for instance.' She looked at Maisie. 'Why not take some time to think it through?'

'You mean leave well alone?'

'I would if I were you.'

Maisie gave no indication of whether or not she would take this advice. She began to make light of her request. 'It's an odd little vanity at my age, isn't it? But it's so awful to grow old; these wrinkles and so on, without ugly brown patches suddenly appearing out of nowhere.'

Laura nodded. 'You look very well indeed.'

She felt that there was mutual satisfaction as the door closed behind Maisie. She had evidently passed a stringent test imposed by her difficult patient, who went to congratulate Gerald on the asset he had found in Laura.

Abbey Grange Garden Centre was not sited for commercial success. Laura found it by taking a side lane, keeping the Abbey itself in view and using her common sense to keep going until she came to a small house behind a high walled garden. She left her car beside a barely legible sign and walked the final few yards up the drive.

A white frost had coated the walls and made the gravel path crunch underfoot. Lilian's wintering plants were shrouded and ghostly, the black earth crusted over. But Laura could see an order and organisation within the walls, and imagined the bare trellises in full summer, amock with climbing roses and clematis, the borders burgeoning with delphinium, lupin and aquilegia. She went up to the front door and knocked loudly.

Lilian emerged from the side of the house, armed with trowel and empty plant-pot. She was dressed against the cold, wrapped in a scarf, her navy blue workman's jacket buttoned to the chin. She wore heavy socks over her trouser bottoms, and sturdy boots. 'It's Dr Grant, isn't it?' She put the pot on a low wall and came forward.

'Hello, Mrs Rigg. I just popped in to see how you were getting on with those tablets for your back.' Laura went to shake hands.

'It's a good job you came out well wrapped up.' Lilian eyed Laura's high brown boots and warm camelhair coat, then she looked up at the dead, grey sky. 'They say it could snow, but I don't think so.'

Laura thought Dot was right; Lilian looked paler and quite a bit thinner than when she'd last seen her at the surgery. 'Did you get any bed-rest for that back?'

'Nay, I'm not as bad as all that.' She beckoned Laura round the side of the house, out of the wind.

'I don't suppose this cold weather helps?'

'Not much, no. Still, I mustn't grumble. You'll think I've no manners, keeping you standing out in the freezing cold. You'll have a cup of tea? Or do you have to be on your way directly?' She moved stiffly ahead into the kitchen, where an old Aga kept the room warm and Lilian's orderly hand was much in evidence. Mugs hung from a rack in an alcove, a teapot stood on a dresser, both within easy reach. When she bent for milk from the fridge she winced and eased herself up.

'Let me,' Laura offered.

'Nay, you sit down. Do you take sugar?'

'No thanks.'

'Bad for the figure, I know. You young women!' Lilian shook her head and placed the steaming mugs on the table.

'So the tablets haven't helped?'

'I can't say they have. But I've made my mind up just to keep plodding on until the warmer weather. It comes of old age, I expect; aches and pains. It happens to us all in the long run.'

'I don't suppose you'd let me take a proper look?' Laura suggested. 'I'm wondering if you've got a touch of arthritis as well.' She was worried about the weight loss. Without her jacket, which lay across the back of a chair, Lilian looked scrawny. 'Are you eating well?'

'When I remember. It's no fun cooking for one, and I've not much appetite these days. I tell myself to stoke up the old boiler, otherwise I'm worse than useless when it comes to digging and lifting and carrying.' She forced a smile. 'I'm an old crock, aren't I?'

'No, it's probably something we can put right without too much trouble,' Laura insisted, as she tried all the logical ways she knew to persuade Lilian back into the surgery. The visit had set alarm bells ringing.

In the end, Lilian agreed. 'I can see you're doing it for my own good. I wouldn't want you to think I'm not grateful.'

'So you'll come?'

'Aye, all right.'

'Good. How about tomorrow at nine?' She stood up and buttoned her coat. 'There isn't anything else, is there?' She sensed that Lilian still had something on her mind.

'Nothing for you to worry about.'

'That's not the point.' Laura smiled. They stood together in the yard, looking out onto Lilian's frozen flowerbeds. 'It's what might be worrying *you* that matters.'

'But it's nothing you can help with.' Lilian clutched her jacket across her chest and gazed over the old wall to the rocky hillside beyond. 'To tell the truth, I doubt if anyone can.'

'It sounds serious.' Laura tried to guess whether Lilian had family to worry about. Somehow she thought not. It was more likely to be business troubles. Times were hard for small set-ups, and Lilian must face strong competition from the big commercial garden centres.

'That depends on your point of view. There'll be some in the village who'll think it's a good idea. More money in the dale. Jobs and such like.' She shook her head.

'I'm sorry, Mrs Rigg, you've lost me.'

'You mean you haven't heard?'

'I'm new round here, remember.' Laura scanned the horizon for the source of the trouble. She saw nothing but the upturned hulk of the limestone cliff and two large, black birds flapping across its face.

'Then you'll not have been following the quarry business?'

It took a while for Laura to make sense of this. 'You mean they're considering starting up a quarry in the dale?' She thought the idea was preposterous.

'That's about the size of it. Mind you, they've been thinking about doing it for years and they've never got round to it.'

'Well then.' Her alarm subsided.

'Only, I bumped into Dick Metcalfe yesterday, and he tells me they're back, and this time they mean business.'

'Who's they? You mean the quarry company? Surely they can't intend to come and ruin the countryside.' She pictured heavy lorries grinding up and down the narrow road, the gradual erosion of the magnificent skyline. She'd seen the man-made mountains of waste, the scarred hillsides caused by quarry works in other parts of Yorkshire. The landscape never recovered, it seemed, from such an assault.

'Like I say, there's big money behind it.' Lilian spoke quietly, trying hard to hang on to her self control. 'I understand what they say about keeping the young people in work. But when I think of the peace and quiet being lost for good, it breaks my heart.' Her voice began to tremble. 'Have you been up Ravenscar to look at the tarn, Dr Grant?'

Laura nodded.

'Well, that's where they'd be, with their blasting and their conveyor belts and machines to break up the rock. Right there.' She grew angry. 'And then what would happen? There's curlews up there, and grouse. There's dippers in the tarn, and I still see the odd kingfisher in the Gill. What would happen to them, once the lorries begin to grind the place to blazes?'

'You mean Black Gill and Joan's Foss?' Laura was stunned. The plan seemed like a personal blow. For the moment, she couldn't look beyond the immediate damage.

'It's the only way up, unless you come at the tarn over the top from Swiredale, but that's National Trust land over that side. They can't touch that. No, the lorries would come right along here and up the Gill, like I said. Dick's seen the plans.'

Laura realised that things must have already gone quite far. 'How do other people feel?'

'Ah.' Lilian gazed at the horizon. 'We may not say much, but folk who've lived here all our lives, we're up in arms over it. We go on year after year without paying much attention to the so-called environment, just busy working the land. But you try and change things and it all bubbles to the surface. We're a stubborn lot, and when it comes to it we'll fight tooth and nail to keep things the way nature intended!'

'But what will you do?'

'We don't know yet. We haven't got ourselves organised.'

'You'll have to have meetings, petitions. You'll oppose the plans before they're passed?' During her life with Tom, Laura had learned how to mount such a campaign. 'List the environmental damage, lodge a complaint as soon as you can.'

'Aye well, best not to be hasty.' Lilian regarded her with new interest. 'I can see the idea of the quarry bothers you.'

'I think it would be dreadful! There's little enough beautiful open space in this overcrowded island. I want to keep Ravensdale exactly as it is.'

'I hear you went swimming in the Foss?' Lilian cut in with a wry smile.

Laura coloured. 'Yes. I don't know why we didn't just put an advert in the local paper and have done with it.'

Lilian grinned. 'You're only young once.' She turned away.

'What would happen to you, Lilian, if the quarry plan went ahead?'

'Me?' There was a long pause. 'I'm slap bang in the middle, see. They'd pull down the Grange to make way for the road. I'd have to close the garden centre and move out.'

CHAPTER TEN

Lilian came to the surgery as promised the next day. Laura examined her and decided straight away on a series of blood tests, having found little evidence of arthritic joints. She was still worried about the weight loss. Her patient kept up a defiant silence about her 'aches and pains', but Laura persuaded her to go through gynaecological tests then and there. She sent the tests off for analysis and resolved to talk to Gerald or Philip about Lilian's family history.

So, when the results came through a week later, there was little surprise. Lilian Rigg had ovarian cancer. It was fairly advanced, with secondary tumours likely. Laura read the hospital information and sighed. Gerald had recalled Lilian's sister, Marjorie, dying of the disease thirty years earlier. A cousin over in Swiredale had died too. There was a definite family link.

'Do you want me to go out to the Grange and have a word?' Gerald offered. They'd just finished an eight hundred and he could see that Laura was troubled.

'No thanks. She's my patient. I'll go.' Typing the results into Lilian's empty file, she pursed her lips. 'I was treating her for lumbago.'

'Don't feel bad. Two or three weeks won't have made much difference if the condition is well established. As a matter of fact, I think you did pretty well to get her in here at all. She's not the most cooperative of patients.'

Laura looked up. 'Thanks, Gerald.' His praise meant a lot.

He shook his head. 'By the way, did you get the call?'

'What call?'

'From the big house. Your invite to Maisie's Christmas do? Mine and Janet's arrived this morning. She's already planning her outfit.'

Gerald's introduction of Maisie into the conversation seemed to Laura to be a step in the right direction. 'Oh, that. Yes. It looks very posh.' She'd put her unexpected, gold-edged card on the bedroom mantelpiece. 'I suppose everyone gets dressed up?' The invitation was for December the nineteenth, just over a week away. On the evidence of one visit to the surgery, Maisie had evidently decided to elevate Laura into the circle of her acquaintances. At the moment, she could hardly tell whether she was flattered.

'It's the big event of the Hawkshead social calendar!' Gerald raised an eyebrow. 'Not that you'll have any difficulty attracting attention, whatever you turn up in.'

Startled, she retreated to her consulting room. She bumped into Philip on the way.

'What's wrong? You look flustered.'

'Gerald's just been nice!' she whispered. 'I think he's just paid me two whole compliments.'

'He must be making up for his huffiness over Maisie.' Philip grinned.

'Hmm. Just wait till I put another foot wrong.' She disappeared into her room, ready to begin surgery. Afterwards, she would pay a visit to Abbey Grange. She would deliver the verdict and discuss treatment with Lilian. It would mean a biopsy, scans, probably a course of chemotherapy rather than surgery. Ovarian cancer needed to be caught early for a good prognosis. She wondered how much to tell Lilian and decided to play it by ear as she drove up the deserted lane to the garden centre.

Lilian received the news with an inscrutable expression. 'Aye, I can't say I'm surprised.'

'You knew?' Laura clasped a mug of hot tea, sitting across from Lilian at her kitchen table.

'I know the signs. It took our Marjorie just the same way.' She spoke quietly. 'I don't want mucking about too much.'

Laura described the modern treatments. 'It depends on what the scan reveals.' She told her there would have to be a short hospital stay while they made a full diagnosis. 'I'm not sure yet exactly when that will be. It might not be until after Christmas.'

'The sooner the better. I'll be busy come spring. I'd like it over and done with by then.'

'I'll do my best.' Laura stood up, taking her tone from Lilian. 'Has there been any more news about the quarry?'

'Murmurings and mutterings, that's all. Nothing definite.' Lilian's gaze was steady. She shook Laura's hand. 'Now, you're not to go worrying about me. I'll manage up here until I get the call from the hospital.'

Laura left on a brisk note, glancing back at Lilian, who stood in her doorway buttoning her blue work jacket, looking up at the leaden sky.

When Laura got back to the surgery just before lunch, Sheila was quick to beckon her into Reception. She held one hand over the mouthpiece of the phone and spoke quietly. 'It's Aimee Scott. She wants to make an urgent appointment. I said if she comes in this evening we could try to slot her in between other patients, but she's refusing to sit in the waiting room.'

'Shall I speak to her?' Laura slipped out of her coat and put her bag on a chair. She took the phone. 'Hello, Aimee, I hear you want to come and see me?'

'Yes. My father isn't there, is he?'

'Not at the moment, no.'

'Well, can I come straight down?'

'There's no surgery right now. I have to go out and see some patients. Can't it wait?'

'Look, if I wait till proper surgery hours, I'm bound to bump into Dad, and that's just what I don't want to do.'

Laura assessed Aimee's tone of voice and picked up a note of panic behind the façade. She glanced at her watch. 'Well, I do have half an hour before I have to set out again. How soon can you get down here?'

'Ten minutes.'

'OK, come as soon as you can. You can tell me what's wrong and we can see where to take it from there.'

The phone went dead and she put it down thoughtfully. Sheila's face had taken on a deliberate blankness.

'Where did Gerald go, as a matter of interest?' Laura asked.

'Merton. He said he'd be a couple of hours.'

'You don't think I did the right thing there, do you?'

'We usually try to keep to surgery hours.' Sheila spoke stiffly, as if she was offended.

Laura saw that she felt undermined. 'You wouldn't have said yes, then, if I hadn't interfered?'

'It sets a bad example. Soon there'll be others wanting to squeeze in at odd times.'

'But I don't think Aimee is likely to broadcast this. After all, she wants to keep it all a secret.'

Sheila broke off from her task. 'To be honest, I don't like going behind Gerald's back. I know Aimee's entitled to confidentiality like everyone else. But I can't help feeling – '

'Disloyal?' This bothered Laura too; the blurred boundary between their professional role and a natural inclination to let Gerald in on any problems to do with his daughter. 'I know what you mean.'

'I've worked for him for eight years. He's bound to be upset once he finds out.'

'Yep, it's hard.' Laura picked up her coat and bag. 'But it's Aimee's choice. If she wants to keep this quiet, whatever it turns out to be, I have to go along with that.'

Reluctantly Sheila agreed.

Before long there was a knock on the door and Aimee came in, pale and edgy, dressed in a grey sweater and black trousers, her long, dark hair hiding most of her face as she sat down. Laura thought that if anything she looked thinner and certainly angrier than the last time they met at Bridge House. Hostility simmered behind her averted eyes and pouting mouth. 'How can I help?'

The small muscles in Aimee's jaw and neck pulled tight. 'That pill you gave me didn't work,' she blurted.

Laura rested one hand against the edge of her desk. 'How do you mean, it didn't work?'

'I mean I think I'm pregnant. I missed a period.'

'How late is it?'

'Over two weeks.'

She made a rapid calculation. 'Did you have unprotected sex any other time before you came to see me?' This would be the only possibility; that Aimee's risky action hadn't been a one-off.

'What do you think I am?'

Silence welled between them. Aimee picked at her fingernails, while Laura tested the way forward. 'Are your periods usually regular?'

'Not that regular. But it's never been this late before.'

'Well, there are a number of reasons for it happening, the least likely of which, you'll be pleased to know, is that you're pregnant.'

She spoke slowly, waiting for the impact of her words to sink in. 'The morning-after pill has an almost one hundred per cent success rate, provided you take it within the prescribed time period. That's why I had to ask about other possible occasions.'

'I already told you – '

' – And I believe you. That's why I'm saying that the chances of you being pregnant are practically nil. In any case, we can't test until a pregnancy is six weeks advanced.'

'So I have to take your word for it?'

'I took yours,' Laura said quickly and firmly.

Aimee clammed up.

Laura steadied her voice again. 'If your periods tend to be erratic in any case, there could be a hormonal reason why this has happened. Are you worried about anything, for instance?'

'What's there to worry about, besides being pregnant?'

'I don't know. You tell me. Exams, perhaps?'

'They're not till next year.'

'Schoolwork in general?' She recalled Mary's account of Aimee scuppering her chances of success.

'Boring.' Aimee's eyes swept upwards, across the ceiling, to rest defiantly on Laura. 'What's this got to do with me being pregnant?'

'Or *not* pregnant? If you're anxious to any degree, it can affect menstruation. Trauma can actually cause periods to stop for several months until a patient recovers from shock or grief or whatever.' She tried to generalise, to show Aimee that her body could be subject to normal stresses and strains.

'I'm not anxious, OK?'

'No problems at home?'

'No more than usual.' By now, Aimee's stare had glazed over. 'Compared with a lot of kids, I have it easy, don't I? Two parents still married, big house in the country. Everything's hunky-dory, isn't it?'

'You have an elder brother, I hear?'

'Brilliant. Amazing. I have a brother. That's very traumatic.'

'That's not funny, Aimee.'

'It wasn't meant to be.' She blushed. 'Sorry. I get all screwed up when you ask me questions.'

'We're trying to sort out if this missed period is significant. Unless you talk to me, I can't help you.'

'I know. But it's always the same if I get asked questions by anyone; at home, at school. I seem to go off the deep end, like I wish they'd drop dead.' She hung her head.

'So you don't discuss things at home?'

Aimee rallied. 'Have you tried discussing things with my father?'

'What kind of questions would irritate you most?' Laura's sympathy was growing, as she realised how Aimee had cut herself off from solutions to her problems. She began to wonder if amenorrhoea were the only symptom.

'Oh, I don't know. He's always asking me about schoolwork. But he asks in this tone of voice, like what I'm doing is useless anyway, because it's not science. He wanted me to do medicine.'

'Like your brother?'

'My brilliant brother.'

'And your mum?' Laura had met Janet Scott several times in passing, enough to exchange pleasantries and general chat. She seemed a patient, mild woman, a foil to Gerald's bombast.

'Mum doesn't mind what I do, but she does go on sometimes.'

'What about?'

'How I dress, I suppose. And what I eat, that sort of stuff.' Aimee bit her lip and looked away.

Something clicked. That was it; weight loss. Under her baggy jumper, Aimee was dramatically thin. Her face, with its wide cheekbones and full mouth, was misleading. Its prettiness distracted from the fact that she was probably severely underweight. 'Your mother thinks your eating is a problem?'

She shrugged. 'I don't eat meat. So what? You can be perfectly healthy without eating the flesh of other living creatures.'

'Sometimes healthier,' Laura agreed. 'As long as you get the balance right. Plenty of protein, calcium and so on.' She noticed Aimee shake her head impatiently. 'I'm sure you know all that. How tall are you?'

'Five-eight and a half.'

'How much do you weigh?'

'Seven-stone-one.' The answers came quick as a flash.

'And are you losing weight?'

'A bit. I don't know.'

'But you do weigh yourself?'

'I'm not on a diet, if that's what you're getting at.'

'But you watch what you eat? You're pretty light, did you know that?' Laura waited, but there was no reply. 'Dramatic weight loss can be connected with loss of periods,' she explained. 'That's the reason I'm interested. Would you have any idea how much you've lost in the last six months, say?'

'A couple of stones, I don't know.'

In fact, Laura guessed she knew to the nearest pound. This linked up with other things; the sudden switch to anti-social behaviour, the concentration difficulties. 'What does your mother say about it?'

'What would she know? Anyway, she's given up saying anything. She just shoves plates of chips at me and I throw them away when she's not looking.'

'You don't ever deliberately make yourself vomit to keep your weight down?'

'No, I just don't eat in the first place.'

The look of high-minded disgust made Laura smile. 'You must be very strong-willed.'

'I don't want to get fat, do I?'

'That's not very likely.' Laura considered the genetic factor. Gerald was thin as a rake, and Janet, though smaller and rounder, was in good shape. 'In fact, it seems to me that the most likely cause of this late period is that you've lost too much weight too quickly. If you want to return to normal, you may have to put some back on again.'

Aimee blinked, and when she opened her eyes it was as if an invisible shutter had come down to close off all expression. 'Right.'

'That doesn't mean you have to eat mountains of chips if you don't want to. Wholemeal bread, boiled potatoes, fruit. Do you eat cheese and eggs?'

She nodded lethargically.

'Plenty of them. I want you to agree to do something.'

One nod, no eye contact. Aimee stared ahead.

'Try to keep a diary showing what you eat each day. An exact record. Check it. Make sure you're including carbohydrates. In two weeks' time, I want to see you again.'

'OK.' Aimee got to her feet.

'You can come at this same time if you like. Come when it's quiet.'

She agreed. But her body had stiffened, her eyes were still expressionless.

Laura risked one last word of advice. 'What you're doing in fact is providing your body with too little energy to cope with all its normal functions.'

This clicked Aimee back into defiant mode. 'But I feel great. How can it be bad for me if I feel OK?'

'You'd feel better if you got your weight back up a bit, believe me.' Laura came from behind her desk and went with Aimee into the waiting room. 'And you might also feel better if you took the plunge and discussed some of this with your parents.'

'What's the point?' Aimee drew the frayed cuffs of her sweater over her hands as Laura opened the door and they stood outside in the cold wind.

'It's good to talk.'

'There's nothing to talk about.'

The shutters were still down and Aimee's face a pale mask as Laura watched her head for the street, avoiding attention yet seeking it with her mane of dark hair, her heavy eye make-up and her hostile stare.

CHAPTER ELEVEN

Each December, Dot's preparations for Christmas included thorough house cleaning from top to bottom, the meticulous sending of Christmas cards bought boxed from Marshall and Highgrove in Wingate, the baking of a cake so huge and rich that it would last well into March, and on the first Sunday of the month a visit to the schools' carol service at St Michael and All Angels.

'Would you like to come?' she asked Laura, who had just returned after a fruitless trawl around estate agents' windows in Merton and Wingate. There were many houses on the market, but so far nothing that she liked or could afford. 'The children from the local schools get together to form the choir, and the church is all decked and ready for Christmas.'

'I'd love to, Dot. Shall we go in my car?'

'I generally walk down. It's not far.' She liked to stick to the smallest details of routine. There would be a nip in the evening air, the village square would be swathed in coloured lights as they made their way towards the old bridge and the Abbey grounds beyond. St Michael's was the restored church attached to the Abbey ruins; a perfect setting for the carols, as the children processed with candles through the old cloisters towards the nave. 'Oh, and Laura, Maisie Aire rang to ask whether or not you would be going to her party next week. I said I'd pass on the message.' This had proved a severe test of Dot's sense of honour; her inclination to ignore all that the owner of Hawkshead Hall did and said was strong, especially since the issue of the quarry had been reopened.

'Damn!' Laura paused wearily halfway up the stairs. 'Don't tell me I forgot to reply.'

Dot had noticed the gold-edged card propped on Laura's mantelpiece. 'No, well, I expect you've more important things on your mind. Shall I ring her back for you?'

'No thanks, I'll do it. What time does the carol service start?'

'Half-seven. We should set off at seven if we want a decent seat.'
Dot looked forward to singing the familiar hymns, and this year to
the added pleasure of Laura's company.

They set off in good time, Dot in her Black Watch tartan suit and
black hat and Laura in her creamy-fawn coat and brown leather
boots. With her hair up and her gold earrings sparkling under the
street lamps, she looked lovely, Dot thought. She felt proud to have
her as a friend and not merely a lodger as they joined up with Philip
and Juliet Maskell at the gates of Bridge House and walked the rest
of the way under a clear, starlit sky.

The ruined Abbey rose in silhouette from the stretch of flat valley
chosen by the monks for its perfect sheltered position by the river.
The old bishop's house stood a little to one side, its yellow lights
glowing through arched, leaded windows. To the other side of the
dark ruins, the wide church doors stood open. Organ music
welcomed them, ushers handed out hymn sheets, the vicar stood
talking to the headmaster from the comprehensive school. Dot
spotted Lilian Rigg with her widowed brother-in-law, Kit
Braithwaite. She still didn't look herself, and no wonder.

'All that worry,' she whispered to Laura as they took their seats
three rows from the front, and only a few seats away from Kit and
Lilian.

Laura looked round, puzzled. 'They haven't decided anything
yet, have they?'

'No, but there's rumblings. Nothing definite until after Christmas is what I heard.' Dot realised that Laura never took her up on
the subject of her patients' health. She respected this and moved
on. 'Wait till you see the children in the procession. They're lovely.
My Valerie was in the choir when she was at school. In those days
the whole village came along. John read the lesson two years
running. He never slept a wink the night before, but he had a lovely
speaking voice.'

As they sat waiting, both took in the high arches, the rich stained
glass, the white and gold lilies painted on the altar screen. Dot
leaned across to Lilian to ask her where she planned to spend
Christmas.

'I shall be over in Swiredale with Kit. Just the two of us.'

'A nice quiet time?'

'I don't know about that.' Lilian bridled. 'There's plenty going

75

off, what with this quarry. We shall be planning our counter-attack, don't you worry.'

'What've you heard?' Dot asked.

'Tot got wind of the name of this new outfit that's showing interest. Frontier Stone Company. There's to be a public inquiry.'

'We'd best be on our toes.' Mention of an inquiry rattled Dot. If public money was to be spent, it made the whole project more real. She was also upset by Lilian's appearance; still thin and ill, with dark shadows under her eyes. She turned to Laura. 'How long will it take?'

'Weeks if not months, I should think.' Laura sounded preoccupied.

'Well, I wish they'd leave the land alone,' Lilian said, summing up what they all felt.

Then the organ notes died away and the congregation fell silent. The pure strains of a boy's voice started up with 'Once in Royal David's City' casting its spell, and the children processed in crimson robes and white surplices into the choir stalls, their voices swelling under the rafters, candles flickering across their round, serious faces.

Later, Dot took Laura along to the Falcon, where churchgoers were to meet up again and join in a more secular pre-Christmas get-together. This year the talk was all about the quarry, and almost all opinion was strongly against the idea.

'I hope the Frontier Stone Company realises what it's up against.' Philip leaned over Laura and Dot's shoulders with the drinks he'd brought to their corner table. 'Tot and Dick are dead set against it, and I take it that you and Lilian will be there to spearhead the campaign, Dot?'

Lilian had gone straight home after the service, but Dot felt able to speak for them both. 'We will that, Dr Maskell. I don't see how they can justify bringing something like that into the dale, not if the local people don't want it.' She had faith in the strength of public opinion, though a vague awareness of a powerful commercial interest about to steamroller them into submission was unsettling. She listened as Philip Maskell and his wife played devil's advocate.

'I suppose we're not immune from modern trends,' Juliet said. 'After all, the farmers had to give way to quota systems, didn't they?'

'Yes, and now hundreds of gallons of good milk get poured back onto the fields as slurry every day.' Dot hated waste.

'I'm not saying it's right, but it's happening wherever you look. Philip's forever coming home and complaining about the GP funding system, but there's not a thing he can do about it.'

'It's a case of accepting the inevitable, worse luck.' Philip took a long drink from his glass.

'We're a long way from accepting anything so far as this dratted quarry is concerned.' Dot didn't like defeatist talk. She broadcast her message loud and clear.

'That's it,' Dick called from the bar. 'No one's going to start shoving us around, are they, Tot?'

'Let 'em try.' Tot rapped his empty glass on the bar top. 'Same again, Brian.'

'I hope you're right.' Juliet got up to go, and Dot let the fighting talk subside. There was no point in jumping the gun and allowing the dispute to spoil Christmas. With her back to the warm log fire that Brian came to stoke, she noticed his daughter, Nina, following him.

'Dad, Aimee and I want to go to Wingate tomorrow night. She just rang to ask me.'

'What did you say?' Brian settled new logs onto the embers.

'I said yes.' Nina ate casually from a bag of crisps, lolling against the stone fireplace.

'What time will you be back?'

'I don't know, do I?'

'Well, remember, the last bus from Wingate sets off at half-ten.'

Nina screwed up the empty crisp bag and threw it on the fire. 'Thanks a lot, Dad.'

'Why, what did I say?'

'You're expecting me to get some poxy bus home before the film has even finished.'

Dot overheard the altercation and saw Alison Lawson hovering within earshot. Nina looked a match for her father; outspoken, with that scorn for adult authority that teenagers saw fit to display these days. She looked like her dad; the same sporty physique, rather square face and grey eyes, but without his affability.

'I don't know why you bother to ask me up if you're so busy all the time.' She sulked as she trailed out of the room.

'OK, OK.' Quickly, Brian gave in. 'I'll fix something. What time do you want picking up?'

'The film finishes at a quarter to eleven. We'll see you outside.' She sauntered off.

He shrugged and made his way to the bar with some empties, where Alison soon collared him and took him out of sight, ready no doubt to argue all the reasons for him to have stuck to his first decision; Nina's rudeness for a start, which Dot would never have tolerated in her own children, and the staffing difficulties it would cause. Alison seemed upset when she reappeared to serve drinks, and there was no more sign of Brian right up until closing time. She handled the rush up to last orders with what Dot thought was a forced cheerfulness.

'She has a lot on her plate, has Alison.' Dot's quiet observation was interrupted by the arrival of Mary Mercer, fresh from the final rehearsal of the school's Christmas play.

'What wouldn't I give for a stiff whisky.' Mary took Juliet's empty seat. She unwrapped a long woollen scarf and slipped out of her heavy black denim jacket.

'Stay there, I'll get it.' Philip shot off to the bar and brought back a double Scotch.

'How did it go?' Laura asked. 'Any disasters?'

'One of our main actors has the flu, the set for scene two collapsed on the chorus, and the member of staff who does front-of-house has had a nervous breakdown. Otherwise, great.'

'You're not serious?'

'No, I exaggerate – slightly. Oh my God, why do I let myself in for these things?' She took her drink from Philip with a murmured thanks.

He sat beside her. 'How's the bedsit?'

'Home from home and already a complete tip.' She smiled at Dot.

'You don't get too much noise from the pub at night?' he persisted.

'I'm never in to notice. By the time I get back from rehearsals I'm so knackered I could sleep through an earthquake.'

'And did you get the landlord to fix that door lock yet?'

'I haven't had time.' She dismissed his worries and turned to Laura's own trials and tribulations over finding a place to live. 'Any luck?'

'Not so far. But I'm like you. I can hardly find the time to turn around, let alone see the house of my dreams. Anyway, Dot makes things far too comfortable at Town Head.'

Dot sat listening happily. She noted not for the first time the contrast between Laura and Mary; like chalk and cheese, she thought. Whereas Laura had set out to prove that she could fit in, Mary seemed to court controversy. Here she was now, catching Tot Dinsdale's eye, knowing how much the old nuisance had enjoyed spreading rumours about t'schoolteacher and t'new doctor after their chilly dip in Joan's Foss. It was as if she thrived on her ability to upset the applecart, approaching Tot and Dick, glass in hand, flaunting herself. 'You'll both come along to see the show, won't you? There's plenty of singing and dancing; you'd love it. Why don't you come?'

'Nay, my singing and dancing days are done,' Tot sniffed. But Dot could tell he wallowed in the attention.

'*You* don't have to dance. You sit and watch. Then we all pop in here afterwards for a drink.' Mary produced tickets from her jeans pocket. 'Alison, how about you? Can you get time off later in the week?'

'Sorry, no can do.' The landlady reached up to replace clean glasses on a rack. 'I'd like to, but some of us have to stay and work.'

'Oh dear, I'm not doing very well, am I?' Mary leaned on the bar.

Philip joined her. 'You can let me have a couple of tickets for Thursday. We'll try and get along.'

'Oh thank you, sir!' Mary went broad Cockney. 'That's real good of you, sir. Any of you other kind gentlemen buy a ticket off a poor girl?'

She approached another figure who had just come through the door. At first Dot didn't recognise him, but when he came under the bar lights, she saw that it was Christopher Aire, looking fit and tanned. He seemed amused by Mary's tactics.

'Who's that?' Laura looked on with interest.

'Christopher, Maisie Aire's eldest. I didn't know he was back. I expect he's here for the party. She'll do well to get him to buy a ticket.' Dot regarded them sceptically. 'He's not a great supporter of things that go on in the dale, not like his father was.' She thought he had a cheek turning up in the pub, the way things stood.

'You don't approve?'

'It's not up to me how much time he spends living abroad. Personally I wouldn't turn my back on links that go back for more than two hundred years. That's how long the Aires have lived at the Hall. When they first had it, it came into the family with lots of land, practically half of Ravensdale. Eventually most of it got parcelled up and sold off.'

'For tax reasons?'

'I suppose so.'

'But they've not really fallen onto hard times?'

Dot grimaced. 'Not exactly. They still own some of the most beautiful parts of the dale.' She lowered her voice. 'And that includes Black Gill.'

Laura took a sharp breath. 'I see.'

'You didn't know the Aires owned the Gill?'

'I'd no idea. But now I realise why you don't like him.'

'I never said I didn't.'

'You didn't have to, it's written all over your face.'

'Well, I'm not the only one.' Dick and Tot had already cold-shouldered Christopher Aire by slamming their glasses down and leaving as soon as he came in. 'It stands to reason, doesn't it? If he just did what his father did and sent the stone company packing, there'd be none of this trouble brewing now.' She shut up then, feeling too upset to continue. It was all right for him standing there in his smart dark suit, with his good looks and charming ways, but he wasn't to be trusted. Goodness only knew what influence he had over his mother and what money-making scheme they would be up to next.

'Laura, this is Christopher Aire.' Mary's deep, velvety voice made the introduction. 'He promised to buy a ticket if I introduced you.'

'I did?' He played along.

'No, I'm lying. But you did ask me to introduce you to Laura, and I thought I might as well shame you into supporting the school while I was at it.' She fanned out the tickets like a pack of cards. 'How many?'

Christopher gave in with good grace. 'Let me have two; no, three. I admire your sales technique.'

'Cheers.' Smoothly Mary concluded the bargain and slid off to talk to Philip.

'Mother gave you a great build-up,' Christopher told Laura. 'As soon as I arrived she was telling me all about the new doctor she'd been to see.'

Laura didn't respond to his flattery. Dot guessed she was embarrassed by it, and once more Laura went up in her estimation.

'She has one black mark against you, though, and that was something to do with not replying to her party invitation.'

'That's right, I'm afraid. Tell her I'm really very sorry. I've been so caught up in my new job that I didn't give it a thought until earlier this evening, when Dot passed on the message.'

'So I'll tell her that you're suitably contrite and that you'll come?'

'I'm still not sure. I need to check with Gerald about which of us is on call that night.'

'If it's you, you can make him change it. He's been to dozens of these things. Tell him to let you have a turn.'

She smiled coolly. 'I can't do that.'

'Yes you can. If you don't come, it'll just be the same old crowd. And what will I do for amusement amongst the tweedy ladies and golfing gentlemen?'

'I'll come if I can. I'll call the Hall tomorrow with a definite answer.' Laura stood her ground. 'Will that do?'

It seemed not, because Christopher stood up and waved at Philip. 'Do you happen to know who's on call on Christmas Eve night?'

Philip thought for a moment. 'Gerald. Why?'

'He turned, triumphant. 'Well?'

'OK, you win. I'll be there.'

'Excellent. I'll pass on the message. It was a stroke of luck, us running into one another like this. I'll see you on Christmas Eve.' He made his exit before she could change her mind.

Dot stared stolidly at her drink, saying nothing.

Philip shrugged. 'Did I rope you into something you didn't want to do?'

'No, it's my own fault, really. I felt too embarrassed to turn him down.'

'You go and enjoy yourself.' Mary breezed across. 'And count yourself lucky. It's not every newcomer who's invited into the inner circle straight off.' She turned down the corners of her mouth.

'Poor Mary. Maybe you're the lucky one. I'm always on edge on occasions like that, and I'm not sure I want Christopher Aire breathing down my neck all evening. You can go in my place if you like.'

As Alison put the towels over the pumps, their group began to disperse. Philip told Laura that she would have a good time at the party in any case. 'Everyone loves the Hall from the moment they set eyes on it. And Juliet and I will be there to keep you company.'

'I'm away to my bed,' Mary yawned.

'I'll see you home,' Philip offered.

'It's only next door.'

'Even so.' He led her out, saying goodnight to Dot and Laura, and nodding to Alison as they left.

Dot buttoned her jacket. The serenity of the carol service had long since dissolved, and as she set off to walk home with Laura, she felt piqued. She didn't blame Laura for giving into pressure from Christopher Aire; that wasn't it. No; the fact was she didn't see why Dr Maskell had to escort Mary home. Not one to let her niggles rise to the surface, she drew Laura into discussion of the carols as they climbed the narrow street to Town Head.

'The children's voices were lovely.' Laura, who'd been entranced by them and the wonderful setting, agreed.

'And the readings came across well.' She put her key in the front door lock.

'The whole thing was perfect.'

'Would you like a cup of tea?' Dot put her handbag on the hall table and took off her hat.

She had quashed her worries and put on a show of normality. She and Laura could settle into a cosy nightcap together. Still, she was unhappy. Trouble of various kinds was simmering; the Lawsons weren't all pulling together as a family, for a start. The quarry business was taking its toll on Lilian, who looked a shadow of her usual self. And now Laura was getting drawn into the Aires' social circle, where she might soon find her loyalties divided. And then there was Mary Mercer. If it weren't for the fact that she was a friend of Laura's, Dot knew she could easily have been tempted to speak out against the woman who was definitely flirting with Philip Maskell, she decided. The attraction could only be skin deep. Mary would go shamelessly for her man when the wife wasn't around, and then wear him like a feather in her cap. She couldn't possibly feel anything serious for him; he was that much older and surely had given her no encouragement. No, Dot blamed Mary.

She went into the kitchen and put the kettle on, apprehensive of what the New Year would bring.

CHAPTER TWELVE

'It's not long till Christmas,' Dot observed. She crossed off a square on the WI calendar with its December picture of robins in the snow. 'Six more days.'

'Oh, don't.' Laura scarcely needed reminding. Festivities had already broken out. There was a brightly lit tree in the village square, carol singers knocked at the door each evening, and cards thudded daily onto the doormat. 'I haven't even made my Christmas card list yet!'

'Well, time flies.' Dot got ready to embark on her Saturday morning shopping expedition. She left Laura still in her dressing-gown, sipping tea.

When she'd gone, Laura crept upstairs, wrapped the eiderdown around her shoulders and sat in the window seat, looking out on the valley. What had been a golden scene of hay stubble and autumn leaves when she first arrived had given way to sombre greys and blacks. This morning, first thing, she saw that frost had glazed the windows and settled in a hoary layer on the fields where sheep stood immobile. Only the birds wheeling over Ravenscar suggested any sign of life.

Today she was off-duty; no visits to geriatric patients with heart failure and osteo-arthritis, no emergency house calls to farmers with sudden chest pain, wives with lumbago, or distressed children with colic. Despite the gallop towards Christmas, she reflected on her first months in the dale, on her new colleagues, patients and friends, and on her surroundings – her untrodden ways.

With the latter she was perfectly happy. She loved the space. Something about the hills, a quality of great stillness, could lift the pressures of her busy life. There was purity and undisturbed beauty in the massive beech trees by the river, their silver grey branches stripped bare, root-tentacles stretching along the bank towards icy, clear water, and an awesome power in the clouds that rolled over the rugged scar of limestone behind the village.

The doorbell rang, jerking her out of her quiet mood. She went down to find Janet Scott standing nervously in the cold.

'You'll have to excuse how I look.' Laura tightened the belt on her dressing-gown and pushed her hair behind her ears.

'I know it's your day off,' Janet began. 'And you will tell me if I'm stepping out of line, won't you? But the truth is, I just had to come and see you.'

'Don't worry. I take it this is private?' Janet's normally unruffled presence was replaced with an edgy urgency. 'Look, come into the kitchen. I'll put the kettle on and you can make us both a cup of coffee while I fling some clothes on. I'll only be a couple of minutes.'

She rushed to change into a warm sweater and trousers, then sat down at the kitchen table. 'Why not tell me what's going on?'

Janet struggled for control. 'It's probably nothing at all. You know what it's like before Christmas; rush, rush, rush to get everything ready, presents to choose, food to plan, family stresses and strains.' She paused for a sip of coffee.

Laura waited. Janet Scott was one of life's copers, she knew; a no-nonsense woman used to managing the quirks of her husband's temper with patience and tact, and able to run their domestic and social routines with minimum fuss. She was a small-boned woman of medium height, with short, straight hair, greying at the sides, and features that were unremarkable except for the light grey eyes and arched eyebrows which gave her a refined air.

'It's not nothing if it makes you anxious,' she assured her. 'You wouldn't be here unless it was important.'

'That's just it, I don't know if I'm exaggerating things. In fact, I'd love to go away from here feeling that I've got everything way out of proportion these last few weeks; that what's happening at home is perfectly normal and will right itself in time if I just sit it out.'

'Perhaps it is.' For all their sakes, Laura found herself hoping the same thing.

'But if it isn't, and I do nothing about it, I would never forgive myself, would I?' She appealed directly to Laura. 'I felt you were the only person I could speak to. You've probably had lots of experience of this sort of thing. I'm told it's very common.'

'What is?' She knew not to jump the gun.

'It's Aimee.'

'Yes.'

'You've met her?'

'At Philip's house. My friend, Mary Mercer, is her drama teacher, and Mary used to live with the Maskells, you remember?' Laura was careful to protect Aimee's confidentiality, but her heart sank as she realised that she was about to be embroiled in further family secrets.

'Yes. Did Miss Mercer say anything?' Janet caught hold of the scrap of information.

'Only that she was helping Aimee with an assignment. I gather Aimee doesn't have much confidence in her own abilities.'

'And what about you? What did you think?'

'That she looked a bit on edge. I didn't have time to form much of an impression. She left soon after I arrived.'

Janet shook her head. 'Do you know, she used to be a lovely, friendly child. When she was small, she had a mop of curly dark hair, and everyone made a fuss of her and said how gorgeous she was. Aimee was the type of child who would go and sit on anyone's lap, never shy and clinging. She sailed through her first years at school. I used to count my blessings; first Nick, who was clever from the very start, then Aimee. We had no problems with either of them, apart from the usual ailments, and even then I considered myself lucky to have a doctor as a husband. He always knew exactly what to do when they were ill.'

'It sounds like the perfect childhood,' Laura suggested. 'But then, there's always more to it, isn't there?'

'I don't say it was perfect. We quarrelled, like everyone else. And Gerald was always busy. Well, you know.' A new idea seemed to strike home. 'Do you think there are some men who put too much of themselves into caring for others, and not enough into making sure that their family feels cared for too?'

Janet sighed. 'In our case, I was the one who was always there for the children. But now I see a certain irony in that situation.'

'How?'

'Well, it wasn't me they needed. It turns out they wanted less of me and more of their father.'

'You can't be sure of that.'

'It's the only reason for what's been happening, ever since Nick left home to read medicine at Edinburgh. Aimee underwent a personality change almost overnight; you know, princess into frog.

No more smiles and hugs, and suddenly she became hypersensitive. She turned every comment into huge criticism, every encouragement was thrown back in our faces.'

'Nothing out of the ordinary so far.' But Laura's own understanding of Aimee led her to believe there was more.

'Teenage rebellion? I know. But Gerald can't tolerate it. It infuriates him when Aimee sulks or makes demands or sounds off about this or that. Being Gerald, he thinks it would be beneath his dignity to show her he's angry, so he puts on a pained expression and buries his head in a newspaper, which makes her ten times worse. She becomes totally outrageous, then he stalks out, leaving us all miserable.'

'Especially you?'

'I can't stand to see them argue. But what I'm really worried about is Aimee's weight. She denies that she's losing any, but I know she is. She doesn't eat enough to feed a bird, and her arms and legs are getting so thin. Didn't you think so? Didn't you see how thin she was?'

'Yes. I didn't know her before, obviously, but I would certainly say she's underweight at the moment. What does Gerald think?' Aimee had failed to keep two further appointments since her second visit to the surgery. Laura's hands had been tied; if an anorexic patient chose to stay away, there was little she could do.

'Gerald's attitude is that she's being silly, but that she'll come out of it if we take no notice. He says the worst thing to do is to force her to eat.'

'I agree that nagging doesn't help. Have you thought about expert advice?'

'He won't discuss it with me. He won't really admit there's anything wrong, you see. If he recognises that she's making herself seriously ill, that would reflect badly on him, he thinks. We'd be one of those families that they call – what's the word? – dysfunctional. He couldn't bear it.'

Laura rested her chin in her hand. She needed to know more. 'How much do you reckon Aimee does eat each day?'

'Less than a thousand calories.'

'Consistently?'

'Yes. She has a chart in her room with calories for every conceivable food. She even draws a graph of her weight loss. I've seen it in her drawer. She charts it week by week.'

'And how much weight is she losing?' The signs of obsessional activity weren't good.

'About three pounds a week.' Janet's anxiety appeared as tears at last. 'She's wasting away to nothing, but I can't say anything. I can't get through to her.'

'Has she ever been overweight?'

'Not in the least. She's naturally skinny, like her father.'

'Look, Janet, I think you're right; there is a problem and I think we should try and do something about it quickly.' Aimee had struck her as someone who would do nothing by halves.

'But what? I came here because I can't bear to sit by and watch it happening any longer, and I knew I could trust you not to say anything. It would be harder for Philip. He's worked alongside Gerald for all these years. But you might have a fresh view. Laura, what can we do?'

'Talk,' she said calmly. 'Tell Gerald how worried you are. Talk to Aimee. Listen to what she has to say. Don't try to make her eat, though. Just do a lot of talking and listening.'

'Is it anorexia? Are you sure?'

'Pretty much. But I'd want to run a physical check-up to rule out other things.' Laura planned their next move. 'Can you try to persuade her to get in touch with me? Say I need to see her.'

Janet nodded slowly.

'One more thing; I'm convinced you should include Gerald in this from now on.' Laura stressed this, then waited for a reaction.

'I should, I know. I would if he was anything but what he is. If he was a teacher or a lawyer, or anything outside medicine.'

'Doctors aren't immune to illness, you know. Nor are members of their families.'

'Laura, I know this puts you in a difficult position, believe me.'

'That's not the point. I just think Gerald should know, for your sake and Aimee's.'

But try as Laura might, she could not extract a promise from Janet to tell Gerald what was wrong. She had to be satisfied that she herself would try to find the opening, and that Janet would try to get Aimee back to the surgery.

'And don't worry too much. Most anorexics respond to treatment. We should see it as a cry for help, not as an act of deliberate self-harm. Get her to come in before Christmas if possible, and we'll take it from there.' She showed Janet to the door.

'Right.' She crossed her jacket over her chest and stepped outside. 'And thanks, Laura. I really appreciate it.'

'Thank me later.'

'I'm so glad you joined the practice. I truly am.'

Laura was touched by her gratitude. 'Christmas cards,' she told herself sharply as she closed the door. Turn to something simple; catch up with old friends and family, instead of taking the problems of the whole world on her shoulders.

That evening, after a day of gentle, pre-Christmas tasks, Laura got ready to go to the party at Hawkshead Hall.

She drove across the dark valley, passed through a stone gateway by an empty lodge, and fell in love at first moonlit sight.

Her headlights swept across landscaped gardens. She caught glimpses of a pale, gleaming stretch of water, and closer to the house acres of rhododendron bushes sloping away up the hill above a formal garden of topiary hedges and stone archways. A cluster of low stable buildings and outhouses stood to one side of a courtyard, next to the solid outline of a Jacobean house.

Laura pulled up close to the stables. Though big, the two-storey building had simple proportions; small windows with heavy stone lintels and mullions, low doorways and a low sloping roof. It formed a sheltered L-shape against the west wind which swept the dale, tugging now at the flimsy clothes of the party guests as they mounted the stone steps in twos and threes, to the brightly lit main door.

She sat a long time, reluctant to break the spell, able to make out gothic arches designed into the stonework of the top storey windows. Massive cornerstones gave shape and strength to the walls, their straight lines broken by porches and irregular additions which gave the house its lived-in, gradually evolving feel. She could imagine generations of Aires whose feet had trodden the flagged paths, hands that had clipped the yew hedges and swept the lawns clear of falling leaves.

'Nervous?' Juliet Maskell's friendly voice interrupted the quiet study of her surroundings. Guests still trickled into the house. Laura had seen Gerald and Janet arrive and enter. Philip and Juliet were among the last. Now Juliet bent towards her window to see if she wanted to join them as they made their way inside.

'Yes.' Laura climbed out of her car. 'Thanks. Isn't this a wonderful place?' She spread her arms in every direction.

Juliet linked arms with Philip on one side, Laura on the other. 'Wait till you've seen the inside.'

Laura, only half listening, had a rapid sense of the interior; oak panels, low ceilings, before they were swept inside by their hosts and the door closed behind them.

Christopher Aire came suavely forward to meet Laura, claiming old acquaintance. He took her elbow and steered her across highly patterned, richly coloured rugs into a long, low room full of guests. 'Welcome to Hawkshead.' Smiling, he handed her a glass. 'Don't feel obliged to pay the usual compliments.'

'Oh no, it's wonderful.' She admired the portraits, the landscapes in their golden frames, mostly Victorian, mostly good.

'My mother.' Christopher followed the direction of her gaze. 'She collects minor Pre-Raphaelites. I try to get her to sell the damn things but she refuses.'

'I agree with her. They suit the house.' Many had medieval themes, the women in velvet gowns and low girdles, with flowing hair.

'But not the pocket.' Christopher grimaced. He looked relaxed, his blond hair set off by a dark green casual shirt. Amidst the many more formally dressed guests he looked at ease and in control.

'Come and talk to Mother,' he suggested. 'She's feeling on edge. This is the first time she's attempted one of these functions since my father died in the summer. I keep telling her there's no need to be nervous. With the caterers in, these things practically run themselves. Come and distract her.' Christopher escorted her towards the window, where a small group of women stood.

Maisie turned as they approached. 'Ah, it's our new doctor. I do so admire young women who take up these worthy professions.' Her greeting was flattering, but measured. 'The medical world is so complicated nowadays, isn't it? You have such wonderful machines to do your scans and make your diagnoses. It quite frazzles my brain.'

'I'm a GP, Mrs Aire. I don't have much to do with the wonderful machines.'

'Quite right, my dear. I know you have the human touch. Anyhow, welcome to our small gathering.' She turned to her son.

'Christopher, your talent for spotting quite the best-looking woman within a twenty-mile radius is undiminished, I must say!'

Laura knew she was being patronised, but Maisie smiled sweetly, head held high like a delicate bird.

'Never mind Mother's outrageous compliments,' he assured her. 'It comes of the American tendency to exaggerate.'

'Oh now, Christopher, don't spoil it. I mean what I say; Dr Grant looks very beautiful.' She studied Laura and went on unabashed. 'You have what I call the modern look; tall, rather more casual than in my day. I do love your dress. So simple. Silk, isn't it? And dark blue suits you.' Maisie went on to compliment the timeless tailoring technique of the gored skirt that sat slim and smooth on Laura's hips.

Laura dipped her head. 'Thank you, Mrs Aire.'

'Oh, you must call me Maisie. It makes me feel so *old* if you don't. Come along with me. Christopher, I intend to steal Laura from you and introduce her to everyone myself.'

'Speak loudly when you want her to hear what you say,' he murmured to Laura. 'She's a little deaf, though she won't admit it. We don't insist on a hearing-aid, however!' He raised his eyebrows. 'See you later.'

Maisie glanced back and gave a light laugh. 'What's he telling you, my dear? Family secrets? Come along and meet some of Geoffrey's old friends, and watch out for the look on their wives' faces. I shall enjoy this!'

Dutifully Laura did the rounds of the mostly middle-aged and elderly guests. She assumed that Maisie's tongue, though sharp, was harmless. She seemed to enjoy taking pot-shots at the peculiarities of the English class system, but none of her guests took offence. 'Oh, Maisie!' they said, chuckling over the rims of their brandy glasses.

'Isn't she remarkable?' they said within hearing as Maisie and Laura passed by. 'One never knew for certain how she would get along – after Geoffrey, so to speak. Glad to see you keeping up the Christmas tradition at Hawkshead, Maisie.'

Maisie smiled, pausing in between guests to recite chunks of her life history. 'You're so sweet to listen to an old lady's ramblings,' she said with a sigh. 'But doctors are good listeners, I'm told. You are, in any case.' They strolled together from one room to another, with Maisie pointing out the better pictures in her collection, her hand resting lightly on Laura's bare forearm.

Listening to the American intonation as her hostess described her arrival in England, Laura wondered how the elegant and sophisticated Maisie Aire had gone down in Ravensdale when she first arrived.

'I came for the tour just after the war and met Geoffrey at a theatre in London. We had a whirlwind romance and I never went back.'

'She fell in love with Hawkshead, didn't you, Mother?' Christopher passed by, hands full of refilled glasses. 'Even though she'd never seen it.'

'I did not. Though I confess Geoffrey would tell me tales about Yorkshire and the house, as he called the Hall. The house. I pictured something quite different. You know, something raw and remote.'

'She'd seen Laurence Olivier in *Wuthering Heights*. That was the start of it all.'

Maisie chose to ignore him. 'Tell me, do you *like* my son?' she asked Laura, elaborately puzzled.

'He's charming.' Laura laughed, ready to join the game between mother and son.

'Incredible. I find him inherently unreliable, an insatiable womaniser and an incorrigible spendthrift. But then, you two have only just met.'

Laura's eyes widened. The jibe seemed to have hit home, though Christopher tried to laugh it off. 'She's right, of course.' He went off to deliver the drinks. Laura saw Maisie follow every movement.

'Christopher has no heart,' she warned. She still sounded angry. 'Or none that I could ever discover. Matthew, my other son, on the contrary, certainly has one. It makes a man vulnerable, don't you think?'

Laura shook her head helplessly. She wondered whether it was the wine or the old lady's stern analysis of her elder son that had knocked her off balance. But then, she thought, she hadn't come to the party to chase Christopher Aire. Why then should she be dismayed by the mother's opinion?

Maisie's voice softened suddenly. 'I'm sorry. You're not used to us, are you? Christopher and I get along very well as a rule. Only, today he told me he plans to fly back to Italy two days after

Christmas. I had hoped to have him here for the New Year.' She sighed. 'However, it's his life. What can I do?'

Laura gave herself time to read between the lines of Maisie's last remark, as Gerald and Janet came up to join them. She understood the mother's disappointment; this was the family's first Christmas since Geoffrey Aire's death and Maisie would need plenty of support. But her brittle manner disguised her vulnerability even from her sons, apparently, and Christopher didn't seem the sort to show sympathy. Between the two of them she imagined plenty of room for misunderstanding.

'Laura, I'm telling Maisie, the winters we get nowadays aren't anywhere near as bad as winters used to be.' Gerald, dressed in a dark suit and light grey tie, drew her in. 'What do you think?'

'Pure nostalgia, Gerald.' She was relieved that he wasn't showing any sign of hurt feelings, but then Janet probably hadn't had the time or the courage to discuss Aimee since her visit to Town Head.

He took her retort in good part. 'I remember winters when snow came over the top of the telegraph poles!'

'And the ice on the tarn was two feet thick, and everyone went skating, and afterwards they roasted chestnuts round a log fire; I know!'

'Cynic.'

Laura smiled at Janet. 'I never knew Gerald had a sentimental side.'

'Oh yes, he watches all the old Bing Crosby films on TV.' She'd come to the party in a long-sleeved cream dress, touched up with pieces of gold jewellery. She looked composed, but not at ease, Laura thought.

By this time, Maisie had drifted on to a different group of guests, still aware of the figure she cut with her beautifully coiled grey hair, her long black dress, the elegant turn of her neck. Laura realised with a start that the offending moles had been removed, privately, no doubt, and to good cosmetic effect.

Then Mary appeared out of nowhere and broke into their comfortable circle, dragging along Philip and Juliet. 'I know, I know!' She flung both hands in the air. 'How did I get here? Don't ask.'

Laura was glad to see her. 'I thought you hadn't been invited?'

'I wasn't. But I worked on Christopher one night at the pub, and lo, an invitation arrived posthaste!'

'Mary, you're wicked.'

'I know. Where's the wine? I've just arrived and I'm dying for a drink.'

Philip stepped in gallantly. 'I know my uses. What would you like?'

'Anything. You choose. Whatever I drink, I'm bound to end up with a dreadful hangover.'

'She's going to disgrace us,' Laura warned, as Philip went off on his mission.

'Naturally.' Mary ran slinky hands down her strapless, shimmery black dress. 'Why else would I be here?'

Wherever she went, she changed the mood, made her mark. Laura admired her for it, and the brave cover-up of any feelings she might still harbour for Philip. Watching her vamp her way through the evening, no one would have guessed that there was anything beneath the teasing.

Towards midnight, with the party in full swing, Maisie came to collect Laura once more. 'There you are. Are you having a good time?'

'Marvellous.' She'd unwound and entered into the spirit of Christmas.

'You dance well.' Maisie took her arm. 'Christopher seemed to think so too.'

They'd spent an hour together, talking then dancing, before Philip had claimed Laura for what he called a golden oldie; a rock and roll number. Meanwhile, Mary had swept Christopher back onto the dance floor and was still there with him now.

'Come along, I'd like you to meet Matthew,' Maisie confided. 'You two should get along, you have things in common.'

Laura suspected she was out to annoy Christopher with this introduction. They passed close by. Christopher was deep in a clinch with Mary.

'I think Laura should meet Matthew,' she told him in her distinct way; her Katharine Hepburn voice, as Laura styled it. 'I'd like him to show her the rest of the house.'

Laura wasn't sure that she wanted to be dragged away from the fun on a guided tour. Still, there was no arguing with Maisie.

'Come with me. I guess I know where he's hiding. You'll like him,

I know you will. Since his father died, Matthew manages things around here for me. He's just the person to show you around.' She led her away from the dancing into a lounge, where quiet music and the hum of conversation filled the room.

CHAPTER THIRTEEN

'Mother.' Someone stood up and came towards them. Tall like his brother, but dark, Laura at first put Matthew in the same category; a man with confidence verging on arrogance, charming but shallow. 'Come and sit down. You've been on your feet all night.' He offered Maisie his seat; a cream-coloured armchair next to the fire.

'Now Matthew, don't fuss. I never sit at parties, as you well know. I circulate.' She brushed him to one side. 'This is Laura Grant. I want you to look after her and show her the house.'

'Don't feel you have to, please.' Laura didn't want to break up their circle.

'Nonsense, he doesn't mind. He'll be in his element.'

'Of course.' He turned to Laura. 'What about you? Don't let Mother bully you into anything that doesn't interest you.'

'No, I'd like to look round. In fact, I'm fascinated by what I've seen so far.' She rapidly revised her opinion. Matthew was nothing like Christopher. His voice was deep and considerate, with a teasing edge. He seemed to treat his mother with amused affection.

'She's fallen for the place,' Maisie told Matthew. 'Why not give her a potted history while I try to find out what Christopher's up to.' Head high, with her studied walk, she left the room.

Laura's smile was embarrassed. 'You don't have to entertain me, really.' She realised that she'd broken up a cosy gathering of younger guests; probably Matthew's own friends. A Paul Simon album from the mid-eighties played softly in the background. She found it hard to meet his gaze.

'Was Mother giving you a hard time?' He insisted that she take his seat.

'No,' Laura laughed. 'She was very sweet to me.' Gradually she relaxed. The others turned back to their conversations. Matthew sat on the arm of her chair.

'Good. The whole Hawkshead experience can be a bit intimidating at first. It's not when you get used to it, of course. But these Christmas occasions are a bit grand. That's why we retreated in here.'

Laura glanced round the room. In pride of place on a wall opposite the window hung a large, richly coloured picture of a woman resting against the bough of an apple tree in full blossom. She was reading a crumpled love letter, her white dress swept the flower-studded grass, and at her feet lay a withered posy of violets.

'Every picture tells a story?' Matthew said. 'That's one of Mother's favourites.'

'It's very touching.' She smiled, conscious of Matthew sitting close by.

'Would you really like me to show you round?' His suggestion sounded too sudden to be casual. 'Mother wasn't making it up when she said you liked what you'd seen of the house?'

'No, and I wasn't being polite either.'

'It puts some people off, I have to say. Too much like a museum. They wonder how we can live in it.' He led her off through another door. 'Christopher told me he had to use all his powers of persuasion to get you to come.' They stood in a cooler, darker corridor linking the two wings of the house.

'That's because I've been so busy these last few weeks.'

'New job. No time for a social life?'

'That's right.'

'But you're glad you came?'

Laura laughed. 'Relax. I'll let you know when I stop having a good time, OK?'

He turned, hands in pockets, looking straight at her. 'Good. Are you ready for a surfeit of samplers and an orgy of oak dressers?'

Together they wandered in and out of rooms, down corridors and finally out into the cold courtyard for a glance at the exterior of the building. 'This huge chimney here is where the original bakehouse would have been.' Matthew was caught up in the details. 'At one time they'd cook and bake here for the entire estate, for the lodge, and all the granges and cottages on the old Abbey estate. It must have been a big job.'

Laura breathed in the sharp air. She'd taken Matthew's jacket when he offered it, and stood now with it slung around her shoulders. Still she shivered. His voice tailed off and he looked at her. In the darkness, with the sound of the party going on indoors, she turned to him, wondering what was going on in her suddenly tumultuous heart.

Matthew bent his head slowly towards her. Their lips touched. She took a step backwards, wrapped the jacket around her and shook her head.

'Sorry,' he said quietly. Then, 'No, I'm not. Are you?'

Years ago she would have kissed a man like this, without preliminaries. As a student at a party, with a kitchen full of beer kegs and Rod Stewart crashing out the decibels. As a teenager on her first date; a fumbling kiss. But that was before Tom.

She shook her head. 'No, not sorry. Not really ready, though, either.' She tried to smile, but the shivers ran through her. She felt like a boxer who'd lowered his guard and been sent crashing to the canvas.

'Let's go back in.' He took her hand.

In the glowing hall guests were preparing to leave. Gerald and Janet paused for a few words with Matthew. They gave Laura a curious look.

'We'd best be off now, Maisie. I'm on call tonight, on the wagon.' Gerald's voice was clipped. He frowned at the man's jacket around Laura's shoulders.

'Have you been called out?' Her smile still wouldn't work. Her jaw was clenched tight.

'No, touch wood. Let's hope it stays that way.' He turned to say his thanks to Maisie. Marvellous evening, as always. Many thanks. Happy Christmas.

Maisie acknowledged her departing guests.

'See you at eight hundred hours,' Gerald reminded Laura. He shook Matthew's hand.

In the lull Laura planned to catch up with Mary and offer her a lift home. She felt Matthew's arm resting on her shoulder as they crossed the hall. Perhaps he'd invite her out, but she wasn't sure enough to make the move herself. Too busy, too complicated, not over Tom yet. She listed the reasons.

Maisie came up from behind to watch the last dancers on the polished floor of the reception room. 'I knew it,' she sighed. 'Christopher would have to let me down.'

'Don't be stuffy, Mother.' Matthew noticed Christopher engrossed in Mary. They clung to one another, oblivious of the departing guests.

'I'm not being stuffy. Who is that he's staggering around with?'

'They're not staggering. He's dancing with Mary Mercer. Leave them alone.' He put out a hand to stop her from going across.

'Don't worry, Matthew, I won't make a scene.' She backed off and went to tend to her other guests.

Laura looked quizzically at him, offended on Mary's behalf. Maisie must belong to a different era altogether if she believed she could control her son's choice of dancing partner.

'She feels he should help her more with the guests.' Matthew shrugged. 'It's been difficult since Father died. She's used to having someone to rely on at these parties, and now she sees it as Christopher's role.'

'Not yours?'

'He's older than me. She's very traditional,' he explained without resentment. 'She refuses to see that he can't be a stand-in for Father. They're completely different, chalk and cheese, and he resents the pressure.'

Mary and Christopher broke apart at last. Laura saw her retort to something he had said or done with a quick sidestep and a flick of her long, dark hair. He slid his arm back round her waist and went on talking, his mouth against her cheek. They were still marooned in the middle of the floor.

'Matthew, please!' Maisie had returned. She seemed genuinely upset.

'What can I do?'

'It's unforgivable.' She turned to Laura. 'I'm sorry, my dear, he seems to have invited you under false pretences.'

'Oh no.' Laura saw what she was getting at. 'I never came as Christopher's special guest or anything like that. I'm not offended.' She might be worried that Mary had taken on more than even she could handle, but that was her only reaction to seeing the two of them entangled.

'But he specifically made a point of getting you to come. And you took so much trouble, I know.'

'Mother thinks a personal invitation is practically an engagement.' Matthew tried to ease the tension.

'But I do think he's behaving badly and spoiling things for all of us.'

'Only if you let him.' Matthew left Laura's side and guided Maisie into the hall, where Laura could hear her remonstrating, him placating.

'I take it Maisie's not happy?' Philip remarked, as he and Juliet passed by. Laura was still waiting for Mary to disentangle herself.

'No.'

Philip glanced across the floor. 'But Christopher obviously is.'

She turned, surprised at his tone.

'Come on, Philip. We're the last to leave.' Juliet made straight for the door.

'And don't look at me like that, Dr Grant.'

Possibly he'd drunk too much, his guard was down. 'Like what, Dr Maskell?' Laura asked him.

'As if you'd caught me doing something I shouldn't. I'm merely remarking that honourable number one son is having a damned good time.' He couldn't carry it off. The flippant comment died on his lips.

'Philip!' Juliet called.

With a start, Laura realised that Philip was jealous. 'You go ahead. I'm waiting to offer Mary a lift.'

He shrugged and began to move off. 'If she needs one.'

'Meaning what?' Everything had turned sour.

'Meaning, why offer to take her home? She looks pretty happy where she is.'

Laura stared after him as he and Juliet left, then waited uneasily in the hall, wondering what, if anything, she should say to Mary.

'Did you realise that Philip didn't like you dancing with Christopher?' Laura delivered the message cautiously when they met up in the Falcon later that week for a Christmas drink.

Mary's expression closed down. 'Laura, please, I'm not in the mood.'

'For what?'

'Jokes. Especially about that.'

The gold streamers, the Christmas tree lights, the fake mistletoe; the pub should have cheered them up after Laura's hard day at the surgery. 'I'm not joking.' Her voice was drowned by a nearby games machine.

Mary was stubborn. 'Nothing happened between Philip and me, if that's what you're thinking.'

'You wouldn't lie to me?' She was relieved; Mary seemed to have everything under control. 'OK, so tell me something else.' She'd brooded over this since the awkward dying moments at Maisie's party. 'Why would Gerald disapprove of me and Matthew Aire?'

'When?' Mary stared back in disbelief.

'At the Hall. He saw us together and gave me a look as if I'd suddenly turned into Lady Macbeth or someone.' There was silence. 'Not that anything happened between us either.'

'Gerald's an old fogey.'

'Yes, but why?'

'Because Matthew's married, OK? He's got kids, the full works. That's why.'

CHAPTER FOURTEEN

'Philip, remember Bean's due in Merton at six this evening.'

Philip heard Juliet call on her way out to work. She was leaving early, hoping to finish by the middle of the afternoon so she could enter the Christmas Eve skirmish at the supermarket before the shelves were completely empty. 'Right. Do you want me to pick him up?'

'No. I plan to be there. I should have finished the shopping by then.'

He went down into the hall. 'Sure?'

'Yes. There's no point us both driving into Merton. The traffic will be murder.' She checked her make-up in the mirror and slung her shopping bag over her shoulder. 'I swear, Philip, after today I am never going to set foot inside another gift shop or buy another scrap of tinsel in my entire life.'

Kissing her, feeling guilty that he'd left everything to her as usual, he stood at the door to see her off. 'The place looks wonderful.' She'd rigged up the tree, the decorations by herself.

'Thanks to Dot. She put in extra hours this week. What time do you finish?'

'After evening surgery. I'll come straight back.'

'OK, I'll have a meal ready. A family meal.'

Ian and Jim would be home for Christmas, there would be a lull before the day itself, then all the ritual exchange of gifts, over-indulgence and regrets. One year soon he would kick over the traces, go to a South Sea island and have a beach barbecue for Christmas dinner. It was Juliet who clung to the family thing, unable to imagine what the boys would do without them.

Philip watched her turn on the headlights and start up the wipers. Fog was forecast on the hills. 'Drive carefully!' The car slid through the gates. For a second he stepped outside the shell of house, wife, routine and saw himself disorientated, discontented. Then the moment passed. He would be late for the eight hundred and the busy morning ahead.

Laura had fitted Lilian Rigg into her crowded schedule in a slot she'd been saving for Aimee Scott. She'd left it vacant, hoping that Janet would be able to persuade her daughter to keep the appointment, but it hadn't happened. It would have to be postponed until after Christmas, a difficult time of year for anorexics. Still, it meant she had a space for Lilian.

'I wanted to let you know there's a hospital bed available at the start of January. There's no point being admitted over the holiday period, but as soon as you're ready in the New Year?'

Lilian nodded gravely.

'I take it you've never been an in-patient before?' She had tracked down a leaflet issued by the hospital, giving information about what she would need to take with her, the procedure when she arrived and so on. She handed it to her.

'How long will they keep me in?'

'That depends. They may want to keep you in to begin chemotherapy, if that's one of the options. Or they could discharge you after a few days and call you back as an outpatient for regular radiotherapy. Or they might suggest surgery. We shan't know until they've made a full diagnosis.'

'It's a good job it's my quiet time of year.' Lilian sat upright, holding Laura's gaze. Her hands lay folded on her lap, her eyes were untroubled. She was dressed as usual in her thick navy blue jacket and corduroy slacks. 'And I expect the rest will do me good.'

'Is there anything you'd like to ask before we send you in? Anything about the equipment at the hospital, or types of treatment?' She guessed that this patient would not want to fudge the issues or break down in public. If anything, she would miss out vital questions in case she put anyone out. 'You must feel free to ask whatever you want to know. It won't be a nuisance.'

'Well, I reckon you know what you're doing.'

'Treatment has changed a lot in recent years,' she continued. Was Lilian's reticence part of her stoical outlook, or was it passive resignation that her time was up, come what may? 'It might be that the doctors in Wingate will want to send you on to one of the big city hospitals where there are specialist oncology departments.'

'I wouldn't want to be away from home longer than necessary. Would you tell them that for me?'

'Sure.' Laura thought for a moment. 'You know there's a system of nursing designed to help you stay at home during your illness? We can put you in touch. The nurses are specially trained to care for cancer patients in the home. It's very good. They're on the end of the phone whenever you need them, with special equipment, advice about drugs, in fact any advice at all. How would you feel about that?'

'I'll bear it in mind, thank you.'

Laura cast around for a way to break through Lilian's defences. 'Have you thought about how you'll get to Wingate?' There were practical difficulties for an elderly woman living alone in a remote dale.

'Kit wants to drive me over, and back again when they've done with me.'

'That's good. And will he keep an eye on things at the Grange?'

'He'll see to the garden side. Dot's promised to pop in and check the house. I said she needn't put herself out, but you know what she is.'

'You'll feel better knowing that someone's calling in to collect the mail and keep things tidy.'

'To be honest, I'm glad she'll be there, what with this quarry inquiry rearing its ugly head. Someone has to check up on these surveyors. And no doubt they'll want to ask questions and write reports. At least Dot knows what she's talking about if she bumps into them.'

'It's set to go ahead, this inquiry?' Here was something they could get their teeth into. So far, Lilian hadn't let her near.

'First week of January, when I go into Wingate.'

'That's why you're anxious to get back?'

'I need to be there,' she said stolidly. 'If they're thinking of turfing me out of my home, the least I can do is put up a fight.'

'It won't come to that, surely?' It was hard to believe that quarrying stone could come before the rights of someone like Lilian to go on living as she'd always lived in a house she'd made her home. Then she thought, why the surprise? It was the old argument; industry versus the environment, profit versus people. Right up Tom's street, for instance.

'It will if Maisie Aire goes ahead and sells her land.' Lilian's hackles rose. 'And the Frontier lot must be banking on that, or else they'd never have gone ahead with these surveys.'

'Has anyone actually tried speaking to Maisie about it?' It struck Laura that a quiet word from the right quarter might swing things.

'You don't know Maisie.'

'I do as a matter of fact. I was invited to her party.' She stopped in her tracks. To Lilian this might seem a piece of blatant disloyalty.

'There's no law against it, so far as I know.'

The tart reply brought a blush to her face. 'You don't think she'd listen to reason?'

Lilian shook her head. 'They say she's short of money. To her it'd be common sense to sell the land; especially with the son to back her up.'

'Matthew?'

'No, Christopher. He's the one with the business brain, apparently.' Lilian looked thoughtfully at her. 'There is one way of getting through to Maisie Aire, and that's if someone said face to face, how would *you* feel if we came along and knocked down your beautiful house to make way for a road? But then, that's not likely to happen, is it?'

'What isn't? Her having to make way for a road, or getting someone to talk to her face to face?'

Lilian left a significant gap. 'I don't suppose you could?'

'I really don't know her well enough,' Laura answered. 'She wouldn't want to listen to me. Perhaps Gerald?' She knew it should be someone with more standing, an insider. 'Or you?'

'She'd see me as biased, which I am.' Lilian frowned. 'Have you asked Dr Scott what he thinks about the quarry?'

'Not specifically, no.'

'You might be surprised.' Pursed lips followed the frown.

'Well, what about Matthew Aire? Wouldn't he have some influence? And I can't believe that he wants this quarry. He didn't seem the sort.' Again Laura gave herself away. 'I'm only supposing.'

'Maybe you're right. I always thought he was a good sort. He comes to me for perennials and bedding plants for the Hall. You know where you are with him.'

'Well then, why not get him on your side?'

Lilian sniffed and squared her shoulders. 'Perhaps I will have a word.' She stood up. 'Thank you, Doctor. I won't take up any more of your time.'

Laura showed her to the door and held it open. 'I'm always here if you need me,' she said. 'Look after yourself, Lilian.'

'Thank you, and Happy Christmas.'

'You too.' She closed the door quietly, shook her head and went to the desk to bring the next patient's file up on-screen.

Philip had disagreed with Gerald at their morning meeting. He'd handled things badly over a question of respite care for a paraplegic patient, an ex-farmhand injured in a climbing accident. His wife needed a break and they were looking for a residential unit to take him in for a few days during January. Gerald had dug in his heels over not being a damned travel agent, as he put it, and Philip had argued back instead of letting him grumble on. Laura suggested a spinal injuries unit in the Midlands which she promised to get onto for them.

Still disgruntled after the meeting, Philip ploughed into a pile of correspondence, then put it to one side until after the holiday. Administrators went to ground for a fortnight over Christmas, though patients didn't stop getting ill. There'd be a backlog, more inefficiency. He left his room to moan to Sheila in Reception before the start of surgery.

'They'll only lie on someone's desk for weeks if we send them now.' He waved a bunch of pro-formas at her. 'That's if they don't get lost in the Christmas post.'

She tutted. 'You're beginning to sound like Gerald.'

'Am I? Yep, I am.' He shoved his hands into his pockets.

'What's wrong, too much Christmas spirit?'

'Don't I wish? No, it's old age, overwork, you name it.'

'You need a break.'

'I know.' He eyed the patients huddled and propped, bandaged and encased in plaster who sat waiting for surgery to begin. 'Fat chance. Who've we got first?' He ran his finger up the list and went through to collect Brian Lawson from the waiting-room.

'Come in and sit down.' He settled into routine. 'Let's see, how many weeks is it since you and Alison came in? How are things?'

'The same.'

'No good news, then?'

'No. You said to come back if there was no joy.'

Philip nodded, wondering about Alison's absence. 'Perhaps it's time we got you to see a fertility specialist. What does Alison think?'

'She doesn't know I'm here. Things have got pretty rough, as a matter of fact.' He clenched his teeth and tapped the desk. 'Alison told me it's all a waste of time. She heard something on the radio. They say it can be a two or three year wait for suitable donor eggs or what have you. And even then there's no guarantee.'

'That's true.'

'And they say it can cost an arm and a leg.'

Philip nodded. 'Treatment at a private clinic is expensive. But the NHS does have an IVF programme.'

'A what?'

'In Vitro Fertilisation. The egg is fertilised outside the womb. But there are many different types of assisted conception. Alison shouldn't write it off just because of something she heard on the radio.'

'Well she has. I came in to say thanks but no thanks. We've decided not to go ahead.'

Philip waited for more.

'To be honest, I can't say I'm sorry. I didn't fancy it. I'd have gone through with it if that's what she wanted. It meant a lot to her.'

'So why change her mind? It's not only because of the waiting list, is it?'

'I don't know what's got into her. There she was, all for it. She'd do anything to get pregnant.' He faltered. 'Anyhow, now she won't even talk about it.' Brian looked close to the end of his tether. His eyes were red-rimmed and bloodshot, a nerve clicked and jumped in his jaw. Despite his physical size, he seemed to shrink into his chair.

'Does she still take the blame for not conceiving?' Philip probed gently.

'No, now it's my fault. Everything's my fault. Problems with Nina; they're my fault. Problems with the marriage, you name it.'

'It sounds serious.'

'It is. We'll be lucky to make it through Christmas. She's practically got her bags ready and packed.' He looked away, pressing one hand over his mouth. 'Sorry.'

'That's OK.'

'It's a mess. Nina's ringing up her mother saying she wants to go back home for Christmas Day. Then her mother gets on to me, wanting to know what the hell's going on. Alison yells and says I should stand up to them, not let them push me around. If it was up to her, she'd pack the kid off on the next train south and good riddance. I'm caught in the middle. On top of all that there's this baby business. I won't spell it out, but now she's sleeping in the spare room and she won't let me near her. Where's the sense in that? And when I say sleeping, I mean walking about and crying and going downstairs to make herself a cup of tea. In the morning I don't know who looks worse, her or me.'

'What about you? Are you managing to get much sleep?'

He shook his head.

'Eating?'

'Not interested.'

'Any other physical symptoms?'

'Plenty. My gut's playing me up. I've got a bloody awful headache, pins and needles. Anything else?' He tried to laugh.

'I want to give you a prescription for an anti-depressant. Quite a low dosage, just one a day.' Philip reached for his pad. 'You're what we call clinically depressed. Mildly. It may not feel mild to you, but believe me I've seen it hit a lot harder than this. It's a reactive depression. That means you're reacting to external problems; the marriage and so on. This treatment is designed to help you through by putting a bit of a distance between you and the problems. It belongs to a modern group of drugs without side-effects, OK?'

Brian breathed out hard. 'I thought she was the one who needed treatment.'

'She may do. But Alison will have to come and see me off her own bat.' An appropriate metaphor for an ex-cricketer, he realised as he filled out the prescription. 'Or maybe you could get her back in here to discuss the fertility problem again?'

'I'll do my best.'

'Don't worry. Depression's common. It's treatable.' He looked up again. 'And no, before you say it, you're not making a fuss over nothing and it's certainly nothing to feel ashamed of.'

'Thanks. I appreciate it.' Brian tucked the prescription into his pocket.

'No problem. I hope it does the trick.' Looked at cynically, the fluoxetine might not save the marriage, but at least Brian wouldn't collapse if it failed. He held out his hand. 'I won't say Happy Christmas.'

'No.' He grinned and shook hands. 'I owe you one.'

'I'll be in later to claim it.'

'It'll be ready and waiting. Double Scotch, is it?'

'You're on.'

The door closed and Philip took a deep breath. Physician, heal thyself. Sometimes he thought depression was the only sane response. His wasn't so much depression as confusion, hitting him from behind, catching him unawares. Why couldn't he get Mary Mercer out of his head? Why was he suddenly dissatisfied with Juliet, or with himself for lacking something? What was it? Honesty, courage. Big words that didn't apply to a small-time GP in a backwater like Hawkshead.

Philip knew that his uneventful life was being turned on its head. He questioned the quality of his marriage, feeling smitten with guilt each time he went home to Juliet, a good meal and a comfortable house. He put all his effort into disguising his sudden dissatisfaction but deceit only made him more jumpy and irritable.

'What's got into you?' Juliet would say, when he lost patience with the video machine or grumbled about the telephone bill.

'Nothing.' He shut her out because it was Mary who had got into him. Deep under his skin; Mary with her mercurial personality and her eccentric, unguarded sex-appeal.

It sucked him in each time they met. The next time he ran into her was at the pub that evening, when he and Laura called in after their long, hard day.

'I don't know about you two, but I'm definitely de-mob happy.' Mary had finished work three days earlier. The pub was crowded with Merton office workers, the usual locals, a few strange faces.

'Ask me again when we've polished off this round.' He placed the glasses on the table, leaning over Mary's shoulder and pushing one towards Laura. Then he squeezed into a seat by the wall. 'These are on the house. Brian says Happy Christmas.'

They raised their glasses to the landlord behind the bar and Mary blew him a kiss.

Laura sighed. 'I must do some serious house-hunting after Christmas.'

'I'll help.' Mary had quietened down, as she often did when Philip was around.

He found himself watching everything she did, though he

scarcely listened to the details of her conversation. He noticed her slim wrists, her long fingers as she ran them round the rim of her glass.

'No thanks. You'd want me to buy something big and extravagant, and I'm thinking small and sensible, easy to clean, that sort of thing.'

'Boring.'

'Yep.' Laura changed her mind. 'OK, then, you can come and help me spend all my money, which I haven't got my hands on yet, by the way.' It was one reason why she hadn't started looking properly. The house sale in Camden had hit difficulties. 'Anyway, Dot makes me far too comfortable at Town Head for me to contemplate moving out before spring.'

Mary glanced at Philip, then hid her face behind her glass.

'How's your flat?' he asked.

'C-c-cold. I spend all my time in here just to keep warm. It's costing me a fortune.'

'Serves you right. Juliet still hasn't forgiven you.' This reminded him that he'd promised to go straight back home. He ignored the twinge of guilt and went off to buy another round. When he came back he stooped to kiss Laura's cheek. 'Here's to you.'

'What was that for?'

'For surviving your first few months in Ravensdale. And you, Mary.' He kissed her too. He brushed her skin with his lips, felt her face go out of focus, smelt her perfume.

She smiled uneasily. 'I know, we deserve a medal. I do, at any rate. All I've got round here is school and bloody sheep.'

Laura leaned across the table. 'It can't be that bad.'

'Worse. Listen, let me be the bearer of glad tidings.' She looked mysterious as she took another drink, launching into a piece of gossip geared to keep Philip on the sidelines. He stared into his glass.

'Yes?' Laura shook her arm. 'Go on.'

'About Matthew Aire.' She drummed her long fingers on the table. 'You know how I told you he's got a wife and kids, the complete set? Well, correction. He *had* wife. Still has kids, of course. Well, wifey has them over in York somewhere. That's right, isn't it, Philip?'

He nodded briefly.

'How do you know?'

'I ran into Christopher the other night. He told me all. The wife's name is Abigail and she runs her own business. Christopher likes her, says Matthew's a fool.'

'They're divorced?'

'Separated. It happened last summer, just after the old man died. Good, isn't it?' She bit her lip. 'Sorry, ignore me. I thrive on misfortune, you know that.'

'No, it's OK. I'm glad you told me.'

Mary seemed to be on form. 'But look on the bright side; at least your coast is clear.' She turned to Philip and waited for his agreement.

'Maybe Laura's a bit more subtle about the way she tackles things.' He'd better watch his drinking, he thought. That remark had come out of nowhere and dropped heavily into the conversation.

'I probably won't do anything about it though.' Laura moved them out of the awkward silence that followed.

'What?' Mary wailed. 'I don't believe this.'

'I'm immune.'

'You can't be. Not to Matthew Aire. He's drop-dead gorgeous.'

'But I am.' Since Tom, since the divorce. 'Passion is dead.'

'Long live passion.' Mary took a long pull at her drink.

'Amen to that.' Philip felt that if he stayed any longer he would say something he would regret. He badly wanted to tell Mary to be more serious, to take her and shake her into a more genuine frame of mind, then to have her in his arms, in his bed, in the centre of his life. 'Home time,' he said abruptly. 'I'm late.'

'Drunk too,' Mary added, eyes wide.

Good, let them think that was why he couldn't string his words together. If only. Drink was something you slept off, and woke up minus a few brain cells but none the worse for wear. Passion, to use Mary's word, was much harder to shake off. Passion, when things spun out of control and turned what had been a quiet, respectable life into a chaotic jumble of desire, missed opportunity, fear and guilt.

CHAPTER FIFTEEN

At home for Christmas with her parents in staid and stately Wingate, Laura spent the day being fed and pampered, catching up on family news.

All was familiar, but nothing quite the same. This was the first Christmas that she and Tom had spent apart in twelve years. Her mother spoke of him in hushed tones, but her father, tongue loosened by an afternoon's steady drinking, spoke his mind. 'To tell the truth, I'm glad to see the back of him. I didn't take much of a shine to him in the first place.'

Laura gave him a quick hug. 'He isn't that bad, Dad. We drifted apart, that's all.'

'Is that what you call it?' George Grant thought that Tom Elliot hadn't pulled his weight. He called himself a freelance journalist, which meant that he was always in and out of work and relying on Laura's income.

'George!' Laura's mother gave him a warning glance and thrust a plate of Christmas cake at him. She trod more carefully over the divorce business; you sometimes heard of people getting back together at the eleventh hour. She steered the conversation towards Laura's new job, saying that she looked well on it.

'Yes, I like it. I'm just beginning to feel that I belong.' She caught herself. 'Well, maybe not quite. But at least I don't feel I stick out like a sore thumb.'

They reminisced about family trips up Ravensdale when Laura was little. They would stop at Merton market on a Wednesday afternoon and drive on up to Hawkshead. 'Do you remember the snow up there?' her mother asked. 'In the winter of seventy-seven. Or was it seventy-eight? Anyway, the year of your GCEs. The snow ploughs had just got through and the snow was banked up at the roadside higher than the cars. Pure white everywhere. Even the river froze over. Do you remember?'

Laura laughed. 'We're hoping it's not going to be like that this year.' She imagined trying to reach the farms beyond Oxtop.

'We don't get the winters any more,' her father noted. 'It's this global warming.' He looked at her and nodded. 'So you're doing all right then?'

'Of course I am.' She told them about visits to patients way up at the top of the dale and over into Swiredale, in hamlets without pub or post office, up among the old lead mines of Ginnersby and Waite.

'And you're sure you're not working too hard?' Margaret Grant asked. 'We hear on the news about doctors working eighty-hour weeks. It worries us.'

'That's in the hospitals, Mum.' Though she had to admit that a GP's hours were long too.

'Well, we like having you close by. That's a real boon for us, you know.'

Laura made a New Year's resolution to see them more often. Her father was retired from his job with the water company. 'You'll have to come up to stay in the summer, when I've sorted out a house of my own.'

'You bet.' He jumped at her offer. 'I can do any little jobs that need doing.'

Margaret smiled as he got up to answer the phone. 'You know him and his little jobs.'

But when he came back he was frowning. 'For you,' he told Laura. 'It's Tom.'

She felt a small lurch and a tightening in her stomach as she got up to take the call. She and Tom hadn't spoken since she'd moved up to Yorkshire. He must have guessed she'd be at her parents' house for Christmas. She went into the cool hall and picked up the receiver. 'Hello?'

'Hi. It's me.'

The familiar voice sounded mellow. She pictured him stretched out in front of a TV somewhere, glass in hand. 'Hi. Are you having a good day?'

'Great. How about you?'

'Fine. I'm at home. Well, you guessed that, obviously.' She faltered. 'How are you?' She gazed around the hall at her mother's

Christmas decorations. There was a tree all lit up in the window of the house opposite.

'Not great.'

She didn't want to feel sorry for him. There was another long pause. 'My job's working out OK.'

'Busy, busy. Doing good works.'

Laura refused to let herself react. He sounded bitter.

'Listen, I just heard the other day, the house sale went through.'

'Good. At long last.'

'Yeah, they took their bloody time. Do you know what rake-off the bloodsucking estate agent gets?' He launched into an attack on the system. 'And the lawyers.'

It meant that her share of the money would soon be through, a decent deposit for a new place.

'You still there, Laura?'

'Yes. I'll get in touch with the solicitor. Thanks.'

'Pissing awful, isn't it?' he said miserably, after another painful silence.

'Yes.'

'I never thought we'd end up like this.'

'Tom, don't.'

'I mean, I knew in the end we'd never make a go of it. But there again, it still hurts like hell.'

'Yes.' Early hopes and dreams, sliding into unfulfilled expectations, unmet demands. Twelve years. Now this great crack in the ice, staring at each other across a widening gap.

'But you're OK?' His voice thickened.

'Yes. Listen, Tom, I want to ask you about a public inquiry they want to set up into a new quarry near us. I thought you might know how it all works.'

'Try me.'

'There's a particular company showing interest.'

'Name?' His brain clicked into action.

'Frontier. Ever heard of it?'

'No. It can't be one of the mega mob. But there's a big issue I've been following up in the Western Isles. They want to start blasting away, creating a super quarry that you could see from outer space, would you believe? Six hundred million tons of rock.'

Laura sensed that he would love to get his teeth into the Ravensdale problem. 'Not the same company?'

'No, but the same issue. *They* say major investment in the community, lots of jobs. The islanders say no way. They don't want the pollution. All that slurry and sludge into the rivers. All that dirt and noise. And what about the birdlife? That sort of thing.'

Laura agreed there were similarities. 'So what do you think?'

'I think you should get good legal backing straight off. Dig the dirt on this Frontier mob. Get all genned up about the environmental damage; you know, giant pyramids of waste, terraces cut into the hillside, great scars on the landscape. And go along to the inquiry well prepared.'

Laura felt her heart sink as she realised the full implications of going ahead with the quarry.

'Not to mention the storage sheds and the metal towers, and the noise and dust and lorries. Have they thought about the accessibility angle?' He was in full flood. This was his sort of thing; local communities taking up arms against mighty corporations. 'Oh, and one more thing.'

'Yes?'

'Get the press on your side. The local press first off. Then, spread the word. That's when I could come in, if you want.'

'Yes, I've got that, thanks.' He sounded more his old self, but Laura wasn't sure how much more of his help they would want.

'No problem. Let me know how you get on.'

'I will. Listen, I'd better be off. And thanks for phoning.'

'Give me a ring, remember.' He was about to replace the receiver. 'Oh, and Laura – '

'Yes?'

'Happy Christmas.'

'You too, Tom.' She put the phone down. That wasn't so bad, she thought. I'm still in one piece. She never imagined being able to say that, not after the last time, when they'd stood across the bed from one another, screaming recriminations, swearing revenge.

On Boxing Day morning, Laura was on call but she dropped in at Philip's for pre-lunch drinks. Juliet had decked the place out like a Victorian Christmas card; swags of red ribbon and real holly hanging across the stone chimney breast, a huge bowl of punch on the kitchen table, an open fire. Two of the Maskell boys, home for the holiday, had made rapid inroads into the punch. The atmosphere was jovial and easy-going.

'A glass of the old orange juice for me, worse luck.' Gerald was there, putting in his order. 'I'm still on the wagon. You got on all right with Maisie, then?' No doubt he fancied that he sounded inconsequential.

'I think so.' Laura went onto the defensive.

'She took a shine to you. Told you she would.'

'You did?' She was prepared to let this pass, guessing he would soon get round to discussing Matthew. She smiled broadly at Sheila Knowles, but Sheila didn't take the hint to come and rescue her.

'I hear Christopher didn't behave too well?' Gerald swilled the orange juice round the glass and took it like a dose of medicine, with a sour face. 'But then, there's nothing new in that. I do think, though, that he could restrict his womanising to the away ground. It's a bit rich to have it going on home turf, right under your nose. Janet insists it wasn't entirely his fault. Your friend, Mary Mercer, was as much to blame.'

'They're all grown-ups, Gerald. What they do is their business.'

He still circled round his main subject, so Laura decided to help him. 'I expect Matthew's more on Maisie's wavelength than Christopher?'

Gerald looked taken aback, then recovered his direction. 'Well yes, as a matter of fact – it's a bit delicate, you see.'

Laura smiled. 'Oh, come on, Gerald. What is this? Are you trying to tell me something I need to know about Matthew?' For a second she enjoyed her senior partner's discomfort. Then she softened. 'Look, it's OK. I know he's married. Mary told me.'

'Ah.' Gerald coughed, put his glass down, and shoved both hands in his pockets. 'Sorry. Like you say, probably none of my business anyway. But it's on a knife edge, you know.'

'What is?'

'Matthew's situation. Maisie was telling Janet all about it at the party.' He studied Laura's puzzled face. 'Trouble; it's often the mother who takes the brunt, isn't it?'

'You're talking about the marriage break-up?'

'Certainly. I mean, no, not quite.' He looked far too hot in his new guernsey sweater. 'Look, what I meant to say is that the whole situation at the Hall is damned delicate. Matthew and Abigail are having problems. He doesn't know where the hell he is with her. It's complex enough without you getting involved.' He paused, then lowered his voice. 'I wouldn't want you to get hurt, Laura. I thought you should know.'

That afternoon, Laura took a walk along the river under a doubtful sky. Clouds had gathered over Ravenscar, heavy with snow. But in spite of the weather she felt she needed to get out and put some real effort into roaming the quiet footpaths. She hoped to enjoy the space without interruption, finding time to think about this latest situation surrounding the Aire family. Heading downriver towards the Abbey, she cut across the valley bottom, over a wooden footbridge towards the sharp rise of Black Gill.

In this lonely mood, she began the steep climb. She paused by Joan's Foss where a heavy hoar frost had transformed clumps of overhanging grass into spearheads and created sharp-fingered icicles on the exposed tree roots at the head of the waterfall. She listened to the gush of the stream as it tumbled into the icy pool, watched the powerful swirl of the clear current, then headed on, planting her feet firmly from rock to rock, feeling an edge of danger as she gained height and discovered that the footholds were slippy with ice.

At last she came out of the Gill into the vast silence and stillness of Ravenscar. Here snow had begun to fall. The expanse of bracken and heather already had a white covering. Snowflakes drifted from banks of cloud, large, soft and silent.

Beautiful though it was, Laura realised that getting lost in freezing conditions on this high ground was a dangerous thing. She remembered the curious limestone pavement and the dizzying pits which formed a feature of the landscape to the west of the tarn.

Deciding to avoid that risk and to keep walking along the single-track road signposted to Hawkshead, she came across distant valley views of Ravensdale Abbey, the Grange and the Hall beyond. She pulled the brim of her hat low over her forehead, glad that she'd come prepared in a good waterproof jacket, scarf, gloves and boots. Twenty minutes' rapid progress should bring her down below the flurry of snow somewhere near Lilian Rigg's cottage, so she set off at a good pace, aware that she was alone in the white wilderness.

Wrapped in her own thoughts and by the falling snow, which cut down visibility and deadened all sound, she was surprised to be overtaken halfway down the hill by a high, four-wheel drive vehicle that slid to a halt some yards ahead. By now, the snow was three inches deep underfoot and drifting higher against the walls. The car's headlights were full on, its tail-lights glowing red in the white snowstorm. Its driver leaned out to ask if she wanted a lift.

Laura recognised Matthew Aire, alone in the car. She hesitated, thinking of all the reasons why not.

'Where are you heading?'

'Home.'

'Hop in, then. It's forecast to get much worse.' He waited until she came alongside. 'I can give you a lift all the way home. Better still, why not come back to the Hall with me for a drink? I can run you over to the village later on, when the snow's stopped.'

The offer was attractive; an open fire in the lounge at Hawkshead Hall, quiet music playing, just the two of them. Laura glanced up at Matthew. As far as he was concerned, there seemed to be no hidden complications. 'OK, thanks.' She went round, pulled off her hat and shook it before she climbed into the car.

It was the weather that had thrown them together, she told herself. If it had been fine, she would have refused the offer and followed her resolution not to get involved with Matthew Aire. Not that she was intending to get involved. This was only a lift and a quiet Boxing Day drink with a neighbour. Seven days earlier, it had been a mere moonlit tour of the house and a light kiss, hardly that. She sat beside him as the car dipped into the valley, through the village, over the river and along the lane to the Hall.

'Do you often walk up there alone?' Matthew asked, once she'd taken off her wet jacket and boots and they'd settled into two deep chairs in the study. He handed Laura a drink and watched her curl her legs under her. She flicked her dark hair clear of the rolled collar of her fawn sweater, leaning back against the creased brown leather. 'It can be a bit risky on the top of Ravenscar at this time of year.'

'What?'

'Walking by yourself. The weather can change pretty rapidly.' He explained that he'd been driving back from visiting friends in Wingate.

'My home town.'

'Is it? I didn't realise.'

He was easy to be with, conversation rose and fell in comfortable waves, the spent logs sank in the grate.

'What time is it?' she said at last. Through the open curtains she saw that it was dark outside, impossible to tell whether the snow had stopped.

'Half-five. Stay for supper.' He stood up, back to the fire. 'You don't have to rush off, do you?' He leaned forward to take her empty glass.

'No. But I don't want to be a nuisance.'

'No problem. Make up a four; Mother, Christopher, you and me.'

She got to her feet, uncomfortable at the mention of the others. 'Oh I don't know, perhaps another time.' It was hard to say no to Matthew.

'Stay. I'll go and fix things up and take a look at the weather, if you like. Do you need to make a phone call to tell someone where you are?'

'My landlady.'

'There's a phone on the desk there.' He smiled. 'Can I take it that's a yes?'

She nodded, then realised that Matthew's hand was still wrapped round hers in an attempt to take her glass. She tried to release it, but instead he leaned closer towards her and kissed her again. This time it was more definite.

She stepped back, trying to look as if contacting Dot had become an urgent priority.

'I won't be long,' he promised. He went to find Maisie. When they came back, Laura thought she looked agitated.

'Laura, I hear you've been risking life and limb up on the moor?'

'Hello, Maisie. Not really.' She received a light kiss.

'Well. He tells me he played the knight errant.'

'He insisted on giving me a lift. I'd no idea the snow could come down so suddenly.'

'Poor thing, you must have been terrified.'

'I headed downhill. I was trying not to panic when Matthew came along.'

'So I hear. Listen, we've been discussing supper, and of course it would be lovely, but not this evening, worse luck.'

'Oh, that's fine.' Laura cut in before Maisie had time to launch into long apologies. 'I really should get back; the snow and so on.'

'I knew you would understand. Matthew had no idea when he asked you to stay that I'd been in touch with Abigail while he was out. I invited them over.'

Laura glanced at Matthew.

'Sorry.'

'No, it's OK.' Her mood plummeted. She longed to be out of the suddenly claustrophobic room.

'It's just that we haven't seen nearly enough of the children over Christmas. And Abigail was very sweet about it. They're on their way right now.'

'You should have asked me first.' Matthew went to look out of the window. 'They shouldn't be driving anywhere in this weather.'

'Oh, darling, you know there was no snow when I invited them. In any case, Abigail loves spur of the moment things. There was no stopping her.' She looked apologetically at Laura. 'It seems I need permission to invite my own grandchildren to stay.'

'Look, I'm on my way.' She slipped her feet into her boots, standing by the fire to dry. When she said goodbye to Maisie, she was aware that Matthew had followed her to the door. 'Don't be angry with her. How was she to know?'

'At least let me drive you home.'

'No, I can walk.'

'It's Sophie and Tim.'

'I know.' She could see he felt a fool. 'Bad timing. But it's OK, I knew about Abigail. I know what it's like.'

'Should I have mentioned it?'

'It never came up. I haven't told you about my lurid past either.' She zipped her jacket and opened the door.

'I have to sort things out with her about the kids. I don't know what'll happen.'

She knew that one too. Will you, won't you, will you, won't you? 'I hope it works out.'

'Let me drive you home.'

'No, thanks.' Her smile was brief. 'The snow's stopped. I'll be OK.'

'I'll ring you.' He walked a few steps beside her.

She breathed in the cold air. 'No.' Other people might handle this; the conflicting emotions, the waiting by the phone. But it wasn't for her. 'Thanks for the lift, Matthew. Bye.'

But it was easier to sound calm than to feel it. In fact, as she left him and stepped out into a white, barely recognisable world, she felt sharply humiliated and hurt. No one's fault, she knew, but she saw how difficult it would be to find a secure niche in Matthew's life, and that somehow Maisie had been satisfied for Laura to realise this.

Well, she knew her own limits; right now she wasn't very resilient, nor ready to take on a fight. The wounds from Tom were still healing. Better to retreat graciously. Goodbye, Matthew. Passion is dead.

Her footsteps made fresh prints in the snow. Only when she was sure that he'd gone inside did she look back at the house; the white roofs, tall chimneys and brightly lit windows of Hawkshead Hall.

CHAPTER SIXTEEN

Philip planned to pull himself out of a post-Christmas slump by dealing with the backlog of correspondence that he'd put off since before the holiday. He chose the morning that Juliet had set by for driving Ian and Jim to the station, complete with fresh laundry and healthy boosts to their student bank balances. When the doorbell rang, he left his desk and went down, telling Dot that she didn't need to break off work to answer it.

'Mary.' He stood nonplussed, one arm resting against the door frame. She was poorly dressed for the cold in sweater and jeans, her big silver earrings making her look exotic even in the dead of winter.

'Philip, hi. I didn't expect you to be here. It was Juliet I really wanted to see.'

'She's taken the boys to the station. Can I help?' He held the door open wide. 'Come in, you must be freezing. Coffee?' He made for the kitchen.

'No thanks. OK, then, just a quick one. I've been an idiot as usual. I think I must have left some stuff in a drawer here by mistake. You know, National Insurance number, P45. The local authority wants to process me. I'm going to be on permanent supply instead of temporary blah blah. Too boring. I've ransacked my flat, can't find the stuff anywhere.'

'So it must be here? Dot hasn't mentioned seeing anything in your room.' He gave her the coffee. 'Jim's been using it, so God knows what kind of state it's in now.'

'I'll go and have a look, shall I?' She got up, but Philip put a hand on her arm.

'No, stay and chat.'

She sat down, letting his hand stay where it was on her arm.

'Why aren't you at work, Philip? You were supposed to be, you know.'

'Why? Are you avoiding me?'

She pulled her arm away.

'No, listen,' he continued. 'I don't think I've got this wrong. I'm not very observant, I admit, but there's something going on, isn't there?' There was for *him* every time he set eyes on her; across the street in the village, through the smoke-filled bar at the Falcon, dancing with Christopher Aire at a party.

'Please don't, Philip. I'm trying to be good, and I haven't had much practice.'

'Why do you run yourself down?'

'I didn't know I did. I always thought I had a pretty high opinion of myself.'

He examined the woodgrain on the table. 'I didn't get it wrong, did I?'

She sighed. 'No. I moved out because of how I was feeling. Satisfied?'

'About me?'

'Yes – and no.'

He didn't fully understand, but she had at least admitted that she felt something for him. She could have said don't be ridiculous, how could you imagine something like that? 'And so there you are, stuck in a freezing flat on the High Street, huddling by a gas fire.' He passed it several times a day, registered when the light was on, whether or not the curtains were drawn, hoping for a glimpse of her.

'Like something out of a Russian novel?' She laughed. 'Do me a favour, Philip.'

'I worry about you.'

'Well, don't. Absolutely don't. I like my flat, it suits me. I didn't get where I am today by hankering after wall-to-wall carpets and dishwashers.'

'I'm not allowed to wonder how you're coping?'

'You're not my father.'

'Sorry.' He stood up and walked away. 'You're right. I was being patronising.'

'Yep.' She too stood up. 'I'd better go.'

'What about the insurance number?'

'Could you ask Dot if she's seen any papers hanging around? Maybe down the back of a drawer or something.'

'Look, Mary. I need to say this. When you decided to leave I didn't try to stop you. I had no right. And I didn't know what I felt. It was afterwards I realised, when I started to miss you.'

'Don't tell me.'

'I have to now.'

'No, you don't. If you tell me how you feel, it'll be agony, believe me.' She backed away.

'It's agony anyway. But I don't want to hurt you.'

'That makes it worse.'

'How does it?' He caught up with her. She stopped. Slowly he put his arms around her, felt her lean against him. He kissed her face and lips. 'I miss your footsteps along the gallery, the coffee cups in the sink, your voice.'

'I know.'

'I would never have believed it.'

She stroked his face with her fingertips.

Untwisting an earring caught in the dark strands of her hair, he cupped her face in his hands and kissed her again.

'Philip, I have to go.' She broke away at last. 'You see, this doesn't change things.'

This time he didn't stop her from opening the front door, letting in a rush of cold air. He knew she was wrong, though. For him, everything had changed.

Dot watched her run up the drive. She stood at an upstairs window, duster in hand, as Mary ran across the bridge, head down, not seeing anyone through her tears.

'Someone's in a hurry,' Dot said out loud, determined to mind her own business. She went back to her dusting. 'If she wants to catch the bus into Merton, she's missed it. It's just gone by.'

She set to, trying to make up the hours she'd missed because of the Christmas break. When she'd finished at Bridge House, her day was still only just starting.

She did the kitchen and downstairs, vacuuming with a vengeance, so that she didn't hear Philip leave for work.

Then she set off for Oxtop, taking the Hopper bus from the old bridge, to call in on Tot Dinsdale who'd been missing from his barstool at the Falcon the night before. It was unlike him to break his routine. In any case, she wanted to confer with the old farmer about their tactics to stop the quarry people in their tracks before an inquiry took hold.

As time passed, Dot had become adamant that the quarry must be stopped. When people talked of progress and moving with the times she stopped her ears. Hawkshead could do without that sort of progress; the upset and the ugliness, all to make a fat profit at the expense of the local people. Above all she blamed Maisie Aire, for being old enough to know better. The trouble was, Maisie wasn't born and bred in the dale; she merely married into it. Her roots didn't go as deep as Dot's, or Lilian's, Dick's or Tot's for that matter.

Stepping down from the bus at the top of the windswept moor, she followed the unmade track to Tot's farm, calculating that she had just under an hour before she caught the Hopper on the return stage of its round trip through Ginnersby and Waite. She went and hammered on the peeling door, waited, knocked again. Tot's old Land Rover stood in the yard; he couldn't be far away. She tried the door handle and found that it turned. 'Tot? It's me, Dot Wilson. Are you there?' She stepped inside, straight into the old man's gloomy and comfortless kitchen.

'Can't you see, I'm over here? Here, here.' He growled at her like an irritable old dog.

She picked him out sitting in a high-backed armchair, wrapped in a blanket, his face whiter than the ashes in his grate. His grey hair was spiky and uncombed, his chin unshaven. 'What's up with you? Are you ill?' She went forward to see what could be done.

'Don't you wait for an answer before you come barging in?'

'Come off it, Tot. What's up? Do you want me to ring for a doctor?'

'I do not,' he insisted. 'I'll soon mend.'

'You can't move out of that chair, can you?'

'Don't ask daft questions.' He huddled inside the blanket, moving only his head. His arms were hidden, but he seemed to be hugging himself, shoulders hunched.

'Right, don't argue, I'll ring for help.' She went for the phone and spoke to Sheila Knowles. 'Sheila, it's Dot Wilson. Can you send someone up to Oxtop? Tot's in a bad way here.'

'Dr Scott's still on holiday, Dot, and Dr Maskell's working at home. It'll be Dr Grant.'

'Tell her I'll hang on here until she arrives. Mind you, he's in a

wicked temper. I expect it's because he missed his pint last night.'
Tot had begun to swear fit to bust.

To get to Oxtop Laura would have to negotiate the infamously
steep and winding incline of Hawk Fell, past Sheila's modernised
barn, and along the bare, scarred hilltop where the mines of
Ginnersby had once been worked for lead. It was a crystal clear day,
with snowdrifts three or four feet deep still bedded into the hollows,
and a fresh sprinkling on the far summits. Most of the snow had
melted, however, and the grey-green hills were exposed once more.

The old lead mines had left their mark in the shape of derelict
smelting mills, tippings of shale now grassed over, and hushes or
dry grooves running vertically from the hilltops. They'd been
formed by damming a stream and diverting the water so that the
beds could be investigated for veins of metal. The mines had left an
atmosphere too. Dot always thought as she rode up on the bus that
Ginnersby seemed haunted by the sad memory of miners' gangs
trudging through the dawn light and filing silently into the shafts,
working like moles underground until eventually the veins were
exhausted and the buildings left desolate.

The land provided little sustenance now. Only a few scattered
sheep farms survived, among them Oxtop, which, Dot knew, had
been with the Dinsdales for generations. Tot's dilapidated home
was perched on the ridge at the end of half a mile of rough track.

She greeted Laura with the warning about Tot's wicked temper,
then led her inside. 'I think he's broken summat, the way he's
going on. He says it's his chest, but he's not wheezing, no more
than usual.'

Inside the kitchen, they were met with a hail of abuse from the
stick-like figure propped in an old armchair. No woman doctor was
coming near him, he said. He'd stay put until Dr Scott or Dr Maskell
arrived. He'd held on long enough before Dot had come and
interfered, and he'd hold on a bit longer rather than let himself be
poked about by Laura.

'He's not had anything to eat or drink for days,' Dot confided. 'I
think he's delirious.'

She pointed to the unwashed crockery in the sink, dead embers
in the grate of the iron range, the glow of a single-bar electric fire
that hardly dented the chill of the large, dark kitchen.

Laura told her quietly that Tot suffered from a degree of heart
failure and hypertension, normal in a man his age. But from the

way he was sitting she suspected a fracture rather than anything cardiovascular. He held both arms across his ribs, reluctant to turn in his seat while he hurled his insults, which were muttered through clenched teeth, as though deep breathing increased the pain. 'Where does it hurt, Mr Dinsdale?' she asked in her best professional manner.

'Nay, it's nowt. It'll mend on its own.' He shook his head, but his resistance seemed to be waning.

Laura changed tack, sitting opposite him, hands in pockets to show that she had no intention of poking him about. 'Do you still farm?'

'Aye, I do. I've a few sheep on the Fell. I shall want to be on the mend for lambing, mind.'

'What happens at this time of year, then? I noticed they stay out in all weathers. But don't they need feeding?'

He looked suspiciously at her, his face grey with pain. 'A bit every now and then. I take extra out in the Land Rover. I've been carrying on as usual right up until yesterday morning.'

'Even though you didn't really feel up to it?'

'Aye well, I gave myself a bit of a knock a week or so back, just after Christmas. Came off the road coming down Hawk Fell into a snowdrift.' He tried to pass it off. 'It were nowt. Just a bit of a bang across my chest.'

'You didn't think to come in and see us at the surgery? You see, if the rib was broken in the accident, and you've been carrying on as usual, trying to lift and carry as well as drive, the fracture might well have become infected. Let's see if we can find any swelling around the site. How much does it hurt?'

'Nay, you'd only stick me in Low Royds,' he announced.

Dot too could see that this was the way Laura's thoughts were tending. Low Royds was the geriatric unit in Merton, an ex-mental hospital of the old kind, on the site of a former workhouse. No wonder Tot resisted the idea.

'Not necessarily. If I'm right, and you're nursing a couple of broken ribs there, it really needs an X-ray to take a proper look.'

'That's right, stick me away in one of them places, and then see.'

'It won't have to be for long, Mr Dinsdale. And I can't make a diagnosis until I've taken a look, can I?' She turned to Dot. 'Have you given him anything to eat or drink since you came in?'

'I made him a hot cup of tea, strong and sweet, as soon as I found him.'

'Good. Look, Mr Dinsdale, I'm probably going to give you an antibiotic for the infection around the fracture. We need to get the swelling down. That might do the trick, so long as you don't try to move about. But I'm worried about you staying here all on your own. Do you have any family who could come in and help?'

He shook his head. 'There's only me.'

'In that case, I don't feel I can leave you here on your own. Even without further complications it's just too risky. Now, why not let me take a look and decide what we should do?'

Dot stood by, admiring Laura's handling of the difficult problem as she moved in quietly and waited for her patient to signal his consent. Then she took away the blanket and held his jacket to one side, peeling away the layers until she came to the bruised and swollen flesh towards the bottom of the ribcage on the left-hand side.

'There's my sheep to think of, see,' Tot said in a quiet, broken voice. 'What's to become of them?'

Laura nodded.

'Don't worry about 'em.' Dot moved forward and spoke firmly. 'I'll get Dick to see to 'em. He won't mind.'

'Well?' Laura prompted.

'Aye, but I'll not budge.'

'But you'll stay put and let Mr Metcalfe look after your sheep, at least?'

Reluctantly he nodded. 'Only for a day or two, mind.'

'We'll see.' Laura turned to Dot. 'Don't worry, I'm pretty sure we can clear up the local infection, which is what's causing him the worst problem. After that he'll need complete rest until the rib heals. I'll have to try to get a nurse up here on a regular basis.'

'Aye, well, I'll pop in as often as I can,' Dot promised. 'It's not so bad on the bus. I can come up after work.'

'Aye,' he said, allowing Laura to strap up his chest and to ease him out of his chair towards a long sofa in the living room. 'But I'm not shifting from Oxtop, not at my time of life.' Slowly he shuffled through and lay down.

They left him as comfortable as they could and Laura offered Dot a lift home.

'Why do the old-timers always reject what we can offer?' Laura

127

asked. 'Can't they see that by putting off treatment, they often make things worse?'

'That depends.' Dot knew that for people like Tot there was nothing worse than giving yourself up into the arms of the system. It harked back to old Poor Law days and their treatment of the elderly.

'On what?'

'On how much you cling to your own way. Folk like Tot were brought up not to rely on anybody.'

'He won't thank me for sending Joy in, then?' Laura drove carefully through the village.

'We'll never hear the end of it afterwards.'

'If there is an afterwards,' Laura reminded her. 'We'll have to watch out for pneumonia. That's the real reason I wanted him at Low Royds.' She sighed.

'Don't take it too badly. I doubt even Dr Scott would have been able to prise him out. He always was a cussed old beggar.'

They arrived home unable to shake off the worry about Tot and his frail bones, possible hypothermia, pneumonia and self-neglect all marching under the banner of independence.

'One thing's for sure,' Dot said as she picked up the phone to get through to Dick Metcalfe. 'It doesn't make your life any easier.'

She didn't admit it, but the experience up at Oxtop had shaken her. What with Lilian ill in hospital, and now Tot, it looked like the old order was crumbling. As you got on in life you had to accept unpalatable truths; that your own joints would ache and creak, that you would become less indispensable to your family as time went by. But it was more of a jolt when your friends began to fall by the wayside. You watched them grow frail and fade. Then came the funerals.

Never say die. She shook herself into a more positive mood as she waited for Dick to come to the phone. There was Black Gill to take up arms for; Lilian's home and livelihood to save, and now Tot to look after. Perhaps she still had her uses after all.

CHAPTER SEVENTEEN

'Any New Year resolutions?' Laura asked Mary over a quiet drink at the Falcon. She was tired after a weekend on call and a close shave with a diabetic patient who was semi-comatose when he was found on the floor of his garage workshop just outside the village. She'd got the paramedics out from Wingate just in time. The mechanic was now safely hooked up on a saline drip, under observation in hospital.

'None that I could possibly announce to the public at large,' Mary replied. 'Anyway, resolutions involve willpower, and I don't have any.'

'Unlike some people I could mention.' Laura had just seen Aimee Scott pass by. She knew that Gerald and Janet hadn't been able to persuade her to go with them on their annual skiing trip, and both Philip and Laura had agreed to keep a discreet eye on her.

'You mean Aimee?' Mary had followed her glance. 'Oh lord, I should be at home to meet her. I promised to see her about some extra tuition.' She gulped her drink. 'Come with me, Laura. I can't cope with an undiluted dose of Aimee right now. You being there will put her off.'

'Thanks a lot.' In fact, she was happy to go along. Knowing that her parents had left word that she should be supervised, Aimee had spent the week avoiding both Philip and herself. Laura had only seen her in passing; still thin, still arresting attention but, at the same time, blocking any approach. She followed Mary out of the pub.

'You know what I mean. It's just that she's less likely to go all intense on me if there's a third party.' They hurried onto the street, to find Aimee standing off the pavement, peering up at Mary's window. 'Here I am. Come on in. Laura's going to make us coffee, aren't you, Laura? You two have met, haven't you? Course you have, I'm hopeless.'

They went up a flight of dark stairs to Mary's room, where despite the clutter there was an airy feel from the big sash-window and some large paper lampshades. A smell of baking bread drifted up from the shop below.

Aimee hovered in the doorway. 'I could come back some other time,' she suggested.

'Of course not. Laura doesn't bite. Come in and sit down where you can. Find a space, move something, tell us about your lousy Christmas. Let's compare family horror stories.'

'Mine wasn't lousy,' Laura said. 'But it's so long ago, it feels like years.'

'Lucky you. What about yours, Aimee?' Mary settled in a big old armchair.

'It was OK.'

'Tucking into the turkey?'

Aimee looked away. 'I don't eat meat.'

'Wise girl. What about cheese and eggs? How far do you go?'

'No. I'd rather not talk about it.'

'OK, boring, I get it.' Mary raised her hands in surrender. 'No, but really, it's interesting. What happens at times like Christmas? It must be pretty difficult for you to join in.'

'Who cares?'

'Right. Anyway, I admire your willpower. I was just telling Laura, I fall a bit short in that department.'

'She's being modest.' Laura handed Aimee a cup of coffee and noted that she refused both milk and sugar. 'In fact, Mary's got a will of iron. She must have, to stand on a stage in front of hundreds of people. I'd rather die.'

'Acting doesn't take willpower. It's all about technique. It's the one thing where I can forget about myself and concentrate on something more important.'

'You can get everything under control. No one's doing anything unexpected.' Aimee agreed, entering the conversation with enthusiasm now.

'Unless the scenery falls down.' Mary regaled them with tales of onstage blunders and accidents.

'Is that what we'd all like? For our lives to hold no surprises?' Laura asked. 'Is that why we build routines?'

'I guess.' Mary shrugged. 'You're the expert.'

'So what if something comes along and demolishes our routine?'

'We turn around and build ourselves another one.'

'To convince ourselves we're safe. Some more than others. I don't think you do that as much as me. What about you, Aimee?'

'Sometimes. I won't follow someone else's routine, though. I've got to decide for myself.'

Mary laughed. 'Is that why you miss all my lessons?'

'And why you're so good at being vegetarian?' Laura chipped in.

'How come you're so interested in what I eat?' Aimee rounded on her. 'Well, we know why.' She turned to appeal to Mary. 'She thinks I'm too thin. I'm not too thin, I just watch what I eat. There's nothing wrong with that. It's better than being fat. And if you must know, it doesn't take any willpower whatsoever. It's dead easy. I just don't eat, full-stop. Oh, who cares? I bet you two have been talking about me. Just get off my back, OK!' She jumped up and stormed to the door.

Mary beat her to it. 'Calm down, Aimee. Laura didn't mean anything. It was me who brought the subject up, remember?' She met her eye. 'And as a matter of fact, I agree with Laura. You are too thin.'

'Look, this is stupid. I'm healthy, aren't I? Fat people get heart attacks, don't they?'

'And anorexics starve themselves to death,' Mary said bluntly.

Aimee scowled, retreating because her way was still blocked.

Laura gestured to Mary to back off. 'Let's just clear this up. Firstly, we haven't discussed you behind your back, so don't think we have. But now that Mary's in on this, couldn't you explain it to us? Why the big deal about your weight? What's it all about, really?'

'Well, it's not about fitting into size eight, I can tell you that.'

Laura knew they had to make a breakthrough, or she would never get Aimee onto any course of treatment. 'So what's behind it?' she said gently.

'What do you want me to say? I count calories. I'm losing weight. I've got everything under control. What's the problem?'

'You're losing too much, you can't stop. That's the problem.'

'What's too much? It's my body, my choice. You're both like my mother, trying to make me eat. I don't have to.'

'No you don't,' Laura agreed. 'What about your father?'

'What about him?' Aimee's face took on a hunted look, her eyes were dark and wide, she was breathing fast. 'I'll tell you what, he'll have to admit I'm good at something, won't he? In the end, he'll have to bloody well admire me for doing something well.'

New Year faded as fast as Christmas, Gerald was safely back at work and Laura heard no more from Aimee after her outburst at Mary's flat. Lilian Rigg was still in hospital, Tot convalescing at home, and news of both the quarry and Matthew Aire had taken a back seat for a few days, when Laura suddenly bumped into Maisie in the supermarket in Merton.

The old lady's greeting was effusive. She introduced Laura to her daughter-in-law, Abigail Drummond, and her two grandchildren, who immediately skittered off down the aisle towards the racks of sweets. 'Yes, I know, it's awfully confusing. Abigail never took the family name, you see, and poor Sophie and Tim are saddled with one of those dreadful double-barrelled things. Drummond-Aire, such a mouthful. What will happen when *they* marry and have children, goodness only knows!' Maisie rattled on, happy to let Laura take a good look at Abigail and vice-versa.

She was curious, as Maisie intended. Slight and small, with a boyish air, Abigail had nonetheless a strong presence. She was carefully made-up, but probably older than Matthew. She was fashionably dressed and looked confident.

'How's Christopher?' Laura steered Maisie to what she thought was safe water.

'Purring in his Tuscan retreat, lapping up the climate, I guess.' Maisie's mouth set in a bitter line.

Abigail stepped in. 'I was telling Maisie, I nipped over to the States on business.' Now she told Laura about the successful East Coast trip. 'I design and build conservatories. They love all the skilled craftsmen, natural wood stuff.'

Maisie puffed up her daughter-in-law's success. 'Your accent alone has got to be worth at least a thousand dollars on each conservatory. I hope you charged plenty?'

'We did,' Abigail assured her.

'And the children. Where did they stay?'

'At home. I got in a temporary nanny. It works out well, so long as you can rely on the agency.'

They said goodbye and chose a check-out at the opposite end to

Laura. Abigail cast her one more curious glance before they reached the car park and she drove Sophie and Tim with their grandma back to the Hall, where they were to stay for half term.

Laura had stopped off at the supermarket in Merton on her way to Wingate to see Lilian. Tests had confirmed the ovarian cancer, with secondary tumours in the lungs. Wingate wanted her to stay in for the course of intensive chemotherapy and reluctantly Lilian had agreed to a week's further incarceration. Earlier, Laura had explained the chances of remission and the quality of life which Lilian might expect to maintain. She'd watched her patient slowly consider the options, answered all her questions, and finally succeeded in getting her to accept treatment. Now this visit would prove how far her judgment had been right. She was hoping to find Lilian rested and free from pain.

In a ward full of flowers and quiet chatter, Lilian sat by her bed. She was dressed in a cornflower blue candlewick dressing-gown, looking good, with some colour and flesh restored to her cheeks after a period of care and a regular diet. She greeted Laura shyly, pulling her robe tight under her chin with a blunt-nailed hand. 'I feel a proper fraud,' she told her. 'I was just saying to Dot Wilson, there's plenty worse off than me in here.' She said she'd been crowded out with visitors who'd bothered to make the long journey to come and see her, and she soon waxed angry over the issue of the day; the threat to the dale of the stone quarry.

'It's not just Abbey Grange I'm bothered about.' Lilian leaned forward and grasped the arm of Laura's chair. 'I know you haven't been long in the dale, but it seems to me you've already a good idea of what Black Gill and Ravenscar mean to us. With this inquiry hanging over our heads, no one can rest easy.'

Laura nodded. 'When does it begin?' They'd been expecting it, day by day, since Christmas.

'Dot says it's going to be next week. She was up at Oxtop lending a hand to old Tot. According to him, there's the first public meeting at the school next Thursday. If they let me out of here, I'll be there.'

Laura said smilingly that she didn't doubt if for a moment.

'Tot swears he'll make it down to the meeting and all, if it's the last thing he does. Rib or no rib.'

Laura made a mental note to drop in on the old farmer, who would no doubt continue to ignore her advice. His injury was healing, thanks to good support from his neighbours and home visits, plus meals-on-wheels, but Tot's impatience to be out and about made him daily more cantankerous. 'There should be a good turnout then?'

'You can say that again. The whole village will be there. We'll give the quarry lot a polite hearing, but then they'll get what for.'

'Lilian, do you know if anyone's leading this campaign?' She had in mind Tom's advice about legal representation. Since their talk on the phone she'd been stuck over how such a thing was to be funded. Now however, with the inquiry imminent, she felt it was time to act.

'I don't suppose we've got a leader as such. And I don't know that you'd call it a campaign exactly.'

'Well, I think it needs a bit more organisation. I'll have a word with Dot. But how about you two getting your heads together as soon as you feel up to it?' It was partly a medical judgment; with something definite to keep her going, Lilian's remaining days would be active and purposeful. It would stop her from moping.

'Nay.' Lilian's natural modesty held sway for a moment. Then, with a glint in her eye, she looked up at Laura. 'We'd need a bit of a hand every now and then. What do you say?'

Laura only had to catch a fleeting glimpse in her mind's eye of the soaring hillside. 'Lilian, I'd be honoured!' She felt the old lady's hand gently cover hers and smiled back warmly.

Lilian chuckled. 'They'll never get their quarry at this rate, you mark my words.'

They went on to discuss details. Lilian hoped to be discharged from hospital on the following Monday. That same day Laura would ask advice on decent solicitors and find one who was strong on land rights, public rights of way, access and so on. She hoped they'd be able to trip up the Frontier people over issues such as this.

'Who'll pay?' Lilian asked, pragmatic as ever.

'Perhaps we could ask for donations, make an official fund? I'll look into it.'

'Right. It's good of you to come, Dr Grant. I'm grateful for all you've done for me. And I'll see you next Thursday at the school?'

'I'll be there.'

'I'll tell you what,' Lilian said suddenly, 'you could go up to the Grange if you like. The whole place is a carpet of snowdrops just now. Do you like snowdrops?'

Laura smiled and nodded.

'Then pay a visit to the Grange this weekend.' Lilian nodded encouragement and patted Laura's hand once more. 'Snowdrops everywhere, thousands of them, along the walls, under the trees. It'll be a sight for sore eyes.'

Laura left the hospital, aching at the old woman's kindness, promising herself the special treat of seeing the brave forerunners of spring nestled in Lilian's garden at the very foot of the threatened hill.

CHAPTER EIGHTEEN

Dot was flattered when Laura asked her to form a committee to oppose the quarry. She stirred tea leaves vigorously and set the pot on the breakfast table. 'Ask a busy person if you want something done. That's what they say, isn't it?'

'You're sure you have time?'

'I'll find time. There's a jumble sale at Church House this afternoon. I'll pass the word around, rope in the vicar and a few others. Now, you mentioned setting up some kind of fund? I'll ask Lilian to be treasurer. She's good with figures, running her own business as she does. Fund-raising is more my line, jumble sales and sponsored walks. Maybe the schools will want to get the children involved.' There was no shortage of ideas once she set her mind to it.

'We'll need a solicitor to look into the legal angles.' Laura spread marmalade on her toast and chewed thoughtfully.

'Leave it to me.'

'Do you know someone?'

'I'll ask round.'

'Me too.' Laura took her time over breakfast. It was Saturday, a weekend off.

'I'm on my way then.' Dot took up her basket, ready for the market. 'I promised Tot I'd pick up a few bits and pieces for him. I'll need to take them up and get back again in time for the jumble sale.'

She went down the hill. It was a dull, damp morning. In the square she passed from stall to stall buying vegetables, cheese, meat, spreading the word.

'We don't want this quarry idea getting off the ground. Now's the time to nip it in the bud, before the public inquiry gets going. We have to be organised.' She approached stallholders and shopkeepers, drew in farmers meeting outside the pub, Mr Hughes, the headmaster at the secondary school, and Marsden Barraclough, the vicar at St Michael's.

'Well done, Dot.' Juliet Maskell took her for coffee at the Falcon. 'You're certainly getting us galvanised into action.' She took out her purse to make a donation.

'Hold on.' Dot made her close it again. 'Lilian's going to be treasurer. She'll be out of hospital on Monday. Give her your money, it'll give her something useful to think about.'

'What are we collecting for now?' Brian Lawson came with their coffee.

'To pay for our quarry campaign.'

'It's a campaign, is it?'

'We've to make a firm stand. We need legal advice, and that doesn't come cheap.'

'No, you're right.' He dug into his pocket.

'Keep hold of your money, Brian. Lilian will be round soon enough.'

'How is she? When's she getting out?'

'Monday.'

'She's the one I feel sorry for.' He wiped the next table and set the mats back in place.

'She won't want your pity,' Dot warned. 'Just your cash.' She glanced around the bar. 'What about your Alison? Will she help with the jumble sales?'

He didn't stop in his stride, but continued towards the bar. 'You'd better ask her.' This was a funny answer, she thought.

'You'll pass on the message?'

'I will when she gets back.'

'Why, where's she got to?'

'Away. She needs a break.' He disappeared behind the bar.

Dot took the hint and turned back to Juliet. 'Who else can we rope in?'

'Me for a start. I'll be glad to lend a hand.'

'What about Dr Maskell?' Dot was dogged in pursuit of influential help.

'Definitely.'

'Dr Scott?'

'I wouldn't hold your breath there, I'm afraid.'

'That's right. He's thick with Maisie Aire, isn't he? Him and

Geoffrey Aire used to go shooting together.' Dot sniffed. 'No, we won't bank on Dr Scott.'

Other customers drifted in off the busy street. Brian emerged to serve them. 'Still at it?' he said as he passed by with a full tray.

'We are,' Dot confirmed. 'Can you think of a good solicitor for us, Brian?' She spotted Laura across the street, going up the step into the office of Warboys and Wychell, Solicitors and Commissioners of Oaths. 'She's wasting her time there,' she commented. 'I should have warned her about that.'

She and Juliet decided to press on. Juliet had shopping to finish and Dot had to catch the bus to Oxtop. They stopped for a few moments when Mary Mercer came by with Aimee Scott and Nina Lawson in tow, and Dot recruited more help for the campaign.

'It's outrageous,' Mary declared. 'Ludicrous. How can they think of ripping the heart out of the dale?'

Even the teenagers seemed partly roused from their apathy. 'I could start a protest at school,' Aimee suggested. 'As soon as term starts.'

Mary looked for Dot's agreement. 'What do you think?'

'We should all pull together. You'd better ask Mr Hughes first, though.'

'No, we should just go ahead and do it,' Aimee insisted. 'It's got nothing to do with the teachers. Most of them don't live here anyway.' She and Nina went off, their interest engaged.

'Don't worry, I'll organise it,' Mary promised. 'It's good to involve the kids anyway. You need the whole community behind you.'

It had been a successful morning; lots of enthusiasm, hardly any dissenting voices. Dot felt cheerful as she climbed into the Hopper and headed up Hawk Fell to Oxtop.

Simon Warboys was the solicitor Laura had chosen to polish off details of the house sale in Camden. He was part of a long-established local firm, handy for her because its offices fronted onto the village square. As she went through the door, out of the bustle of the market, she hoped to kill two birds with one stone.

Simon, grandson of Edward, the original Warboys, was a conservatively dressed, middle-aged man of medium height with receding grey hair and a light handshake. He gave the distinct impression that he preferred paperwork to people. His desk, scrupulously neat and tidy, set up a sturdy barrier between him and his clients, and all his mannerisms suggested distance; from the flick of an invisible speck from his lapel after he'd shaken hands, to the pressure of forefinger against glasses at the bridge of his disdainful nose. Quickly he offered Laura the forms to sign regarding her share of the spoils on the Camden property.

'All we need now is your ex-husband's signature, then we can transfer the deeds into the hands of the buyers' solicitor. The agony should all be over in a matter of days.' He withdrew the papers from Laura, hovering over them in his half-moon specs.

Laura doubted that the business of extracting a signature from Tom would be quite that painless, but she went on with her other piece of business. 'There was something else, Mr Warboys.' She did her best to iron out a frown, experiencing a twinge of Tom-type resentment towards these professionals who charged so much and cared so little. 'Some of us in the village intend to form an action group against the Frontier Stone Company's plan to begin quarrying on Ravenscar. We need legal advice on how best to oppose them, and it seems to me that, as the local law firm, someone here might be in a position to help us set out our stall.' She hesitated, waiting for his reaction.

'You want to set up an action group?'

'Yes. Dot Wilson and I feel there will be a lot of support. People stand to lose their homes if they live on the route of the proposed access road along the valley bottom and up Black Gill. The dale would never be the same again.'

Simon Warboys shook his head. '*Other* people might think that it was a fair price to pay for progress.' He paused, studying Laura's earnest face. 'Forgive me, Dr Grant, but this business of the quarry mustn't be taken at face value. My own opinion, for what it's worth, is that the opposition argument may turn out to be rather lightweight in comparison with the benefits of jobs and revenue which the quarry would bring. New industry, new housing and so forth. The cosmetic aspect would then surely pale into insignificance?'

Laura sat firm in her seat. This was the first voice she'd heard raised in defence of the quarry and she was taken unawares.

'I suppose you've assessed the level of support for your little group?'

Blushing, she had to admit that they were at a very early stage.

'And you've considered how your opposition to what I have to say I believe to be an admirable plan would split this community right down the middle?' He paused. 'Just think of it; professional protestors rampaging into Ravensdale with every intention of disrupting a legitimate enterprise. You've seen them in the newspapers; the sort who build tree-houses on the quarry route and sling banners from the rooftops. All that they achieve is to attract wide and acrimonious publicity. They prolong affairs by seeking individual glory or martyrdom, then fizzle out as another cause takes their fancy.'

Her own argument dismissed out of hand, she stood up, nodding stiffly. 'Thank you. We'll consider what you say.'

He stooped across the desk to shake her hand. 'Why not wait until you hear Frontier's point of view? When is it, next Thursday?'

'That's the first public meeting, yes.'

'Well then. I'm all in favour of people going along there with an open mind. Listen to what they have to tell you first off, and I think you'll be pleasantly surprised by their enlightened stance on the environmental issues that you people are getting worked up about.' He gave her what might pass for a smile as he showed her to the door.

Laura left the office seething. Pompous . . . opinionated . . . ass! Each step she took towards the surgery brought forth another spurt of anger. Cynical . . . uncaring . . . callow . . . If she had her way, she would dump people like Warboys in a planner's nightmare of high-rise industrial wasteland and then hear what he had to say about the irrelevance of preserving the quality of the environment. Run a railway under his window, build him a hovel over a motorway interchange, see how he liked it!

'Anyone know of a good, honest solicitor?' She burst into the surgery. Gerald and Philip were both in their consulting rooms, catching up on paperwork. 'Or is that a contradiction in terms?'

'Whoa, steady on!' Gerald emerged, swinging his glasses between thumb and forefinger. 'House sale fallen through, has it?'

'No!' Laura was still fuming. 'I've just had the unedifying experience of talking to Simon Warboys about this quarry business. I've never been so patronised in my entire life!'

'Hmm, gave it to you hot and strong, did he?' Gerald twiddled his glasses.

'He actually turned away business. Can you believe that? He refused to help.'

Gerald glanced at Philip. 'Whose business? Yours?'

'The campaign's. We're getting up an opposition group to present a case to the inquiry.' Exhausted by her anger, she sank into a chair. Philip ambled out of his room. 'Now let's see, what were his exact words?' She recalled them with fresh indignation. 'That we should all go to the public meeting next week with an open mind!'

'Good old Simon; he of the open mind.' Philip sympathised with Laura. And he was afraid she was in for a few more unexpected knocks. 'What he really means is, wait and see who's going to win before you place your allegiance!' He sat down beside her. 'Listen, Laura, as a matter of fact, you couldn't have chosen anyone worse than Warboys to talk to about your campaign.'

She realised that Philip was trying to let her down gently. 'Why? What should I know about Warboys and Wychell?'

He cleared his throat. 'They work for the Aire family. Always have.'

'Oh, what an idiot,' she said faintly. She felt two inches tall, then she tried to look on the bright side. 'Well anyway, he didn't seem too much of a hotshot. Maybe it's a good thing he's representing Maisie Aire, when it comes down to it?'

But Gerald began to shake his head and pace up and down the oblong space in the centre of the waiting-room. 'I'm not so sure. He's no fool.' Slotting his folded glasses into his jacket pocket, he came to a halt in front of Laura. 'I hope you didn't tell him where to get off?'

Already angry, Laura bridled again. 'Give me some credit, Gerald.' She considered she'd made a dignified exit in the circumstances.

'That's one good thing, then.'

'What do you mean, that's one good thing?' She ignored Philip's restraining arm. 'You make it sound as if you're on his side!'

'I'm saying it's not clever to go around wearing your heart on your sleeve over something like this.'

'No? Look, Gerald, it's Ravenscar we're talking about here. They plan to churn it up with this scheme of theirs. Ravenscar! Have you taken a walk up there lately? Have you seen what it is they'd be destroying?' If her heart was on her sleeve over this, then she was proud. 'And people's homes and livelihoods. Far from bringing work, it could destroy it. There's Lilian's place, for instance. They'll raze that to the ground!'

'Ah.' Gerald gave a short, sharp grunt and a look that warned against unprofessional over-involvement. 'Lilian Rigg. How is she coming along?'

'Gerald, that isn't the point! Lilian just happens to be one of the ones worst hit by the plans. But the whole village will suffer, you must see that much?'

'I don't see anything. Not until we've had the meetings and let everyone have their say, including Maisie Aire, who, I suppose, knows what she's doing in all of this.' He looked steadily at Laura, waiting for this angle to sink in. 'She must need the money from the land to make ends meet at the Hall. It's not a decision anyone would take lightly.

'Listen, Laura, I've lived here in Hawkshead since before you were born. I've known patients whose memories went back to the old lead-mining days, and you should have heard them on the benefits and miseries of *losing* industry from the dale. Nothing changes that much, believe me; the issue will come and go like everything else. And then we'll all get on with keeping our heads above water, living together, surviving, with or without the quarry.' He backed away, nodded several times, expecting her to calm down. 'Like I said, in our position we have to take a back seat, not get too involved.'

'Why?' She had listened to the long speech, incredulous. She glanced at Philip for help.

Gerald stepped in again. 'Because we can't afford to upset one side or the other by adopting too radical a stance. The patients on our list will come from both camps, and we don't want to lose their trust over it.'

Laura knitted her brows. 'You wouldn't be saying this if I happened to be in the pro-quarry group, would you, Gerald?' What seemed to him like perfect logic sprang in fact from old Tory leanings. He was a professional, like Simon Warboys, both of whom had no doubt gone onto the grouse moors and golf links with the likes of Geoffrey Aire. By radical, Gerald meant left-wing and populist. 'Whose side are you on, as a matter of interest?' She saw clearly that not only was the quarry set to divide the community as the solicitor had predicted, but that it would divide the practice too.

'That's beside the point. My advice is to stay out of it altogether, and don't go barging in. It doesn't go down well.' He looked at Philip, who stayed silent. 'I'm on my way up to Oxtop,' he announced. 'I haven't dropped in to see Tot since I got back from my holiday.' And he left in a swirl of cold air as he swung open the door and strode out.

He'd ignored the nicety of liaising with Laura over the old farmer's progress. She felt the slight like a slap in the face.

Laura knew that she'd let her emotions get the better of her during the walk from Warboys' office to the surgery. Now she regretted it. She should have been more circumspect, instead of sounding off like that and expecting people to agree with her. But though she'd been naive, she hadn't been wrong.

'So, do you know a good solicitor?' she murmured to Philip. 'More to the point, do you know one slightly to the left of Ghengis Khan? Or does no such beast exist in the wilds of Ravensdale?'

'Good to see you've recovered your sense of humour.' Philip took an emergency call, then came back. 'Listen, you could try Luke Altham at Bootham and Wood in Merton. You might have better luck there.'

'Thanks. And what do I need to know this time?'

'Luke's a junior partner. He was involved in a protest against a trunk road coming through the valley in the late eighties. They won. He could be your man.'

'Right. I appreciate that.'

'No problem.' He nodded, picked up his bag and left hard on Gerald's heels.

CHAPTER NINETEEN

'I came to give you these.' Philip stood in the narrow corridor outside Mary's bedsit. Inside the room he glimpsed low lampshades and patterned covers thrown over comfortable old chairs. 'They're your National Insurance papers. Can I come in?'

She stood to one side. 'That's some chat-up line you have there.'

'I know. It must be fate. Dot looked and couldn't find them. I went in there an hour later, pulled out the drawers and out they dropped.' He put them down on the table.

'You could have sent them by post.'

'I wanted to talk to you.' She wore a black silk robe embroidered down the back with gold and red flowers. Her hair was freshly washed.

'Look, Philip, I've been in this situation too often to count. It doesn't work.'

He ignored her. 'Shall I tell you how it felt when I saw you with Christopher that night at the party?' He kept his distance, though all he wanted to do was to hold her.

'No, I told you; no!'

'It was like someone thumping at my rib cage with a hammer. I had this extraordinary feeling that my ribs would cave in. For a couple of minutes I could hardly breathe. I told myself it was nothing, he meant nothing, it was just a game you were playing with him.'

'It was. It always is.'

'And after that, when I calmed down, I told myself that I had no claim, no right to be jealous. I knew that's what it was. I was jealous of him being free to flirt with you. I wanted it to be me.'

'Philip, for God's sake.'

'I'm telling you the truth.'

144

'I know you are. What do you want me to say? You know how I feel.'

'No, you never said.'

'I moved away, didn't I? That's how bad it was. I wanted us both to be safe.'

'And now you've gone, I spend all my time thinking about you, wondering who you're with, trying to prise information out of Laura without making it too obvious. It's driving me crazy.' He hung his head, stranded amongst her shelves of books and pottery, her old furniture, the long shadows cast by the paper lampshades.

'What can I do?' She moved closer, clasping the neck of her robe.

'Nothing – tell me you love me.' He'd come to hear her say it. Nothing else would save or satisfy him.

Her hands dropped to her sides. She stared at him, eyes wide and dark, her mouth slightly open.

'You do love me, don't you?' He put his arms around her.

She kissed him, eyes closed, head back. Her damp hair swung out of its twisted knot down her back, covering his own arms in a scented mass.

'You do.'

'Yes. I must be mad.' She rested her weight back, her arms still hooked round his neck. 'I swore I wasn't going to let this happen.'

He was kissing her, pulling her back towards him. 'So what?'

'So now it gets complicated.'

'No, don't turn away. I don't care.' He would be strong enough to deal with complications. There was an energy in breaking the rules after a lifetime of playing it safe. He wanted more of her.

'Are you ready to lie and feel guilty? Are you willing to see me at the pub, in the street and ignore me?'

'I know. I've thought about it. But I needed to hold you. I need to now.' He kissed words out of her mouth, thoughts out of her head. She took his hand and led him into her bedroom.

Under her silk gown was the smoothness of her skin in the lamplight, the long, curving line of her back. He ran his hands over her body, slid the robe off her shoulders, took his own clothes off swiftly, never taking his eyes off her, until they lay, nothing between them. Her eyes watched him, half-scared.

'You drive me out of my mind, you know that?'

'What did I do?' she begged. 'Whatever it was, I never meant to.'

'You don't have to do anything.' He kissed her neck, shifted so that she lay beneath him, arms pinned against the pillow. He wouldn't let her turn away. Her body was softer and more vulnerable than he'd pictured so many times in his mind's eye; the gentle rise of her breasts, the curve of her waist. He let his own weight rest against her, slowly, gently.

Then she was kissing him, mouth open, holding tight to his neck, his hair. Her body rose to meet him and he slipped his hand into the warm gap between sheet and supple spine. Her mouth came onto his neck, his chest, her face hidden against him.

With his free hand Philip drew her hands together above her head, which she turned sideways on the pillow, tilted back, the side of her neck, her breast exposed. It drove him beyond himself; the defencelessness, the creamy softness of her flesh.

'Philip.'

'Don't. Don't talk.' He felt her arch again, turn her head this way and that. Warm and soft. Wanting him. And he was sure in his lovemaking, driven on, arousing her and finding his own satisfaction after Mary; very soon, very urgent.

'Philip.' Her voice was a whisper. She stroked his face.

'My darling.' His fingers rested on her mouth. 'I know.' He would love her and look after her, make sure she would never be afraid again.

Before she went to see Luke Altham at Bootham and Wood, Laura made up her mind to ring Tom for more advice. She checked with Dot first.

'He knows a lot about this sort of thing. He's good at getting to the nitty-gritty of government policies on anything to do with the environment. He's been writing about it for years.'

'And you think he can help us?' Dot was suspicious.

'I'm sure he could if we wanted him to.'

'Do we? What about you?'

'Do I want him to help?' Laura thought carefully. 'I think I can separate off the two things. Our divorce has nothing to do with the quarry when you think about it.'

'It's feelings, not thoughts I'm worried about.'

'No need. It was listening to Simon Warboys being so negative about our point of view. It made me see there could be a strong argument for selling the land and starting the quarry. We're going to need all the ammunition we can get.'

'It's up to you.' Dot went away, held her own counsel.

Soon Laura was on the phone to London. 'Hi, Tom, it's me. You know you said you would lend a hand over this quarry?'

'Yes, hi. Make it quick, would you? I'm on my way out.'

'OK, listen. We need to know more about the Frontier Stone Company; who's on the board of directors, what links they have with anyone in powerful positions, and so on.'

'Got that. Leave it with me.'

She could hear the TV playing in the background. 'Before this Thursday? That's our first public meeting.'

'Sure, no problem.'

'Thanks, Tom.' He was brisk and businesslike, just as she'd hoped. The nostalgia of his Christmas phone call had disappeared.

She went straight out to meet Luke Altham, to outline the situation and see if he would represent them.

'I've had an eye on developments,' he told her. 'I was planning to show up at Thursday's meeting in any case.'

'What are our chances?' Laura had already begun to think in terms of all-out war. It was easy to do when she thought of the pompous Warboys and imagined what the quarry would really mean to the beauty and peace of the valley.

'That depends. If you want me to work for you, I'll start looking into things like possible preservation orders on the affected houses, such as Abbey Grange for a start. Then there's the right-of-way angle. The Aires can't do away with a public footpath if one does exist up Black Gill.'

'Tot Dinsdale's convinced it does.'

'We need more than hearsay. One of our strongest arguments will probably be difficulty of access. Ravensdale's a pretty narrow, steep-sided valley with only one way in and out. That's in our favour.'

Laura had taken to the tallish, good-looking solicitor. He pitched straight in, was down-to-earth and approachable, not cut off by acres of polished desktop and old-boy mannerisms. She explained their plans to raise money to pay him. He promised to keep his fees as low as possible, and they shook hands on it.

'Good to meet you,' he said as she got up to leave. 'I've heard a lot about the new doctor up at Hawkshead.'

'All good, I hope?'

'Let's say you've certainly made an impact.'

She laughed. 'And let's just say that from my point of view I'm enjoying the challenge.'

'I'll be in touch, Dr Grant.'

'Laura.'

'Good. I'm Luke.'

They said goodbye and she drove home in an upbeat mood. That same evening, Tom came back on the phone. This time he was more intense.

'Laura, I've got one or two things for you. Ready? Not good news, I'm afraid.'

'Go ahead.'

'The chairman at Frontier has a brother in the Department of the Environment. No law against that, but I thought you should know. Second, the company pays substantial amounts into party funds. Thirdly, the government road-building plan is fixed years ahead, as you know. I hear they're going for stone quarried here at home. It's cheaper than the imported stuff. But they need more of it.'

'So they're planning new quarries?' Tom's news gave her a truer impression of the scale of things. This was no little local dispute.

'Not exactly. But it's likely they'll look favourably on planning applications. Are you with me?'

'Yes. Thanks.'

'Listen, it could be worse. What else do you want me to do? I can get in touch with that Scottish outfit, the one that's fighting the quarry you can see from the moon or whatever. They'll have useful info for you.'

'That's OK. We can do that ourselves, thanks.'

'Let me. Now that I've got stuck in, I want to see it through.'

He was the old mixture of energy and commitment to a cause. Every phrase was familiar to her. She knew Tom when he got stuck in. 'Yes, fine. Thanks.'

'And listen, honey, how are you doing? It's time we caught up. Did you find a house yet?'

'No, still looking.' This was an exaggeration. 'Well, not really looking yet. In spring, probably.'

'How's the job?'

'Good. Listen, Tom, I'd better go.' It was her turn to fend him off.

'Great to hear from you, Laura. Still some social conscience lurking in there somewhere, I guess?'

'Difficult as it is for you to believe, yes.'

'So. Maybe I was wrong.'

She smiled to herself. 'Impossible.'

'Yeah, yeah.' He had the grace to laugh. 'Leave it with me, OK?'

He hung up. But before she could go upstairs to bed, the phone went again. It was Mary, desperate to talk, hardly making sense, telling her something about Philip, something she must swear never to mention, and could she come down to the flat before she, Mary, went completely crazy?

CHAPTER TWENTY

'Laura, how soon could you get out to the Hall?' Sheila rang through to her room in between patients.

'As soon as I've finished here. Say twenty minutes. Why?'

'I've got Matthew Aire on the line. His mother's collapsed with some sort of migraine attack, he thinks. He wants someone to take a look at her.'

Laura drew breath. 'Yes, OK. Say I'll get there as soon as I can.' Not for the first time, she reminded herself of the boundaries between her personal and professional life.

She'd heard nothing from Matthew since Boxing Day; glad on the whole not to have the complication, especially since the quarry inquiry had begun to take up her time. The more she learned about the plan to take stone from Ravenscar, the more she saw the Aires as the enemy. And then there had been Maisie's strange obstructiveness, and Abigail, Sophie and Tim. Stacked up like this, any feelings she might have for Matthew could only plunge her into the sort of chaos that Mary was living through over Philip.

She dealt with her last patient, then headed across the river towards the Hall. It was a rare day of brilliant sunshine, blue sky and crisp horizons. The hills rolled into the distance, solid greys and browns. The ruined Abbey stood pale against its green bend in the river, which ran full and swift.

As she drove up the drive towards the Hall and parked in the old stable yard, Laura saw Matthew come out of the house. He was holding the car door open as she reached across for her bag.

'How is she?' Laura followed him inside and straight up the wide staircase into part of the house she hadn't seen before. Maisie's bedroom was at the far end of a low corridor. The curtains were drawn, the patient lying still on a large double bed, her head turned away.

Matthew shook his head and spoke in a murmur. 'She didn't want me to call you. But I've never seen her as bad as this. She didn't sleep last night because of the pain, and now she can hardly move. She's not keeping anything down, not even liquid.'

Maisie's face was cold and damp, her skin had a yellowish tinge. 'Hello, Maisie, it's Laura Grant.' The pulse was rapid. 'I'm going to take your temperature. Matthew tells me you've been nauseous.'

Still she didn't move, but she spoke. 'It's a migraine. I have tablets, but they didn't work.' Her dry lips trembled, her voice was slow and slurred.

'Where does it hurt most?'

'Everywhere. Across this side of my head. I don't think I can bear it.'

Laura took the thermometer from her mouth. 'What about visual disturbance? Flashing lights, blurred vision?'

'Yes.'

'Right. I'm going to give you an injection for the pain. It's also a muscle relaxant, so it will stop the vomiting. It'll make you sleepy, OK?' She saw a tear trickle down Maisie's cheek. 'Don't worry, it'll soon pass.' She put a hand over the old woman's, and felt it clasped weakly in return.

'I have to be better for Thursday, for the meeting.'

'You will be.' Laura prepared the injection of methysergide and administered it. 'This will make you more comfortable.' She waited until she was satisfied that the drug would take effect, then left the bedside.

'Thanks.' Matthew stood by as she packed her bag. He followed her out, walking down the corridor. 'What brought it on? Could it be stress?'

'Migraine can be stress related. The important thing is to counteract the nausea so that she doesn't dehydrate. Give her plenty of liquid when she wakes up.'

They stood in the main doorway, looking out over the grounds towards the lake. 'I wish she wouldn't get so worked up. It's the inquiry, she's obsessed by it. I don't know what she'll do if it turns out against her.'

Laura frowned. 'I'm not the best person to talk to about that.'

'I know. Simon Warboys told us. You've got Luke Altham on your side. He's pretty tough. Give him a decent cause and he'll fight his corner. It's a good choice.'

'It was Philip Maskell's idea.' She went down the steps into the full glare of the sun. 'I hope you realise it's nothing personal.'

'I do, but Mother doesn't. She lives in a different world, a kind of feudal society. She thinks Gerald should take you to one side and warn you not to interfere. I tried to explain that people follow their own consciences over something like this.' He was apologetic, unwilling to let her leave.

'Tell her that Gerald did his best.' She shaded her face with her hand. 'What about you? Where do you stand? No, sorry, I shouldn't ask.'

He shrugged, leaned against her car. 'It's difficult. I've managed this place for the last few years, since it got too much for Dad. Christopher wasn't interested. I've looked after the grounds, restocked the lake, maintained the walls all down the valley and up the Gill onto the moor. I suppose I know every foot of that land.'

'Does Maisie know how you feel?' He didn't have to say any more.

'Maybe. But she needs to raise capital. She's not a sentimental woman, you know.'

'Is that what you think? That wanting to save the land is pure sentiment?'

'It's what she thinks that counts. And Christopher. He's flying over tomorrow specially for the meeting.'

'I get the picture.' Laura was ready to leave it at that. There was part of her that wanted to keep the black and white division: No Quarry Good, Quarry Bad. Talking to Matthew would make her realise that it was far less simple.

'Do you?' He put out a hand to stop her. 'Laura, will you come back later? This evening?'

Suddenly it seemed impossible to refuse. Her composure deserted her; she felt dazed, dazzled. 'Why?'

'I want you to. Say you'll come.' He held onto her.

His closeness confused her. 'Yes. What time?'

'Any time. Eight?' He stroked her cheek, and bent forward to brush her mouth with his lips.

Laura tried to argue herself out of seeing Matthew at least three times during the afternoon. In the end she left home without telling Dot where she was going, and arrived at the Hall convinced that she'd come partly to check on Maisie, partly to hear Matthew's side of the story behind the family's money worries.

Nevertheless, she was nervous and she had chosen her clothes with care; a cream shirt over black trousers, hair loose, her favourite perfume.

'How's your mother?' They went quietly up the steps into the hall. He took her jacket.

'Better. She's sleeping.'

'Good. Do you want me to check?' The sitting room was warm, firelight cast flickering shadows, there was a lamp on a table by the window, but no other lights.

'No thanks. Best not to disturb her.'

Laura sat in a chair away from the fire. 'I nearly didn't come.'

'I nearly didn't ask you.'

She followed his movements as he fetched drinks, sat on a chair by the table, cupping his long fingers round his glass and resting his elbows on his wide-apart knees. 'I'm glad you did.'

'Me too.'

There was a silence. The burning logs cracked, a wall clock ticked.

'I realise this is – '

'I wish it wasn't so – '

They laughed.

'Let's skip that bit,' he suggested. He stood up and began to wander across the room, the sleeves of his dark blue shirt rolled back at the cuffs, his face half in shadow. He was taller than she'd realised, broad across the shoulders. Graceful. The word surprised her. 'I don't want this to be another false start.'

'No.'

He stopped by her chair and spoke. 'Can we clear the air? Without wishing things away.'

'Where shall we start?'

'With us. Can there be an us? That's what I want to know. It's what I'd like.' He deliberately kept his distance, waiting for her answer.

'You want to know how I feel? OK. I hardly know you, there are half a dozen reasons why I should keep it that way, but I'm here. Is that enough?'

'No. I want to know more. You were married. What happened? Your life story.'

She raised her eyebrows, then leaned her head against the back of the chair. 'Is that all? I grew up in Wingate, an only child. Parents wanted the best for me. I tried to please. Went away, passed my exams. Succeeded. Started work, got married, tried to please. Failed. Got divorced.'

'Name?'

'Tom Elliot. He's a journalist.'

'He's crazy to let you go. OK, here's mine. Born here at Hawkshead, lived here most of my life. Spells away at school and college. Older brother you know about. Abigail and I married when I was twenty-five, she was thirty-three, significant factor. Two children; Sophie, nine, Tim, seven. Abigail left one day in July last year, found a place in York. Nice place. Kids are settled in new schools. Abigail has something going with her marketing manager, Dave Worthing. I found out just before Christmas. Sophie let it slip, poor kid. Course of true love apparently does not run smooth. Back here, Mother still disapproves of divorce, misses grandchildren. You probably know that already.'

'I met them once in the supermarket. Maisie introduced us.'

'She would enjoy that.'

'They must have been staying at the Hall.'

'Every other weekend, more in the holidays. That's the hard bit.'

'Tom and I never had children. I suppose that's just as well.'

'I never wish Tim and Sophie away. I'd like to see more of them. Every day I think of them setting off to school dressed up in their new uniforms, playing rugby and netball, getting into fights, hating their school dinners, watching television.' He pressed a thumb and forefinger to his forehead.

'But they're OK?'

'I hope so.' He stared at the floor. 'I don't want to make it sound too grim. There's money to make sure they're well looked after. Abigail and I try to keep things civilised so the kids don't get messed up in the middle. That's the main thing.'

'But it's hard, I suppose. I don't think money makes a lot of difference in the end, so long as they're still loved.' It was easy for her to say, without having to scrap through the courts for maintenance to buy food and clothes. Still, she felt it was true. Children of divorced parents only ended up in her surgery if they felt they were no longer loved, or if they were used as pawns in the adult game. That was when they got nightmares, allergies, became withdrawn, refused to eat. 'Are you angry with her?'

'Who, Abigail? I can't afford to be.'

'No, but are you?'

'The marriage didn't work out. I don't blame her. Then, deep down, yes, I wish I never had to set eyes on her again. Then again, she's the mother of my two kids. But then she's taken them away from me. Yes, I'm angry.' He stopped himself. 'I didn't think I was until just now.'

Laura got up from her chair and put down her glass. 'Tom never wanted children. He had things to do before he settled down, big causes to fight for. He didn't see himself as a father.'

'How about you?'

'For a while that was OK. I was finishing my training, getting jobs. Being a doctor is important to me.'

'You're good at it.'

'Thanks. It doesn't seem that hard. People are needy when they come to see me. I find that straightforward. It's great when I can give them what they ask for, and when I can't I try to let them down gently. I don't mind them depending on me.'

'So why did you and Tom split up?'

'Which do you want; my version or his?'

'Yours.' He lowered his voice, came nearer.

'Mine was a kind of anger as well, really. It started off with me respecting him, admiring him in a big way. He was big. I mean, he thought big. These battles against giant organisations, rejecting what other people took for granted. He's a powerful man. I suppose I was under his spell; young medic meets campaigning journalist, gets inspired by his battles for the underdog.' She fell silent.

'And then?'

She closed her eyes. 'Something to do with scratching below the surface and finding that what was underneath was contempt. Tom doesn't really fight for the underdog. He hates little people, he thinks they should all be as big as he is. He occupies the moral high ground every inch of the way, everyone else has got it wrong, including me. I often disagreed with him. He didn't take to that. We fought.'

'How do you feel now?'

'Disappointed, let down. Relieved that I was able to break away.' It was like any other injury; it took time to heal.

'You know, the impression you make isn't at all how you tell it.' He put his arms round her waist.

'Don't tell me. I might not like it.'

'Let's see.' He kissed her. 'How do you seem? In control. Unscarred.' He kissed her again.

'See!'

'Practical, full of energy, kind, dedicated, funny, unselfconscious, beautiful.' He kissed her many more times.

'Remind me to ask you to write my next reference.' She was laughing, kissing him back.

'No more false starts?' He made her promise. 'You don't know how desperate I've been to do this since I first set eyes on you.'

'You did, as I remember.'

'And you said you weren't ready.'

'That was then. This is now.' She was the one to kiss him, to sink into the moment.

'What about tomorrow?'

'Oh no, do I have to plan ahead?'

'I won't let you go until you do.'

'Why? What would happen?'

'I might lose you. I might never get the chance to hold you again. Seriously, Laura, I want you right here.' He held her close.

'You can hold me again,' she promised. 'But not tomorrow. Not until after Thursday.' She stepped back, still felt his arms around her waist.

'Yes, that's something we still have to sort out. The quarry.' He led her back to her chair, sat her down and went to rest his arms along the back. He leaned forward, his chin on her shoulder. 'This is where I have to declare my hand?'

'Tell me seriously.' She lifted her head to see his face.

'OK. I have a loyalty to my family. Mother wants to sell the land. Christopher does too. In fact, it was probably his idea in the first place. But now she sees it as the only way of raising money, her only asset besides this house and its contents. Her life is here in the Hall. I can see why she won't sell that.'

'And is selling Black Gill the only other choice she has?'

'For her it's the least painful. You've got to understand, she never had to manage money until Father died. She's lonely, she wants to travel back to Boston to spend some time with her sister. See?'

Laura nodded. 'But I'm still wondering. I know you must feel hemmed in by her problems, but I don't believe that this is what you really want. I've only lived here for a few months, but I feel as if the Gill is at the heart of this dale, a magic place. We ought to leave it as it is, and Ravenscar. You've lived here all your life, you look after the land. How much does it mean to you?'

'It's part of me, like a limb.' He stood up straight and shook his head. 'What does it matter what I think? Mother's already asking if Christopher's got here yet. Once he does, they'll get together with Warboys again to discuss moving a right of way up the Gill from here to there, compensating and rehousing Lilian Rigg –'

'Lilian's ill,' she said quietly. 'Did you know?'

'No.'

'But she'll fight to stay on at Abbey Grange, till her last breath. I'm not exaggerating.' She looked sadly at his troubled expression. 'And I'll help her.'

CHAPTER TWENTY ONE

'Nervous?' Mary and Aimee called for Laura on the evening of the first public meeting. Dot had gone on ahead to join Lilian and some other committee members, Marsden Barraclough, Juliet Maskell and Andy Hughes amongst them.

'Terrified,' Laura admitted. 'How long have we got?'

'Half an hour.'

'Let's not get there too early. I don't fancy bumping into the Aires before the meeting gets underway.' She turned to Aimee. 'How did things go at school?'

'Good. I put up notices telling people where to meet to collect banners and placards. Some of us got together at my house to make them. About a dozen of us in the sixth form are really keen. Well, more. But only a few who'll actually get up on their hind legs and do something.'

'Do they all look as frightening as you?' Laura had already noted Aimee's black jacket, tight trousers and boots, her ringed fingers and the splash of crimson on her lips.

Aimee glared.

'Joke,' Mary reminded her. 'Relax. Anyway, what do you expect? How many of you get up onto Ravenscar to see what we're actually protesting about? Most of you can't wait to get out partying and discoing. Don't you all detest the countryside?'

'So? Why bother to try to organise us?'

'Another joke.' Laura took her jacket from its hook in the hall and put it on. 'Don't worry, we're glad you're on our side.'

'Thanks.' She stood awkwardly by the door. 'That's more than Dad is.'

'Be thankful he lets you express your point of view.'

'Don't you believe it. I had to nip out the back way to get here.'

'Now *you're* joking.' Laura wasn't sure how much pressure

Gerald would have put on Aimee. She imagined them at daggers drawn.

'No way. I had to wait until he left. Then I gave Mum the slip and came up here. She had strict orders not to let me out of the house.'

'What on earth for?' Mary protested.

'He says if I'm not fit to be in school during the day, I can't be well enough to go out at night.'

'That's right; you missed my lesson again.'

'It's just one of his excuses.'

'But what was wrong?' Laura thought that she looked paler and thinner than ever.

'Dunno. Some sort of virus probably.'

'She could hardly get up the hill. We had to stop to sit down twice.'

'Is that what Gerald said it was, a virus?'

'He probably thinks I'm just skiving.'

'Things are no better?' Laura knew they weren't. Janet had phoned twice since the New Year to say that she was no nearer getting Aimee to eat sensibly, or to talking to Gerald. She sounded close to the end of her tether.

'No. Lousy.'

'Would you like me to talk to him for you? I don't promise I'd get anywhere, but I could try to put your point of view.'

'No.' Aimee jumped in bitterly. 'I don't want him involved. It's bad enough having Mum going on.'

'But you realise why you can't walk up hills any more? It's because you're not giving your body enough energy.'

'Don't you ever stop? I'm going. See you down at school.'

'Shall I follow her?' Mary looked at Laura.

'No, leave her.' She sighed. 'Damn.'

'Not your fault.'

'I must be losing my touch. She's making herself seriously ill, and all I seem able to do is wait until she actually collapses at someone's feet.'

'Is that what'll happen?'

'Unless we can get through to her. Right now she thinks she's still in control. That's what this illness is all about. Not weight, not really.'

They set off slowly and reached the square, joining a steady stream of people all heading for the school on this cold and windy night.

'Still nervous?' Mary linked arms with Laura, spotting Aimee again with her banner-waving friends.

'Not so bad now. At least there's a decent turnout.' She could see Dot helping Lilian out of the back seat of Kit's car. She looked frail but determined.

Marsden Barraclough was there, a small, bald man. She'd met him for the first time earlier that week. He was dressed in civvies, but his mild smiling manner never deserted him, and his handshake reminded people of the church porch. They treated him with deference and gave him a wide berth as he stood talking with Andy Hughes, the head teacher.

Brian Lawson had hauled several of his customers out of the Falcon and persuaded them to attend. They all kept an eye on Tot, who had reluctantly agreed to be driven down from Oxtop. 'They're making a heck of a fuss,' he complained to Laura, as she and Mary passed him in the entrance hall. 'I tell 'em I'm on the mend, but they keep chuntering on about convalescence. Dick here won't hear of me getting out of a morning to see to the sheep.' He coughed and winced. 'Aye well, it's knocked the stuffing out of me, else I'd be out there before him.'

'Aye, even if it's siling down,' Dick put in, lending the old man a hand into the building. 'We know you, Tot. Daft as a brush.'

'What's up wi' that?' he grumbled, moving stiffly, resenting his neighbours' help, though he obviously needed it.

Dick negotiated him through the crush to a seat in the assembly hall near the front. He made sure his friend could see and hear, and signalled to Lilian and Kit to come and sit close by.

At the back of the hall, Laura parted from Mary and got her bearings amongst the crowd of two hundred or so people. On the platform she recognised both Luke Altham and Simon Warboys, together with four other middle-aged and elderly men, and one woman. Searching the floor of the hall, she soon spotted the Aires. Maisie, in a smart black coat and seemingly recovered, was seated further along the same row as Tot. Christopher sat next to her, leaning forward to speak to Simon Warboys. He looked relaxed as usual, with his midwinter suntan setting off his fair hair. Beyond him, she saw Matthew's quieter, more subdued figure.

She thought that the Aires camp looked isolated amongst the

swell of opponents. Apart from half a dozen faces which Laura recognised from Maisie's Christmas party, the hall seemed packed with people from her own group.

There was Gerald, of course. He was talking loudly to Joy and Sheila, still unaware that Aimee was protesting noisily outside. Juliet Maskell kept slightly to one side, explaining to people that Philip had been called out to Askby to attend a patient.

'Open mind, eh?' Gerald echoed Simon Warboys' advice. 'Let's wait and see what develops.'

Laura made a point of stopping nearby to say hello to Juliet. All week Gerald had stubbornly refused to talk sensibly about the quarry. His position was clear from the start, he said. Now he intended to stay above and beyond it all, a kind of benign spectator. His disapproval of Laura's hands-on involvement in the opposition had permeated the surgery for days.

Seven-thirty came and went. The hall filled up, the doors were closed. Still there was no let-up in the noisy exchange of opinion. At twenty-five to eight, the chairman of the committee called everyone to order. Laura steadied her nerves and listened closely as the chairman described the procedure. He stressed the information-gathering nature of the exercise, and did his best to dampen down what he could see were already heightened feelings.

But his smooth, characterless style didn't go down well, Laura felt. His audience knew they were being patronised and resisted his bland introduction. 'Old windbag,' Dot's voice cut through the shuffling feet and restless coughing. On the platform, Simon Warboys riffled through his papers, while Luke Altham looked composed.

The chairman gave way to a spokesman who put the case for Frontier. A solid, no-nonsense sort, he delivered a polished and reasonable argument on the merits of the quarry. His strong, gravelly voice carried a hint of Yorkshire and his manner inspired confidence.

He told them frankly of industry's need for good quality limestone for metallurgical use, chemical works, and road stone. He described how the rock from Ravenscar would be quarried and broken down into rubble before transportation. 'All the processes will be carried out right here in the valley. I don't need to point out the potential for the community. Look around here in the school at the young members of this audience. How many will have a future in the area unless people like us bring them the jobs, the investment, the income? Far from being a threat to Ravensdale, what Frontier is offering is an opportunity, especially to the young; an opportunity which it would be foolish to turn your backs on.' He went on with further details about employment and wealth creation; solid facts and benefits.

In the front row, Dick turned uneasily to Dot. 'Well, he has a way with him, you have to admit.'

Dot looked straight ahead, waiting for their own man to have his say.

Next, Simon Warboys got to his feet to speak to the inquiry about legal niceties concerning rights of way on behalf of his clients, the landowners who wished to sell Ravenscar to the developers.

He roused a disapproving murmur from the onlookers. 'Cold fish,' was Dot's audible opinion this time. Lilian continued to sit in silence, arms folded, as Luke Altham got up to speak.

'No one here is against change in itself.' He began his address to the committee, quiet but firm. 'Make no mistake, dales people can move with the times. The evidence is all around; conversions of old farm buildings, the construction of good schools and sports facilities, the acceptance of new farming systems and of tourism. It would be entirely wrong to see Hawkshead folk as dyed-in-the-wool reactionaries.'

He paused for the inquiry panel to study the audience, the teenagers standing in a gang at the back, the old-timers sitting in the front row, the farming families and professional people who filled the hall.

'But one thing we do have is pride in our valley.' He glanced sideways at the spokesman from Frontier. 'You can talk about jobs and profit to folk round here and we'll turn round, look you straight in the eye and ask you about the mountains of waste, the gallons upon gallons of sludge and slurry that you'll be pouring daily into the clear streams of the River Raven. We'll want to know about the devastation to landscape and wildlife, and how many houses must be knocked down for the multi-million pound road developments. We're not interested in how much profit Frontier would plunder from these hills. We want to keep our right to roam up Black Gill and onto Ravenscar, without quarry workings on a massive scale to destroy our peace. That's what matters round here; the quality of life.'

He ended his speech to a volley of applause. Laura could see Maisie Aire sitting ramrod straight. Then Christopher rose to his feet to ask a question from the floor. 'How many people here tonight came from Ginnersby and Waite?' He seemed unperturbed, waiting patiently for a reply.

Twenty or thirty hands went up.

'And how many from Askby?'

This time, response came from a dozen or so.

'Now, as we know, Ginnersby and Waite are old lead-mining villages, and Askby was built in the early part of the last century around the textile mill on the lower falls. True?'

There was slow, murmured assent.

'Without the lead mines, without the felling of trees on Ravenscar, the tall chimneys of the smelt mills, the huge water wheel that powered the looms of the textile works, the villages in which you now take such pride wouldn't even exist.

'If the lords of the manor in earlier days had been reactionaries, refusing to move with the times and open their lands to the new industries, how many of you would be here tonight?' He waved his hand to the chairman to show that he didn't expect a reply.

'Hear, hear,' cried one or two voices.

'There's a heck of a difference between Askby Mill and a great stone quarry,' Dot retorted, without signalling for permission to speak.

'All points must come through the chair,' an official remonstrated from on high.

Slowly, amidst a sea of hands all vying to speak, Lilian raised her arm. The chairman spotted her close at hand and indicated that she should make her point. The others fell silent as she stood up and cleared her throat.

'You'll think I have an axe to grind,' she began, 'since I'm one of those who would lose my house and living to the quarry if it goes through. I suppose I'd better come clean on that score. At my time of life, I've no desire to move and start all over again.' Her voice gathered confidence as she got into her stride, standing in her heavy blue woollen jacket, hands in pockets, facing the inquiry team.

'But let me tell you something. I look out of my window one way and I get a view of the river and the Abbey ruins across the other side. I see the stepping stones the monks used and the great arched windows, the roof open to the elements.

'I look the other way, towards the north, and it's Ravenscar I see. That hill looms over us, and the birds soar over it, day in, day out. I follow the season by that hillside. When I see the white tops begin to thaw in a week or so, I shall know that spring is on its way. I'll see it in summer covered in purple heather, turning brown and gold in autumn.' She paused to let them picture the scenes she described. 'Ask anyone how much that hill means to them. Ask anyone. And then ask those that mean to destroy it how they would ever repair such a beautiful thing.'

Lilian spoke with slow dignity, committed to every word she said. Listening, Laura couldn't help wondering how many more such springs and summers Lilian would see. And she thought of the nodding heads of the snowdrops forming a thick white carpet on the lawn at Abbey Grange, which Lilian had sent her especially to see.

After Lilian, the debate picked up fast and furious. Simon Warboys painstakingly pointed out that the area had no legal protection from use for development purposes, falling just outside the National Trust boundaries of the Abbey estate, and well beyond the limits of the National Park. Luke Altham countered with their strongest point about the public footpath up the Gill. Brian Lawson pointed out the inevitable loss of tourism if the quarry got the go-ahead.

The Frontier spokesman, on the defensive now, promised minimum disruption to the village by keeping access roads well to the east, out of sight. Most of the blasting would be carried out unheard and unseen.

Laura's spirits rose and fell with each successive speaker. She was full of admiration for Lilian's calm courage, brimming with scorn for Warboys' clinical analyses. By the end of the evening, when the chairman drew proceedings to a close, she felt emotionally drained.

'It went well.' Luke Altham came down from the platform to speak to her as people began to file from the hall. 'We got our message across loud and clear. Now I think we should use the feeling generated here to collect signatures for a petition. We can send it to the county council, the Department of the Environment. Perhaps you could encourage Dot Wilson to organise that?'

'She won't need much encouragement.' Even as they spoke, Laura could hear Dot talking with a group of their committee members. She shook hands with Luke and set about finding Mary somewhere in the entrance hall, as arranged.

But it was Matthew who intercepted her by the door. Their meeting attracted curious glances.

'Laura, wait.'

Out of the corner of her eye she could see Maisie and Christopher. Gerald had also noticed them together. She tried to be her normal self. 'How do you think it went?'

'Fair enough. Both sides had their say. But listen, we have to meet. You said after Thursday. Give me a date, then you can go away and think of all the good reasons not to turn up.'

'Go through agonies of indecision?' She led the way out into the cold, dark night.

'If you like. Then you can let your heart rule your head and meet up with me as planned. How does that sound?'

'Dreadful. Where?'

'Anywhere you like.'

'Wingate.'

'When?'

'I've got Saturday off. I'm going house-hunting in the morning. How about the afternoon?' She began to shiver in the wind. Already a host of reasons why she should back out filled her head. Already, she knew that she would go.

CHAPTER TWENTY TWO

'It's good to have you back home,' Dot told Lilian. She'd finished her Friday routine at Bridge House and come straight over to Abbey Grange to chew over events of the night before. She discovered Lilian pottering in her garden, moving slowly down the rows of hibernating plants.

'It's grand to be back.'

'And how are you?'

'Plodding on.'

High walls sheltered them from the worst of the wind, but there was a touch of frost and the air was raw. 'You're still taking your medicine?' Lilian never mentioned to Dot how the treatment was going, but she could guess that her friend was in a fair amount of pain.

'I'm taking so many pills I rattle.' She took hold of a straggling rose. 'I should have pruned this climber back before now. It's a nice one. New Dawn, creamy pink flowers all summer long. You can come and cut some for the house in summer. Don't wait to be asked.' She took her secateurs and clipped at a branch.

Dot heard her breath come short. 'Here, let me.' She stretched to pull the top shoots within reach. 'You spoke up for us last night, Lilian. They'll have to listen to us now.'

'I'm not so sure.' She kicked the clipping to one side and walked on. 'The inquiry has to consider other things, like jobs. It's not easy. Christopher Aire has his angle, remember.'

'If you ask me, he had it off too pat.'

'You can't blame him. I'd run through my own little speech beforehand. Now it all depends how that committee sees it.'

'Laura says we need a petition with as many signatures as we can get.'

Lilian agreed. 'Get it typed up and give me a copy. I'll pin it up here for people to sign. How does she think we got on?'

'Laura? She's like you, she wants to wait and see. I'd say she has her mind on other things though.' Dot and Laura had kept strictly to business when they arrived back at the house after the meeting. No mention of Matthew Aire.

'Now, you're to leave her alone,' Lilian warned. 'She can talk to who she likes, can't she?'

'I know she can. Did I say anything?' She did wish Laura would steer clear of complications, but she knew to mind her own business.

'You don't have to, not if you give her one of your looks.'

'Now, Lilian, I can't help how I look.'

'You know what I mean. You can send people to Coventry at the drop of a hat. Laura's on our side, whatever happens.'

'You're probably right. But she's young, she doesn't always see it our way. Personally, I wouldn't give anyone in the Aire family the time of day, Matthew included. He could very well get the wrong impression, for a start.'

'That's up to her. She's done a lot for me, and everyone says the same.' She paused to gaze up the hill. 'Her heart's in the right place, that's the main thing.'

Kit Braithwaite arrived soon after, and Dot left Lilian with him. Neither he nor Dot wanted to acknowledge how ill Lilian was, though Dot could read the worry in his face. She hurried away, resorting to the usual comforts: Lilian was bound to be weak after her treatment, but she would soon pick up. No one knew the full answer, but people did recover from cancer. Lilian was a fighter. If anyone could beat it, she would.

She passed through the village, stopping to answer well-meaning queries about Lilian and to discuss the inquiry. She heard that the team was out and about asking questions.

'Better get that petition drawn up, Dot,' Brian reminded her from the pub step. 'If you give me a copy I'll put it in the bar.'

After the event, there seemed to be a general waning of confidence. They'd heard the pro-quarry argument and it sounded reasonable. Frontier would certainly make a good case. 'We have to be on our mettle,' Dot warned. 'We need more than sentiment on our side. We need proof of the harm the quarry would do.'

Determined to think positively and not be downhearted, she

concentrated on the men sitting in government offices, making decisions that could turf Lilian out of Abbey Grange and bring dirt and noise to the whole dale, day in, day out. It made her furious.

She went home and sat down to compose the wording for the petition. One sentence beginning, We the Undersigned; one short, sharp sentence to sum up all the indignation and hurt she felt about the quarry.

By tea time, Dot had done as much as she could. She'd taken her handwritten petition along to the Church House office, where it had been typed and photocopied. She took copies around the village, to the playgroup, schools, pub, shops and cafes. After a short rest at home, she planned to go on up to Oxtop to get Tot involved in this latest stage in the campaign.

A knock at the door interrupted her. With the kettle boiling, the tea in the pot, she put down her tea towel and went to answer the door.

'Hello, I'm looking for Laura Grant.' A stranger stood there, heavy canvas bag slung over one shoulder, the collar of his brown leather jacket turned up, a street lamp behind throwing his thin face into shadow. 'My name's Tom Elliot.'

'She's not home from work yet.' Dot tried to hide her surprise. 'Is she expecting you?'

'Not exactly.' He let the bag swing from his shoulder onto the step. 'You must be her landlady?'

She introduced herself, stiff and on guard. 'Would you like to come in and wait?'

'How long will she be?'

'She's usually back before six, unless there's an emergency. Shall I ring the health centre and tell her you're here?'

'No need. I know she doesn't like being bothered at work. She never used to anyway.'

He was too casual for Dot's liking. He put his bag on the bottom stair and walked ahead down the hall without waiting for her to show him the way.

'Don't worry, she won't throw me out. I've got some more news on the quarry business. As a matter of fact, I'm on my way down from Scotland. Hawkshead was only a stone's throw off my main route, so I took a detour.'

Dot offered him tea. 'Laura mentioned that you wanted to help.'

'It's my kind of thing. I can get a good piece out of it, linking up the two protests, yours and the Scottish one. It's looking like there's some kind of hidden agenda to get as many quarries up and running as they can. Did Laura explain?'

'No. It's good of you to take the trouble, Mr Elliot.'

'It's what I do, make myself a nuisance and call it investigation. Anyway, it means I can catch up with Laura.'

Dot suspected it would have been wiser to check this with his ex-wife first. But, as Lilian had reminded her that morning, it was none of her business. She decided to stick to the quarry, since this was why he said he'd come. 'How have they been getting on with their campaign in Scotland?'

'They're into their third inquiry. Everything's stalled. It's been rumbling on for years. It's because of the hold-up over the big one up there that the stone companies are having to look round for various smaller sites, including Ravensdale.'

He gave the impression that he had a lot of useful information. 'What will you do, write an article?'

'That'll do for a kick-off. To be honest, the campaign up there has gone stone cold.' He grinned. 'No pun intended. I'm hoping for more action here. How did last night's meeting go?'

'We managed to have our say. The whole village turned out. Now we want to get up a petition.'

'You need to work hard to get that off the ground. What about the legal side?'

Dot filled him in on more details.

'The best thing for me to do is keep on digging the dirt. There's bound to be more we can get on the company, or on these people who want to sell off the land; the Aires, isn't it? I'll try to drum up interest among the news editors, but you'll have to stage a big event to get them all the way up here. We'll think about that later.' He yawned and stretched. 'It's an idea, anyway.'

Dot sat precise and polite, suspecting that their cause was about to be hijacked, worried about Laura, but partly disarmed by Tom's confidence.

He glanced around the room. 'I must say, I wondered where Laura had landed. A bit different from what she's been used to. How's she finding it?'

'She seems to like it. And we like her.'

'That's good. You know, she always used to swear wild horses wouldn't drag her back North.'

'She must have changed her mind.'

'Mellowed in her old age, taking it easy?'

'I wouldn't say that. She hardly has a minute to herself.' Hearing Laura's car pull up, Dot stood and looked out of the window. 'Here she is now. You can ask her all her news.' She hoped to intercept Laura before she went upstairs, but when Dot reached the hall she saw that Laura had already spotted and recognised Tom's bag. She stared at it, taken aback.

'He's in the kitchen,' Dot whispered. 'Did I do the right thing?'

Slowly she nodded and put down her own bag. She unbuttoned her coat, smoothed her hair at the mirror, then Tom came out.

'Hello.' He stood, head to one side, a smile spreading over his face.

'Tom.'

'Sorry, I should have phoned.'

'No, that's all right. I didn't expect you to show up, that's all.' She hung her coat on its peg.

'You look great.'

'Yes, I'm fine.' She pushed a strand of hair from her face and gave Dot a faint smile. 'Thanks.'

'I'm on my way to Oxtop,' Dot told her. 'I'll leave you two to talk.'

'Not on my account. We could always go and find a quiet corner in a pub.'

'No, really, I do have to go and check on Tot.' She reached for her coat. 'If I dash I'll be just in time for the bus.' She couldn't tell if the shock had been entirely unpleasant for Laura, but she still looked white as a sheet, poor thing. As if she didn't have enough to contend with, without her ex-husband turning up uninvited. She set off down the hill, saw the bus waiting at the bus stop, and hurried on. 'Damn.' With one foot on the bottom step, a thought struck her and she stopped.

'Are you getting on, or not?' the driver asked.

'I meant to bring that petition for Tot to sign. Too late.' She got in and sat down as the bus pulled away, and began to wind and grind its way up the fell.

At Oxtop, Dot knocked on the farm door and went straight in. She knew Tot was still well under par, without a lot to say for himself. Last night at the meeting, for instance, he'd been uncharacteristically silent. She'd thought his spare frame was more stooped, his face more gaunt.

'Tot?' She advanced into the kitchen. There was no sign of him. Grumbling to herself, she went to the bottom of the stairs and called again. 'He must be bad if he's missing another night at the pub and taken an early night.' She thought she'd better go on upstairs and knock on the bedroom door. She found him there, on the bed, hardly able to breathe. He drew in rough gulps of air as he lay there, half delirious.

'You stay where you are, Tot,' she told him. He tried to raise his head. 'I'll go and fetch Dr Grant.'

She ran to the phone, hoping and praying that Laura hadn't left the house with Tom.

She was lucky. Within minutes, Laura's car was there, its headlights swooping over rough fields along the track to the farmhouse. She came upstairs two at a time.

'I never knew he was this bad.' Dot had both hands over her mouth, standing beside Tot's bed.

'It's OK, Dot,' Laura said gently.

Dot nodded with tears in her eyes as Laura gently took her to one side. 'I'll do what I can,' she promised. 'But it may be what I've been afraid of; pneumonia may have set in.' Tot lay, his eyes closed, propped up on cushions and pillows, taking long, painful breaths.

'Now, Mr Dinsdale, let's see what we can do.' Laura took out a stethoscope and held it against his sunken chest. She confirmed the worst.

'Nay, I'm only a bit rutley,' he protested, half coming round, but submitting to having his blood pressure taken with scarcely a word of complaint. 'What time is it?'

'It's ten past seven. Now try and stay quiet.'

'Where's my watch? What time is it?'

Fever made him semi-delirious. Dot had seen this before; the obsession with time as it finally slipped away from an old friend's grasp. She went and took his hand. 'Just rest, Tot.'

After a short struggle he relaxed. Then he opened his eyes and looked straight at Laura. Gone was his satirical, hardbitten look, but not his blunt approach. 'Am I pegging out at long last, Doc? You can tell me.'

In spite of her anxiety, Laura smiled. 'I don't know about pegging out, Mr Dinsdale, but you've certainly got pneumonia.' She discarded the thermometer she'd just used.

He wheezed. 'Never say die, eh?'

'Not while there's treatment they can try, no.'

Dot sat holding the old man's hand, glancing round the room at the bare bulb hanging from the centre of the cracked ceiling, a row of old hardback books on a rough shelf, the grubby red candlewick bedspread on the double bed. Tot looked wizened and shrunken, his short white hair rubbed all ways by the pillow.

Laura broke into Dot's quiet vigil. 'Can you wait here to see if he needs anything? I want to call Gerald.'

She nodded, and when Laura returned a few minutes later, she slipped her hand out of Tot's and went softly to the door. 'Well?'

'I've told Gerald it's pneumonia. He's off-duty but he insisted on coming up.'

'Tot's his patient, when all's said and done.'

'We may have to try to get him over to Wingate.'

'It's an emergency, then?' Not that Dot needed to ask. She'd felt how weak Tot's pulse was when she held his hand between hers.

Gerald arrived at last and came straight upstairs. 'Now then.' He spoke firmly and calmly.

His voice seemed to rally Tot, who tilted his head towards him. 'Now then, Dr Scott. What's the damage?'

Gerald examined him. 'Not so good,' he admitted. 'We ought to get you right over to Wingate, Tot, quick as we can.'

'Nay.' The old man's chest heaved under the bedclothes. 'Not tonight.'

'Morning might be too late.'

'Aye.' There was a long pause. 'What'd they do for me in hospital that this young woman didn't already do?'

Gerald stood with his head to one side like a wily bird. 'Not a lot.'

'Aye, well then, like I said, if it's owered wi' me, I'd rather stay here in my own bed, if that's all the same to you.'

Slowly Gerald gave ground. 'I thought you might say that, Tot. Right then, you're the gaffer.' He nodded to Laura and Dot, warning them not to try to dissuade the old man. 'We'll keep you here and make sure you're comfortable, don't you worry.'

'Aye, I know you will, Dr Scott.' He turned to Dot and spoke faintly. 'You'll do one thing for me before you go?'

'What's that?' She moved in close.

172

'You'll fetch my old watch from the mantelpiece. That's it. Lay it down where I can keep my eye on it. Aye, that's just the job.'

Dot did as he asked then stepped back. She could hear the murmur of conversation between Laura and Gerald.

'We'll take it as it comes,' he said. 'I'll stay here with Tot. You take Dot home and get some sleep.'

'Sure?'

'Yes. Thanks for calling me in.'

'I knew you'd want to take a look.'

Every breath seemed to come more slowly. The three of them watched as Tot sank into a state of semi-consciousness.

'To tell you the truth, I was worried myself that he might not stand the journey into town,' Gerald said.

Still they watched. 'You'll give us a ring?' Laura said at last.

'If there's any news.'

Reluctantly they left the room. They walked out together into the cold, starlit night. Dot knew they were losing Tot and there was nothing anyone could do. A more cantankerous, suspicious old man you could never hope to meet. But they would all miss him at the Falcon, and chugging down Hawk Fell in his old Land Rover. His farm would stand empty to the wind and rain.

At three on Saturday morning Gerald rang to say that Tot had died peacefully, his watch in his hand, as if ready, even anxious, to make his final journey.

CHAPTER TWENTY THREE

'How long will you stay?' Laura asked Tom.

'I don't know yet.' They stood on the old bridge, ready to walk up Black Gill together. 'It depends what I can unearth. If things get interesting, I'll stick around.'

They set off through a thick, wet mist, crossing the main square before the Saturday market had got underway. They walked along the river bank until they came to Lilian's house and the track up to Ravenscar.

'You OK?' He turned as she bent to tie her lace.

'Yes, fine. I didn't get much sleep, that's all. We lost a patient last night.' She caught up and tried to walk two abreast along the narrow, dripping path.

'Who was it, someone you liked?'

'Yes; a crabby, cantankerous, miserable old sod, all of eighty-six years old. He died in his sleep.'

They walked on. Tom held open a gate. From here, the path grew steep and slippery. 'Watch your step.' There was a tangle of brambles, a stretch of mud. He offered his hand as she leapt across.

'It's a pity the weather's so bad.' She looked away and walked swiftly on. 'The idea was to show you exactly what the quarry would spoil, so you can see why everyone's up in arms.'

'Is this a public right of way?'

'Yes, up here past Joan's Foss.'

'What's that?'

'A waterfall and a deep pool. They used it as some kind of sheep dip in the old days. You can still see the remains of a wall where they penned the sheep.'

'I can hear the water now.' He scrambled ahead through the fog, moving nimbly. 'I brought my camera, but I don't know how much use it'll be.'

They came to a halt by the edge, silenced by the crash of water over rock, gazing up the long drop. Tom nodded. 'Pretty impressive.'

'They would cut a road up from the valley right through here, in a diagonal route up to Ravenscar. It would be the only access.'

'Come on, let's go up.' He took her arm again. 'Lead the way.'

After another hard climb, with the fog clearing as they came out of the valley onto the limestone plateau, Laura paused to catch her breath. Below, the village lay hidden, to either side thin mist drifted. 'Better not go that way,' she warned as Tom set off towards the dangerous chasms. 'It's a long drop.'

'Is this it, then?' He stood, hands in pockets, turning full circle.

'Like I said, you can't see much today.'

'No, but it's great.'

'When I first saw it, through the window at work, it took my breath away. Funny, now it seems part of me. I hardly notice it unless I'm showing it to someone.'

'Do you come up here a lot?'

'Whenever I can. It keeps me sane.'

He came and stood close to her. 'No regrets?'

She knew every gesture, every intonation. His voice had a distinctive, caressing quality that made her want to trust him again. 'Dozens. Hundreds.'

'About us?'

'Of course. I didn't walk away undamaged.' She must resist. 'But one thing I don't regret is taking the job. It's been good for me, and I love all this.' She spread her arms.

'Is it ever not windy?' He hunched his shoulders and pulled up his jacket collar.

'That's what I asked. Come on.' She turned. 'Let's go down by the road, it's easier.' For a moment she was sorry for him. 'Look, Tom, I don't know about you, but I'm trying to build a new life. I can't afford to keep looking back, dwelling on what might have been.'

'Does that mean you don't want me around?'

'I didn't say that. I must have known that you'd turn up in Hawkshead eventually, when I first told you about the quarry. I know you too well.'

'That works both ways.'

'Meaning?'

'I can read you too. Shall I tell you what I see right now?' He linked arms.

'No, I don't think so.' She walked quickly, following the sign down to the village.

'It looks like you're making out OK,' he persisted, easily keeping up. 'The job's going well, you're busy making yourself indispensable. You're good at that.'

'I said I didn't want to know.' She could feel him getting under her skin, churning her up.

'Exactly, you're keeping your distance, playing safe. Laura, listen.'

'No, Tom.' She stopped to face him. 'You're here to help us fight this stone company. That's what you said last night. That's why I asked Philip and Juliet if they would put you up for a few days. Your being here has nothing to do with us. I don't want to get involved, it's too painful.'

'OK.' He grimaced. 'OK, OK, I won't muddy the waters. Anyway, maybe you're jumping the gun. I have a life of my own as well, you know.' They walked into a belt of fog. It swirled around them, clinging to their hair and faces. 'Well?'

'You're saying I'm wrong?'

'Could be.'

'No, you wouldn't be being nice unless you had ulterior motives.'

He laughed. 'Maybe I've changed.'

'Not that much.'

They parted in the square. Tom had phone calls to make, Laura planned to meet Mary to trawl the estate agents' and spend the morning looking at property.

In her mind's eye Laura could see the place she wanted; an old stone farmhouse in a sheltered spot, already worked on by builders to update the facilities, but with plenty of scope for her own ideas. 'I'll probably end up with a brand new box on an estate,' she prophesied, as she drove with Mary past the Maskells' place by the old bridge. The estate agents always made wrong assumptions; that as a woman on her own she would want an easily managed property, a small garden and a built-in garage. She would go for neighbours and street lights and security alarm systems. In the end, Laura had given up trying to explain and simply accepted whatever details they offered.

'What about Ravenscar Hall?' Mary said with a glint in her eye. She'd dressed for the occasion in a black coat and matching cossack hat trimmed with fur. 'I noticed in Addys' window that it was up for sale. Price on application.'

Laura swung across the bridge, following signs to the Abbey. In the distance, Hawkshead Hall sat in a patch of sunlight. 'It's a bit on the large side, wouldn't you say?'

'Pity. It'll be going for a song.'

'That's what the quarry's doing to property prices.' Laura frowned as she changed down into third gear to negotiate the bends in the narrow road. 'They've hit rock-bottom. Everyone's moaning about their houses losing value. Except me, of course.'

The fog began to lift as they took the road out of the village along the river, through a copse of tall, straight beech trees. Farm dogs barked as they passed, straining at their chains. Half a dozen grey geese darted from a ramshackle yard and called out raucously. Laura's hopes rose; perhaps the house of her dreams lay at the end of the lane.

But Dale Chapel, described by Addys' blurb as imaginatively converted and in need of some finishing touches, was no more than an empty Methodist shell. Builders' rubble lay piled up in the overgrown garden, and a bright blue plastic tarpaulin flapped across the half-exposed roof beams.

'Hmm.' Mary strode up the steps and pushed open the door. 'Someone ran out of money, methinks.'

'No wonder it's a bargain.' Laura stepped across bags of cement, solidified by the damp that seeped under the door. A steel kitchen sink stood abandoned against a wall in a downstairs room. She turned to Mary and sighed. 'Give me a box on a modern estate,' she moaned.

Three houses and three major disappointments later, they gave up. Cold, jaded, hungry, they headed back to the village for coffee. 'It's my shout,' Mary volunteered. 'Let's order the biggest, creamiest cakes on the trolley,' she suggested as they sat at a window-table in a cafe overlooking the market square. 'Millions of calories and loads of saturated fats to clog up the arteries. What the hell.'

Laura settled in for half an hour of self-indulgence before she drove off for her meeting with Matthew.

'You're not really going to Wingate?' Mary wanted to know. 'Will you tell Matthew about Tom?'

'Tell him what? Yes, of course, if it comes up in conversation.'

Mary put on a good imitation of Laura's voice. 'Oh, by the way, my ex-husband's turned up and he's going to help us stop you from destroying the dale.'

Laura stirred her coffee and pushed away her half-eaten cake. 'Thanks a lot.'

'I jest not! The whole thing could look pretty strange. What's Tom doing here, anyway? Does he want you back?'

'Shh. You always oversimplify.'

'*Au contraire*, you over-complicate. I'd have thought it was pretty obvious. Tom's had six months to realise what he's missing and he's come to Hawkshead to get you back.'

'He would deny it.'

'Men always lie about their emotions, you should know this.'

'You're great, you know that, Mary?' Laura rested her chin in her hand. 'No, I mean it. You blunder in where angels fear to tread.'

'Tactless, eh?'

'No. Listen, if Tom does think he wants us to try again, and you may be right, I need to sort out what to do.'

'Keep a clear head.'

'Yes. Remind me, will you, that living with Tom was not a pleasure. He's an angry man; deep down angry. It's a corrosion eating away at whatever we try to build. He can't help it. And in the end, I can't stand it.'

'Well, that sounds straightforward. I don't see any problem about wavering there. No way would you be seduced into thinking it would be worth having another go. Would you?'

'The thing is, it still hurts.' Her voice was a whisper. 'I lost a lot when we split up.'

'I know.'

'When I married Tom, I thought it would be forever.'

'Nothing is,' Mary said gently. 'You know the cliché. Nothing is forever.'

'But we still want it to be, don't we? If it isn't forever, where does that leave us? Yesterday I loved him. Today I don't. Last year, this year. What is it that changes?'

Helplessly Mary shook her head. 'You're asking me this question?'

'No, I suppose I'm asking myself. And not coming up with any answers.'

'Let me know if you do. Meanwhile, tell me what to do about Philip!'

Before she left for Wingate, Laura took it upon herself to pay a special visit to Dick Metcalfe's place. Highfield Farm sat halfway up Hawk Fell, well off the beaten track. Dick had lived there alone since the death of his wife, Peggy, two years earlier. She knew Tot's death would be a hard blow. He opened the door, reading bad news on her face. 'What's up?'

'It's Tot.' She stepped inside the kitchen. 'Last night. There was nothing we could do.'

'I told him to go easy, but he was a stubborn bugger.' Dick sighed and turned his head away.

'Like someone else I know.' Laura spoke quietly, leaving a long pause for Dick to regain control.

'When's the funeral?'

'Thursday morning. Shall I get someone to call for you?'

The old man coughed. 'Nay, I'll make my own way.' There was another pause. 'We'll give him a decent send-off.'

'Good.' Laura judged it was time to go. 'And you'll be all right?'

'Me? Right as rain.' He showed her out, and stood, holding onto the door handle long after Laura's car had driven out of the yard, looking up at the skyline and the empty space of rocky Hawk Fell.

Wingate seemed to offer a solid, safe meeting-ground for Laura and Matthew. A Victorian spa town of gardens and open spaces, it demanded restraint. Visitors kept to the footpaths and didn't run amok among the acres of crocuses whose spear-shaped tips of purple, white and yellow signalled the start of spring.

They met, and walked quietly through the immaculate park, talking inconsequentially. It was a dull, damp afternoon, still very cold. She was glad when Matthew took her hand as they walked along, and he quizzed her about her own childhood in the genteel town.

'Not so genteel, actually,' she confessed. 'I don't remember many stately Sunday afternoon walks in the park. Climbing trees and rampaging through woods was more my style.'

He said he liked to imagine her rampaging. 'You're so cool and collected now.'

'Am I?' That was the second person who had said that to her today.

'On the outside at least.'

'It must go with the job.' She wanted to tell him that the calm exterior didn't give the full picture. 'As a matter of fact, I sometimes feel I don't know what on earth I'm doing with my life.'

'But you don't regret the move to Hawkshead?' He kept her hand in his as they walked out of the park, towards bare winter woodland.

'No. I love the place. I suppose it's the idea of buying my own house. It's making me nervous for some reason.' She told him about the morning's fruitless search.

He promised to keep a lookout for the kind of place she might like.

They'd begun to follow a track that led still higher up the hill. Last autumn's leaves still lay soggy underfoot. Clean green shoots of crocuses clustered round the roots of trees.

'You know, while you were rampaging through these woods, I was busy doing my prep and getting good at science. To impress my parents. Especially Maisie.' He paused. 'It wasn't that easy.'

'No,' she agreed. 'It's strange how she seems vulnerable now.' They walked on in silence. 'What will happen if she loses?'

'Over the quarry? Christ knows.' Matthew stopped in his tracks. 'I don't know. She's not used to it. I wouldn't put it past her to sell up lock, stock and barrel. I guess she might go back to the States.'

'She'd give up the Hall?' Laura realised that he'd let go of her hand. He stood with a troubled look, staring up at the grey branches.

'There's always a chance of that, yes.'

Laura's heart turned over for him. She pictured the lovely, mellow house being sold to strangers. 'Isn't there any other way she could raise money?'

'That's not the point. You don't know my mother. If she doesn't get the decision she wants over Ravenscar, she could well give up on Hawkshead altogether. She would see it as a personal affront, she'd feel humiliated. And she would never want to speak to anyone in the village ever again.'

'And what about you and Christopher? How do you two fit in?'

'Christopher wouldn't give a damn. He'd hole up permanently in Italy. He loves the ex-pat lifestyle, and as long as he can make ends meet by selling an odd painting or two he's happy.' Matthew couldn't prevent a note of bitterness from creeping into his voice. 'I haven't been thinking about much else since you came to the house; the Hall and the land. Not so much the Hall as the land, as a matter of fact. I know every square foot of it. I suppose somehow I've always expected it to be there, outside my four walls.'

She could see how shaken he was by the prospect of another loss, coming hard on the heels of his father's death, his wife, his two children. 'So, in a way it's better for you if Maisie does manage to sell the land to Frontier? At least the family would be able to stay on at the Hall.' This was a complication she hadn't bargained for.

'Better for me? Yes, I suppose so.'

'But?'

'But look what it's doing. It's ripping the heart out of the place.' Matthew strode up the path until he came to an open area of dark rocks which overlooked a steep, wooded valley. 'You were at the meeting, Laura. You saw how people felt. If my family sells that land, we'll be murderers in their eyes. I mean it. We'll be killing something vital. It's the place, Ravenscar. We'll destroy it forever.' The ground seemed to fall away beneath his feet. He stood at the very edge of the cliff.

'Matthew!' She caught hold of him.

'It's OK. I'm OK.' He turned back towards her.

'No, you're not. I'm sorry!' She took both of his hands. 'I never realised.'

He held her, folded his arms around her and drew her close. 'It doesn't seem so bad, now that I've got you.'

She kissed him, held onto him, as the wind swept around them, making the day wild and unruly.

'Don't talk,' she said softly, hiding her face against the warmth of his jacket. They both knew how they felt, that she wanted Matthew and he wanted her.

CHAPTER TWENTY FOUR

Thursday, the day of Tot's funeral, started cold and rainy. At the medical centre Gerald rushed through the eight hundred so that they could begin surgery and be finished in time to get to church.

'I'll see you there,' Philip reminded him. He knew Gerald hated funerals and had to be dragged along.

'If I find the time. I'm needed over in Wingate later today. First things first.'

There was no time to argue. Philip went in to see his first patient; a tearful child of seven who had accidentally swallowed a coin.

'A five pence, Dr Maskell, part of his school bus money.' His anxious mother presented him for examination.

'Now let's see.' He shone a light down the boy's throat. 'What's the matter, didn't your mum give you enough breakfast?' He sat back and explained. 'We'll send him for an X-ray to be on the safe side, though nature will probably take its course.' The boy was beginning to calm down. 'The hospital will take a special picture of your insides to see where the money is. With a bit of luck it'll pop out all by itself.'

He nodded, his face still damp with tears.

This was routine, as was the next one; a heart patient with recognised aortic stenosis, who was waiting for angioplasty treatment. Then there was a farm lad with a gashed hand, who also had to be referred to the General. 'No chance of stitching it here, I'm afraid. We don't do it any more, you'll have to go to Casualty.'

The lad said he preferred it, since it gave him the morning off work.

Between him and Mary nothing was resolved. He made the running, snatched time with her, turned a deaf ear to her warnings that Hawkshead was a small place where sooner or later someone would suspect. She'd already told him that Laura knew of their affair.

'Has anyone noticed, the days are getting longer?' Laura sounded a cheerful note after surgery, as the three of them came and went through Reception.

'Don't go taking your shovel out of the boot just yet,' Gerald warned. 'We'll be digging ourselves out of more snowdrifts before we're through.'

'Pessimist.'

'Realist,' he insisted. He regaled them with the time he'd been caught in a deep drift on his way up to Oxtop. 'Wind whistling through me like a knife. Had to start digging myself out. When I got there, old Tot was at his gate in an open-necked shirt and an old jacket, demanding what had kept me.'

'He was tough all right,' Philip agreed. He offered Laura a lift to the church. 'I hear Dot's done the funeral arrangements?'

'Yes. She's determined it should go exactly as he would have wanted.' Laura told him that her landlady had rounded up some distant relatives; a niece from Scarborough and a younger half-sister who'd defected over the border to marry a butcher from Burnley. 'She says the two of them will split the proceeds from the sale of the farm.'

They arrived at St Michael's moments before the hearse and slipped into a space at the back of the church. Dick, even later, grumbled when Dot put him in the pew alongside the chief family mourners, but she brooked no argument. 'You'd do the same for Tot,' she told him, defying logic.

From the back of the small church, Philip kept an eye on the old farmer, done up in his best navy blue suit and collar and tie, with something raw and helpless about the hunch of his shoulders, the set of his close-cropped head. The funeral march struck up and the bearers carried the coffin down the aisle.

'Gerald never made it,' Laura whispered.

'He'll be along afterwards,' Philip assured her. 'It's just the hymn singing that gets to him.'

He understood why. A rich swell rose into the ancient roof beams. 'The Lord is My Shepherd.' 'There is a Green Hill Far Away.' Tot's death brought people together in a robust bout of mourning.

The vicar packed his sermon with affectionate, good-humoured anecdote. Marsden Barraclough told the apocryphal story about the young Tot, who, suddenly stricken with toothache in the midst of one lambing season, went from barn to toolshed for a pair of pliers. He promptly pulled out the offending molar and went back to the business at hand. 'Heck, I got the wrong tooth,' he muttered five minutes later. Onlookers swore that he went back a second time to get to work with the pliers.

'Now, we all know Tot suffered pain gladly, but by no means fools,' the vicar continued amongst more wry smiles. 'Most of us experienced the sharp side of his tongue on more than one occasion. And we know he enjoyed the taste of a pint better than the Communion wine. But I think we all felt somehow that Tot was indestructible, as much a part of the scenery as Black Gill and Hawk Fell. He was always on the go, through thick and thin, and we were so used to seeing his familiar figure in the out-at-elbow jacket that we imagined we would always have him with us here in Hawkshead. In the end, of course, even Tot was not ague-proof.'

At the front of the church, the niece bowed her head. Her two children stared at the coffin. Many of the mourners had given way to tears, but Philip noticed that Dick stood, head up, mouth clamped shut as the final hymn began.

'I never coughed up for flowers,' he told him afterwards. 'I don't believe in it.' He insisted that Tot had been an old grumbler and skinflint in his time. The story about the tooth was true enough, but only because the miserly beggar begrudged the price of a visit to the dentist. Still, he'd had a hard life, Dick gave him that much. 'Tot would hate to lose any beast to the weather. And you always knew where you stood. He never gave you no flannel.'

'Salt of the earth,' Dot confirmed, also dry-eyed. 'Still, he had a good innings and went the way he would have wanted.'

Gerald did show up, in time for a gathering at the Institute. Philip saw that he headed straight for Lilian Rigg, standing beside a trestle table piled high with tea urn and sandwiches.

'I thought he'd outlast the lot of us,' Gerald said, tea in hand.

Lilian reflected. 'No, I saw over Christmas he was failing. He wasn't himself.'

Throughout the service, Philip had felt keenly for Lilian. She'd stood in a pew beneath the window of St John the Carpenter at work against a green hillside under a cloudless blue sky. The window commemorated Geoffrey Aire's older brother, Michael, killed in action in 1943. Lilian sang serenely. There was already an other-worldliness about her which seemed to shield her from curious glances and impertinent questions about her health. There was no sign of struggle on her face, no fear, or plea for sympathy. She seemed to be living in the minute, raising her voice with all the rest, remembering Tot Dinsdale as she herself would wish to be remembered.

Now, among the Institute crowd, she was listening intently to talk about the inquiry; how those individuals worst affected by the quarry plans were due a visit from members of the inquiry team. Luke Altham had backed Tom Elliot's idea of a build-up of press interest, so that the campaigners could gain a wide public platform for their views.

'How do you think the campaign is going?' Philip wandered across to join them.

'I'll carry on the same as always,' was all she would say. 'Busy in the greenhouse planting and labelling, getting ready for the spring.'

She had chosen to fight her battle against cancer alone, vetoing discussion of her treatment and progress, so he plied her instead with questions about when to prune his lavender bushes, and what were the best soil conditions for a new clematis given to him by a grateful patient.

Lilian gave it to him chapter and verse; the acid-alkaline mix, how much sun, when to cut back, maximum height and susceptibility to disease. 'If you look after it properly it'll see you out, Dr Maskell. Mind you, it'll take some holding back. Fine, velvet crimson flowers from May to September, but only on new growth. Cut it well back in October and it'll do you proud.'

She turned to ask Laura how her house-hunting was going along, taking a full interest in all that went on. When she grew tired, she made her quiet excuses and left, touching Dick gently on the elbow and offering soft words of condolence.

Later that day, after a phone call from Juliet to remind him that she was staying in Merton for the evening to play badminton, Philip went for a drink at the Falcon.

At least, this was what he told himself, not allowing himself consciously to hope that he would find Mary there, but trying to stave off a feeling of gloom that perhaps Tot's funeral had brought on. It was unlike him to be aimless and on edge. A good book and a stiff drink by the fire at home would usually have seemed the perfect ending to his busy day.

As soon as he walked into the pub he knew it was a mistake. Mary was there all right, talking to Tom Elliot, amongst a crowd who were all hot under the collar about the quarry, the main topic of conversation these days.

'Dr Maskell, what can I get you?' Alison Lawson was on duty behind the bar, looking happier than when he'd last seen her.

'A double Scotch, please. Did you have a good break?'

'Yes, thanks. I went to my sister's in Glasgow. It wasn't a holiday exactly.'

He sat down at the bar, his back to Mary. 'Brian said you needed a rest.'

'That's putting it mildly. I thought Brian and me would split up over the New Year. Things were getting us both down.'

'I know. But you're looking better.' She had a new, shorter hairstyle, her eyes were clear, she'd lost weight.

'That's because my sister Susie gave me a good talking to. She said I'd better get myself sorted out. She told me to stop worrying about Nina and what she might be saying behind my back. She said, what did I expect, a medal for taking her dad away?'

'Susie sounds like a natural born therapist.' Philip took a long drink. 'What else did she say?'

'Are you sure you don't mind me going on about it? Busman's holiday and all that?'

'Alison, believe me, I'm glad to see you back. Talk to me. Tell me something that will cheer me up.'

'It's like that, is it? Well, she made me take a long look at things and I saw she was right. Nina's not my problem, is she? I mean, when it comes down to it, I don't even have to like her. And there was me thinking I had to be a mother to the kid when she came to stay, making a proper family for her, which is probably just what she doesn't need.'

'Since she's already got one, you mean? Is she back at home now?'

'Yes, but she's due up this weekend. And my New Year resolution is to be myself with her, and leave Brian to sort it out if she starts being moody.'

'Sounds good. What about you and Brian? What did Susie have to say about that?'

'Plenty. She has a different way of looking at things. Mind you, she's already got three kids. When the last one was two weeks overdue, she went round saying she wished it would carry on taking its time; it was far less trouble in than out.' Alison worked on, stacking clean glasses. 'She says, sure it's great if you want kids and you can have them. But she says what makes me think it's my right? Like ordering a takeaway family. It took me ages to see what she meant. I mean, I've wanted a baby ever since I was a little girl. She was the tomboy, she never wanted them. Now she's got three.'

'In other words, she doesn't believe in babies on demand?'

'If it happens, it happens.'

'That could sound a bit hard. How do you feel about it?'

'Let's say I'm not as desperate as I was.'

'And Brian?'

'You'd have to talk to him. I put him through the mill, didn't I?'

'A bit. It takes two, though. Maybe he's had time to rethink too? Listen, I think you should ring up for another appointment.' Philip could feel the group behind him breaking up. He glanced round to see where Mary had gone.

'You think it's worth it?'

'I do. Whenever you're ready.'

'I'll talk to him.' She sidled away to serve fresh customers. 'Thanks, Philip.'

He smiled back.

'Hey, Philip, what's yours?' Tom came up from behind and ordered two drinks. Philip realised that the martini was for Mary. 'Come on, Doc, let me buy my landlord a drink.'

'Make it a pint of bitter, thanks.'

'Here, come and join us.' Tom nodded his head sideways. 'Mary was just telling me that we've shared a bed.'

Reluctantly Philip followed. This was the situation he hated most; being close to Mary but unable to own up to how he felt. He knew he would sit there stilted and uncomfortable, while Tom Elliot's witty conversation flowed on.

'We shared a bed, but I must have been too drunk to notice.'

'Pity, you missed a treat.' Mary couldn't resist a look at Philip.

'Was it at a student party? Were we smashed?'

Philip looked restlessly round the bar. He nodded at Dick and Dot ensconced in their corner.

'OK, I'm joking,' she confessed. 'When I say shared, I use the word loosely. It's a serial share. No, a consecutive share. You're staying in the room I was in before I moved to my flat.'

'Now it's my turn to say what a pity.' Tom was gallant. 'You were always my favourite, Mary; easily the most outrageous of Laura's friends.'

She made a lemon-sucking face. 'Let me tell you, that wasn't difficult.'

'Boring medics?'

'Well, they can be a bit earnest.'

Philip shifted on his stool. He knew he was being hypersensitive.

'Don't worry, she doesn't mean you.' Tom downed his drink. As he put down the glass, he looked from Philip to Mary and something clicked. 'Listen,' he said hastily, 'I have to talk to Brian. The company surveyors were in this lunchtime. He probably picked up some useful information, off the record.' He dismounted from his stool, swinging one leg and rotating on his backside. 'Catch you later.'

They nodded and fell silent.

'Can't I have a joke with an old friend?' she complained.

'It's not that.'

'Tom's OK. He's harmless.'

'If you say so.' He thought her judgment had deserted her. As far as he was concerned, Tom Elliot's motives in stoking up the quarry debate were mixed. He was crashing it into a higher gear with his conspiracy theory that the inquiry was really a cover-up for a decision that had been taken well in advance. Philip suspected that at least part of it was switched on to impress Laura.

'Why let him stay at your place, then?'

'Because Laura asked me, as a favour.' He ran a hand through his hair. 'Look, I don't want to argue.'

'Me neither.' She looked miserable, her lip trembled as she turned away.

'Let's get out of here,' he urged.

'We can't, Philip. It's too obvious.'

'Come on, Mary. We have to talk.'

'Where?'

'At the flat. You go, I'll follow in a couple of minutes. Please.'

At last she agreed. She picked her bag off the floor. 'But wait, don't rush out after me, OK?'

He promised. She slipped away across the crowded bar without meeting anyone's eye. Tom noticed her, and Dot watched with her eagle eye.

'Cheers, Tom.' Philip took his empty glass to the bar.

'Are you off already?' Brian broke off from serving.

'I'm away to my bed.'

'Right you are.'

''Night, Dick. 'Night, Dot.' He rattled his car keys ostentatiously.

'Would you tell Mrs Maskell I'll be in early tomorrow morning to make up for today?' she called, equally deliberately.

Dot knew. He felt it in his bones. She knew about him and Mary.

'Guilt.' Mary tried to explain it away when he told her how Dot had watched him leave. She lay in his arms, still cold under the bedcover. 'She probably didn't suspect a thing.'

'I'll soon know tomorrow morning.'

'She won't tell Juliet, will she?'

'No, I'll probably get a lecture on family values while she's polishing the table.'

'Seriously?'

'No. I expect she'll just give me one of her looks.'

'I know those. She gives me them already.'

'Quite right too, you scarlet woman.' He pulled her close and gently turned her face towards him. 'We're both as guilty as sin, you know that?'

'Philip Maskell, I warned you!'

'And I wouldn't listen.' He kissed her. 'I needed you too much. I still do.'

When she opened her eyes, they were still troubled. She stroked his cheek with her fingertips, then his eyelids, tracing the shape of his face.

'Don't be sad,' he said.

'I'm not. I'm happy.'

'Don't cry. Mary, I don't want to leave you, I want to stay here.'

Her sigh turned into a sob. He lifted himself onto one elbow to shield her, to let her bury her tears against his chest. Then he kissed her again and she clung to him, her arms wound around his body, her fingers grasping him. She was racked with dry, thin cries.

'Don't!' He could only hold her and kiss her until they grew calm, tell her she was beautiful, murmur the words and listen to her sigh again and take him to her and make love. He said she was the most precious, the most exciting and wonderful thing that had happened to him in his whole life.

CHAPTER TWENTY FIVE

'I'm sorry, I truly am.' Mary sounded distraught. 'I must have mentioned you and Matthew to Tom without thinking.'

In silence, Laura rearranged things on her desk: prescription pad, pen, calendar.

'To be honest, I don't know what I'm doing half of the time. But once I'd let it slip, he made damn sure everyone else found out. It was after last night's meeting at Church House. Dot was there, and Aimee. It was Aimee Tom passed it onto, I think.'

'What did he say?'

'Something about your halo slipping. Sleeping with the enemy.'

'I'm not sleeping with him.'

'That's just Tom's way of getting the knife in. Anyway, I heard Dot telling him you could see who you liked. It didn't make any difference to the work you were doing for the campaign.'

'Never mind, Mary. It was bound to come out. I remember Gerald warning me that it was impossible to keep a secret round here. And we weren't being particularly furtive about it.' Since the time in Wingate, Laura had gone on seeing Matthew. Tonight she was due to fulfil the long-delayed dinner invitation to the Hall. 'So you don't think I'm in danger of being blacklisted?'

'Not by Dot, at any rate. I'm not so sure about Aimee.'

'Maybe she'll ask to be transferred to Philip.' She knew, though, that Aimee was on her list for a half past ten appointment that morning.

'I doubt it. You haven't seen Tom yet?'

'Since last night? No.' She'd left the meeting early.

'I thought I'd better warn you. It's just that, with this complication over the quarry, Tom could easily use it against you.'

Laura put down the phone, trying to assess how Tom would react. If he meant what he said about the quarry being his only reason for being here, her going out with Matthew would make no difference. But he was devious. He might seem laid back about it, yet still want to retaliate.

The knock on her door made her start. It was Gerald, on his way to visit a patient in Ginnersby. 'Here's that list of nurses to call on if Lilian Rigg decides she needs one.' He put it down on her desk. 'Laura?'

'Oh, thanks. Actually, she still says she doesn't need help.'

'Well, they're there just in case.'

She thanked him again, then signalled to Sheila that she was ready for her next appointment. By the time Aimee arrived, her mind was on the job, and she was ready to handle what looked like being a tricky situation.

'Thanks for coming.' She'd rung Aimee at home to ask her to make an appointment. 'It's about the results of those tests we sent you for.' They were back-ups to her diagnosis of anorexia, intended to eliminate other causes of the weight loss. Aimee had submitted with bad grace, but had at last allowed Janet to take her through to Wingate. Laura knew that Aimee's mother sat outside now. 'Well, the blood tests didn't show anything significant.'

Aimee sighed, as if she'd known this all along. She was dressed in her oversized jumper and black trousers, looking pale and aggressive.

'But the chest X-ray's a different matter.' Laura re-read the radiographer's report. 'They've spotted a problem; a small shadow in the corner of one lung.' She looked up. 'They say it needs investigation.'

'What kind of shadow?' Aimee gripped the edge of her chair.

'That's what they need to check. As far as they can tell from the X-ray, it's not a malignant growth. It's more likely to be TB.'

'How can it be? I had the jab.'

'Not according to your file. You tested immune which means you could have already had the disease as a child. People sometimes get it without knowing. What the hospital wants to do is make absolutely sure that everything's fine now.' She waited for the news to sink in.

'I don't believe I'm hearing this.' She shook her head, arms locked at the elbow, hands still anchored to the seat of her chair. 'It's a trick, isn't it? To get me into hospital, so they can stuff food down me.'

'Believe me, it's not.' Laura moved out from behind her desk. 'If the problem is TB, we can deal with it. No need to go thinking about consumptive heroines in Victorian novels, fading away in agony. These days it means a short stay in hospital, some blood tests and a very simple treatment.' She put a hand on Aimee's shoulder and tried to break through her daze. 'Shall I go and fetch your mother, so we can discuss the arrangements?'

She nodded slowly. Laura went to explain to Janet, whose reaction, after a gasp of surprise, was calm and practical. 'She'd like you to come in when you feel ready.'

Janet sat down next to her daughter.

'If it's TB, it's infectious, so they'll want to isolate you. You'll be in a small side ward.'

'I thought you said I had it ages ago when I was a kid?' Aimee was trembling.

'They need to make sure.' Janet reached out, but Aimee jerked away.

'What about the campaign?' she demanded. 'They're relying on me to organise it at school. And there's going to be a sit-in. I can't miss that.'

'This is the first I've heard of it.' Laura glanced at Janet. 'A sit-in where?'

'At Black Gill. We decided on it last night. I said I'd get it all set up with the other kids at school.'

Laura frowned. 'Whose idea was this?'

'Everyone's. We were sitting around in the pub afterwards. Tom says it'll really help get the public on our side.'

'Well, you won't be sitting-in anywhere unless you get your health sorted out,' Janet warned. 'Now, you must listen and do as Laura tells you.'

'Yes, and aren't you glad?' Aimee lashed out, jumping to her feet. 'Dead easy, isn't it? TB's a whole lot better than anorexia. TB isn't anyone's fault.'

'Aimee.'

'Why not just stick me in hospital and forget about me? That's what you'd like. I know it's a pain having me around. Aimee, do this, Aimee, do that. Eat this. Eat, eat, eat!' She stood marooned in the middle of the floor, tears streaming down her face.

'Now you can send me off for a TB cure and I'm supposed to come back chubby and cute, like a good little girl. And you can stop worrying, and I'll behave perfectly and I won't let you down ever again.' She sobbed, no longer angry, hardly knowing where she was or what she said.

'It's not true.' Janet stood up and appealed to Laura.

Laura eased her back into her seat. 'Aimee, no one thinks you're letting them down.'

'They don't say it, but they think it. I'm not going to be a doctor, I'm a failure; get it? Everyone in our family who's any good is a doctor, aren't they, Mum? It's the only thing to be. Well, I hate it. It's morbid. People die on you, they get horrible diseases and you have to sit there and watch them suffer. Doctors kill themselves more often than in any other job, did you know that?'

'It's not all like that.' Janet tried to reason. 'Daddy saves lives as well.'

'Yes, but he's a doctor. He lives, breathes, eats and sleeps like a doctor. He's never off-duty, he's never been a normal everyday father.'

Janet began to cry too. 'What do you want from him? From us?'

'To notice me,' Aimee muttered after a long pause.

'But we do.'

'No, me! Notice me! Not a carbon copy of Nick. Why can't you realise that what I do and think is OK too?'

Janet took the tissue handed to her by Laura. 'You don't give us the chance to get close to you any more. You block us out, Aimee, not the other way round. I've been sick with worry about you lately, you know that. And you won't even let me tell Daddy you're ill.'

Aimee made an effort to get her voice under control. 'I still don't want him to know.'

Laura's internal buzzer went. She picked up the phone.

'I thought you'd better know, Gerald's car's heading back into the car park,' Sheila said. 'It looks like he's forgotten something.'

Laura felt her stomach lurch. It was true; through the window she could see Gerald getting out of his car and coming towards the surgery. He'd spotted Janet's car parked close to the door. She heard his voice rumble through the building.

Aimee heard it too. She looked round, startled. Janet ran to the door, but he pushed it open and stood looking at them, his face setting into angry lines.

Laura moved to intercept him. 'I need to have a word with

Aimee, Gerald. Janet, can you go out and explain to him what's happening?'

'No.' He stood firm. 'No, this time I won't be fobbed off.' He closed the door behind him. 'How long has this been going on?'

'Nothing is going on,' Laura protested. 'Nothing against the rules. I've been trying to find out why Aimee's losing so much weight.'

'Behind my back.' He looked from one to the other. 'How long?'

'Since before Christmas. Aimee wanted to keep it confidential.'

'And you let her?'

'What else could I do? You know the confidentiality principle.'

'Damn the principle. This is my daughter, my family, not just any old patient on your list.' He turned his anger against her. 'How would you feel?'

'Bad,' Laura admitted. 'But Aimee didn't want to tell you and there was nothing I could do.'

'You mean, I'm the problem?' He raised his voice. 'That's the trendy thing, isn't it? Blame the parents. She wants to be thin, so that's my fault. How the hell can an obsession with dieting be my fault?'

'I'm not saying it is anorexia. There's a possibility of TB.'

'Oh, come on, Laura. Have you asked her what she had for breakfast this morning? And every morning this week? A carrot for lunch, maybe cottage cheese, or maybe thin air again. And when did she last sit down for an evening meal?' He drew a sharp breath. 'If you must know, I've had her down as anorexic since last October.'

They stood in stunned silence.

'You knew?' Janet whispered.

'Of course. The only thing I didn't know was that she was coming here.'

'Why didn't you discuss it with me?'

'Why didn't she discuss it with us?'

'I'll tell you why I didn't, Daddy; because you never listen, that's why. You only hear what you want to hear. I say something, and you say don't be ridiculous. What's the point of talking to you? You wouldn't understand the first thing.' Aimee finished scornfully, with no trace of tears.

Gerald looked at Janet, while Aimee enjoyed her moment of

bitter triumph. Laura decided to leave the three of them to sort it out.

'We'll talk about this later,' Gerald warned as she opened the door and walked across the waiting room to look for Philip.

Laura drove quickly to Bridge House, but was disappointed to find that Philip's car wasn't there. Instead, she spotted Tom heading on foot towards the house.

'Where's the fire?' He hailed her car and peered in as she wound down the window.

'There isn't one. I'm looking for Philip.'

'Too late. I saw him heading out of town. Will I do?'

She hesitated, desperate for someone to talk to.

'Come in for coffee. You look as if you need one.' He opened her door and waited for her to get out.'

'OK.' She followed him inside and sank into a chair at the kitchen table. 'I've just had a terrible morning.'

'Tell me about it.'

'I can't. Only that Gerald's just done his *et tu Brute* act.'

'On you?'

'I shouldn't joke. He feels badly let down, but I was in an impossible position.'

'No position is impossible if you're young and healthy. Who said that?'

'Tom!' She laughed out of tension and relief. 'You've no idea what it's like, all these ethical dilemmas.'

'Don't I? If anyone does, it's me, sunshine. I had twelve years of it.' He put an arm round her shoulder as he handed her a drink.

'Thanks.' She turned her face to accept a kiss on the cheek. 'I just feel there must have been something I could have done to avoid that scene back there. God knows what will happen now.'

'Exactly.' He met her gaze as he sat down opposite. 'And you're not He, though you may sometimes think you are.'

'Do I?' She closed her eyes and let out a long sigh.

'In the nicest possible way,' he said in the voice that made her recall how much she had loved him. 'Relax. There's nothing you can do. Gerald will soon get over whatever it is that's eating him, and you'll go on having your crises of conscience. Nothing's new, nothing changes. I thought you would have realised that by now.'

CHAPTER TWENTY SIX

Philip called at Town Head later that day, as Laura was finishing getting ready for her evening at the Hall.

'Aimee's refusing point blank to have the TB tests.' He caught her up with events. 'Gerald's not talking to anyone, and Janet's at her wit's end, poor woman.'

Sitting in Dot's front room amongst the orderliness of her ornaments and dressed in a fitted cream wool dress and high heels, Laura took the news quietly. 'It looks like we'll have to wait for things to calm down before we can do anything else. To be honest, the chances of finding active disease in Aimee's lungs are remote. It's more the atmosphere at home; it could heighten the anorexia problem.'

'I do see Gerald's point, though.'

'Me too. He's been left in the dark for months. It must feel dreadful.'

'It's hit him hard. I saw him at the centre before I came here. He's lost his fizz, just hanging around looking for something to do to avoid going home, I suppose.'

'Is he still angry with me?'

'Not according to him. He says he feels a fool, and he hates that more than anything. Losing face.' Philip tapped the arm of his chair. 'How about you? Are you all right?'

'More or less. I bumped into Tom and he soon sorted me out. He's got clear ideas on how far a doctor's responsibilities go. He wrote me right out of the central role and left the stage clear for the Scotts to sort things out for themselves.'

'Wise man.'

'Mary warns me that his motives are impure.' She wanted to know what Philip thought of this.

'Wise lady.' He refused to be drawn.

'I'm beginning to think she's right. It was sod's law that I ran into Tom instead of you. I just hope it didn't give him ideas.'

He stood up. 'From what I've seen, the ideas were already there. It's pretty obvious that he's interested in you two getting back together, and the quarry campaign slots nicely into place alongside that major ambition. Not that it's any of my business, of course.'

His tone, kind but brisk, drew further confidences from her. 'So what should I do about Matthew? That's why I'm all dressed up; I'm going to the Hall tonight. He's finally managed to persuade Maisie that I don't have two heads.'

'There's been a cessation of hostilities, then?' Philip asked. 'Or are you planning to infiltrate behind enemy lines?'

'Oh come on, this isn't open warfare. We can still be civilised.' She was disappointed that he took the simplistic view.

He shrugged. 'Feelings are running high, you know. You heard about the sit-in?'

'Aimee told us.'

'Take Dot, for instance. She'd love to get her hands on the opposition if she got half a chance. She overheard one of the local builders in the pub last night saying he'd jump at the opportunity to build starter homes for new families who came for jobs in the quarry, and sod the environment.'

'So going out with Matthew is a dumb thing to do? What if I happen to like him? Quite a lot.'

'That's harder,' he admitted. 'Don't tell me about it.'

'I know, I'm sorry, Philip.' She followed him to the door. 'If *you* ever want to talk, you know –'

He looked up at her from under knotted brows. 'Thanks.' He gave her hand a pat as he showed himself out. 'And have a good time, OK? Take no notice of us, we're a bunch of old Jeremiahs.'

'One day perhaps you'll see the Hall in the daylight.' Maisie smiled across the dinner table at Laura. The evening had gone off well so far, with the focus firmly on Laura's job and recent efforts to find a house. Maisie went on to share her own experience of arriving in the dale, a complete outsider.

'It was just after the war. I guess they thought we American girls were spoiled. You know, the GIs always had money in their pockets. And then there was the Hollywood thing; all that glamour. It didn't go down too well.' Maisie's dark eyes glittered in the candlelight. 'I guess people round here looked down their noses at me for quite a few years.'

'Where did you spend the war?' Laura was glad to concentrate on Maisie.

'At home in Salem, which is a very proper town, despite its gory reputation.'

They talked of witchcraft and Arthur Miller, of Marilyn Monroe and the Kennedys. Maisie still admired Rose Kennedy, the great American matriarch. They discussed the British royal family, and the Duke of Windsor's affair with Mrs Simpson.

'That's who you remind me of, as a matter of fact,' Laura confessed.

'Am I to take that as a compliment?' Maisie smiled. 'Of course, I always thought that the scandal over the Duke of Windsor may have had something to do with my own reception in this charming country. I think they thought I was some sort of gold-digger. They hated Wallis Simpson by this time. He, Edward, was seen as the poor innocent seduced by her worldly charms.' She shrugged. 'They would see it that way, I guess. And then there was her jewellery, and her clothes.'

'She looks fabulous in all the photographs and newsreels.'

'It's strange, the twists and turns in all our lives.' Maisie gestured carelessly around the room. 'Imagine, if Geoffrey's brother, Michael, had survived the war. He would presumably have married, had children, and none of this would have belonged to us.'

'And what would you have done?' Matthew refilled the wine glasses.

'Who knows? Drifted around the Mediterranean, maybe, or lived in Paris.'

'I can't imagine Father drifting.'

'You mean his Wesleyan streak? No day is worthwhile unless you've achieved something measurable? Yes, you're right. Geoffrey was no slouch.' In the pause that followed, Maisie let her smile drop. 'No more am I, actually. That was one of the things I found attractive in Matthew's father,' she told Laura. 'His solid determination. What do you call it, northern grit? I guess it struck a chord with my New England puritanism.'

Laura nodded, encouraging her to go on, finding Maisie's reminiscences unexpectedly touching.

'All the other young men I met in London had pots of money,

inherited wealth mostly. But they swayed with the wind. Matthew's father was a true rock in comparison. And he was handsome. He told me about his wild native county, he warned me I would never stand the winters. I said he mustn't underestimate me; I came of good pioneering stock. So we came up here and I stuck it out for fifty years.'

She broke off, lifted a strand of hair from the nape of her neck and patted it into place. 'I don't mean to make it sound so grim. Only, I wasn't used to it, and it was much more difficult to travel in those days. I didn't go home for five years, until 1950. And after that, there were the boys.'

Laura picked up her wistfulness. 'You must have been lonely.'

Maisie turned her wine glass, tilting it against the candlelight. 'Homesick, yes. Lonely, no. I had my new family, and Geoffrey was a wonderful father. Matthew takes after him.'

'Not according to Abigail,' he said shortly. 'To hear her talk, you'd think I was the father from hell.'

'Don't be silly, darling. Sophie and Tim are perfectly happy in York, aren't they?'

'That's the official line, yes.'

Laura wondered why the cracks had appeared. This was the first time she'd heard Matthew introduce the children into conversation, and she wasn't convinced by his flippant tone.

'But they like their new schools? Their house? Abigail has great plans for the house.' She turned to confide in Laura. 'Matthew has paid for it. He can't reproach himself.'

'I'm told now that money isn't everything. There are other forms of neglect, apparently. Not enough quality time.'

'I'm sure Abigail can't think that you neglect them, Matthew. She's never hinted at it to me. They can come here whenever they like; she knows that. Are you sure you're not being hypersensitive to some remark or other? Something she let slip in the heat of the moment?' Maisie sought for excuses.

'Yes, you're probably right. She's under pressure at the moment, making a go of the business. I was probably in the wrong place at the wrong time.'

'Let me talk to her,' Maisie decided. 'Whatever it is, I'm sure we can help her out.' She stood up from the table. 'You'll see to coffee, won't you, Matthew? And Laura, you don't mind if I make myself scarce?'

She pleaded tiredness, though Laura guessed that the conversation about her grandchildren had upset her. She thanked her for a lovely evening.

'Once you start me talking about the old days, there's no stopping me,' she said sweetly. 'Nice, safe waters. Thank you, my dear.'

Maisie went up to her room, while Matthew left Laura in the lounge and reappeared a few minutes later with the coffee.

'I'm sorry,' Laura murmured, taking her cup.

'About the kids? It wasn't your fault. Abigail's been bending my ear all afternoon, so Mother caught me on a sore spot. I went over on a visit. First I got into trouble for taking them to the playground in the rain and trailing mud back into the house. Then there was a problem over school fees. You name it, I'd committed the crime.'

'I agree with Maisie, you shouldn't take it to heart.'

'You two got on like a house on fire.' He sat beside her on the cream sofa in the room where they'd first met. A tape played soft piano music.

'No need to look like that.' She curled her legs under her. 'I enjoyed myself, I really did.'

'Me too.' He smelt the perfume in her hair, took her head in both hands and kissed her.

'Strange,' he whispered.

'Weird.' She sighed. 'It does feel like some kind of madness.'

'Have I known you all my life, or just since Christmas?'

She kissed him on the mouth. 'Matthew, this is serious.'

'What is?'

'The way I'm feeling.'

'That's good, isn't it?' He wanted to gather her up.

'I don't know.' She began to laugh.

'I thought you said you were serious.'

'I am, I think. Stop kissing me.'

'Why?'

'I can't talk. I can't think.' She struggled free. 'Come on, Matthew, let's talk. Let's walk. Anything.' When she stood, it was like stepping off the waltzer at the fair.

'Walk!' He lay back against the sofa. She tugged at his hand. 'I don't think I want to walk.'

'Yes you do. It'll be bracing.' She pulled him up.

He groaned. 'Laura, you're kidding.'

'No. Look, if we stay here, it'll be one of those things we might live to regret.' She couldn't get rid of the thought of Maisie's refined disapproval. The house, the pictures on the wall shouted her presence.

'OK. Where do you want to walk to?'

'Outside by the lake.' She thought the fresh air would steady her spinning head.

'It's the wine.' Matthew linked arms and led her out through the french windows. 'Are you sure about this?' The night was cold and Laura's wool dress was light.

She nodded, aware of the immense dark space of stars and moon. They stepped onto the stone terrace and down to a lawn touched by frost. He wrapped his arm around her shoulder and pulled her close.

'Talk to me,' she whispered. The grounds of the Hall rolled away towards the glittering expanse of the lake. Gradually her eyes grew used to the night. There were dark bushes up one hillside, and tall, straight beech trees lining the drive.

'Talking sounds dangerously like thinking to me.'

'But why are we doing this?'

'See. "Why", that deadly little word.' He steered along a footpath leading to the water's edge. They followed it, leaving the house behind. 'We're doing this because it makes us happy, I guess.'

'Happy? Now, there's another deadly little word. It's short and sort of breathy and it shifts around inside your mouth. God knows what's coming next.'

He stopped and held her again. 'Who did this to you?'

Laura sighed. 'Life, the whole damn thing, I expect.'

'Meaning, your ex-husband?'

'The two of us. Like a chemical reaction that goes wrong. Sudden explosion followed by poisonous fumes.' She looked down at the smooth, cold water, and up at the crowded skies.

He led her on to a summerhouse, built on stilts over the water, housing a long, narrow rowing-boat, upturned and beached for the winter. Up the wooden steps, inside the chalet, the air was damp, the room empty except for several folding chairs stacked in one corner, and the oars for the boat, which hung on metal hooks from a wall. The place held a faint smell of creosote, an air of Swallows and Amazons; of girls in shorts with innocent tomboy names, and rough-haired terriers. Laura smiled and sat crosslegged on the floor. 'What a wonderful place!'

'Are you cold?'

She nodded. 'And happy, dare I say?'

He was stunned by her vulnerability. 'You look so young.' He bent down, tilted her chin towards him, confident that he could give her what she wanted. Stroking her face, her shoulders, he felt her shiver as he took her to him. 'Do you want me?' he whispered.

'More than anything.' Her hands went up to meet his. She wrapped them around his wrists. The strange setting; the sound of the lake lapping at the sturdy wooden supports, the musty childhood smells of canvas and creosote, disorientated her.

'Well then?'

She sighed. 'I'm scared.'

'I promise not to hurt you,' his lips murmured against her hair. Looking up, she believed him. She entwined her fingers with his and eased them down the length of her body until they rested on her hips. Then she reached up and put her arms around his neck and kissed him.

His loving was gentle at first, and generous. He didn't rush to prove anything; no showing off, no glib tricks. As they undressed he touched and stroked her and she admired his grace, the smooth, clean width of his shoulders, his strong arms. Her fears left her. Matthew's body was beautiful.

'Still happy?' he whispered.

For answer she smothered him in kisses.

She revelled in his touch, lay back in this cold play-house and glimpsed the stars. She loved his sureness as he aroused her and felt at last that she had come home.

CHAPTER TWENTY SEVEN

Purple and yellow crocuses burst out at the foot of Black Gill in early March, before the dark earth seemed ready for them.

Dot and Lilian strolled upstream towards Joan's Foss. It was a heavy, grey day, damp with mists, but the flowers were like beacons heralding the spring.

A nice, smart young man had come to call, Lilian told Dot. 'We talked and he wrote things down. I showed him round the garden and the greenhouse. He took an interest.'

Dot gathered that the young man had been no gardening expert. She pictured him in his neat city suit, clipboard in hand, assessing Lilian's small business against the capital benefits of knocking down the Grange to make way for the quarry. 'Did you bring him up the Gill?'

Lilian shook her head. 'He wasn't dressed for it.' She gave a small grin. 'Not a country lad, you could tell.'

'But you made it clear why you were against the quarry?'

'I told him straight. I said me and my husband had run this little place for nearly fifty years. It may not be much, but there's a lifetime of work behind it. Good, solid work, I told him. I don't want to see it all taken from me at the drop of a hat. I said my husband would turn in his grave if he knew what was going on.'

'What did he say?' Dot looked steadily up at the waterfall, watching it slide over shiny black rock and crash into the pool below.

'Not a lot. He said he understood I rented the place from the Aires. That gave me less say. But he did tell me they'd found out it was a listed building.'

'That's good!'

Lilian was unimpressed. 'Nay, they list owt these days. Dick's old barn up Hawk Fell is listed, so he says.'

'Still, it puts one more obstacle in the way of the stone company.'

Lilian agreed. 'But by all accounts, these big companies with a lot of brass behind them can do anything they want. If they want one of these supermarkets, down come whole rows of houses. If they want to put a motorway right through a town, who's to stop them?'

'But they didn't get the go-ahead to put one through Swiredale, did they?' Dot was afraid that Lilian was beginning to waver.

'No, because when they finally got together and did their sums, it turned out it would cost too much. That's why they scrapped that one.'

'What about us local people having our say?'

'I don't say it doesn't have its place. Don't get me wrong, I think we're putting up a good scrap, and that our man, Altham, knows his stuff.'

'And that journalist, Tom Elliot. Say what you like, he's brought us a lot of publicity.'

Lilian frowned. 'I don't know about this sit-in they're planning when the weather improves.'

'We have to go by what he says. Laura says he's trying to wrongfoot the inquiry, looking for leaks and suchlike.' Dot was still willing to believe that Tom would prove influential on their behalf. For the past few weeks he'd been dividing his time between Hawkshead and London, staying with the Maskells whenever he came to Yorkshire.

'I had another visit late last week, a young woman reporter from the *Star*. She said it would be written up for this week's front page.'

'You're turning into a celebrity.' Dot followed Lilian down the grass track towards the house.

'She took a photograph of the Grange,' Lilian said proudly. 'With all the crocuses just coming through.' She stopped at a distance from the walled garden, suddenly silent. Then she turned to Dot. 'Tell me what you think about this chemotherapy business. Should I go in for it or not?'

'I really can't say.' Taken aback for once, Dot tried to sidestep. 'I don't know enough about it.'

Lilian looked her steadily in the eye. 'What would you do if it were you?'

'You're surely not asking me to make your mind up for you?'

'I'm asking your advice. I never said I'd follow it. I'd have to go to the hospital every week and get hooked onto a drip all day. The best I'd get out of it is a short remission.'

They went and stood inside her garden, looking back up the wooded hillside. Dot shook her head. 'It's always going to be your decision, Lilian, but I know the side effects can be nasty.'

Lilian nodded. 'I knew, right from the start.'

'What?'

'There'd come a time to say no. It seems we're there already.'

'What does Laura say?'

'She says the problem is they diagnosed me late. But at any rate, I'd rather be going on as I am, working for as long as I can. In my right mind. Mind you, she doesn't know how long I've got. I've noticed my breathing comes shallow these days. I have to pace myself and go gently.'

'Nay –' Dot began to protest.

'I mean it. I can't get out and dig as I used to. Laura tells me I need to get someone in and work for me, an Easter school leaver.'

'And so you should. You need to look after yourself.' Dot was more upset than she let on. As they parted, she looked over her shoulder at Lilian standing in her garden, her back turned, hands in pockets in characteristic stance, staring into the far distance. Her heart squeezed as she set off along the track, past the mist-blurred walls of the old Abbey, under the rain-stained, indefinite hills.

'Right, I've managed to get hold of Frontier's detailed access plans.' Tom Elliot arrived at their meeting fresh from London. 'Frontier has already submitted these to the inquiry team, but we weren't supposed to get our hands on them until the next public meeting in April. There's also a copy of how they propose to limit the environmental damage.' He dropped both documents onto the table. 'They've certainly been doing their homework. It's a pretty good case they're presenting.'

Dot had come away from Abbey Grange that morning dead set on victory for Lilian's sake. Knowing now that she would decide to refuse further treatment only made things more urgent as far as she was concerned. 'We still have the right of way up our sleeve,' she insisted to Juliet Maskell, sitting beside her. She took up the copy of the plans and studied it.

'And!' Tom held up a preview edition of one of the weekend colour magazines. 'In here you'll find a double page spread written

206

by yours truly, putting Ravensdale into the national context, complete with stunning photograph!'

His news received the exclamations of admiration and surprise that it deserved. Hands made a grab for the article as he placed it in the centre of the table.

Dot nodded her satisfaction; a nod was sufficient, she felt. The picture of Ravenscar appeared as a grainy, remote landscape, free from the hand of man.

'That certainly does it justice.' Juliet gave her verdict. 'Look Mary, can't you just see mile upon mile of rolling heather?'

Mary, quieter of late, took it up to examine it.

'I tried to get across the level of local opposition,' Tom explained. 'That's what gives the piece its clout. And the idea that what Frontier is up to amounts to a good, old fashioned rip-off. I make it clear they're riding roughshod over a whole community, and I've flagged up the sit-in as the next space to watch.' He turned to Laura. 'What do you think?'

'Good.' She seemed to hold back from saying any more.

'It's brilliant,' Aimee chipped in, grabbing the magazine from Mary and poring over it.

'I'm hoping for some spin-offs; local radio news, maybe the nationals will pick it up, maybe even the telly. It's the sort of issue that gets the local news stations hopping around.'

'This is just what we need.' Luke Altham read the piece over Aimee's shoulder.

'Yes, we want Ravensdale to be a household name, hundreds of protest letters to MPs, outrage and idealism. That's the way to win this fight.' Tom was happy with the response.

Amidst the buzz of admiration, only Marsden Barraclough struck a warning note. 'I don't know how wise it is to fan the flames of conflict. Isn't it enough to sign petitions and organise our sit-in? Remember, we still have to co-exist when all this is over and done with.'

Dot found herself edging towards his point of view. Talk of radio and television filled her with dismay.

But Tom was intent on carrying them with him. 'The way I see it, the legal arguments still have a long way to go.' He paused to glance at Luke, who nodded. 'Sure, we'll carry on with the behind the scenes work, but this extra press coverage should make all the difference. There's a definite lobby inside parliament; pro-roads, pro-development at all costs. The men from Frontier will already have the ear of these people by projecting how much stone the builders will need for a potential road-building scheme which has already been approved by the Department of Transport and already been costed out on the basis of using local stone.'

Aimee spoke out. 'That's disgusting!'

'It's how it works, I'm afraid.'

Dot watched them grab the bait.

'It's all wheels-within-wheels. That's why my advice is to kick up a god-awful stink. Remember, it's not a fair fight we're talking about here.'

'That's exactly what I think!' Aimee was fired up. She described the demonstration which she and her friends had planned for the next public meeting. 'We're going to stand in the entrance with big placards, wave them in the faces of the Frontier lot when they arrive. Then when they get inside, we're going to shout them down.'

'Great. Put plenty of energy into it. If you plan to disrupt an event, make sure you're convincing,' Tom advised.

Dot glanced at Laura, who frowned out of the window onto the dark, wet street.

Slowly the meeting broke up as Tom suggested an adjournment to the pub.

Marsden Barraclough was teetotal. Luke Altham pleaded work next day and offered Dot a lift home. 'Laura, why don't you hop in too?' he said.

'Thanks, but I've got my own car. In fact, I can take you,' she told Dot.

'You'll have a drink first?' Tom was stooping over the table, collecting his papers. His offer to Laura, spoken quietly, had the effect of excluding everyone else in the room.

'I thought I'd get an early night, thanks.'

She looked weary. Dot knew that things between her and Dr Scott hadn't improved since their blazing row over Aimee. She herself was in favour of straight talking to sort out the girl's problems, but at the same time she realised this theory was hopelessly out of date. In any case, Aimee Scott did look very ill indeed. She was skin and bone beneath that baggy jumper. Surely she didn't imagine she looked well on this ridiculous diet?

'Come and wind down over a pint.' Tom took Laura's arm. 'We can fill Brian in on what's been going off.'

She sighed and gave in. 'Just one, then.' She picked up her belongings and he took them from her.

'Philip said he'd try and join us,' Juliet added on her way out. 'He had an emergency call. He's going to love the article.'

One by one they filed out.

'Ready?' Luke waited for Dot at the bottom of the stairs.

'I'm sorry, I'm a bit slow these days.' She had to take her time down the steps.

He smiled and offered his arm. 'Personally, Mrs Wilson, I'd say you had your feet firmly on the ground.'

'Flattery will get you nowhere with me, Mr Altham,' she responded gamely. She must learn to stop worrying about the messes other people made for themselves.

'I meant metaphorically speaking.' They paused under a street-lamp, watching the others cross the road and disappear into the Falcon. 'You carry on with your petition, steady as you go. It'll pay off in the long run.'

'I hope you're right.' They walked slowly across the square. 'You don't think it's all getting out of hand, do you, Mr Altham?'

'I'll keep an eye on it,' he promised. 'Publicity is a double-edged weapon and we must be absolutely sure of our ground.'

Altham was someone to rely on and Dot was glad of his steady arm and reassuring voice. On the drive home, she told him about poor Lilian, and how the quarry hung over her head like a double death sentence.

CHAPTER TWENTY EIGHT

'Laura, what's this?' Gerald strode into an eight hundred a few days later, waving a batch of forms.

'They look like the night time call-out claim forms to me, Gerald.'

'The point is, what are they doing here? They should have gone off at the month-end, you know that.'

'Yes, I'm sorry. I haven't had time to fill mine in yet.' She would not react, she told herself.

'And meanwhile we all have to twiddle our thumbs? Sheila can't put them through until they're all done.' He gave them to her with bad grace and began the meeting, sifting through mail on his desk as he talked. 'Philip, the psycho-geriatric unit at Wingate is full. We'll have to find an alternative for Joe Henderson. Alzheimer's is ten a penny, they don't want to know. Laura, you were on duty last Sunday?'

She nodded slowly, ready for trouble.

'What's this entry here? Something about stitches to a cut chin?'

She leaned forward. 'Yes. There was a woman walker who had an accident up Black Gill. Her friend brought her in here. All it needed was a couple of quick stitches.'

'But we don't do them any more.'

'Not as a rule. But she had no transport to get over to Wingate and there was nothing else happening here at the time.'

'We can't claim for it.' He unhooked his glasses and stared in her direction. 'You know that better than anyone.'

'But Gerald, what was I supposed to do? Send her off with her chin pouring blood to hitch a lift? It was Sunday, remember. No buses.'

'I think I've got the answer for Joe Henderson.' Philip looked up from consulting a file on Gerald's desk. He put his finger against a name and telephone number. 'It won't be as handy for his family to visit, but beggars can't be choosers.' He waited for Gerald's response. 'Shall I go ahead?'

Laura breathed again. This was more than she was prepared to take. Ever since the row over Aimee, Gerald had picked her up on the least thing. It was time for a showdown.

So, during a mid-morning lull, she sought him out. 'Wish me luck,' she whispered to Sheila, smoothing her skirt and straightening up as she knocked at his door.

'Come.' He glanced up and assumed a breezy air. 'I've only got five minutes before I have to dash. Make it snappy, would you?'

'This is important.' She went to look out of the window, more nervous than she'd expected. In an odd way, she still wanted to spare his feelings. A man, she thought, would have gone in guns blazing.

'Gerald, there's been a whole series of little things bugging you lately. Unless we have a talk, they're going to build into a serious problem.'

'Not for me,' he assured her. 'As far as I'm concerned, they're small irritations, part of the daily ebb and flow. I take it you mean the non-referral to Casualty? Don't give it a second thought.'

'If it was nothing, then why haul me over the coals in front of the others?'

'If something needs to be said, I'll say it. You shouldn't be so thin-skinned.'

He'd turned it around and she was in danger of losing the initiative. 'Well, I expect that to work both ways.'

He looked up more sharply. 'Meaning?'

'I expect to put my point of view and have it taken seriously. Look, Gerald, I don't mind a decent discussion about whether or not we should bend the rules occasionally to help out a particular patient. But I do object to being ticked off like a schoolgirl.'

'I think you're blowing this out of all proportion.'

'No, this is something you've deliberately set out to do to me ever since you walked in on my consultation with Aimee.'

'Now you're being ridiculous.' He snapped a file shut and stood up, looking at his watch.

'That's what all this is about, isn't it? You think I was wrong to treat her without bringing you in.'

'No link whatsoever. Now, if you don't mind –'

'But I do. I mind very much how we work together. What I want to know is what you think I should have done.' She stood by the door, determined not to let it drop.

'You're in my way.'

'I know. I need an answer.'

He leaned back against his desk, folding his arms. 'You talk about bending rules to help a patient. But you fall back on a rule when it suits you.'

'Which rule?'

'Confidentiality. You make it your excuse for not involving me in Aimee's case. But what about the people behind the rule? I'm her father, for God's sake.'

'But it was up to her to discuss it with you.'

'Anorexics don't discuss things, you know that. It's the nature of the illness; dishonesty, deception.'

'That's a bit hard.'

'All right, then, secrecy. Anorexics keep secrets.'

'So, if you knew she was ill and you also knew she would try to keep it a secret, why didn't you come to me to talk about it?' This was what Janet had done, after all.

He paused. 'Because I don't mix personal problems with my professional life. Never have.'

'Now *you* want it both ways.' She turned away in exasperation. 'You want me to overcome my professional scruples and tell you about your daughter's condition, while you keep your own life in nice safe compartments. That's hardly fair.'

'OK, I didn't want to talk about it. Maybe I should have, maybe things wouldn't have got into this mess.' Hurriedly he began to stuff his file into his briefcase.

She caught the altered tone. 'How much of a mess?'

He cleared his throat. 'Aimee will end up in hospital before Easter, whether she likes it or not. There isn't a thing we can do.'

'Gerald, I'm sorry.' She went up to him and touched his shoulder.

His head was bowed, his voice breaking. 'You know, it's the most excruciating thing to watch your child slowly destroy herself, knowing in some way she's doing it to get back at you. She's angry with me, Laura. I see it in her face every day. She hates me.'

'She loves you. She needs you to notice.'

He slumped into his chair and put a hand over his eyes.

Laura fought against the pity she felt. 'Listen, Aimee's a girl of extreme reactions, deep sensitivity. Other kids cope with life's pressures and injustices, but Aimee takes them all on board. Look at the work she's doing to save Black Gill. She doesn't do things by halves.'

'She never has. Janet always said she threw the most spectacular tantrums she'd ever seen. Later on, when she could read, she would disappear for hours. We'd find her in the garden shed, curled up with a book. She'd forgotten the time. Not like Nick. He was more organised.'

'More like you?'

Gerald pressed his forehead with his fingertips, then looked up. 'She wants to join this sit-in. Janet's worried to death about it. We don't think she's strong enough.'

'I think you should let her do it. She's put her heart and soul into it.'

'We probably couldn't stop her if we wanted to.' He caught himself out. 'Don't be so negative, eh? What she needs is actual encouragement.'

'If you can bear it.'

'With my old fogey views? But what about us, where do we go now?' He looked at her.

'We press on.'

'The air's cleared?' He got up to leave once more. 'Can I just admit something to you in complete confidence?'

She nodded warily. What now? She and Gerald had been through enough revelations for one morning. The buzzer on his desk sounded.

He picked up the phone. 'Yes, Sheila, she's still here. Hang on a second.' Handing it to her, he shrugged. 'Another time.'

Relieved, she took the phone.

'There's a call from the Hall. They need someone out to Maisie right away. It's Christopher making the call this time. It sounds urgent.'

She was on her way, stepping from one crisis to the next, wondering when Christopher had got back from Italy, and whether it had anything to do with the inquiry, which dragged on from week to week, gathering information, weighing the pros and cons.

Matthew came down the steps to meet her. He kissed her quickly and led her upstairs.

'Not a migraine this time?' She unbuttoned her coat as they hurried along.

'No. I got back from York to find that Christopher had called you out. He's with her now. She's had a fall, apparently.'

'Whereabouts?'

'At the foot of the stairs. As far as we can tell, there's nothing broken. But she's very vague, doesn't seem to remember how she got there.' He opened the bedroom door and waited for Laura to go in before him.

She walked towards the bed, putting her bag down at the foot. Christopher moved his chair to one side to let her through. 'Maisie?' She tried to rouse her. 'Has she come round since she fell?'

'Not completely.'

She watched Maisie's shallow breaths, her eyelids fluttering with restless movement in that half-waking state between dream and reality. 'Come on, wake up. What have you done to yourself?'

'Laura?' She opened her eyes.

'We'll leave you to it,' Matthew volunteered. He led the way. 'Give us a shout if you need anything.'

With enormous, dark eyes, Maisie watched them leave the room. Her long grey hair had fallen loose over one shoulder. 'I am such a fool,' she sighed. She made an effort to sit up. 'I've never done anything like this before.'

Helping her, Laura noticed extensive bruising down her right arm, from elbow to wrist. There was another slight injury high on her cheek, where the skin was scraped but not broken. She made her comfortable, then checked her pulse. 'Now move your fingers for me, Maisie. One by one. That's right. Did you bruise yourself anywhere else? On your leg, or your hip?'

'I don't remember.'

'Let's take a look.' Carefully Laura folded back the duvet. Maisie was still dressed in her skirt and blouse and was shaking slightly. 'Wiggle your toes; that's it.' Gently she replaced the cover. 'And you've absolutely no idea how it happened?'

'I had a blackout.' She turned her head away.

Laura reached for her stethoscope. 'I want to listen to your chest. That's fine. The memory loss is probably connected with slight concussion. My guess is that you tripped and fell down a couple of steps, banged your arm, hit your head.'

'Yes, that must be it.' Maisie sounded relieved.

'No bones broken, though, and you were lucky that Christopher was around.'

'No.' Maisie was adamant. 'No, Christopher was out.'

'But he rang the surgery.'

'I'm sure I was alone when I fell.' The confusion seemed to agitate her.

'It doesn't matter. The good thing was that you didn't lie there for long. And there's no serious damage. You'll probably be a bit stiff for a few days.' One last thought occurred to her. 'You don't have any headache or blurred vision, do you?'

'No.' Maisie grew subdued, but not calm.

'You can see perfectly well?'

'Yes.'

'And nothing else is worrying you?'

The questions set off a chain reaction. Sympathy produced tears which glistened at the corners of her eyes. She sighed and turned her head away again.

Laura began to suspect this wasn't a straightforward fall. Certain things didn't fit. There were no marks on her legs and hips and the position of the bruises on her arm suggested something had hit her from above. Then there was her patchy memory recall.

'We need to keep an eye on you for a couple of days,' she continued. 'You must take it easy. I'm going to go and talk with Matthew and Christopher. Are you OK now?'

'You won't tell anyone how silly I've been.'

'Not a soul.'

'I don't usually cry.' Maisie reached for a tissue. 'Don't tell Christopher. He likes me to be strong.' She dabbed at her eyes and blew her nose.

'Don't be too hard on yourself. You've had a bad shock.'

Maisie held out her hand for Laura to grasp. 'You're very kind. Kinder than I deserve.'

'Nonsense.' She eased her onto the pillow. 'Sleep. I'll call by and see you tomorrow.' Sliding her hand free, she collected her bag and left the room.

Her main impression, as she looked back at the big bed, the drapes and gold-framed paintings, was one of isolation. Something had happened that had cut Maisie off; something that she didn't want to talk about. Puzzled, she went to look for Matthew.

There was no one in the lounge or kitchen, but a back door stood open, and she went through it into a corner of the stable yard. She could hear raised voices at the far end, where a trailer stood hitched to Matthew's Land Rover.

'It's a bloody mess, isn't it?' Christopher was in hectoring mood. 'You mean you haven't sorted out proper access to the kids yet? Isn't that what you pay solicitors for?'

Laura couldn't hear Matthew's reply. She hesitated in the yard.

'Listen, mate,' he continued. 'There's nothing amicable about divorce. You have to fight your corner. Mother might fall for Abigail's line, but I was never fooled. I fully expected her to take you to the cleaners.'

He sounded drunk. A door banged and she saw Matthew emerge from the empty stable and fling open the Land Rover door. He jumped in without seeing her, edged it forward, jammed on the brake, then jumped down again, ready to start loading logs from the yard into the trailer. They landed in the metal container with loud thuds.

Christopher came and leaned against the door. 'Mother was upset,' he said casually, arms folded, watching the logs fly.

'She's not the only one.'

'You know why, don't you?'

More logs, more angry silence.

'She was looking forward to spending some time with the kids. They are her grandchildren, after all.'

Matthew grunted with the effort of stooping to fling the dry logs onto the trailer. Bark flaked off, the dust made him cough. 'Then she should know better than to stir things up between me and Abigail.'

'I expect it's because she disapproves of Laura.'

She took another step forward. But the row careered on, out of control.

'Anyway, what's the woman playing at, going out with you if she has a bee in her bonnet about the quarry?'

Matthew stopped work. He ran his forearm across his brow, jutting his chin and narrowing his eyes. 'It's not a game, you know.'

'Bunch of romantics.' Christopher kicked one heel against the door. 'Why can't you get someone else to do the logs? And while we're at it, I don't think going out with Laura is the best move you could have made either.'

Matthew swore and pushed past him.

'It's beginning to give Mother second thoughts. I worked hard to push her into putting the land up for sale. Now I come back and find her having doubts. That's down to you, Matthew, and your lady friend.'

Again Matthew swore.

Christopher pushed himself clear of the door and came face to face with Matthew. 'You'd better bloody listen to this, little brother. Maisie needs you screwing around with Laura Grant like she needs a hole in the head!'

Matthew stood his ground, teeth clenched. 'You don't give a stuff, do you? You see pure profit, pound signs, and never mind that they'll blow the whole place sky-high.'

'It isn't bloody Hiroshima.' Christopher took a step back and injected irony into his tone. 'It's not lives we're counting. It's stone. Dead, ugly bits of stone. That's all.'

'Not according to the people round here, it's not.'

'Oh, don't go on about the beauty of the landscape. What is it, when it comes down to it? A useless, hulking great rock that we can't farm, we can't build on, nothing. Frontier comes along and offers us the ideal solution to Maisie's financial problems. Sure I said go ahead, snap their hands off. We'd be crazy not to.'

'Even though Dad wouldn't have wanted it?'

'Spare me,' Christopher groaned and turned his back, then felt himself swung round as Matthew grabbed hold of him and hurled him against the trailer. He put up his arms to shield himself from the punches, then he kicked out.

Laura ran across the yard. The sound of the fight turned her stomach, her hand went to her mouth at the sight of them both, as they groaned and heaved punches into each other without knowing she was there.

'For God's sake, stop!'

Her voice halted them in their tracks. Matthew stepped sideways to hang onto the trailer. He dragged air into his lungs, folding his arms across his bruised ribs.

Christopher staggered out towards the door. 'Get out of here. Go on!' He too fought for breath.

Matthew pulled himself upright, shoulders heaving. He walked towards her. 'Let's both get out,' he said. 'I've had enough.'

He pulled her into the Land Rover, started the engine and swung

CHAPTER TWENTY NINE

It was to her landlady that Laura eventually turned for advice. Dot said it would take time for the brothers to make up their quarrel. 'A lot's been said that shouldn't have been said. You'll have to wait and see.'

Once he'd calmed down, Matthew had agreed to go back to the Hall to make sure that Maisie was all right, and to collect a few possessions. 'He's staying with friends in Wingate for the time being,' Laura told her.

'It'll give them both a chance to cool off.' Methodically Dot went through a box full of Valerie's old Girl Guide stuff, looking for useful items for the sit-in. She found a camping stove, some plastic mugs and plates. 'Does this mean Christopher will have to be on the spot to look after his mother?'

'Mm.' Laura took the plates and washed them for her. 'She's back on her feet, but still a bit weak. I dropped in earlier today.' It was three days since her fall and Maisie was insisting, unconvincingly, that she was fully recovered. She hadn't said a word about Matthew, and there was no sign of Christopher, though his car was in the yard.

'And how's Matthew coping?'

'In one way he's glad it's out in the open. He doesn't have to pretend to be in favour of the quarry.'

'But he feels awful about letting his mother down, I expect?'

'Right. When he calls the Hall, Maisie won't even speak to him. She just puts the phone down.'

'That's time again, you see.' Dot began to pack a box for the protestors; camping equipment, matches, torch. 'Time will either make her come to her senses or it won't. One thing I am sure of, though. She has the solution in her own hands if she wants to use it.'

'There.' Laura finished the drying-up. 'Shall I run this stuff over to the Gill for you?'

'That'd be lovely. I promised it by teatime. What's the weather doing now?'

'It's fine. It'll probably be wet underfoot though.'

'I hope they've got their long-johns.'

'And plenty of pullovers.' Laura lifted the box. 'How many tents will there be?'

'There's room for about six around the Foss.' The idea was to run shifts of about a dozen people, willing to take it in turn to sleep out. 'I'm in charge of the food. Juliet's providing extra blankets and pillows. Everyone's doing their bit.' She followed Laura down the path.

'Rather them than me.' Laura pulled her jacket collar up under her chin.

'I suppose there's no backing off now?' Dot asked.

'Not once the sit-in gets underway. We'd look pretty silly if they gave up after a couple of days because they missed their warm beds.'

Dot waved her off down the hill, then went inside to answer the phone. It was Tom Elliot to tell them what to expect once they got themselves over to Joan's Foss. 'It's all coming good,' he exclaimed. 'We timed it right for the local TV news boys, radio, the lot. Get over here quick.'

It was too late to flag Laura down, so Dot put on her coat and hurried down on foot, getting only as far as the town square before she stopped to take stock of exactly what was going on.

The media teams had gathered there; the high vans, the clusters of journalists and cameramen in brightly coloured padded jackets. She noted the effort and expense that went into a sixty-second news item and tried to convince herself of the old saying that any publicity was good publicity.

Dot weighed up their chances for the hundredth time, then braved the *mêlée* in the square. 'The traffic's bad,' she warned the Maskells. They parked their car and joined her in the walk to the Gill. At Abbey Grange they met up with Kit Braithwaite and a frail-looking Lilian and, amongst a band of regulars from the Falcon, there was Brian Lawson with Mary Mercer.

'Look at that.' Brian pointed out the TV lights and camera crews who had staked out the entrance to Black Gill.

'I wish we could have done without this nonsense,' Dot muttered to Juliet.

'Don't you think it's exciting?'

Journalists swarmed everywhere. Two policemen tried to cordon off private property to either side of the footpath. 'Flipping circus.' She stalked past the cameras.

She was evidently in a minority, however. Lights flashed, the crowd thickened, excitement rose as the newsmen caught sight of Aimee Scott and her group of noisy young protestors – leather-clad, braided and booted, with their placards and chants.

'Isn't that Nina?' Philip asked Brian as the teenagers advanced.

'She's a recent convert,' he admitted.

Everyone stepped aside to let them pass close to the mob of cameramen.

'To be honest, Alison thinks she's got a crush on Tom Elliot and that's why she's suddenly come over all fanatical. Hands Off Our Land.'

Dot spotted Tom standing in the thick of the bunch of journalists, enjoying every moment. Aimee marched by him at the head of her team of demonstrators, her black hair tucked under a small cap, her pale face set at a defiant angle.

'Save The Scar,' Mary added. 'You should hear them at school; they don't talk about anything else.'

'I only hope they stay on the right side of the law.' Lilian sidled close to Dot.

At the point where they would have to break into single file to climb the Gill, the teenagers drew to a halt. They spread across the footpath and set up a new chant.

'What don't we want?'

'The quarry.'

'Where don't we want it?'

'Here!'

They held up their placards and shouted.

'Fresh Air Is Our Right,' Dot read, and, 'Leave The Land Alone.'

More police arrived, driving fast across the field. Half a dozen men stepped from the cars and made their way towards the noisy protestors. Cameras flashed again.

'Stand back. Keep to the path.' Their orders punctuated the steady chants.

'Stop the Slurry. Stop the Sludge.'

Microphone heads bobbed and swooped over the crowd as the policemen made a human chain to force the protestors onto the path.

'Oh, dear,' Lilian sighed.

One protestor thrust a placard in a policeman's face. The policeman shoved him off. Aimee turned on the man, screaming at him until she too was pushed back. Infuriated, she kicked out. The scene attracted cameras like a magnet.

'Wait here.' Before they could stop her, Mary had slipped away and pushed towards the sixth formers. Some of them saw her and let her through. She grabbed hold of Aimee. 'You said no violence!'

Aimee spun round. 'No, you said no violence. I never did.' She struggled as Mary pulled her roughly into line. 'Let go of me!'

From a distance, Dot summed things up. 'I know what I'd like to do to that little madam, showing us up like that.'

'Come on, Kit.' Lilian shook her head wearily. 'I've seen all I want to see.' Slowly she turned her back on the protest and went home.

On the news they said that feelings at the sit-in were running high. They showed the scuffle with the police, of course, then an interview with Luke Altham on behalf of the campaign.

The committee had gathered around the television in Church House to judge the impact of the day. There was unease over the demonstration, but when Luke came on camera, they murmured their approval.

He quoted statistics about the amount of rock which would have to be trucked out of the dale each day and the pollution which was to be pumped into the River Raven from the quarry works.

They showed Simon Warboys admitting that Joan's Foss would have to be destroyed, but there would be a new right of way created beside another fast-running stream to the east. All the quarried land would in time be landscaped.

'Landscaped!' Dot spoke above the mutterings in the room. 'Did you ever hear owt so daft? What do they want with landscaping Ravenscar? Isn't it landscaped enough already?'

Then Luke reappeared beside the interviewer. 'Frontier promises land restoration. Our group wants land conservation. The loss of Ravenscar can't be calculated on any spread sheet. We want people to challenge the notion that the land beneath our feet can be stolen from us and turned into profit.'

Everyone clapped. 'Let them put that in their pipe and smoke it,' Dot said.

'They won't get it through now.' Juliet was excited by what they had achieved.

'Well done, Tom.' Marsden Barraclough shook his hand. 'I said it was a risk, but it seems to have paid off.'

'It's only the beginning,' he promised.

'This talk is all well and good.' Dot scraped her chair as she got to her feet. 'But isn't there anything we can do to gee up their decision?'

'No, just pressure and more pressure, I'm afraid,' Luke told her. 'We should expect to see their preliminary findings by the end of May.'

The news threw a dampener on proceedings. As they went their separate ways and Dot joined Laura for a lift home, she explained her frustration. 'Eight weeks is a long time when you think of Lilian.'

'I know.' Laura drove slowly through the village. The TV vans were gone, all was quiet. 'Did you hear her say that she's agreed to get someone in to help her run the garden centre?'

Dot saw this as a significant admission by Lilian that she could no longer cope. 'How long has she got, Laura?'

Laura looked across at Dot. 'I don't know.'

'Will she see the May blossom?'

'No,' she said softly, as the wipers whirred back and forth. 'I don't think she will.'

Dot's heart ached as they pulled up outside Town Head. As usual she tried to hide her feelings, but her expression must have let her down.

Laura touched her arm as they stood on the path outside the house. 'I know; there's nothing fair about it, is there?'

'What's fair got to do with it?' She patted Laura's hand. 'Life's never fair. I knew that long since.' She tried to smile. 'You're a lovely girl, you know that?'

The smile she had back was worth a thousand words. Dot didn't know what she'd do without Laura, to help with the quarry, with Lilian, and poor Tot when he was on his last legs. 'And kind with it,' she added. 'Lord knows what we did to deserve you.'

CHAPTER THIRTY

By late March the cold winds and night frosts had begun to give way to bright, light spring days. As Philip drove out on calls he saw farmers ploughing their fields and taking lambs to graze on the hillsides. In the villages, people emerged from their stone winter shells to dig their gardens.

This year, however, he wasn't filled with the joys of spring. His affair with Mary continued, a series of highs linked by long spells of doubt. He questioned himself constantly, wondering what had driven him to her in the first place; not unhappiness with his marriage, not boredom. He and Juliet still made a good team, still had interests and attitudes in common, and a lot jointly invested in the welfare and happiness of their three sons.

He liked his job, his home. There had been nothing to account for the sudden impulse to fling it all overboard. Except Mary. Every time he set eyes on her he fell under her spell. Her voice, deep and dramatic, often sorrowful these days, worked its magic, drugging his reason, undermining his willpower. Her personality, intuitive and unabashed, held him fast, and her body awoke every nerve ending and pulled him back even when his doubts were strongest, his guilt most profound.

He'd finished his calls and was back at the medical centre in time for evening surgery when he crossed swords with Gerald.

'This subdural haematoma –' Gerald made his usual entrance while Philip was in the middle of trying to sort out yet another admission to a geriatric unit.

'*Suspected* haematoma.' He put the phone down abruptly. The patient was a fourteen-year-old girl who'd sustained a head injury playing hockey at school that morning. When she was brought into the centre, Philip suspected a possible blood clot. He'd referred her immediately.

'This haematoma. Why the delay?'

'There was no delay.'

'It says here the incident happened at ten. She was referred at one.'

'That's right.' Another bad day for Gerald, he told himself. These days he seemed to have taken Laura's place as chief whipping-boy.

'Well?' He scratched his head with the end of his pen. 'A patient can die in circumstances like that. I would have taken prompter action myself.'

'Read the form, Gerald. The fact is, the girl told her teacher she was fine at first. She played on until the end of the lesson. She was back in the classroom before she began to feel any symptoms. By the time they brought her in, she was already in a poor state.'

'Vomiting? Stiff neck?'

Philip finally ran out of patience. 'Leave it alone, will you?'

'I don't want them clobbering us for negligence. I've got enough on my plate.'

'And I've got a surgery to run.' He glared at him until Gerald backed out of the room.

Philip plunged into his list of patients, hoping to get through quickly and head home. Neither he nor Gerald had come out well. He kicked himself for making no allowances for his partner's problems at home, and wondered whether his state of mind had contributed to the row. Then Brian and Alison Lawson appeared at the head of his list and he deliberately slowed his pace. He would give them some time, see if here at least he could make progress.

'Good to see you.' He waited for them to sit down. Alison still looked bright and trim, Brian less stressed than when he'd come in just before Christmas.

'It was good of you to fit us in at the last minute.' Alison kicked off.

'Thank Sheila for that.'

'Yes, well we've been thinking we'd like to go ahead and see that specialist. We've talked things through and we both agree about wanting a baby.' She smiled broadly.

Philip checked with Brian.

'Whatever keeps her happy.'

'Brian!'

'No, only joking. What she says is right. We both want to start a family. I was just a bit wary before. When you've had a kid and then

225

you lose them because your marriage breaks up, you feel lousy. I didn't want to go through that again.'

'So you're both sure?'

'We're hoping it's something simple that the specialist can put right straight away.' Alison was upbeat, thinking ahead. 'And if we have to go on a waiting-list, well the sooner the better.'

'That sister of yours did a good job on you.' Philip typed onto their file.

'Susie? Yes. She's expecting again.'

'Four now, is it?'

'Doesn't it make you sick?'

'How about you, Brian? How did you get on with those anti-depressants?'

'They saw me through. I don't want any more, though. I reckon I'm better off without them.'

'That's fine. Things are looking up. I'll write to Professor Spillars in York, and you should get a letter giving you an appointment. Let's hope it won't be too long.'

'We'd like one more little bit of advice,' Brian began after a reminder from Alison. 'Last time we were here we mentioned Nina.'

'That's right. You didn't think she'd take to the idea of you and Alison starting a family.'

'As it happens, we talked to her and she doesn't seem to give a damn. But now we – well, me really – I'm worried she's too involved in this sit-in. When she's up here she spends every minute up at the Foss with Aimee Scott. I don't mind Aimee, don't get me wrong, but she's a bit intense about the whole business. I'd like Nina to keep it a bit more in proportion.'

Philip heard him out. 'I don't really see it's anything to worry about.'

'You don't think Aimee could be a bad influence?'

'In what way exactly?'

'I mean, I don't want Nina catching a bad case of hero-worship from her. Before we know it, she'll be refusing to go home and I'll have her mother on my back again.'

'Hero-worship?'

'Yes, Aimee and Tom Elliot. I mentioned it, remember? She worships the ground he treads on. It's a bit dangerous at that age, don't you think?'

'It can be. On the other hand, I don't see what you can do.'

'That's what I told him.' Alison nodded firmly. 'I said just be thankful it's not some pimply pop-star. She'd be spending a fortune on CDs and concert tickets.'

'I just don't want her getting into trouble.'

Philip gave it some thought. 'I'll tell you what, if I notice her getting involved in anything she shouldn't, I'll let you know.'

They went off satisfied. But it had left Philip with another problem. If Aimee really did admire Tom as much as they said, he could see her going to great lengths to attract his attention. Should he warn Gerald? With their own recent differences hanging over them, he decided to leave it.

He discussed it with Juliet later and she thought so too.

'You know Gerald, he hates you to interfere in family problems. And we've no idea how things are between him and Aimee right now.'

They sat quietly over their evening meal in their dining-room overlooking the river.

'We don't know how serious this crush is,' Philip pointed out.

'With Aimee it'll be life or death. It always is.'

'Literally, if the anorexia goes much further.'

'Don't.' Juliet shuddered.

'Are you OK?' He took his attention off the grey water sliding over the smooth boulders.

'I'm fine. There's a letter from Jim on the mantelpiece, did you see?' She got up to clear the plates. 'He's got a new girlfriend.'

'Never mind Jim's new girlfriend.' He made her put down the plates. 'I want to hear about your day. What have you been up to?' She seemed lonely in the big, empty house.

'The usual. Work this morning.' She lifted his hands from around her waist. 'Do you have to go out tonight?'

'Afraid so. Seminar in Wingate.' In fact, he'd arranged to see Mary.

'So you'll be back late?'

'Not too late.' He wondered how good a liar he was.

'Well anyway, I think I'll go to badminton.' Turning away, she went on clearing the table. 'Jim would like to bring Kathryn home at Easter.'

'Kathryn?'

'His girlfriend. She sounds like a nice girl.'

He picked up the letter from the fireplace and wandered off with it, his heart in turmoil. For a second he imagined that Juliet knew about him and Mary. There was something in her eyes when he said he had to go out, as if she knew exactly where and who with.

He took a deep breath, steadied himself and changed to go out, calling to Juliet from the hall, anxious to avoid seeing her, knowing that he wouldn't be able to meet her gaze. He was almost running as he made for the car. He slammed it into gear and drove away as fast as he could.

For his visits to Mary he had a parking place behind the bakery, where no one could see the car from the main street. He ran up the steps to her flat.

In his mind he raced through all the reasons why they should break off; how the hurt outweighed the delights, guilt over Juliet, jealousy when he saw Mary talk to another man. But he turned his key in the lock to find her waiting and pretending that she wasn't as she looked up from her book as though she'd forgotten about him. He loved her.

'Hi.' She stood up, stretched and came to put her arms around his neck.

'Were you working?'

'No, just playing at it. You're hot. What have you been doing?' She put her hand on his chest and felt his heart thump.

'I've been running.'

'Who from?' She swayed away, suddenly ironic.

'Not from anyone,' he lied again. 'I was running to see you.'

'Well, here I am.' She moved in closer.

'What shall we do?'

'Let me see, there's so much choice. How about a quiet evening in?'

'Suits me.'

They sat on the sofa, Mary's legs across his lap, his arms around her waist. 'You've had a bad day?'

'You can tell?'

'It's written all over your face. What is it?'

Philip stroked her bare legs and ankles. 'I had a bit of a row with Gerald, that's all. Nothing really.'

'Sure? You're not a very good liar, you know.' She spoke softly, wryly. 'I reckon a five year old could suss you any day.'

'Mary, do you love me?'

'If you stop fiddling with my legs and look me in the eye, I might tell you.'

'No, seriously?'

'I love you, Philip. What's this about?'

'Do I make you happy?'

'Some of the time.'

'When do I make you unhappy?' He drew her towards him.

'When you're not here. Why?'

'I'm trying to understand. Why does someone as lovely and talented as you get stuck with me?'

'Boring old GP, ultra-respectable, never puts a foot wrong?'

'Right.'

'I ask myself that question all the time. Mary, I say, go out and find someone unattached. Where's your dignity, woman? Sitting waiting by the phone isn't where it's at. Hiding in a corner, never on show, it's bad for the ego.'

'Don't,' he whispered. 'Am I doing this to you?'

'There you go, thinking you're the only one. I didn't say you were doing this to me. I'm doing the choosing here as well, remember.' She thought for a bit. 'I knew what I was letting myself in for.'

'I don't want to hurt you.'

She sat up, suddenly intense. 'Philip, that's a killer. "I don't want to hurt you" is the exit line in B movies. Meaning, things are getting too tough. Woman breaks down, pleads with him to stay. He leaves anyway.' She searched his face for a response. 'You're a kind man, Philip, and decent. I can trust you. For me, that's rare.'

'I don't feel kind.' He held her close again. 'I feel like an absolute shit.'

'A kind man with a conscience. What on earth are you doing with me, Philip Maskell?'

'I don't know. I love you.'

But he saw his decency as a kind of weakness. He had no courage. When he wiped away her tears and kissed her, he was only selfish, falling deeper into deception, taking whatever joy he could.

CHAPTER THIRTY ONE

Next morning, as they met for the eight hundred, Sheila took a phone call from the Grange. Kit had arrived to find Lilian breathless and 'rambling', as he put it. He thought Dr Grant should come over right away.

Laura had been expecting this sort of crisis for some time. She excused herself from the meeting and drove quickly to the Abbey. Kit came to the door of the Grange to greet her, stiff and stuttering with shock. 'I never saw her like this before.'

She remembered that Kit Braithwaite had lost his own wife to the disease; he must be reliving some terrible scenes. 'Let's see what we can do.' She put a hand on his arm and led him inside. 'Where is she?'

'Upstairs in bed. That's when I first knew summat was up. She's not one to lie in, you see.' He trudged up the narrow stairs ahead of her.

'No.' Laura went into the bedroom. Lilian lay in her high bed, unaware of her surroundings. Her eyes, blank and dull, were open, her lined face struggling to suck in shallow breaths. The marked deterioration signified a toxic confusion that often set in when a patient needed a high dosage of morphine to manage the pain. Laura found that Lilian had a fever, plus a degree of heart failure which needed immediate treatment with both intravenous and intramuscular drugs. 'I think she'll be all right shortly,' she told Kit. 'You did the right thing. Now let her sleep. When she wakes up, she should be more or less her old self.'

He nodded, his hand trembling as he held onto the end of the bed.

'I'll come back this afternoon to see how she is. In the meantime, if she wakes and says she wants to get up, that's fine. She may need a blood transfusion to counteract probable anaemia, but we'll see.'

Quietly she cleared away her syringes and packed her bag. By now Lilian was sleeping peacefully.

'She were rambling, see.' Kit led the way downstairs. 'She kept calling me Walter. She weren't half mad at me and all. Called me all the names under the sun because I'd forgotten to pot on some seedlings or other. It took the wind out of my sails, I can tell you.'

Laura stayed a while to listen. She knew it was often as difficult for the relatives as for the patients themselves. They saw their loved ones slipping away and still hoped for a miracle.

The old man talked on. 'It were only yesterday she were out in the greenhouse, right as rain. She was going on about that lot up at Black Gill. She's not keen on them camping out, she says they'll leave a right mess.'

Laura nodded. The sit-in had gone from strength to strength now that the weather had taken a turn for the better. The protestors' small circle of ramshackle tents at the bottom of the Gill proved an ideal spot. The dozen, including Aimee, who were living rough were determined to stick it out until the end of May, when the first report would be issued. 'I think most people have mixed feelings about the sit-in,' she said, taking the proffered cup of tea from Kit.

'According to Lilian, they've no idea of how to behave in the country. And they've no – what d'you call 'em – facilities and such like.' Kit's anxiety was easing. 'You say she'll soon be up and about?'

'Probably. But you do realise she's going to need plenty of help from now on?' She wondered whether he would be able to take on the responsibility and edged towards a practical suggestion. 'It's good that she's got you to keep an eye on her, but why don't I let Dot know that you'd be glad of a bit of help every now and then? Dot only works mornings. I'm sure she could spare some time.'

'Aye, all right then.' He seized the offer with both hands.

'Good. Dot could probably organise a bit of a rota.'

Kit struck a snag. 'Aye, but you know Lilian. She's a bit stubborn, like. She said no to one of them visiting nurses when it was on offer. She'll want to be doing it all, no matter what.'

'And I think she should, for as long as she can. She's an amazing lady, your sister-in-law. But Dot can be standing by just in case. I'll pass the word.' She stood up, ready to move on.

Kit shook her hand. 'Thank you, doctor.' He felt his eyes filling up and turned away.

Laura saw herself out. She noticed the bluebells, their shiny, spiky green leaves, the tight flower heads almost ready to open. The daffodils were already nearly over for this year. Hawthorn sprouted green in the hedgerows, the elder bushes were coming into leaf.

Lilian rallied, as Laura expected, but by now they'd exhausted most available treatments. She discussed further possibilities with Gerald, who suggested a Hickman tube into a main vein to administer drugs directly to the circulatory system. They both knew it was a last-ditch measure.

'Do you think she'll live to see the decision over Black Gill?' Gerald asked the question on everyone's lips. The weeks seemed to crawl by, the entire dale lived on edge, awaiting the inquiry team's verdict.

'It's what keeps her going.' Laura was about to set off for Wingate, to call in on two geriatric admissions, visit her parents, and then meet up in the evening with Matthew. She hovered by the reception desk, grateful for Gerald's help.

He shook his head. 'This is what the Americans call being between a rock and a hard place.'

'How come?'

'Well, if Lilian's struggling on in the hope of getting the right decision from the inquiry, we ought to be glad in one way. It keeps her with us, soldiering on. On the other hand, say the decision goes Maisie's way instead, it'll break Lilian's heart and she'll pass on knowing that her beloved Gill will be torn apart and the Grange smashed to rubble.'

'Exactly.' Laura's position on the quarry hadn't wavered since Luke Altham's rousing statement in front of the cameras.

'But what about Maisie? It would knock her for six. And if you look at it in the cold light of day, how long will Lilian hang on at the Grange, even if she wins the quarry fight?'

Knowing the two elderly women as she did, Laura's sympathies were clear. 'I'm still on Lilian's side,' she said quietly.

'Hmm.' Gerald studied her.

'And don't you hmm me, Gerald Scott!' she laughed. 'Either way, I agree it's hard.'

'And has the errant son returned to the Hall yet?'

'If you mean Matthew, no he hasn't.' She remained tight-lipped about the flat Matthew had found by the park in Wingate. He spent much of his time anxiously negotiating access with Abigail and looking after one or two business interests. She knew he hated to be cut off from the Hall and its land; his land, the cause of all the trouble.

'Isn't it about time they kissed and made up?'

'Easier said than done.'

'How sharper than a serpent's tooth it is to have a thankless child.'

Laura raised an eyebrow. 'I suppose that must be the way Maisie sees it. She won't even talk to Matthew now. And I've a feeling that's the way Christopher prefers it.'

Sheila came out of her small back office and stood, looking from one to the other, concerned about the raised voices.

'You don't think she deserves his support?'

'I don't think so, no.'

'So, you'd desert your parents in their hour of need, would you?'

'That's different. They would never do what Maisie's proposing to do to Ravenscar.'

Sheila stepped forward.

'Hmm.' Gerald took his glasses from his top pocket and swung them to and fro.

'You're doing it again, Gerald, hmming.'

'You two, you're as bad as one another,' Sheila remarked loudly. Philip was also hovering. 'They need a referee in with them when they get talking about that quarry.'

Laura and Gerald broke off.

Philip grinned. 'Where would you place your bets, Sheila?'

'Oh, I never gamble.'

'No, but if you did, where would you put your money? On Gerald or on Laura?' He sifted through some case notes.

'Where would *you*?'

'As far as the quarry goes? I'd put it on Laura,' he said firmly. 'There's none so fanatical as a recent convert. And Laura's only been with us a few months. She's hopelessly in love with the place.'

That evening, Laura went to Wingate General to visit her two patients, then took the opportunity to call in on her ever-welcoming parents. They quizzed her about houses; had she seen one she liked, were prices very high, what effect were the quarry proposals having on property values? Her dad got involved in the minutiae of the plans. He'd saved dozens of cuttings from the Yorkshire papers and watched out for it on the local news. The story had faded from the nationals, pending the inquiry's report, but George Grant followed it closely. He supported Laura's view that the quarry would destroy something that could never be replaced. He was the man to ask about the problem of river pollution, he said. Seeing him get hot under the collar, his wife tried to divert the conversation back to houses, but Laura and her father gave their attention to the main issue of the day.

'I don't know, just like a couple of bookends.' Margaret disapproved of political talk.

'Are we?' Laura smiled.

'Just the same, always getting your teeth into things and refusing to let go.' Deep down, she approved of Laura's efforts on behalf of the dale.

'Laura does right,' her father said. 'I'm proud of her.'

'Let's just hope all the effort's worth it.' She got up to go.

'And you'll let us know when you find something suitable?' her mother reminded her.

'What? Oh, a house. Yes, I'm going looking again this weekend.'

'That's tomorrow.'

'So it is. I'll give you a ring if I find anything I like. I'll probably need your advice.'

'No need to soft-soap us.' Margaret gave her hand a squeeze. 'We'll be handing out the advice whether you like it or not.'

Feeling relaxed, Laura drove into town. She and Matthew intended to go out to eat, and his new flat in Prince Albert Square was a good, central meeting place. She bought two dozen red tulips and took them up to him. 'These will brighten up the room.' She offered them with a kiss. 'Not that it needs brightening up, with a view like this.'

The flat, on the second floor of a grand Victorian house, overlooked acres of green, open space. Trees framed the grassy squares, which were intersected with footpaths, in turn lined with cherry trees just coming into blossom. At the far side of the park was a tall church spire, with more nineteenth-century opulence to either side.

Prince Albert House, with its ironwork balconies and ivy-covered tower, was a local landmark, and the apartments hard to get hold of. Matthew had moved in without fuss, renting the place fully furnished on a short lease.

He went to the kitchen and looked aimlessly for a vase.

'Try the cupboard under the sink,' Laura suggested. She took off her jacket and let down her hair, kicking her shoes off and sinking into a chair.

'Found one!' He ran the tap, looked doubtfully at the tulips, then jammed them into the water. 'That's what I like about you.' He wandered in with the flowers.

'What?'

'Your female logic. You know exactly where another woman would store a flower vase.'

'This is lovely, Matthew.' She leaned against the cushions, taking in the polished table where he placed the vase, the high marble fireplace. Everything was rich and mellow, from the ornate ceiling-rose to the Persian rugs.

He came to the back of her chair and folded his arms along the top of it, his face close to hers. 'It feels good.'

'What does?'

'Having you here.'

For a while they let the silence swim around them.

'How hungry are you?' she whispered.

'Not very.' He moved in close, raising her to her feet. She was amazing, the way she folded her long, slender arms around him.

'Shall we stay in?'

He nodded. 'When do you have to get back?'

'Tomorrow.'

'Sounds perfect.' He kissed her then led her into the bedroom. 'I love making love to you.'

'Tell me why.' She undressed and lay on the bed.

'You're beautiful. And you don't play games.'

She gave herself to Matthew easily and gladly. It was true, she had no inhibitions about her body, but she'd been wary at first of the sexual attraction. Since Tom, she'd learned to dampen her desire.

Tom, she knew, had used sex to bridge the gap between them. They would row; she would be hurt by his insults and go reeling off into a lonely world of wounded self-esteem. They would make love;

235

she would cry with relief that there was still some warmth between them after all.

He would say he was sorry for all the hurt he'd caused; he knew his temper was bad, he said things he didn't mean. She learned to recognise the blinkered, switched-off expression, began to resent the power of the bedroom to draw them back together. In the end, the sex was all wrong for her, but she lacked the courage to say so.

But with Matthew she felt free to express herself. She could be funny and affectionate, not always intense. There was still nothing desperate, nothing to prove. It was hard work that kept his body in good shape, he said. She told him that she liked to look at him. She ran her hands up and down his back, watched his expression unfocus as his desire took over and he loved her urgently, not always tenderly, but aware of her and wanting to carry her along.

To lie in bed with him after they'd made love, one arm across his chest, her head on his shoulder, was an indescribable pleasure. If there was a centre of the universe, she felt she'd arrived at it. Here was where everything came together and had meaning and richness. For a while she would see no point in ever moving, ever striving, ever seeking anything else. Then she would lift herself onto one elbow, suggest some music, a drink, or she would begin to talk. He might want to kiss her back into silence and stillness, but she would move away from him, and life would go on.

To sleep the night with him for the first time felt like heaven.

Next morning, a Saturday, they drove together from Wingate to Hawkshead, conscious of being a couple when they stopped in Merton to scour the estate agents' for more house details for Laura. She found half a dozen places which seemed to have some appeal; older properties in out-of-the-way areas, with what the agents described as magnificent views of Ravenscar.

'Look, if you sit here in this window and crane your head all the way forward, that's Ravenscar over there.' Matthew pointed it out from a third-floor attic.

This was their fourth house. They stood in the bare, musty room, where a poor crow had fallen down the chimney and lay dead in the grate. Outside, the birds' nests swayed dangerously in the bare tips of some ash trees.

'It's certainly remote,' Laura admitted. The lie of the land would mean she would have to drive from here down to Merton, and back up the dale to Hawkshead to reach work; a thirty-five minute journey. Reluctantly she realised it was impractical.

'You wouldn't mind being this far out?' Matthew led the way downstairs and used the agent's key to lock up the empty house. He stared up at the stone gables and the blank windows.

'No, I don't feel as if I would.' Laura looked out over the trees to the hills beyond. 'I think I'd like the freedom.'

He said nothing for a while, then, when they were in the car, driving to their next destination, he said what they'd both been thinking all morning. 'It feels strange.'

'What does?'

He gazed intently at her. 'You looking for a place of your own. I suppose it's too early for us to start trying to find somewhere together?'

If he'd phrased it differently, if he'd swept her along and told her all his hopes and fears, it might have worked. But his diffidence locked into her own doubts. 'Yes, I think it is too soon,' she said sadly.

During the following week, Laura kept a close eye on Lilian. She was glad it was spring, so that her patient could enjoy these warm, sheltered afternoons in the sun after the long, cold winter. Lilian herself seemed to revel in it, content much of the time to sit and watch Kit potter between the rows of hostas and euonymous shrubs, watering, weeding, getting pots ready for sale.

One morning in early May, however, Laura was taken aback to see a new helper at work in a far corner of the garden. The figure was digging over an empty bed that had already been transplanted.

Lilian greeted her with a smile as she walked gingerly down the path towards her. 'I followed doctor's orders, I got myself that help.' She nodded towards the gardener, half hidden by a cluster of apple trees on the lawn.

'Isn't that Aimee Scott?' Laura recognised the jet black hair and skinny figure.

'It is. I took her on just the other day. I got talking to her, see. She happened to say she needed a job. She's got herself into hot water at home, it seems. I said she could earn a bit extra here if she'd set to and do some digging and lifting.' Lilian paused to scrutinise Aimee's technique. 'She's stronger than she looks. Mind you, I'd like to feed her up a bit.'

Laura smiled to herself at Lilian's version of events. 'I hope you're not overpaying her.' They went slowly across the lawn together.

'I pay her the going rate.' No one would pull the wool over her eyes, she implied. 'By the hour. I set her a fair amount of work to get through.'

'Hello, Aimee.' Laura greeted her. 'I didn't expect to see you here.'

'So?' She shoved the fork vehemently into the earth and stood up straight.

'Lilian was just telling me, she's glad of the help.'

Aimee shrugged.

'How's the sit-in going?' Getting information out of Aimee was like pulling teeth.

'Fine.'

'Tom says we should get the council on our side by going to lobby City Hall. He's already recruited a couple of local MPs.'

'Is he here?' For the first time Aimee dropped her guard and sounded eager.

'No, I was talking to him on the phone. He's due up this weekend.'

'Meanwhile, you'd better knuckle down and earn your keep,' Lilian reminded Aimee. She took Laura into the house. 'She's a good girl really. She may look hard but they all do these days. When did young women give up wearing dresses, I'd like to know? I used to watch the group of them going up and down the Gill with bags of food and such like. Never a smile on their faces. Until the other day, she came to the house to ask for drinking water, and I told her to help herself from my kitchen. Then we got to talking about the Gill and she asked me how I was getting along and said she was sorry I was ill, just like that. Took the wind out of my sails. But there's no nonsense about her. She just comes out with things.'

Laura could imagine this meeting of opposites: indomitable, old fashioned Lilian and truculent, up-front Aimee. 'You like her, then?'

'You should see her dig. She puts her back into it. Even Kit has to admit he didn't think she had it in her.' She smiled and eased herself carefully into a chair. 'Those days are well gone for me, worse luck.'

'No more digging?'

'I haven't the strength. Look at me, I'm weak as a kitten.' Lilian sounded cross with herself. 'There's one thing that bothers me about that girl, though. I think she's much too taken with this journalist chap.'

Carefully, Laura disguised her reaction.

'She goes on and on about him. Tom Elliot this, Tom Elliot that.' Lilian bore Laura's silence. 'Well, you're right, it's none of my business, and I know they do things differently these days. But my point is this; she hangs on his every word. If he says this sit-in is a good thing, then she throws herself into it. If he says, lobby City Hall, she'll be there at the front of the queue.'

'You think she's a bit naive?' This hadn't struck Laura before. But Lilian had spotted Aimee's lack of experience beneath the tough image.

'That's the word; naive. She really thinks we're going to win the day.'

'And don't you?' Again, she was surprised.

'I try to keep an open mind, so as not to be too disappointed.' She spoke wistfully.

Laura leaned forward and touched her hand. They talked about her sleeping pattern, and remembering to eat regularly and doing just as much work as she could easily manage.

'Nay, I'll be right,' Lilian sighed. She took Laura outside once more to offer her a choice of plants for her new garden.

'I haven't even found a house yet.'

'Aye well, if you hold your horses and we get the decision we want over the quarry, you might just find the Grange here would suit you?' She looked at Laura, sharp as a robin. 'Nay, Doctor, we'd be daft to think I'll keep on going right through the summer.'

'Let's just see how it goes, Lilian.'

'I've been wanting to mention it for some time. I've got this picture in my head of the old Grange being saved from the bulldozer, standing in all its autumn glory. You've not seen it during back-end, have you? Well, the whole garden lights up with colour; orange, red, yellow chrysanths, red-hot pokers, all brilliant in the sun. It breaks my heart to think of it standing empty.'

'It's my perfect house. I feel honoured, Lilian.' She hesitated, overcome.

'But we'd better not count our chickens, is that what you were going to say? We don't know yet if the quarry will get the go-ahead.'

'No, it wasn't that.'

239

'You don't want to take it on, then? It doesn't have all the mod cons and so on?'

'No, not that either. It's Maisie Aire. She owns the house. I can't see her wanting to rent it out to me, not under any circumstances.'

'You don't mean to say you think she'd turn down your brass?' Lilian was incredulous.

'She would.' She explained the situation between herself, Matthew and Maisie.

Lilian sighed. 'I never knew. I don't bother much with the gossip.'

'You must be the only one in Ravensdale who doesn't.' Laura was touched beyond words by the innocent offer. 'Thank you for thinking of me, Lilian.'

'Nay, I was thinking of myself too.' A long silence developed, then Lilian closed the subject. 'Too many ifs and buts.'

'I'm afraid so.'

'Well, it was just an idea.' She led the way to the gate. 'You can see things fair shooting through now.' She pointed to lily-of-the-valley growing in the shelter of a nearby wall. 'It's a grand time of year.' Unafraid, she looked deep into Laura's eyes. 'But it's a picture in autumn. People say it's past its best, but that's when I love it. Golden, and all the work done for the year.'

CHAPTER THIRTY TWO

They were at dinner at Bridge House: Philip and Juliet, Laura, Matthew, Luke Altham, Aimee, Mary and Tom. It was Friday night, the windows were open onto the river, and a wonderful bank of pink clouds drifted over the sheer white face of Ravenscar.

Once the food had been cleared away, they turned to Tom for the latest news on the campaign. He'd heard that the value of Frontier's shares had been given a sudden boost. 'It seems that someone knows something we don't.'

'Back to the conspiracy theory?' Philip eased back in his chair. Mary sat out of his line of vision, only there because Juliet had pressed her into coming. Conversation during the meal had been stilted; Tom made no secret of his dislike for Matthew, while Philip himself was beginning to be irritated by Tom's dogmatic political correctness.

'Why would shares shoot up in value otherwise? Look, there are two possibilities. One, someone in the inquiry team has leaked a verdict in favour of the quarry. Two, less likely, is that the sale of the land has gone ahead, signed, sealed and delivered.' He glanced at Matthew, challenging him to tell them all he knew.

'I don't think so. Frontier will only pay the high asking price if they get the go-ahead for the quarry. Without planning permission, the land's practically worthless. It wouldn't be in Mother's interests to sell it yet. Everything hangs on the inquiry,' he explained calmly.

'I also heard that your brother was busy buying up shares in Frontier before the price went sky high. Mind you, he probably knows about the pressure from the Ministry of Transport for cheap road-building materials. Nice inside information, wouldn't you say?'

'Yes, and nothing to do with Matthew.' Laura sat between them feeling the temperature rise.

Tom leaned across. 'Blame Laura. She asked me to use my investigative powers, so I did. Turned up with your brother's name as a major shareholder.'

Laura took his hand off her arm. 'What we really have to concentrate on is the environmental damage.'

'And the idea that the whole inquiry is one big sham,' Aimee agreed. 'That's what gets me.'

'It means we have to work even harder. When's the protest at City Hall?' Philip was practical as ever.

'First of May.' Tom traced ridges in the tablecloth with his fork. He turned to Aimee. 'Your little lot will have to be all set up to decamp for the day. Mind you, it would be good to have as many there as possible, Joe Public as well as the fanatics.'

Laura detested his carelessness. She was sure he was behaving badly because of Matthew. Nothing had been said, but he'd acted lately as if he had rights over her, as if he were the injured party.

'We'll be there,' Aimee promised.

'Not me, I'm afraid.' Philip glanced at his pocket diary. 'Fundholders meeting with the health authority.'

'I'll go along if I can,' Mary said quietly.

'And me,' Laura and Matthew both added.

'Tell Dot I can give her a lift if she needs one. And you too, Mary. Should we lay on a coach for people without cars?' Juliet made eager plans.

But Laura sat back, unable to muster enthusiasm about the protest march. She watched Aimee's face come alive at the smallest scrap of attention from Tom. And as the evening wore on, she saw that he encouraged her infatuation; a joke shared at someone else's expense, a whispered comment. Aimee lapped it up.

Then, for a short time, Tom and Aimee disappeared together. The group had split into various rooms; Juliet with Luke and Philip still in the dining room, Matthew with Laura and Mary in the lounge.

'I'm going home,' Mary told them, her face pale and drawn. She hovered by the door.

'I'll give you a lift,' Matthew volunteered.

At first she resisted, then wearily accepted. 'Thanks.' She smiled wanly at Laura. 'Make my excuses, will you?'

Laura followed them to the door and watched the car drive off. She was about to go back inside when she saw two figures caught in the glare of the headlights. It was Tom and Aimee.

They broke apart as the lights illuminated them, but as soon as the car drove off, Tom put his hand on the wall above Aimee's shoulder, trapping her against it. He stooped to kiss her roughly, leaning against her, pressing her against the wall.

Laura stared. Then she turned, went in and slammed the door.

She made for the kitchen and furiously began to tidy dishes for Juliet; anything to take her mind off what she'd seen. Soon she heard the door open and close and caught sight of Aimee grabbing her jacket from the hall stand, pushing Tom off as he tried to move in on her again. He overbalanced and Aimee made a dash for the door, leaving it open as she ran. In righting himself, Tom looked up and caught Laura's eye.

'So?' He stood, elbow resting high against the door frame, blocking her way out.

'I'm not saying a word.'

'No, but you want to. I can see you getting on your high horse, tut-tutting at me. Do I say anything about you and the lord of the manor there?'

She was sick of him, of his dishonesty. She turned to confront him. 'Tom, Aimee is sixteen years old.'

He darted a callous look over his shoulder at the open door. 'Jesus, Laura, I don't need you hassling me.'

'What did you do to her?'

He shrugged. 'She scares easily, that's all. I've been getting the green light from her all evening, then when I do something about it she acts like a little kid.'

'That's because she is. And she's having a hard time at the moment.' If Aimee needed tenderness, she'd chosen the wrong man.

'And how come you're her minder all of a sudden?' He brought his own sense of outrage into play. 'You don't own me. And I didn't ask for your advice.'

She knew it was useless to argue. 'OK.' She backed off.

'No, not OK.' He grabbed her arm. 'You should hear what she calls you. Your own choice of boyfriend isn't up to much, remember. And she thinks you're a stuck-up bitch.'

Years of crumbling marriage reared up again; Tom's self-righteous anger, her going quiet, crying when he hurt her instead of fighting back. 'Let go of me. I don't have to listen to this. Why are you doing it, for God's sake?'

She stopped struggling and he dropped her arm. 'Because I can,' he said coldly. 'Because I know it upsets you.'

This was what she was most afraid of. 'Is that why you came here in the first place, to see how much harm you could do?'

His voice was clear, stripped of emotion. 'Not at first. I came because I wanted to see you, to see how you were. You had a new life. I guess I wanted to see what it was like.'

'And you don't give a damn about the quarry?'

'Course. I never like to lose an argument, you know that.'

'And if you do?' She thought of Dot and Lilian, and all those who were fighting to save the dale.

'The story will be dead in a month in any case.' He shrugged and turned over a page of the newspaper lying on the table.

'You're a user, Tom. You use people . . . You use people and you don't even like them. You've spent too long in the dirt, digging it up.'

'That's not difficult. The dirt's there. It always is.' He stood amongst the debris of the dinner party, surrounded by plates, glasses, bottles.

'Still the cynic, Tom. Still the rebel.' She moved past him. 'Now that you've seen my new life and made it plain what you think of it, would you please go away and leave us all alone?'

Philip walked into the kitchen at the tail-end of their argument. Laura looked ashen. Tom poured himself a drink and strolled out of the room.

'Where's Matthew?' Philip stood, hands in pockets.

'Taking Mary home. She asked me to tell you.'

He nodded and closed the door. 'Don't let Tom upset you, Laura.'

'Don't be nice to me, Philip. I might break down.' She tried to laugh, steadying herself at the table.

'Was he having a go at you about Matthew?'

'Partly, yes.'

Well, we all know Tom's prejudiced against the Aires. He's pretty black and white, isn't he? I'm beginning to think it's true what they say about the extreme ends of the political spectrum meeting up in the middle again. He can't begin to see that Maisie has her reasons for what she's doing.'

'No.' She flicked tears from the corners of her eyes. 'Sorry.'

'How are things between you and Matthew?'

'Good. He's very considerate.'

'Makes a change?'

'Yes. Do you know, I remember something Tom once said. We were in company, a couple of friends round at our place. They said that what it was all about was the art of compromise; the secret of living happily together.' She felt her lips tremble as she remembered Tom sitting there with hooded lids, waiting to pounce.

'And?'

'And Tom said he didn't believe in compromise. He said he'd never compromised in his entire life.'

'Funny,' Philip said. 'I see everything I do as a sort of middle way. Or did, until recently.'

'And now?'

'Just for once I played it a different way.'

'With Mary?'

He nodded.

'And?'

'Chaos. The world's falling apart. I'm falling apart. I want to stay; I want to leave. Juliet's my life; I can't stop thinking about Mary.'

'Philip –'

He shook his head. 'I'm not asking for an answer, Laura. I know this can't go on. Pretty soon this whole thing is going to go smash. Everyone will get hurt.' He walked quickly up and down, his face shadowed with contradictions.

'I can see that.' Being taken into his confidence threw her, so soon after Tom's bludgeoning. 'Mary's my friend, you know.'

'You know her best, Laura. How is she coping?'

'Ask her. You must talk to her.' She interrupted his restless striding. 'I know one thing. Doubt is the worst of all. Being in doubt; I hate it. Wondering what will happen if you do this or this, being convinced that if you do one thing this person will fall to pieces, but if you choose the other way someone else's life will be in ruins. The truth is, it probably won't be.'

'You don't think so?'

'No, it's a kind of arrogance. I'm not saying it's not painful. It hurts like hell when people break up. I remember walking out on Tom finally, just walking out of the door and getting into my car and driving, and thinking what the hell am I going to do now? This second, this minute, for the rest of my life?'

'Nowhere to go?'

'It was the first time I realised what being alone meant. Really alone. I was frightened deep, deep down.'

'How did you get over it?'

'I don't think I did. I got used to it. And now I think I can be alone and happy. That's the difference, I suppose.'

'And what about Matthew?'

They heard his car come crunching down the gravel drive.

'I'm not sure, Philip. I really am not sure.'

Philip and Juliet lay side by side. They liked to sleep with the window and the curtains open, to hear the sound of the river, the wind in the trees.

He turned gently on his side to look at the clock. 'Sorry,' he whispered, as she stirred and sighed.

'I wasn't asleep.'

The seconds slid by. Clouds covered the full moon, then cleared.

'Juliet?' Perhaps now she was asleep. He'd left it too late.

'Yes.'

'I need to tell you something.'

Neither moved. They stared into the darkness.

'It's about me and Mary.'

She didn't question or cry, she didn't say anything. The silence hammered at him.

'Did you know?'

'Yes.'

'How long?'

'Since the beginning, I suppose.'

'Juliet, I'm sorry. I didn't mean – neither of us meant –' He remembered all the times Juliet had made a point of including Mary, inviting her, offering her lifts.

'I know you didn't.'

'Are you angry?'

'Humiliated, hurt. Yes,' she whispered.

He got out of bed.

'And now you're angry. Yours wasn't the only secret, you know. I kept one too. All this time I knew. Does that make you feel silly?' She sat up to challenge him.

'That's not the point.'

'It is, partly. Anyway, mostly I'm sad. I wondered when you would tell me.'

'It should have been earlier, I know.' He stood by the window exhausted, chilled by the draught.

'Now you have. I'm not going to get hysterical or shout, not right now. I need to think.'

'I'll go and sleep next door.'

She didn't try to stop him. As he turned the handle she said quietly, 'What are we going to do, Phil?'

'I don't know. We'll talk tomorrow.'

But he couldn't sleep. The doubts hadn't ended; if anything they'd intensified. He was choked, almost strangled by them, turning this way and that until morning when he got up to face a new day.

For the time being, Matthew's flat was a haven for Laura. The view from the high window was new and green; horse chestnuts in leaf in the park, May blossom blowing across the grass like confetti.

Bruised by her confrontation with Tom, Laura longed to ease her worries in Matthew's arms, to have her poor, dented confidence restored. She felt sanity return as she sat by the open window, a glass of wine in her hand, the remnants of a meal on the table.

'Stay there, don't move,' he said softly, noticing that she was about to move out of the warm evening light. Her arms were bare, her thin gold necklace pulled askew by the top button of her cream blouse. He reached forward to release it. Then his hand stroked her neck. She dipped her head to kiss his palm.

'You're the doctor, explain something to me,' he whispered.

She held his hand. 'What?'

'The healing power of love.' He smiled. 'No, I don't really want an explanation. I'm just amazed. Before you, life was empty, dead.'

'You were in shock,' she said. 'It was only a couple of months after you'd split up.'

'I didn't think I had a future.'

'Only a painful past? I know.'

'It might have looked as if I came through unscathed. Most people said Abigail and I weren't well matched in the first place, you know how they do. She's seen as jumpy, intense. I'm supposed to be more easy-going, wanting a quiet life like most men. It's not true, of course.'

'You'd lost Sophie and Tim.'

He nodded. 'And then I found you.'

They sat together for a long time. Matthew's silences soothed her. His short, straightforward expressions of love were delightful. So was his smooth, strong face with its straight brow and clear grey eyes.

'Don't cry.'

She shook her head.

'Laura, don't.' He held her very gently, stroking her hair, kissing her softly.

Later, in bed, he told her of his latest problems with Abigail. 'I got a letter this morning from her solicitor. It's to do with access. Apparently, she feels that Sophie and Tim are reacting badly to my visits. She called in a child psychologist, and the verdict is that they need a period away from me, to let things calm down.' He uttered the sentences without making full contact with them, shaking his head in disbelief.

'She won't let you see them?'

'Not for a while, no. Isn't it weird?'

'Oh, Matthew. What good is that supposed to do?'

'It's to give them a chance to settle down in the new house. She says Tim's school has contacted her to say they're worried about him. He's too quiet, turning into a bit of a loner, that sort of thing.'

'I thought he'd joined the junior rugby team?'

'He's decided to give it up. He told me the other boys in the team were all boarders. He felt left out.'

'What about Sophie?'

'She thinks her friends are laughing at her behind her back because Abigail's a single parent.'

'Do they talk to you? I mean, about anything important?'

He shook his head. 'They're like a couple of clams. I ask them if everything's OK, and they look at me with their big eyes and nod. Sophie asks for ice cream, Tim plays Superman up and down the stairs. I take them home. Abigail's stiff as a board; hello, goodbye, don't talk to me! How am I supposed to know whether or not they're OK?'

'What about Maisie? Will Abigail let them go to Hawkshead eventually?' Laura could see that his ex-wife might see advantages in keeping the contact with the children's grandmother, behind Matthew's back.

'I don't know. The letter doesn't mention it.'

'And what will you do? Will you have to reply?' She stroked his forehead, imagined the pain he must be in.

He sat up and slung his legs over the side of the bed, then hunched forward. 'Either I accept it, say OK, no contact with the kids. Or I fight. I demand my rights. She resists. The kids get caught in the middle. Social services are brought in to ask them questions, the full works. Some official somewhere decides if I'm fit to see my own kids. The whole bloody thing drags on for weeks.'

'But you'd win in the end.'

'Win what? The right to take them to McDonald's once a fortnight?'

'Better than nothing.'

'Is it?'

'It would be for Sophie and Tim.' How would they feel if their father simply stopped visiting them? 'Listen, Matthew, you have to keep up your contact with them. Social services will have to take into account what they say; the children's interests always come first.' She leaned her head against his back and talked him through it.

He turned his head towards her. 'I can't bear not seeing them.'

'Abigail's wrong. They need to see you.'

'I can't get them out of my mind,' Matthew said. And he told her how Sophie would look, fresh out of the bath, wrapped in a giant white towel, leaving a trail of wet footprints. And about Tim running towards the lake in summer, darting through the trees to the water's edge; his pointed face and quick, dark eyes, his brown schoolboy hair unruly in the wind.

CHAPTER THIRTY THREE

Dot decided to drop in on Lilian the morning their group was to travel into town to protest outside City Hall. She knew that these days her old friend scarcely went beyond the walls of Abbey Grange.

'There's going to be a march, then we present our petition. The idea is to force the Council to come onto our side.'

Lilian looked in dismay at the crowd gathering at the foot of the Gill. 'It's not much in my line,' she confessed.

'You're not the only one. Still, it's meant to put us back in the headlines and get the city bigwigs to take some notice.' Dot and Lilian looked askance at the dozens of people trampling the ground.

'I don't mean to sound ungrateful, Dot, but you don't think somehow we're missing the point?'

'How do you mean?'

'Well, what's happened to the peace and quiet?'

They took in the shabby tents, the muddy circle of ground and the trail of people strung out along the public footpath carrying placards and posing for the cameras. The march was to start here. Then, everyone would get onto two specially hired coaches, drive into the city, and continue along the main streets.

Lilian frowned. 'How can anyone even begin to see what we're trying to hang onto? The magic's all gone.'

'I know; it looks like a lot of fuss over nothing. Just a bit of a stream and a waterfall, and miles of bare rock.'

'We're spoiling what we love.'

'But not for long.' Dot tried to revive their spirits, upset by Lilian's appearance. Every ounce of flesh seemed to have gone from her body, and her face was white and thin. She stooped, leaning on a stick at the gate of the garden centre, searching in vain for the lost spirit of the place. 'Once the battle's won, we'll be back to normal.'

'I hope you're right.'

They stood watching the knots of people; the children in wellingtons, the women gathered like day-trippers with their sandwiches and thermos flasks, the students emerging sullen and scruffy from their tents. Aimee Scott came up from the garden.

'All done back there?' Lilian asked.

'Yes. I've finished planting out. Tell Kit there's just the greenhouse to water.' She wiped her hands on her jeans and zipped her jacket with dirt-ingrained fingers. But she looked better. There was colour in her face, and for once she was cheerful. 'You're sure you won't come?' she asked Lilian. 'We need you to support us.'

'I am. I'm thinking about you. That'll have to do.'

Aimee glanced at Dot, who gave the slightest shake of her head. 'OK then, we'll do our best. Wish us luck.' She was eager to join her friends.

'Off you go.' Lilian nodded and smiled. 'And take those dratted cameramen with you.' She turned to Dot. 'Shouldn't you get a move on too?'

'I'm cadging a lift with Mrs Maskell, so I've got a few minutes to spare. Shall I make us a nice cup of tea?' She helped Lilian up the path. 'You're finding Aimee's a big help, then?'

'I like the girl. You know, Dot, when we were her age, we were digging for victory in the Land Army.'

'In a natty uniform, remember? Snug britches and a felt hat with a badge. I've still got mine somewhere. The badge, that is.'

'We thought we were the bee's knees.'

'We were in those days, Lilian. But you were a bit of a rebel, you know.' She brought the kettle to the boil.

'Like Aimee there? Well, my sister Marjorie was the pretty one. She married Kit at twenty and never looked back. But I made a meal of it. I wouldn't get married, though I wasn't short of offers. My poor father thought he'd never get me off his hands.'

'Hanging on at home.'

'I only went to grammar school thanks to my mother. He reckoned no one would want a girl like me, with my head stuck in a book.'

'Well, he was wrong. Walter did.'

Lilian sighed happily. 'I was twenty-five. He was thirty-three, head gardener at Burleigh Hall. And a married man.'

Through the window they saw the protestors filing along the

path towards the waiting coaches. 'They think they're the first to throw over the traces, these young ones.'

'Yes, but love could always knock you for six. It took Walter three years to decide to get a divorce.'

'And you never told a soul. I know it was a bombshell to us all when he upped and left Burleigh and you and he settled in here at the Grange.'

'Well, we didn't talk about it so much then, did we? The less said the better. There's always someone getting hurt when a marriage breaks down.' She fell into deep thought.

'Did you know, we've got eleven thousand signatures for our petition?'

'You've done a good job, Dot.'

'Not just me. I've had letters from all over the country saying how they visited the Foss once years ago, and how it's stuck in their memory ever since.'

Lilian drummed her fingers on the table. 'Will Dick be there?'

Dot gave a short laugh. 'I asked him, but he said he didn't know a blind thing about local politics, thank you very much.' She didn't pass on Dick's following dark forecast that he knew plenty about human greed, however, and that in his opinion the bulldozers would soon be moving up the Gill.

'He tells me he's not hopeful.'

Trust Dick. 'When did he say that?'

'He called in here the other day. He says we can shout and march and camp out all we like, but if the powers that be say they want that stone from Ravenscar, that's what they'll get.'

'He always was a miserable old beggar.' Dot drank up and put her empty cup in the sink. 'It's a good job Tot's not around to hear him.' She prayed that Dick was wrong, that Lilian's last days wouldn't be spoiled by noise and dirt. 'And if it was him being up-ended at Hawk Fell to make room for this quarry, he'd be out marching with the rest of us, let me tell you, instead of going round upsetting people.'

'He didn't upset me. He thinks old Tot had the right idea, turning his face to the wall before they got their hands on the place.'

'He never said that.'

'He did. Dick always gives it to you hot and strong.'

'And I'll give it to him when I see him.' She got up to go. 'What's he want us to do? Roll over and let them in?'

'Nay, we can't do that. Go on, you'd better dash to catch your lift. Come back and tell me how you got on.'

Dot nodded. She wasn't one to show her feelings, but as she hurried to Bridge House, she had to fight the tears that welled up when she thought of Lilian going downhill day by day.

The demonstration in town took place in a blur of movement and noise that Dot found hard to take in. There were the coaches organised to drop off more than a hundred and fifty people near the city centre, the special traffic restrictions around City Hall, the watchful presence of the police. Camera crews jostled for position as the marchers reached City Square and mounted the steps of the municipal buildings. Tension made the scene unreal; this was their last chance to get the message across, so they marched grim-faced, chanting their creed. Curious bystanders, attracted by the noise, lined the steps of the huge, soot-blackened Hall.

An official emerged through revolving glass doors to take their petition. Dot had been chosen to hand it over with due ceremony; they wanted the world to see that this campaign was not led by extremists, but by a group of ordinary people fighting to save their dale. Dot stood proudly at the head of the procession.

But scuffling broke out at the base of the steps. Someone in the crowd had jeered at their efforts and one of their group, standing close to Aimee, retaliated. Soon others joined in. As Dot posed for photographs the procession broke up. People tumbled down the steps into the mass of fighting bodies.

There was no sense to it, Dot admitted later. A couple of hot-headed protestors had reacted to ignorant comments. But the situation quickly got out of hand. Only a minority were involved, mostly youngsters, more onlookers than protestors. The cameras had a field day.

She'd watched the police move in. They made several arrests. A few resisted. They were seen on television writhing and kicking, midriffs bare as the officers hauled them into nearby vans. There was a roar of protestors chanting, people thumping the sides of the police vans, orders yelled, women beginning to scream.

The police may have been heavy-handed. Certainly Dot, standing at the top of the steps with Laura and Matthew, could see force being used to separate the bodies and haul them off. Some people, trying to get out of the way, found themselves herded into narrow spaces, and reacted by hitting out in panic. There were more arrests than were perhaps strictly necessary.

Then she heard an order to close the van doors and to move down a channel which the police were struggling to keep clear. But the vans could only crawl as protestors and crowd alike yelled insults and hammered at the windscreens.

A student clinging to the first van was wrenched free by a policeman on foot. He fell against an iron bollard and rolled sideways into Aimee. Someone tried to grab hold of her before she too fell, into the path of the second police van which accelerated without seeing her.

Aimee lost her balance and fell forward. There was a terrible moment when Dot knew the van would hit her. It was white, its blue light flashing and wailing, and it was going to knock her down and roll over her before she could crawl out of its path. Then there was silence.

Laura rushed down the steps as the driver reversed the van to reveal Aimee lying face up.

'Don't move her. Get an ambulance, quick.' She bent over, felt for a pulse, cleared her mouth and propped her jacket under Aimee's head. Quickly she pulled a card from her bag and handed it to a policeman. 'Call this number. Tell her parents to get to Casualty as fast as they can.' There was blood trickling from a wound on Aimee's forehead and bad injuries to the left side of her body.

Dot watched the policemen hold back the surging crowd. Two or three of Aimee's friends struggled to get close, but they too were pushed back. Within minutes, an ambulance's blue light flashed above the heads. People parted, two men jumped out and Laura handed over, telling them what they needed to know. 'I've cleared the airway, kept her still. Pulse is weak, there could be haemorrhaging.'

Then Aimee was on a stretcher, covered in a red blanket and being lifted out of sight. The ambulance door closed. Camera lights flashed from the scrum of pressmen who had charged down the steps for the best picture.

By the time Dot and Matthew reached Laura, the ambulance had driven away and the police had control. Laura's clothes were covered in blood.

'Will she be all right?' Matthew took her gently by the arm.

'I don't know.'

They were stunned. Demonstrators drifted away, leaving placards strewn on the ground. Mary and Juliet came and stood nearby, hoping that Aimee's injuries weren't as bad as they looked.

'Touch and go,' Laura told them. 'Broken bones, head injuries. We'll have to wait and see.'

Matthew drove Laura to the hospital, while the others forlornly took to their coaches and cars. Dot drove back with Juliet in silence, thinking of how the family would take it. Dr Scott hated the protest, she knew. Now there would be all sorts of recriminations.

'It all got out of hand,' Dot sighed. They'd agreed to meet up at the Falcon to wait for news.

'It's not anyone's fault.' Alison Lawson quietly served her shocked customers.

'Except Maisie Aire's.' Dick Metcalfe held court in his corner of the bar. 'None of this would have happened if she'd let well enough alone.'

'But Aimee will make it, won't she?' Alison pieced together the accounts.

'She's in the operating theatre right now.' Juliet had been in touch with Philip, who had the latest from the hospital. 'There's a haemorrhage close to the brain, but not inside the skull.'

'It's just been on TV.' Brian came through from the back and put his arm around Alison's shoulder. 'They say she's critical.'

'Bloody vultures,' Dick muttered. 'Them cameramen getting in the road.'

'Yes, and they're down at the medical centre this very minute,' Dot added. 'There's a couple of them camped on the doorstep at the Scott's house as well, waiting for an interview.'

'The place is crawling with them.' Dick growled on.

'And what about Tom Elliot? He got his front page exclusive all right.' Brian voiced the opinion that was gradually emerging.

'Least said about him the better.' Dick slammed his empty glass on the table. 'From what I hear, he's the one who led the poor girl on. If he's any sense, he'll bugger off out of here.' He put on his cap and nodded at Brian, then shoved past the newcomers towards the door.

The phone rang. 'There's complications,' Alison came back to tell them. 'That was Dr Maskell.'

'How long has she been in there now?' Brian looked at his watch.

'Five hours,' Mary answered automatically. 'Has anyone been along to Abbey Grange to tell Lilian?'

'I'll go,' Dot volunteered. 'She's probably seen it on the news. I'd better get over there.' She was glad of something to do.

When Dot finally reached home it was well after dark, and she was worried and tired. She noticed Laura's car as she climbed the hill. She was back from the hospital.

'Aimee's in intensive care. They stopped the haemorrhaging, but the tissue around the brain is very swollen. It's still a matter of time before we know.' Laura sat down at the kitchen table. Neither tried to conceal their feelings.

'What now?' Dot could see the shock written all over Laura. Her clothes were still stained with Aimee's blood.

'A bath and a stiff drink, I think.'

'It'll do you good. And get plenty of rest.'

They said goodnight. Dot went off to bed, but not to sleep. At eleven o'clock she heard a knock on the door and Laura, by this time wrapped in her bath-robe, going to answer it. She stayed where she was, hearing the voices rise and fall in the room below.

'Tom.' Laura held tight to the door. She'd guessed who it would be even before she opened it.

'Can I come in?' He looked drained.

'Just for a minute.' She led him into the lounge, forcing herself to sound calm. 'What is it?'

He took a deep, jolting breath, his mouth working to stay steady. 'I've just called in at the Falcon.'

He had incredible cheek coming here like this, seeking her out as a shoulder to cry on.

He breathed out. 'I can't say that I was surprised.'

'What happened?'

'Nothing. Zero. No one said a word to me.'

'So why come here?' When she looked at him now he was a stranger; someone she glimpsed in the distance and thought, there's a man in a battered leather jacket, he has nothing to do with me. It was strange.

'There was no one else. How is she?'

'Critical. In intensive care.'

'I wasn't to know that this would happen.'

She looked at him coldly. 'I said she was vulnerable, remember?' For all her knowledge, her old love for him, she wouldn't salve his conscience now.

'But not like this,' he insisted.

Something snapped so that she could no longer contain her anger. 'You're outrageous, Tom, you know that? It's never your fault, always someone else's. I expect you think Aimee walked under that van on purpose, just to grab sympathy.'

He turned away. 'Lay off, will you?'

'No, not this time. Aimee's in hospital critically ill. She might die. And she's there partly because of you.'

'How do you work that out?'

'Because you led her on and let her worship the ground you trod on.' Her eyes challenged him so that he couldn't look away. Then she lowered her voice. 'I know that one all too well, Tom.'

'You're saying I did it on purpose?'

She grabbed his arm and held onto it. 'You always do. You used that girl to get back at me.'

He wrenched himself free. 'Don't flatter yourself. Anyway, she was willing, let me tell you.'

'That's not how it looked at Bridge House. You disgust me.'

'Please yourself.' Tom's face set in harsh lines as he shrugged and headed for the door.

But Laura hadn't finished. 'You don't create, you destroy.'

'And you don't know what you're saying.' He fell back into self-righteousness, his usual defence. 'The whole media business did get a bit out of hand today, I have to admit. But why blame me?'

'Because if the cameras hadn't been there, if you hadn't organised it as some extension of your own ego, there'd have been no crush, no scuffle with the police, no accident.' She clutched her dressing-gown round her neck, standing in front of the door.

'And no chance of defeating the stone company.' He kicked at a chair with the side of his foot. It scraped across the stone floor.

'Tom.' She faced him for what she knew would be the last time. 'I'd like to say that I know you meant well. So why do I think you only came here to get something out of it for yourself?'

'And what about you and all the rest? Are you saying you're not in it for yourselves? Everyone is.'

'I won't argue with that.' She tried to turn away.

'You'd better listen then.' He held her by the arm. 'Say you get Frontier to back off and you keep your precious hill. What do they do? They go and get stone from somewhere else. Fine, so long as it's not in your back yard.'

'But we're not like you, we can't solve the big problem. We can't change the world.'

'So you just hide away in this backwater?' He was incredulous. 'And you blame me because some girl falls over and gets run down!' He pushed her away and she reeled against a cupboard, thudding it with her shoulder.

'But she's not just some girl!' He never saw the individual; they were all just part of a pattern he'd arranged for his own benefit.

He turned away, hunching his shoulders. 'I'll see you, Laura.'

'No.' She beat him to the door again. 'No, you won't.'

He stared at her through narrowed eyes. 'Fine.'

She stepped aside and he swung out down the hall, out of the front door, out of her life.

CHAPTER THIRTY FOUR

On a still day in late May, three days after Aimee's accident, when the dale had come alive with new greens, and the farmers sent out their black dogs on long fetches across the soaring hillsides, Laura drove to Wingate to see Aimee.

From the top of Ravenscar she could see for miles across Swiredale to the misty purple slopes beyond. Slowly she wended her way into the valley.

She knew from Philip that Aimee's recovery would be gradual. Gerald and Janet had stayed constantly by her bedside, held her hand, talked her back into consciousness. As for Tom, she'd heard that he'd retreated to London the day after the accident, scorn and earnestness intact. She was glad to be left in peace to take root in Yorkshire, amidst the powerful, no-nonsense appeal of its people. She knew in her heart that she was unlikely to see Tom again.

She parked her car outside the hospital and went in. Its corridors echoed with the sound of trolleys and the soft shoes of the nurses. Outside Aimee's ward she found Gerald talking to a nurse.

'How is she?' She walked up eagerly.

'Stable. Officially out of danger.' He was off-hand.

'That's brilliant, Gerald.' She too kept her distance. 'How's Janet?'

'Relieved. Tired. She's in there with her now.'

The nurse slipped tactfully away. Laura saw him for the first time outside the context of work and family; unsure of himself, frowning, awkward.

She dipped her head towards the bunch of pink roses she'd brought for Aimee. They smelt of crisp, green apples. Through the door she caught sight of Janet smoothing down the sheets on Aimee's bed, beginning to brush her daughter's long dark hair. 'Could I see her?'

Gerald cleared his throat, but he didn't speak.

'Or should I come back later?'

He didn't have time to reply before Janet saw her and waved her in. Gerald turned away, shoulders high and rigid with tension. Laura sighed, then entered the ward smiling.

'Laura, here you are! I've been trying to tell Aimee how you helped to save her life. We can't begin to thank you –'

'That means a lot to me, Janet. Thank you.'

Aimee sat up in bed surrounded by flowers and cards. 'Another visitor?' a nurse said, checking a chart at the foot of her bed.

She frowned and gave Laura a puzzled look. 'You're my doctor?'

Laura stood close by the bed and nodded.

'Did you hear about my accident?' She leaned forward and asked in a confidential tone.

'That's why I'm here.' She placed the roses on the bedside locker, recognising the exaggerated expressions, the confusion of a patient recovering from a head injury. Aimee looked scrubbed and small, propped on her pillows.

Janet, looking worn out but calm, gave up her seat to Laura. 'She doesn't remember much about the accident yet. It's all coming back gradually.' She took the roses.

Laura perched on the bed. 'Don't worry, they won't dare tell me off,' she assured Aimee. She began to browse through the cards on the bedside locker. There were get-well wishes from Aimee's friends in the sixth form, from the teachers, from Mary, and from families in the village.

'Tom hasn't been to see me yet,' Aimee said, with a sudden breakthrough into clarity, as she watched Laura go through her cards.

Laura explained that he must be busy.

'But I thought he would visit. Does he know I'm here?'

'Yes, but he's not in Hawkshead. He's gone back to London.'

Aimee's face clouded over. 'He can't know how ill I've been.'

'I'm sure he wants you to get better, Aimee. We all do.'

'What about the campaign? Don't we need him here?'

Janet leaned forward to brush her hair from her face. 'Keep still, love.'

'We'll have to manage without him,' Laura told her. 'We're not giving up, don't you worry.'

Slowly Aimee absorbed this. 'Who will we get to write about us now?'

'There are lots of newspapers interested. Did you know you were a heroine?' Laura spoke brightly. 'Everyone wants to know about you.'

She refused to be diverted. 'Maybe Tom will send me a card?'

'And meanwhile you have to get better, that's the main thing.' She pulled her chair in closer. 'How are they treating you in here? How's the food?'

'Disgusting.' She wrinkled her nose.

'All the more reason to get out of here as fast as you can. Back to home cooking.'

'Yeah, yeah. Have you seen the calories in one of Mum's cakes? Nightmare.'

'That's more like it. You don't have to eat it. Tell them what you'd like.'

'Anything!' Janet promised. 'Absolutely anything. The sooner we get you home the better.'

'Sure?'

'Aimee, we were never more sure of anything in our lives,' her mother said softly. 'So you just do what the doctor ordered, you hear?'

'I can't help it, I'm surrounded by them.'

Laura went back to the cards, leaving them to talk, aware that Gerald was coming back. He brought news of a promised visit from Nick at the weekend. She touched one card in particular and lingered over it; a picture of a cottage garden in spring, a haze of pink and white. Inside, the message read, 'To Aimee, with very best wishes for a speedy recovery. Kind regards, Lilian Rigg.'

It was to Abbey Grange that Laura walked with Dot that same evening.

'She'll be glad of some good news,' Dot told her. 'She doesn't get out now, you know, but she still takes a lively interest. She's as sharp as a pin.'

They went up the path through the open door, to find Lilian sitting in a chair by the window, her sturdy figure reduced to skin and bone, her dark grey eyes glittering in the half-light.

Laura adjusted to the shadows in the sitting-room; the room of a woman with plain tastes, as the white walls, the strong oak furniture and rows of hardback books showed. Early, brick-red geraniums glowed on the windowsill.

'Shall I get Kit to make us a cup of tea?' Lilian was hospitable. 'He's here somewhere.'

They declined and sat in the twilight with her. Laura told her that Aimee was getting better slowly, though it would be some time before she was allowed out of the hospital.

'And what about her mother and father?'

'Coping. As a matter of fact, the accident seems to have brought them all closer together.'

'A crisis often does. And they're keeping up with the sit-in at the Gill. Did you tell her that? They're sticking it out for her sake, that's what they say, come hell or high water.'

'That's good. We're still waiting for news from the inquiry. It's due at the beginning of next week.'

'Well.' Lilian sighed. She looked placidly across the garden to the hills beyond. 'Who's this arriving now?'

'Isn't that Maisie Aire's car?' Dot stood up in astonishment as the car stopped at the gate and Kit went to investigate. They saw him point to the house, listen and nod. 'I'll go and stop her, shall I?'

'No, let her be.' It was all one to Lilian. Things ebbed and flowed. 'Let's see what she has to say.'

Maisie came in, visibly taken aback by the other visitors, not registering at first how frail Lilian was.

Laura stood and greeted Maisie who, in a fawn checked suit, was as beautifully turned out as ever. Quick to hide her surprise at seeing Lilian's visitors, Maisie acknowledged them with a brief nod.

'Sit down, Mrs Aire. Is it about the quarry?' Lilian gestured to an empty chair.

'Yes.' She sat upright, on guard.

'We could make ourselves scarce, Lilian.' Laura edged away.

'No, you sit down too, Laura, Dot. Let's hear this.' Lilian sounded set to enjoy an interesting situation.

'Now, this quarry,' Maisie began, faltering as she began to realise how ill her tenant was. 'I came to reassure you.'

Lilian put her head on one side. 'How could you do that? You know we won't have it.'

Laura loved her for her categorical nature.

'At least hear me out.'

'Talk's cheap, talk away. What do you want to discuss? My

future? Well, there's precious little of that left, as you can see. To tell the truth, I'm glad I won't be here to see you knock the old place down.'

'Don't say that.' Maisie's eye on death wasn't as steady as Lilian's. 'There are things I can suggest. It's true, the road would run through here, but I wouldn't put you out with nowhere to go.'

'You've left it a bit late in the day.'

'I had no idea, believe me, of the trouble this would cause. And when that poor girl got run over and everything seemed to have run way out of control, that's when I finally took stock.'

Lilian listened patiently. 'I think we all did.'

'My own position hasn't been easy.'

'It never is when you lose your husband.'

'Christopher is convinced that selling the land is the answer. He has a good head for business.'

'And no compassion.' She shrugged at Dot. 'I can speak my mind, can't I?'

Laura wondered what Maisie's offer would consist of. In the weeks since her fall, all contact with the Hall had ceased. She knew only that Christopher was still living with her, waiting for the inquiry's report and presumably stoking up the feud between her and Matthew.

'The fact is, you will need somewhere to live, and for a long time now I've been wondering what to do with the lodge at the Hall. It's been empty for years, you know. But it could be done up, ready for you to rent very cheaply.'

'The lodge?' Lilian smiled and eased herself to her feet. 'Come outside with me, Mrs Aire.' She moved slowly on Laura's arm towards the door. 'Kit's busy planting out bedding plants. I have to keep him right over colours, you know.'

Mystified, Maisie and Dot followed them into the garden.

'He'd put red alongside salmon pink without a second thought. I tell him our customers like to buy busy lizzies all one colour.' Slowly she walked down the rows of plants towards the greenhouse.

The garden was a picture; perennials were coming into flower, delphiniums towering over the heavy crimson heads of peonies. Lilian bent to shake silky, spent scarlet petals onto the earth.

Maisie breathed in the scent of a rose. 'My dear –' She held out a hand towards Lilian.

'Here's my answer, Mrs Aire. This is my garden, this is it.' She turned and seemed to look a long way off. 'Now, you'll excuse me.' She nodded to Laura to be taken back into the house, where there were adjustments to be made to the tube which fed drugs directly into her chest.

Laura worked quietly at resetting the dosage, then taped the tube back into position.

'Has she gone?' Lilian sighed.

'Yes. I heard the car drive off. Dot saw her out, don't worry.'

'The lodge.' Short of breath, discomforted by the contraption, Lilian managed a short laugh. 'Coming to me with her leftovers.'

'I think she got the picture. There, are you all right now?' She tucked Lilian's blanket around her legs.

'If she thinks she can sweet talk me, she's got another thing coming.' She looked up at Laura with the old, firm nod of her head.

Laura took a step back. 'You're a wonderful woman, Mrs Rigg.'

'I don't know about that, Dr Grant.' She looked out over Ravenscar. 'But I do know I'm planning to end my days here in my own place, and I don't care who says otherwise.'

CHAPTER THIRTY FIVE

'Meet me at the Foss. No, on second thoughts, meet me on Ravenscar, by the tarn. It's quieter there.' Mary caught Philip as he came in from work. 'I know it's difficult and risky and all the rest, but come anyway.'

'You shouldn't ring me here.'

'I know. Is Juliet there?'

'No, but still.'

'Look, drop everything and come, will you?'

'OK, I'll be there in half an hour. You go up by the footpath, I'll arrive by car.' Again he had the sense of being overtaken by events. He and Juliet had talked, they'd been as honest as they could. He admitted that Mary was fresh and exciting, she conceded that their marriage had become dull and predictable. She explained how it felt to be overlooked, let down, deceived.

'Deep down, I feel that somehow I must deserve it. There's something about me that leaves you dissatisfied, and there's nothing I can do.'

'That's not true.' He'd been unable to take her in his arms and soothe away the hurt that he himself was inflicting. 'It's me. I'm the one who has to work something out, not you.'

'It's both of us.'

There were times when she was angry, when she talked of walking out on him and finding a place of her own, and then she grew bitter and demanded why she should be the one to leave after what he had done. But she showed no self-pity, and she never once blamed Mary.

Now, as he drove onto Ravenscar on an evening of high winds and sudden cold showers, he saw too clearly the weakness of his inability to say no. Perhaps, after twenty-odd years of uneventful marriage, he'd become addicted to twists and turns of emotion, to the rush of adrenalin when the phone rang, to the drama of these secret meetings. Could it be this as much as Mary herself?

He pulled up in a passing-place on the single track unfenced road high on the summit, locked the car and headed across rough heather and bracken towards the tarn.

He reached the water's edge; still no sign of Mary. He'd expected to see her in the distance, waiting for him. Staring across the brackish lake at a couple of white-headed coots zig-zagging over the surface, his back to the wind, he decided he would wait ten minutes then drive back home.

'Hello.' She slid her hands over his eyes from behind. That voice, that touch. 'Did I make you jump?'

'Mary.' He turned around, kissed her, felt her cold lips. 'You're wet.'

'I got caught in the rain.' She shook drops from her hair. Her wet shirt stuck to her shoulders. 'How long have you been waiting?'

'Not long. God, Mary, come here.' When he kissed her this time, he wanted everything to stop dead, never to start again. 'Mary, Mary.' He ran his fingers down her wet cheek, along her chin.

'Philip, I've got something to tell you.' She pulled away.

'Good or bad?' He wanted her back in his arms. Why had she rung him at home? Why did he feel another change about to overtake him?

'Both. The good news is, I read for a part in rep in Birmingham. I got it.'

'What part?'

'A good part in a new play.' She watched him carefully, every move, every flicker of reaction.

'When?'

'August. I finish at school in July. It fits in perfectly.'

'For how long?'

'I don't know. It could lead to other things. It's a good break for me, Philip.'

'What about us?' He was seized by panic. 'We'll still see each other?'

'It might be difficult. That's the bad bit.' She looked at him, waiting for his response.

He wouldn't let her go. 'Is this it? You get a career break, and that's the end of us. Finish?'

She nodded. Rain trickled through her hair, down her face.

This had never occurred to him. 'I don't mean as much to you as a part in a play?'

She flinched. 'I didn't say that.'

'No? That's what it looks like to me.' Fear turned to anger. 'I put everything on the line for you. Every damn thing. Marriage, family, even my job if people get to find out.'

'For me?' She stared back.

'For us, then. I even told Juliet about us, did you know that? Weeks ago, I told her!'

'I know you did. If you were to ask me the precise night, I could probably tell you to within two hours. You're behind the times.'

'How did you know?' he asked bitterly. 'Have you two been talking?'

She opened her eyes wide. 'Do me a favour. No, it's written on your face, in your eyes. It didn't take much figuring out. And if you confess to Juliet and she doesn't kick you out, you enter into negotiations. What chance the other woman then, eh?'

'You're not the other woman –'

'I am. I'm familiar with the role.' She took his breath away with the cold slap of reality.

'You don't love me?'

'I never said that.'

For a moment he believed again. 'God, I love you, Mary. Juliet says I should make the break and come to you, did you know that?'

She gasped and shook her head.

'You don't know everything, then. Come here.' He moved towards her, but she backed away.

'Listen, Philip. Say you make the break with Juliet's blessing? You come to me for a few days of intense passion, bliss. I'm hooked. I'm yours forever.

'But, then, guilt gets to you. You can't bear to walk down the street in case you see Juliet. Everyone's talking about you behind your back. You ring her and say you need to collect a few things from the house. You tell me you'll be back in half an hour. I never see you again.'

'No.'

She held him at arm's length. 'Anyway, what about my big break? Birmingham, here I come.'

'I don't believe you.'

'Just watch me. I'll send you a couple of tickets, shall I?' She'd begun to shake.

'Mary, I can't lose you, please!' Rain soaked them through, driven by the wind.

'I have to go.' She turned.

He ran after her. 'I'll give you a lift. Let me take you home.' She pushed him away again. 'What will I say when I see you?'

'You'll say hello, we'll be friends. And then in August I'll be gone. Read the papers for the reviews.'

She walked away from him across the rough ground, over the narrow road towards the footpath, until her slight figure disappeared between the trees and the rain filled the landscape. He stood, soaked to the skin.

Later that week – a time when Philip worked through on automatic pilot, with Sheila and Joy to put him back on the rails whenever his mind wandered or routine slipped – he registered a morning appointment with Brian and Alison Lawson. They came in looking relaxed and happy.

'Don't tell me.' He sat back and swivelled his chair towards them.

'You guessed it. You can cancel that appointment with the specialist. We got tired of waiting.' Brian confirmed the pregnancy.

'I bought the kit, tested positive. We're both thrilled to bits.' Alison sat basking in the limelight.

'Congratulations.' Their news shifted the block of gloom sitting on his shoulders. 'Really, this is very good indeed.' He shook hands with them both. 'We'll do a test to make absolutely sure, then we'll get you on the ante-natal list.'

'We wanted to come in and tell you personally,' she said. 'You went out of your way to help us and we're very grateful.'

'You know what I'm going to say; you owe me one.'

'Ready and waiting,' they promised. 'A large Scotch?'

Philip had spotted Laura coming in from her car. 'Do you mind if I spread the glad tidings?' He was on his way to the door. They nodded and followed him out, beaming all over their faces.

'Laura, congratulations are in order. Brian and Alison are pregnant.'

She came and wished them luck. 'I'm very pleased, well done.'

It was only when the Lawsons had gone and Philip followed

Laura into her room that he saw something was wrong. She sat heavily at her desk and stared into space.

'What is it, Laura?'

She pressed her lips together and took a deep breath, then she looked up at him. 'I've just come from the Grange. Lilian died an hour ago.'

CHAPTER THIRTY SIX

Dot watched through the curtains for Laura to arrive home. She knew as she saw her step out of the car then lean for a moment against it, looking up towards the head of the dale, that Lilian was gone. She went quietly to the door and opened it.

'When?' she asked.

'This morning. Kit was with her.'

'Was it peaceful?'

Laura nodded. 'She was lucid, she said she wasn't sorry.'

Dot helped her with her bag and coat. 'Here, come and sit down. You're right, she wouldn't want to linger.'

'No.'

'And we'll always think of her striding on those hills, digging that garden.' Her voice broke.

'It's all right, Dot.'

She shook herself and raised her head. 'It's a terrible, terrible illness.'

'It is.' They sat under the ticking clock, gazing out of the window. 'I just wish she could have hung on until we knew Black Gill was safe.'

'Then perhaps it's just as well.' Dot had held back her own news. 'I had a phone call this afternoon.'

'From Tom?'

'He said you wouldn't want to speak him, but he left a message.'

'Has he got hold of the report?' It was due out in three days, and Tom had the contacts to enable him to see it early.

Dot nodded. 'What he said, word for word if I can get it right, was that the report encourages the Department of the Environment to decide in favour of Frontier. There's nothing in it to show that the environmental arguments outweigh advantages to the community in terms of new jobs, income and industry.' She had rehearsed it, and delivered it pat.

Laura listened in silence. All for nothing. They would lose the most precious thing they had.

'He did say he was very sorry, Laura.'

'Well, it's not over.' She rallied. 'There's still the sit-in.' The protestors, who had sworn not to move from the Gill, were their last-ditch effort.

'It looks like he was right about the inquiry. It was a sham.'

'We'll never know. We did our best with all the legal moves. Now I suppose it's down to who shouts loudest.'

The mood at the Falcon that evening was gloomy when Laura and Dot went to meet Mary. Sadness over Lilian's death mingled with bleak anger about Frontier.

'She's best off out of it,' Dick said the moment he heard. 'She'd never have been able to stick seeing them knock the old place to bits.'

'Do you reckon she knew? A kind of sixth sense?' Brian served the three women.

'I don't know,' Laura answered. 'In a strange way I think she just rose above it and enjoyed the dale as it is now. She always asked to sit next to the window. In fact, she was looking out when she died.'

'And she never mentioned the quarry?'

'Not after Maisie's visit. She put it from her mind.'

Dot took her drink from the bar. 'If you don't mind, I'll keep Dick company,' she said.

As she edged between the tables, Laura and Mary chose a quiet spot by the window, where Mary talked brightly about her plans. She'd told them at school that she definitely wouldn't be back for the autumn term, and was already looking round for a flat near the theatre in Birmingham.

'You sound as if you can't wait.'

'It's a fresh start.'

'I know all about that,' Laura agreed. 'What about Philip?' She'd noticed his face these last few days; strained and pale, turned in on himself, struggling to cope.

'What about him?'

'How did he take it?'

Mary shook her head. 'He'll get over it in the long run. He'll feel hurt for a bit, but then he'll think about it and see what a lucky escape he's had.'

'Says you.'

'He had a lot to lose.'

'Yes, and a lot to win.' Laura looked at her. 'You let him off the hook.'

Mary's eyes filled with tears. 'It was the only way out.'

'But you loved him.' Mary's face conveyed total misery. 'You do love him.'

'Yes, and where did it get us? Anyway, let's not talk about it. Ask me about my glittering future, will you, Laura?' She lifted her glass, inviting a toast.

'Cheers, Mary.' Laura watched her drink. 'I'm going to miss you.'

'I'll send you tickets,' she promised. 'First night, front row. You and Matthew.'

When a call came through to the busy surgery the following day that Maisie needed to see Laura again, she responded reluctantly. 'Is it urgent?' she asked Sheila.

'Sounded it. It was Maisie herself. She said to tell you she was there alone. Christopher's in Italy.'

'Another migraine probably. Did you tell her someone would call?'

'I said you would, Laura. She asked specifically.'

'OK, I'll make it as soon as I can.' She put aside her feelings and resolved to get it over with.

Now, as she drove through the gates of the Hall past the lodge towards the mellow stone roofs, she couldn't help remembering her first visit at Christmas. She climbed out of her car by the broad front steps and glanced at the low yew hedges, the slope of lawn towards the lake. The boathouse stood over the still, clear water.

'Thank you for coming.' Maisie was composed as she came to answer the door. She led Laura across the hall into the study.

'Are you ill?' She rejected the offer of a seat. 'Why did you want to see me?'

'I want us not to fight.' Maisie stood behind the wide desk. 'There's been enough of that already.'

With her patient evidently well, Laura made it plain that she considered the visit a waste of time. 'You haven't blacked out or fallen again?'

'No, but I need to talk to you.' She stepped from behind the desk. 'It's very important.'

'But if you're not ill; no fall or anything – ' Laura turned to go.

'I never did fall.'

Laura stopped.

'I didn't lose my memory. I never fell.' She repeated it, paused, then took up the thread again. 'It was best at the time to let you think that I had.'

Laura put her bag on a chair and went towards Maisie. 'Has this got something to do with Christopher?'

Maisie closed her eyes. 'Didn't you guess?'

'I might have suspected something, just for a second, but you were adamant that you'd fallen. What really did happen, Maisie?'

'I was having second thoughts. We argued. He said no one could afford to hang on to an asset like Ravenscar in this day and age, out of some sentimental attachment to the landscape.' She sat wearily in a leather armchair. 'In the beginning I guess I was only looking out for myself. Somehow, when Geoffrey died, the whole world turned cold. If I didn't look out for myself, then who would?'

'Matthew,' Laura said quietly. 'He would have taken care of you.' She saw now what Maisie had been afraid of; loneliness, old age, death. She was vulnerable, like everyone else. 'You only had to ask.'

'I made a mistake. I trusted Christopher and he panicked me into thinking that I needed money. No, I shouldn't blame him entirely. I wanted to be able to spend, to make myself safe. Money does that.'

Laura said nothing, imagining Christopher's anger when he discovered that Maisie wanted to change her mind.

'He said it was a choice; either I sell the land or my paintings. He knew I would never part with them.'

'So he went ahead and invested his money on that basis?'

'He bought shares in Frontier, yes. I didn't like it. It felt like he was making money on the backs of everyone I knew. Then there was the inquiry, and I found out how you all felt. But he was angry. And I gave him too much of his own way.'

'Did he hit you?' She remembered him at the bedside and Maisie's insistence that he wasn't in the house when she fell. A clumsy confusion.

'Oh, Laura.'

'What is it? Tell me.'

'He stood on the stairs. I was in the hall looking up at him. I told him that I didn't want to sell Ravenscar any more. Please, I said, please try to understand. He swore and hit out at me. I put my arm up like this to save myself. And I fell. Afterwards he denied it. He said it was ridiculous to imagine that he had done such a thing.'

Laura knelt beside Maisie who trembled as she spoke. 'Have you been living in fear all this time?'

She nodded. 'I couldn't tell anyone. He said no one would believe me and people would think I was crazy. And I was so ashamed.' Tears streamed down her face.

'So you protected him. You should have told us.'

Maisie took Laura's hand. 'After a while I began to think I had dreamt it all up in a kind of nightmare. He said over and over that it wasn't the way I said. Was I crazy?'

'No.' Laura was clear. 'There were bruises on your arm, none on your legs. Just the kind of injury that fits in with your version.'

Maisie sighed. 'I got mixed up. Then there was the terrible fight between him and Matthew. I was alone with him, trapped. Eventually I did think of something I could do; not much, but it was something. I went to see Lilian Rigg.'

'You made a move.'

'But it didn't work out. She wouldn't listen, and she was so ill.'

'She died, Maisie.'

'When?'

'Yesterday.'

She sobbed aloud. 'I wanted her to keep her garden. I couldn't bear it. I came home and faced up to Christopher at last. I told him that if he dared to hit me again I would tell everyone. I would call the police.'

'He believed you?'

'He had to. That's why he went away.'

'And what did you do?' Laura's arm was round Maisie's shoulder.

'I wrote to Simon Warboys. I showed Christopher the letter before he went. I want things to stay as they are. I've withdrawn the sale of the land.'

Black Gill recovered its tranquillity. Grass grew where the tents had been. Celandines, wild garlic and violets carpeted the slopes and Joan's Foss shone a clear green-blue.

Laura walked there with Matthew on the day of Lilian's funeral.

They buried her under white lilies and carnations. Her coffin disappeared under a mound of flowers. Gerald came to the service with Janet and Aimee, still in a wheelchair. Philip came with Juliet. Their voices rang through the church and the vicar reminded them that it was Lilian above all who had symbolised the spirit of the dale; unswerving, steadfast and brave.

Laura rejoiced for her old friend on the bank of the Foss. She felt the spray freshen her face, breathed in the green smells. In memory of her they climbed the side of Black Gill onto Ravenscar, where the rough heather caught at their feet, the sheep scattered and the limestone faults gaped deep and dangerous.

On the walk across the moor, Matthew told her that his own agony of waiting was over. 'Abigail's had a change of heart. She says I can go on seeing Sophie and Tim after all. I had a letter this morning.'

Laura breathed in deep and slow. The air sparkled, the sky was cloudless. She put her head back, closed her eyes and felt the sun.

He held her. 'We still have to go through the official business. They'll have to define access. But it looks better now that I have a stable base for them to come to back at the Hall. The kids can come and stay in the holidays.'

'What made her change her mind?'

'Who knows? Maybe she just didn't want the hassle.' He didn't care. Now he wanted to get it down on paper; time with the children.

'What does Maisie say?' Laura tugged at his collar and kissed him.

'She's thrilled. It cheers her up and takes her mind off her money worries.' Gently he took hold of her wrists. 'You know she's all set practically to dismantle the whole place?'

'No, why?'

'She's having to grit her teeth and get everything valued; furniture, paintings. It's her plan of action number two.'

Laura grew thoughtful. 'She's not thinking of selling up completely?'

'No, she wants to stay on. She's surprised that people are still talking to her.'

'Did she think we'd hold a grudge?'

'It's been an eye-opener to her, the whole thing.'

'So, she'll love seeing the children again, even if they have to sleep on camp beds in empty rooms?' They walked hand in hand down the narrow road towards Hawkshead.

'I don't think it's quite that bad.'

'Neither do I.' Laura said she wanted them to go and see Maisie. She had a specific reason which she would tell him about when they reached the Hall.

The three of them sat out on the lawn overlooking the lake. Maisie welcomed Laura with special warmth. 'You look well. Are you having a day off? You deserve it.'

'We've been onto Ravenscar and had a long walk.'

'And an idea,' Matthew warned. 'But don't ask me. She won't tell me.'

Laura was excited. 'It suddenly struck me as we were walking; have you thought of selling Abbey Grange?'

'Rather than rent it out again?' Maisie tuned in straight away. 'But it's so out of date.'

Matthew agreed. 'It would need a lot of renovation.'

'There's no central heating. It must be awfully cold in winter.'

'Would we do it up first, then try to sell it?'

Laura let them talk it through.

'We would have to spend some money on it,' Maisie surmised. 'Who would want to buy it in its present state?'

'I would,' Laura said simply. 'And I would want to move in as soon as possible.'

CHAPTER THIRTY SEVEN

They carried out the surveys and the searches. In the late summer, Luke Altham finalised the details.

At odd times, when Laura could snatch a break from the surgery, or whenever a house call took her out past the Abbey, she would drop in at the Grange. Kit kept up the garden by trimming the lawns and dead-heading the roses, but the commercial side had lapsed, the sign outside the gate was gone. The old house, square and uncompromising, stood waiting. At last, in early autumn, the key was hers.

She took it straight to the medical centre and held it up for all to see.

'I can see you can't wait to get your hands on the place.' Sheila tidied up at the end of another long and busy day.

Philip went up and gave her a hug. 'Well done, Laura. If you need anyone to climb a ladder or paint a door, give me a shout.'

'Thanks, I'll need lots of willing helpers.'

'You hear that, Aimee?' Philip called into Gerald's room. 'How fit are you?'

'Not that fit. Why?' She came out smiling.

Laura waved the key at her. 'Are you any good at papering ceilings?'

'Dream on.' She wrinkled her nose. 'I wouldn't mind helping in the garden, though.'

'Done.'

'Watch out, she'll have the entire village working for her if we're not careful,' Sheila warned. 'I bet Dot's over there already with her dustpan and brush.'

'How did you guess?'

'Just don't forget we've a practice to run.' Gerald emerged from his room, glasses dangling between thumb and forefinger. 'All this euphoria might just blind you to the fact.' He still hadn't forgiven her, still maintained a disapproving air. He went back in and made much of shuffling papers on his desk.

'Ignore him.' Philip was halfway through the door. It swung to after him.

'I intend to.'

Then Matthew arrived and they walked along the river together to Abbey Grange. She used her key to open the door.

'Happy now?' He stood with her on the doorstep.

Between them they'd resisted the speculation in the village that they would take the decisive step and move in together. Laura knew that Maisie almost expected it. Even Mary had assumed it was on the cards. People said they were the ideal couple and the Grange was perfect.

Only Dot chipped in with a quiet word of caution. 'I should hold your horses if I was you. There's been a lot of changes lately, and you've got your whole life ahead of you.'

Laura knew she was right.

'I'll see you tomorrow.' She kissed him then watched him down the path out of sight. Then she turned and went through each room, opening the doors and windows to let in the sun.

She walked out into the garden, into the flame of September colour. A shadow swept up the hillside. In the distance Ravenscar held its mighty place on the horizon. Laura nodded once and went back into the house.

All Orion/Phoenix titles are available at your local bookshop or from the following address:

Littlehampton Book Services
Cash Sales Department L
14 Eldon Way, Lineside Industrial Estate
Littlehampton
West Sussex BN17 7HE

telephone 01903 721596, *facsimile* 01903 730914

Payment can either be made by credit card (Visa and Mastercard accepted) or by sending a cheque or postal order made payable to *Littlehampton Book Services.*
DO NOT SEND CASH OR CURRENCY.

Please add the following to cover postage and packing

UK and BFPO:
£1.50 for the first book, and 50P for each additional book to a maximum of £3.50

Overseas and Eire:
£2.50 for the first book plus £1.00 for the second book and 50p for each additional book ordered

----

BLOCK CAPITALS PLEASE

name of cardholder ....

address of cardholder ....

delivery address
(if different from cardholder)

....

....

....

....

postcode ....

postcode ....

☐ I enclose my remittance for £............................

☐ please debit my Mastercard/Visa (delete as appropriate)

card number ⬚⬚⬚⬚⬚⬚⬚⬚⬚⬚⬚⬚⬚⬚⬚⬚

expiry date ⬚⬚⬚⬚

signature ....

prices and availability are subject to change without notice